COVETOUS

THE MARKED MAGE CHRONICLES

BOOK 2

VICTORIA EVERS

Cover Art By: CivilAnarchy
Photography By: Irina Alexandrovna

Background Artwork © to Sean & Ashlie Dawn Gillis-Nelson at Ashensorrow
Designs.

ashlienelson.deviantart.com

ashensorrow.deviantart.com

https://www.facebook.com/AshenSorrowDesigns

Starline / Freepik Transparent White Light Effect Vector: Designed by Freepik

0melapics / Freepik White Light Flash Effect Vector: Designed by Freepik

Hair By: KLLGraphix

CONTENTS

2 Samuel 22: 38 – "I pursued my enemies and destroyed them, And I did not turn back until they were consumed.

PROLOGUE

Sprawled naked across the musty cement floor, the bloodied man merely coughed. The simple effort propelled the unspeakable agony in his fractured ribcage only deeper. He didn't even bother attempting to sit upright, even as the footsteps echoing across the cellar walls drew nearer. Eighteen hours. That's how long he'd been down there. He knew this, because the beatings came in bihourly intervals, and he was about to receive his tenth. He wondered if they would break his nose this time. It would be a welcomed relief, not having to smell the pungent odor of mildew permeating the dank crypt, not to mention the added putrefaction from what he could only assume was the decay of a rodent. At least, that's what he hoped it was.

"Well, well, well. Look at what we have here."

The unfamiliar lilt in the stranger's voice forced the man to incline his head, if only slightly. He still couldn't see out of his left eye, as it had swollen shut hours ago. Through the bleary gaze of his remaining eye, he could only make out a blur of brown hair and fair skin from the other side of the bars.

"Bring him to me."

The cell door clanked open, and beefy hands seized the

1

VICTORIA EVERS

bloodied man by his biceps, prying him off the filthy floor. It took everything in him not to cry out as broken bones seemed to shift from head to toe. The two brutes holding him up didn't bother setting him on his feet as they dragged him across the cellar to the lone iron chair seated in the center of the room. They didn't even trouble themselves with putting restraints on him anymore. After the last beating, he'd lost the feeling in his legs, and the bone protruding from his left forearm wasn't helping him either. One more strike to the area, and he knew it would pierce through the skin.

The stranger laughed, discarding his tweed jacket. "I must say, you have definitely looked better, mate."

With the singular light bulb dangling overhead and the haze lifting from his vision, the stranger's features at last came into focus as the bloodied man was thrown into the chair. The Englishman spoke as if he knew him, but there was nothing remotely familiar about his face, which meant one thing.

Demon.

More like *parasite*.

And he was the worst kind. Demons couldn't possess human vessels for any long length of time, so even though his features may not have been recognizable, the assertive saunter and iniquitous smirk never changed.

"Raelynd." The simple declaration had the prisoner choking on the blood slipping down his throat.

The Englishman merely smiled as he plucked out a cigarette from the pocket of his tailored vest. Taking in a long drag, he strolled over to the other end of the room, only to return with a folding chair in hand. He propped it open and took a seat, not the least bit tentative about being within strangling distance of the man. It only served as a

2

cruel reminder to showcase how pathetic of a shape he was in.

"Are you finding your new living conditions to be hospitable?" the demon cooed.

The man answered with nothing more than a bloody spit on the floor.

"Then let's not waste anymore of our time, shall we? Just tell us what we want to know, and you can be back on your merry way."

Despite the effort stretching the cut in his busted lip, the prisoner laughed. "As if *you* of all people would let me walk out of here."

"Killing you would serve no purpose. Why give you a one-way ticket to Eternal Paradise when things are about to get so much more interesting down here?" The demon leaned forward, pressing two fingers down on the protruding bone in the poor man's arm.

White flashed in his vision as the man doubled over, biting back the scream threatening to break loose. He wished he could say it was because he didn't want to give Raelynd the satisfaction, but he knew better. That kind of strain to his cracked ribs would have them puncturing into his lungs.

"Altruism doesn't suit you, Gabriel. Why protect a woman who couldn't give a toss about you?"

Unable to mask the agony, the man's entire body convulsed. "You don't know shit!"

"She rejected you, had another man's child, and yet you still choose to be her whipping boy? Now, forgive me, mate, for saying so, but that's just sad." Raelynd only laughed harder, prying Gabriel's chin up to look him in the eyes. "Where is Katalin's daughter?"

"Fuck. You."

The demon sighed, resting back in his seat. Upon waving a dismissive hand at his cohorts, the other men filed out of the room. Raelynd rose up from his seat, retrieving his discarded jacket, and removed the cell tucked inside an interior pocket. "Tell me, was she really worth losing your wings over?"

Gabriel didn't dare answer.

"I figured as much. It doesn't exactly take a genius to work out the details. If you were willing to fall from grace in order to protect her, using physical brutality to get answers would be a long shot. That's why I took extra measures, just to be certain." The demon strolled back over to him, seemingly far more interested by his phone than the very man in front of him. "I must say, you certainly seemed to have moved on rather quickly after your banishment. Not two months later, you found a new ladylove, and based on my calculations, already had her with child."

What little color that remained on Gabriel's face paled away.

"Handsome young man, your son. Looks just like you." Raelynd gave the beaten man another onceover. "Well, on a better day, that is. What's his name again? Reese, I believe." He didn't need confirmation, seeing the man before him tremble. "Ah, yes. And by the exquisite artwork decorating his arm, he's quite the Mage as well."

Gabriel could barely bring himself to look at the screen as the demon paraded it in front of his face. Indeed, the young man was a damn-near reflection of him, merely on a twenty-year delay, down to the coffee-toned hair and amber eyes. "What do you want with her?"

"With Katalin? Nothing. Our only interest is with her daughter."

"Why?"

"Let's just say there's a Prince waiting to meet her."

"None of the dukes' heirs have ascended," Gabriel scoffed. "Except one, and we know how well that ended."

The demon no doubt frowned at the mention. "Yes, well, *that* was unfortunate, but we've found an alternative. A better one, in fact. Stronger, and dare I say, even more attractive. Quite the catch for whichever one of the lucky ladies he chooses to be his bride. He is proving to be rather finicky though. But something tells me that any spawn of Katalin's would no doubt be fetching. And trust me, she'll be in far better hands with him than with Samael."

Raelynd admired whatever image was on his screen, and as he turned around, Gabriel caught a quick glimpse. It was not of his son, but another young man, with raven black hair and pale blue eyes. His heart thundered at the sight. The new Crown Prince...

"You feeling alright, mate? You don't look so well," the demon taunted.

"I don't know where she is," Gabriel muttered.

"You sure about that? Because we can always bring your boy down here," the Englishman offered, pulling out the dagger holstered inside his vest. He admired it under the harsh light, allowing the angel to observe the encrusted brown residue staining the blade. No doubt dried blood. "Perhaps it'll help freshen your memory, watching my Hounds peel the flesh from his bones."

The external agony was nothing compared to what brewed within the beaten man. Gabriel forced his eyes shut, letting the tears burning behind them to pour down his face.

"Ah-ha." The demon outright simpered at the sight. "Have we come to a compromise, then?"

1

I Put A Spell On You

an you go any faster?" I pleaded, choking on the billowing herbal cloud. "This is gonna set off the smoke detector."

Reese laughed. "Relax. It'll only take another minute."

He continued to wave the smoke around me and the rest of the sunroom, eventually pressing the bundle of burning sage into a heat-proof container. I handed him the drawing he'd brought, watching him reproduce the symbol on the page with salt across the floor around me.

Satisfied with the outcome, Reese joined me in the middle of the makeshift protection circle just as his watch sounded off, declaring it midnight. "Ready?"

Following each step as instructed, we both took a seat and added the ingredients into the very same container with the burnt sage. A sprig of rosemary, one ginger root, a stem of devil pod, and a dash of paprika. He nodded.

I looked at the sheet in front of me, and rolled my eyes. "Why do these things always have to rhyme?"

"Just read it," Reese insisted, unable to resist a small smile.

"'Thy enemy of mine. Thy evils that bind. Hear these words to banish your Rite. Undo this prince's hex, the spell undone. Break thy unholy bond that forever unites us as one.'"

I took the candle Reese just lit, letting the flames flicker over the section of parchment in my hand. I dropped the burning paper into the container, watching the name *SITRI*, the official name of Hell's Crown Prince, slowly blacken over with soot as it set the other ingredients ablaze as well.

Reese took hold of my hands, both our eyes focusing on the burning pot until everything was reduced to a pile of ash. Neither of us breathed as he finally released his grip, letting me unfold my left hand.

I immediately groaned, practically collapsing onto the hardwood floor. "This is hopeless."

Reese bit the inside of his cheek, clearly unhappy with the results—or rather, lack thereof—as well. "Madsen *did* say these things don't always enact immediately. It could take a few minutes, or even a few hours."

"Yeah, *if* it worked at all." I rubbed angrily at the skin on my ring finger. That blasted "mating rune" was still tattooed there, just as black and permanent as ever.

"Just give it a little time—"

"Who are we kidding, Reese? We've already tried over two dozen different casts, and it's the same damn outcome—nothing. I'm still linked to that...monster." It had been two months since Blaine had bitten me, infecting me with the demonic virus that had turned me into not only a Dark Mage, but also his eternal Mate.

Yep, I was officially his Runaway Princess Bride from Hell. Mere months ago, I was just a normal seventeen year old. Now, I was up to my ass in demonology and covered in ancient rune tattoos. After that bastard bit me, fang marks weren't the only souvenirs he gave me. With the demonic virus in my blood now, my runes were far easier to enact—particularly on accident. They were controlled purely by emotions, so anytime I'd get angry or upset or even too happy, my arm would light up like a freaking Christmas tree! And it was anybody's guess as to what would happen. I'd ripped doors clean off their hinges, shattered drinking glasses with a mere touch, and even set off every car alarm in a hotel parking lot with a flick of the wrist...

And if Dr. Madsen's research was correct, I couldn't risk triggering *any* of them. Since my runes were linked to Blaine's, they could act as a homing device, leading him right to me. I'd finally settled into a new home, and I didn't want to have to uproot again just to keep running.

But it didn't end there. I'd gained what I later learned was referred to as clairsentience. I could now sense people's emotions, smell them even. If someone was upset, a faint metallic scent would waft in the air. Anger was bitter. Happiness was floral. And lust...lust was by far the sweetest, like apple dipped in sugar.

The last proved the most problematic. It appeared to be the most common sin, which seemed to trigger my own new pair of fangs. As soon as the tang hit my nose, I knew to close my eyes and cover my mouth, or else risk having others see my elongated canines and glowing red eyes.

And you thought *you* had problems...

Plus, you know how in all those movies and television shows where a vampire can't come inside someone's house without an invitation? Yeah, well, I quickly learned the hard way that the same went for anything demonic, including me. Only once someone told me that I could come in could I. Otherwise, it felt like hitting a brick wall.

At least it wasn't as bad as I feared. Seeing how other demonic creatures like Hellhounds and demons acted — crazy, murderous and without empathy — I thought for sure after being infected that I'd wake up one morning, having turned into an evil bitch. Yet, eight long weeks had gone by, and I had yet to turn to the "Dark Side." And although I may have been part 'vampiric,' given my fangs and whatnot, I hadn't yet suffered from blood cravings, and I didn't burst into flames when I stepped out into the sun. Silver linings, I supposed.

But this...*thing*. This damn mating bond, I had to — *had to* — find a way to break it. Not only could Blaine use it to possibly track me, but it *linked* us. Our lives were tethered together, which meant that if I died, so would he. And vice versa.

How could you defeat an enemy like that? How could you overcome someone who would keep hunting you down till he claimed you as his own? If he'd use you to awaken powers confined to Hell? How could you eliminate such evil if you couldn't *kill* it?

Reese and I crashed into my bed after cleaning up the salty mess in the sunroom. The heat of his body warmed my back as we lay beside one another on the plush mattress.

"What time do you have to go?"

"We still have a few hours," he assured, pressing a kiss to my shoulder blade.

"I wish you could stay longer."

"I know." His lips trailed up into the crook of my neck. "We'll break the bond soon enough."

"That won't change things though with Mr. Reynolds," I murmured. "Every Reaper on the east coast is probably out looking for me. Even without the mating bond, I'm still a threat to them as long as I'm infected—"

Reese pulled away, angling my face to meet his. "Every disease has a cure. We just need to find it. Dr. Madsen's already looking into it."

"Like he's looking into fixing *this*?" I scoffed, still seeing the despicable tattooed band wrapped around my ring finger.

"Trust me, he's taking this seriously. Anything to stop Blai...uh, I mean, you-know-who from unleashing hell on earth, he'll do it. We'll sever the bond, find a cure for the virus, and then I won't have to sneak off to make four-hour round trips in the middle of the night to come and see you." He playfully chafed the whiskers from his five o'clock shadow across my face, and I finally laughed, wrestling against him to break free from the ticklish attack.

"Oh, you're not getting away *that* easily." His arms snaked around my waist, pulling me up so that I was lying on top of him.

"Is that so?" His lips claimed mine, cutting my laugh short.

"You have a problem with that?" Reese smiled, exposing his adorable, boyish dimples. And the action only highlighted the magnificence of his striking amber eyes.

"Oh, I'm not about to complain," I whispered, feeling his fingers sliding up underneath the hem of my camisole to the bottom of my back.

Reese sat upright, bringing me with him so that I was sitting in his lap. He continued planting soft kisses along my jaw, only scrambling my thoughts in the most delicious way. My fingers teased through his thick chocolate brown locks, and the act immediately impelled his mouth to reclaim mine. God, he tasted good.

He fisted my hair, slowly bringing my neck back to trail more kisses down the length of my throat. I tried to stifle my moan, but the pressure of my thighs tightening around his waist gave me away. Before either of us could think this through, we both started clawing at each other's clothes. I may have loved Reese's peculiar Gothic-meets-Steampunk choice of fashion, but all the buttons keeping me from him were near maddening. If I didn't get them undone in the next few seconds, I swore I'd just rip the brocade vest right off. My frustration only fueled the angst as I finally pried the waistcoat away. Just as I fed his shirt out over his head, Reese suddenly stiffened, feeling my hand settle on the back of his neck.

And that's when I noticed it, too.

A gentle vibration coursed through my palm, forcing me to pull my hand away. I groaned, burying my face into Reese's shoulder.

This was another serious downside to the whole "Blaine ordeal." As long as I was at risk for setting off any of my runes, we couldn't do this. The moment things got at all heated, I could feel the gentle vibration humming over my left hand. Lust. The rune thankfully wasn't glowing—yet, but the pulsation was always a sign that it was about to. For the time being, Reese and I were restricted to some playful kissing and cuddling. But nothing more.

"At least I know I make you all hot and bothered," Reese chuckled.

I finally pulled away, attempting a feeble smile. "Well, you definitely have the 'bothered' part right."

"Is that so?"

I squealed as Reese suddenly flipped us over, now pinning my back to the mattress. He peered down at me, that lopsided grin of his in place. How badly I wanted to touch him, to trace the plains of his face, the angles of his lean frame, the taut muscles of his stomach.

He kissed me again, this time gentle. "We'll find a way through this. I promise."

And I wanted so much to believe him. But the deep ache in my gut convinced me otherwise.

Sunlight flooded my vision the moment I awoke. Still drowsy, I rolled over onto my stomach and closed my eyes again, letting the rays beat the side of my exposed cheek. And I smiled at the soft caress of fingertips stroking down the length of my bare back.

"I thought you left," I sighed softly, nuzzling deeper into the sheets.

A breathy whisper of a laugh warmed my skin as kisses replaced the touch of hands. My back arched into the sensation. All the hair was brushed away from my neck as well, and goose bumps immediately raked over every inch of me as his lips settled into the crook of my neck.

"Bonum mani, o venusta."

I stilled, feeling those lips curve into a smile as they bore down into where those scarred fang marks rested.

Heat flushed me from head to toe. I angled my head up, meeting those familiar blue eyes, so pale they were nearly translucent. His hair wasn't the processed blonde I'd last seen him sporting, though. It was its natural shade of midnight black again. And that smile. Simultaneously delighted and hungry as his eyes took in the sight of me.

I shot up from the mattress, gasping for air, relieved to find myself in my bedroom. Alone. Nightmares weren't anything unusual—especially ones featuring Blaine, but this particular dream was definitely new to the repertoire. It had felt so real… My entire body trembled so hard, I was forced to clasp my hands together just to steady them enough that I could look at my left ring finger. Sure enough, the spell hadn't worked. Hours later, and the rune was still there.

A note rested on the pillow beside me.

"Didn't want to wake you. Call you later.
– Reese xoxo"

I'd wanted to spend as much time with Reese as I could, since we had very little together these days, but I'd obviously dozed off sometime after two.

Still feeling my aggravated pulse pounding in my ears, I climbed out of bed and got ready, too terrified to return to sleep. The moment I entered the kitchen, my stomach growled something fierce, insisting I needed salty meat, STAT. And to my good fortune, my Aunt Jenna always kept microwaveable bacon stored in the bottom drawer of the fridge. With my heightened metabolism, I needed to eat more than usual, so it served as a perfect excuse to heat up the entire packet.

"I smell bacon," declared Hanna the moment I opened

the front door for her.

She snatched up a fistful of bacon from the plate on the kitchen counter and moaned blissfully as the first slice settled on her tongue. "Damn, why can't I start off every morning like this? All we've got at home for breakfast is that puke-inducing whole grain crap my mom calls cereal."

"It's healthy food for healthy people," I mocked. That was always the response Hanna's mom returned to her daughter when she'd make the same observation.

"It's freaking cardboard is what it is. Insulation would be more appetizing."

Evermore, Massachusetts was honestly the bizarro version of the stuffy hamlet known as Mystic Harbor, Maine. Unlike my previous hometown, Evermore was an artisan's den for free spirits and all things inventive. Bohemians, gothics, and all. So my current outfit of leather leggings and a "Mz Hyde" t-shirt fit in perfectly with this town. It was a nice changeup in style, compared to the evening gowns and cardigan sweaters my mom had always forced me to wear, and the edgier look helped make the rune tattoos on my arm look less polarizing.

My new friend and across-the-street neighbor, Hanna, rocked out in one of her usual paint-stained t-shirts as she continued pushing her large, round-rimmed glasses back up the bridge of her nose, scarfing down the last of the bacon. Despite all her artistic talents with a brush, the girl's culinary skills definitely needed some work. I opted to whip us up some omelets while Hanna ~~burned~~ cooked some toast.

"Did you know that there's a museum shaped like the Titanic in Tennessee? It's half the scale of the original ship, and you can seriously walk the grand staircase! We totally need to go there!" Hanna said between mouthfuls.

"You say that like it's a trip to the mall," I chuckled. "How long would that drive even take?"

She winced. "Thirteen hours, give or take...one way."

"I think we'll have to put that journey on the backburner for now," I laughed.

"Yeah, but it's fun to think about." Hanna surveyed me, getting that little twinkle in her eye I'd quickly become accustomed to.

"What?"

"You should let me dye your hair."

"Again, *what*?"

"Don't get me wrong. It's nice as it is, but you need a little excitement. You know, liven it up a bit. I was thinking...maybe some purple highlights. It'll compliment the brown really well."

"I think I'll pass." Unbeknownst to her, I'd dye my blonde locks the most generic bottle-brown for a reason. I wanted to blend in as much as possible.

Hanna further insisted, and I just laughed, fortunate to hear the groan from the old garage door rattle the whole downstairs. My aunt was home. Sure enough, thirty seconds later, the door rattled noisily again as Jenna came inside through the laundry room.

"Hey, girls," she called out, donned in fitness gear.

"Hey, Jenna," Hanna and I happily replied in unison.

I climbed off the couch at the sight of seeing her juggling armfuls of grocery bags and paperwork. "Here, let me get that."

"Thanks," Jenna sighed, planting a kiss on my cheek. "So happy to be home. You wouldn't believe how crazy the market was this morning."

"I didn't hear you come in last night," I said, unloading

the groceries into the pantry and fridge.

A blush immediately painted Jenna's cheeks, and she whirled around, pretending to preoccupy herself with sorting through the mail on the counter. Hanna and I took another look at her outfit and laughed. My aunt always kept a bag of spare clothes in her backseat for emergencies, and it appeared she was rocking that very same set.

"So I take it your date went well then?" I teased, already knowing the answer. Anytime she went out with her new boyfriend, she *never* came home the same night.

"Oh, shut up," Jenna finally laughed, tossing a loaf of pumpernickel at me. "What can I say? I'm a sucker for a man in uniform."

Neither Hanna nor I could disagree. Officer Hernandez was fifty shades of blue-blooded hotness. And unlike my previous personal experience with the law, he didn't appear to be possessed by a demon, which was most definitely an upside.

Jenna covered her mouth to bury a massive yawn, which only made Hanna giggle all the more.

I looked at the grandfather clock beside the mantle and sure enough, it wasn't even ten in the morning. "Already in need of a nap?"

"I didn't sleep much last night," my aunt confessed, biting her lower lip.

I'd been living here for six weeks, and it still surprised me just how divergent it was in contrast to Mystic Harbor. Being around my mom always felt like walking on eggshells. But with Jenna, it was like hanging out with one of my girl friends. She treated me like an adult, and in return, I acted like one. The household functioned on mutual respect, a system which seemed to be working just fine.

Jenna gave me a playful shove with her elbow. "Just hope the ruckus next door isn't going to keep me up."

"Next door?"

"Yeah, our new neighbors are here."

"Neighbors? Someone finally bought the Swanson house?" queried Hanna, drawing back one of the front window curtains to see several moving vans parked out on the street that hadn't been there when I'd invited her inside. "That place has been vacant for, like, ever."

"Well, it was bought at auction last week." Jenna wasn't particularly thrilled by the news. The last owners had fallen on hard times, forcing them to abandon the property and move out of state. The lot had been sitting vacant for the last year and a half, which meant it had been quiet since I moved here. With our luck though, our new neighbors would probably be a fraternity.

"I really should make a welcoming dish or something. It would be the neighborly thing to do. Perhaps *you* wouldn't mind bringing it over?" Jenna perused the cabinets as if a recipe would jump out at her.

"Come again?"

"Oh, didn't I mention it?" Jenna's grin was all mischief. "I ran into Mrs. Rutledge as I was pulling into the driveway, and by her account, you girls should be pretty happy. One of our new neighbors is a young *man*."

"Age?" asked Hanna urgently.

"Same as you guys."

Hanna squealed. "Thank God! We finally get some fresh meat around here."

"Don't get too excited," I said flatly. "That 'fresh meat,' as you call it, could very well be bologna."

"Way to rain on my parade," she laughed.

"Anybody home?"

17

The three of us turned to see Sam standing in the front entrance, sporting another one of his infamous sloganed t-shirts. Today's read, *"Book Nerd? I prefer the term 'Literary Badass.'"*

Another rule around Evermore: no one locked their doors. People freely came and went as they pleased, which despite my wholly justified fear of strangers, I was actually okay with this, since anything demonic couldn't enter the house without an invitation.

It was just another thing I had to get used to. Like moving to a new town, for instance. Apparently, having a freak for a daughter didn't fit in with my parents' perfect family portrait. After the whole demonic home invasion, Mom and Dad did the only thing they could. Put distance between us and Mystic Harbor.

And then me from them.

They didn't come outright and say that they were scared of me. No, it was all in the subtlety. Like when we fled from town. After taking a train down south, my folks checked us in to a hotel where we were to stay in hiding. Despite the fact that they purchased a suite that was spacious enough to house an entire baseball team, they insisted on getting me my own room. On a completely separate floor.

And it went downhill from there. First chance they got, Mom and Dad shipped me off to stay with my mom's half-sister. I hadn't seen my Aunt Jenna for more than a decade, when she moved to Vegas with her tattoo artist boyfriend, Will. The relationship apparently fell apart, because about a year and a half ago, she relocated to Massachusetts, solo. Mom and Dad told her the bare minimum about my…situation. I had a crazy, angry ex who was looking for me, I was in a car accident that killed a "friend," and my parents' marriage was strained, to say the least.

They failed to mention said ex was a dark prince of Hell. Or that demons were real. Or that there were angelic hunters called Reapers, all of which wanted me dead, including my childhood best friend, Adam Reynolds, along with his father, the alpha of the pack. Come to think of it, the only supernaturally-inclined person who wasn't out to get me, apart from Reese, was Dr. Madsen, a college professor and fellow Mage. You knew things weren't looking good for you if your list of allies was shorter than your options when playing *Rock, Paper, Scissors.*

When the 'rents asked my aunt if she would take me in temporarily, Jenna didn't think much of it. After everything that had happened, it wasn't too odd that I'd want to get away for a little bit while my parents "worked on repairing their marriage." Thankfully, she took me in with open arms…and an open mind. Finally, someone didn't treat me like I was either a freak or a porcelain doll. The two of us got along well, but Jenna wasn't stupid. She knew something wasn't right.

Not with me.

With my folks.

For parents who seemed so determined to protect my "wellbeing," Jenna found it odd that they barely, if ever, checked in with me. She eventually called up Mom, asking when she planned on coming to see me. The massive-ass check in the mail pretty much answered that…

Nothing says "I love you" like a good old-fashioned payoff.

"Whatcha got there?" I asked Sam, seeing the bulk of a plastic bag tucked behind his back.

He smiled, tossing its bound contents at me. I outright squealed. After seeing Reese's setup in his basement, I'd fallen in love with the idea of stringing up some Christmas lights across my bedroom. The only ones I'd come across though were all colored.

But not these.

I tackled Sam with a hug. "They're perfect!"

"It was no problem," he assured. "Found 'em buried in the back of my garage. Figured you'd get better use out of them than we would."

"Thank you."

The three of us scoured the kitchen, eventually finding some adhesive decorating clips to hang up the lights on my bedroom wall. What would've been a twenty-minute task soon turned into an hour-plus ordeal as Hanna and Sam continued arguing over dimensions and what constituted for the appropriate amount of space between clips.

After adjusting the last section of Christmas lights up on the wall, I collapsed onto my mattress. "Is it kinda warm in here, or is it me?"

Both my friends just shrugged.

"I feel kinda weird," I muttered, fanning myself with my shirt.

"Probably just need some caffeine," said Hanna, hopping to her feet. "What'd you want? Mountain Dew, Dr. Pepper, Cherry Coke?"

"Doesn't matter."

Hanna happily took her leave, practically skipping her way downstairs. The girl had a bit of a caffeine addiction, and any excuse she could find to consume more, she took it.

"Talk about bad timing," laughed Sam.

I rolled over on my mattress to see him staring out my side window. "What is it?"

"Your new neighbor's just arrived."

Hanna had spent most of the past hour stealing looks, hoping for even a glimpse of the guy in question with no such luck. Despite the humor in Hanna's horrible timing, I still groaned. The view in question looked literally right out into the neighboring window not ten feet away, guaranteeing zero privacy. So it was official. I'd have to keep my window shades permanently pulled from here on out.

"Sure it's not just one of the movers? They're all pretty young," I said.

Sam chuckled. "Trust me; this guy isn't dressed for the job. He's not really *dressed*, period."

"What?" Curiosity got the better of me. I climbed off the mattress, joining my friend at the window.

Sam sidled aside and flipped on the light switch to admire my new setup as I went to the music dock, using its location below the window as an excuse to steal a casual look across the way. I didn't even have to make a song selection. As soon as I touched the radio, Arctic Monkeys' "Do I Wanna Know" suddenly started playing. I scooped up my phone, which was synced with the device, searching for the song in question. Since when was this on my playlist?

"What's wrong?" asked Sam, clearly noting my bafflement.

Before I could so much as articulate a single syllable, my eyes instinctively shot up to the window at the sight of movement across the way. That building heat in my chest roared to life, making my knees out-and-out buckle.

Sam wasn't kidding. My new neighbor wasn't wearing much of anything, apart from a pair of black jeans that hung dangerously low, revealing the chiseled V-shaped section of his lower abdominals that rivaled Apollo himself.

I outright gawked, feeling my phone slip from my limp fingers. It clattered on the hardwood, but I didn't care. I just kept staring.

This couldn't be.

This couldn't be.

This *couldn't* be.

My new neighbor slipped on the matching black dress shirt in his hands, but didn't bother buttoning it. Instead, he simply rolled the cuffs up his sleeves just enough to display the black metallic tattoos brandishing his left arm.

"You okay?" Sam reiterated.

I didn't move—*couldn't* move.

My neighbor.

He all so casually looked up, not the least bit surprised to find me ogling at him, and straightened the collar to his opened shirt. That taut frame flexed as he raised his arms, lazily resting them on the top of the opened window. A slow, devious smile pulled at his lips.

Finally regaining control over my body, I stumbled back a step, still unable to peel my eyes away from him. I whirled, preparing to bolt for the door. I was cut short though, smacking into something—hard.

Sam.

I'd run right into him.

"Geez!" he yelped.

My momentum toppled us over, and I landed on top of him as he smacked down on the area rug.

"Owww." He winced with a laugh, and I rolled off him with an apology. "What's with you?"

Ding dong!

Shit!

He couldn't possibly have gotten over here that fast…

I shot up from the carpet, ignoring Sam's insistency, and raced for the staircase.

"Don't answer the—" I rounded the banister, just in time to see my Aunt Jenna pull the front door open. Crashing to a halt at the bottom of the landing, I was paralyzed in place as magnetic icy eyes and bleached blonde hair greeted me on the other side of the entryway.

"Hello, lovely," Blaine purred.

Bad Romance

oth Hanna and Jenna stole a look over their shoulders at me, seemingly waiting for a response from my end. I just stood there, open-mouthed and stunned silent.

My aunt cleared her throat, turning back to Blaine. "What can I do for you?"

"I'm your new neighbor," he announced all too merrily. That pirated grin of his ticked up a notch, seeing both Hanna and Jenna light up at the revelation.

I dashed to the door, swiftly slamming it shut in his face.

"Kat!" Jenna bellowed. "What the hell?"

I'd warned my aunt about Blaine—well, as best as I could—when I moved here. And I'd shown her a photo of him, just in case something like this ever happened. As far as Jenna knew, he was a crazy ex partly responsible for the massacre at my previous school. There was no way she'd be entertaining him, unless…

As the Crown Prince of Lust, he had the power of biokinesis. It was the ability to project illusions onto ordinary humans. In particular, he could change his appearance. Eye color, hair, you name it. And the fact that Jenna stared stupidly at me like I was cuckoo for Coco-Puffs, it was safe to say that Blaine had glamoured the heck out of himself. To her and Hanna, he probably looked liked a freaking altar boy.

"Well?" my aunt insisted.

Well what?

What could I tell her? That our new neighbor was a High Prince of Hell that just so happened to wield dark magic? Yeah, because that didn't sound delusional or anything…

Jenna shook her head, brushing me aside. To my complete and utter horror, she pulled the door back open.

Sure enough, there Blaine still stood, batting eyelashes and all, his face masked in perfect innocence. "I'm sorry. Did I come at a bad time?"

"No, no, not at all," Jenna assured. "You'll have to forgive my niece. She's, ah…"

"In need of some serious caffeine," Hanna declared, gesturing him inside.

My aunt seemed to share in the sentiment, because she stepped aside from the door as well. "Would you care to come—"

"NO!" I didn't care how crazy I looked. There was no way this nutcase was getting an invitation into *my* house. Jenna and Hanna cast me another matching set of mystified glares. "I mean…uh, we were just about to leave," I said, looking to my friend.

"We were?"

"Yes," I growled, cutting Hanna a glare of my own. "And my aunt had a rather long night, so she was hoping to actually get a little rest."

"It's not that big a deal," clarified Jenna. "Really."

Another set of footsteps galloped down the stairs, and I turned to find Sam by my side.

"Where's the fire?" he laughed, wrapping an arm over my shoulder. Blaine's brows immediately piqued at the gesture, his calculating gaze seeming to scope out this new addition to the crowd. He didn't seem particularly pleased.

Good.

"I guess we're heading out," said Hanna, snatching up her jacket from the coat rack. "Would you like to join us? I'm dying for a mochaccino, and the Wilmount Shopping Center has the best coffee house in town."

My spine stiffened as I looked to Hanna, realizing she was addressing Blaine.

That mocking smile of his returned with a vengeance. "Oh, I'd be delighted."

I wasn't sure what I was expecting, getting into the same car with the homicidal sociopath that ruined my life. A fatal stabbing, a sinister speech, a drive off the bluffs, perhaps...but certainly not *this*. Five minutes into the car ride, and Sam seemed to have formed a bromance with his newest passenger as he and Blaine discussed manga—at great length. By the time we reached the shopping district, it was clear Hanna and Sam had fallen under the dark prince's spell. The three laughed and chatted all the way to the coffee house.

"God, he's so cute," Hanna squealed, stealing a glance over at the guys parked in the corner booth.

I snuck a peak as well, my skin immediately crawling at the sight of Blaine as he gave me a little wink.

"And it's about as subtle as a TNT bomb that he's crushing on you," she further laughed.

My stomach roiled at the thought. Oh, he was more than crushing on me. His affection was so strong, in fact, that he'd happily start the apocalypse. Seriously, one roll in the hay with him, and all Hell would break loose—literally.

"Oww!" I flinched, more out of surprise than actual pain. An invisible force coiled around my left ring finger, sending a warm tingling sensation to radiate across the tattooed band covering the skin.

"You okay?" asked Hanna.

"Ah...yeah. I just cut my hand is all," I lied, curling my fingers into my palm. "I'm gonna go clean it off."

I stepped out of line and made my way to the back hallway. The employee entrance was at the end of the corridor. I could make a run for it.

But what about Sam and Hanna? Would Blaine do something to them in retaliation for me running again? He knew all about Reese and Carly and even Mark helping me, and he had more than ample opportunity to go after them if he really wanted to. Yet, they were all okay.

And we *were* in the middle of a public setting.

My fight or flight response kicked in like a MoFo, and I took off down the hallway, ducking out of the back door.

What was the plan?

We'd taken Sam's car to get here, so driving wasn't an

option. I could take the bus, though public transport wasn't exactly known for its speedy service. It wouldn't take Blaine too long to realize that I'd fled, and with that damned connection between us, he'd be able to track me down almost immediately. I needed the fastest way out, one that would take me far enough till our connection was too weak for Blaine to trace.

Taking the long way around the building, as to avoid the front windows of the coffee shop, I made it back to the parking lot, spotting the bus stop just a couple blocks down. I couldn't risk just sitting here, waiting for a car service to come and pick me up. So I'd call them before grabbing the bus, taking it down to Main Street where I'd meet the hired driver.

Sounded like a plan.

I continued stealing glances over my shoulder to make sure I wasn't being followed. Nothing. A soft blue light emanated from the stupid rune on my ring finger, forcing me to shove my sleeves down to hide it. As soon as I reached the sidewalk on the other end of the lot, the redline bus pulled out onto the street up ahead. Crap. The last thing I wanted was to draw attention to myself—which sprinting in the middle of a public venue tended to do—but I really didn't have a choice. I took off down the sidewalk, managing to reach the stop in time. A half dozen other passengers filed onboard, and I slinked inside as well, taking a seat in the back.

I still debated over what car service would have the fastest pick-up as I pulled out my phone.

"Who ya' callin'?" purred a silvery voice beside my ear.

I shrieked, practically falling off my seat as I whirled around—to see Blaine seated in the row right behind me, his chin perched on his arms as they rested across my backrest. He beamed an angelic smile that had me bolting out of my seat, scrambling against the flow of traffic as people entered the bus.

Everyone yelped and hollered, but I didn't stop, issuing out an endless reel of apologies until I finally fought my way back off. How the hell had he found me? How had he gotten on without me seeing him? How the hell was I going to get away…?

Darting across the sidewalk, I leapt over the lofty bushes blocking my path to the nearest parking lot. There were countless shops I could take cover in, but that wasn't really a plan. I couldn't just sit and wait for him to find me. God, I wished Reese would answer. I'd left him countless texts during the car ride here, explaining what had happened, but he hadn't answered yet. Not surprising. He usually worked Sundays, and wasn't in reach of his phone.

Reentering the shopping district, I rounded the large manmade pond in the axis of the south wing, finding ample crowds to get lost in. There were at least a hundred different retailers in the massive outlet center, so I had my fair share of options. Turning the corner towards the food court, something tempted me to cut through the loading entrance. It led back out to another section of the parking lot, but on the opposite side of the center. Not until I yanked the heavy iron door open at the end of the dank hallway did I recognize that *pull*. That inexplicable urge humming beneath my skin…

Crap.

"Well, now, aren't you just a feast for the eyes," Blaine drawled as the heavy iron door slammed shut behind me.

I spun around, yanking desperately at the handle. It was locked! The only thing on this side of the lot was a bunch of empty loading trucks. And no people. Except one.

"You know, you could at least try to look happy to see me," he chuckled, stuffing his hands into his pockets.

"What do you want?" I growled, recoiling back a step until my spine met the locked door.

Blaine tilted his head in appraisal, as if to get a better look at me. "What are you offering?" he mused, his gaze scoping every inch of me.

"How about a kiss with my fist?" I snarled.

He clicked his tongue. "Temper."

My own gaze shifted behind him, and he rolled his eyes, knowing full-well I was going to try making my getaway again.

"Relax, alright. I come in peace," he assured, holding his hands up in mock surrender.

"Coming from a psychotic murderer? I highly doubt that," I growled.

Blaine's brows knitted. "And who exactly am I accused of 'murdering'?"

I gawked at him. "Uh, ME!"

"I beg your pardon?" He glowered at me, as if insulted. "I brought you back to life."

"Yeah, *after* killing me!"

"I brought you back," he reiterated with such casual indifference, like that made it okay.

I bolted sideways, making it not more than two steps before he cut me off.

"Will you at least give me a chance to explain myself?"

Pretending to sidestep in the other direction, I lunged at him with the fists of fury.

"I'll take that as a no, then." Of all things, Blaine laughed, only fueling my rage. He threw his arms up, deflecting each blow with an effortless grace.

You have to be kidding me…

Delivering a perfect roundhouse kick, my foot halted mere inches from Blaine's chest.

"I appreciate the moxie, love," he chortled, keeping hold of my caught ankle. "But you're a bit out of your league."

"Is that right?" I leaned in, throwing an elbow at his face. He instinctively released my foot, unaware that he'd just given me the opportunity to sneak to his right side. I grabbed hold of his shoulder and bicep, using his weight against him as I jackknifed my legs up. I wrapped them around his neck and threw my body toward the ground. The angle forced him down with me, sending him somersaulting onto the lawn beside us.

"Holy shit." Blaine let out a breathy laugh as his back hammered into the grass. "I stand corrected."

"Hardly," I scoffed, eyeing his current position. I pried my leg out from beneath his neck and prepared to make a run for it. I got as far as the old Civic three parking spaces down before Blaine's arms hooked around my body, driving me into the side of the hood. The impact set off the car alarm, making my ears nearly bleed as the whaling ignited by my head.

I silently thanked the Lord. Someone was bound to hear this.

Not four whole seconds passed before Blaine slapped his hand on the hood beside me. Electricity surged through his fingertips, and the alarm suddenly died.

Damn it!

Why hadn't I thought of that? I'd actually ~~stolen~~ borrowed a car using the same demonic technique once before. I could've hotwired any car in the parking lot and just driven off! My frustration didn't go unnoticed.

31

"That's what happens when you try to suppress your powers," Blaine remarked, prying me off the hood. He kept my hands pinned to my sides as he rested me against the passenger door. "It really is a shame you insist on doing this to yourself."

"Doing *what?*"

"You escaped from the confines of your parents, only to knuckle down on yourself twice as hard. You've been given freedom, yet you insist on climbing into an even smaller cage, and it's one of your own making."

"Screw you!" I managed to snake enough room to slam my knee up, preparing to nail it into his groin, but he missed nothing. Before I could even lift my foot off the ground, his thighs pressed against mine, trapping me in place.

"I have to admit, though, I am impressed with your fighting abilities. You been taking classes?" His smile turned feline as his gaze dropped down to my neck, to the faint scars left behind by his fangs. "Or, were they, too, passed onto you?"

I bared my teeth at him, wrenching my weight uselessly under his hold.

"I take that as the latter."

I *had* been taking self-defense classes, but my out-of-the-blue knack for kung fu definitely came from...someplace else.

But how did he know that I'd stopped using my runes?

That Cheshire grin of his eased into a smile so full of fascination and childlike delight as his eyes studied the curves and details of my face. "God, I missed you."

"The feeling's not mutual."

"Don't tell me you haven't been thinking about me, dreaming about me..." His gaze drifted down my body.

"And I see you've made some changes. Definitely liking the whole rocker chick vibe. Reminds me of the night of your Rite. Remember?"

"How could I forget?" I growled. Not only had he ruined my life that night, but also my beloved Sex Pistols top. First time I'd worn it out in public, and it wound up tattered and drenched in my blood. And his evil Hellhound crony had even taken my favorite leather jacket.

Considering all the murder and throat slitting that night, it was safe to say, good times were definitely *not* had by all.

Blaine scowled however, seeming to find something to his distaste. "Not really feeling the hair, though. Natural is a far better look on you."

He let go of my wrist, only to finger a section of my brown locks. His thumb rubbed over the ends, and I swiftly slapped his hand away, but it was too late.

Where he just touched rested a smudge of blonde hair, as if he'd rubbed the brunette dye right off.

"What did you do?" I shrieked, slamming a hand against his chest.

He didn't put up a fight, taking a healthy step back. "I fixed it."

I looked back down at the ruined section of hair, seeing the natural blonde coloring underneath extending up the rest of the untouched strand, melting away the dye. *"What the hell?"*

I whirled around to face the side mirror of the Civic. Sure enough, that blemished section of blonde spread across my entire scalp, ridding me of every speckle of brown. In not even half a minute, my long locks were wholly BLONDE again!

VICTORIA EVERS

"Can't say that it doesn't look better," Blaine remarked lazily, leaning against the side of the car behind him. I opened my mouth, but he just gave me a pointed stare. "You know you hated it."

I did, but... "Get out of my head!"

He merely sighed. "Look, I didn't mean to upset you—"

"Then leave me alone!"

"I can't do that either."

"So, what then? Are you gonna kidnap me, throw me in the back of some creepy van?"

"Wow." He rocked back on his heels, running a hand over his face. "You really think that little of me?"

"Well, you haven't exactly given me much better to go on," I gritted.

"I'm not here to take you by force. I want you to come with me, of your own volition."

"Not gonna happen."

He shrugged. "Never say never, love. You *could* change your mind."

"Well, if you're not here to abduct me, then why are you *here*?"

"I have it on good authority that you're in danger."

A high-pitched hiss sounded beside us, and both our eyes were ripped from each other. Not ten feet away stood... Well, I wasn't quite sure. But it definitely didn't look like something I wanted to piss off. Whatever this creature was, it was stark naked, though void of distinguishable genitalia. Gangly limbs jutted out at awkward angles, its skin the color of powdered milk with a shiny texture that best matched stretched latex. And it didn't have any eyes, or ones that were visible anyway. It looked as if the top of a mushroom was jammed over its face, concealing everything above the mouth.

And what a mouth.

Blood red lips pulled back to reveal the gaping jaw of a piranha, accompanied by three rows of jagged teeth that could rival a great white shark.

"Case in point," muttered Blaine.

Raise Hell

riend of yours?" I whispered, shrinking back slowly.

Blaine followed in suit as the creature snapped its jaw. "You really think it would be eyeing me like a Human Happy Meal if it was?"

"Fair point." I looked behind us, noting there was nowhere to go—unless Blaine had some serious Superman-leaping skills I wasn't aware of. The only door was locked, and the façade of the building was at least twenty-five feet high. "You packing?"

"Got a couple daggers."

"That's it?"

Reese never left the house without an array of hardware that would make a ninja blush.

"Well, forgive me, love, but one doesn't typically require longswords to grab coffee," Blaine jabbed.

Before he even rolled up his sleeve, I could see the pale blue light burning bright through the fabric of his shirt. A rune I, myself, had never managed to ignite before roared to life as Blaine extended his hand out. The air literally rippled outward as an invisible force slammed right into the creature. All the trucks and cars caught in the crossfire rocked from the momentum. I waited for the alarms to go off, but…nothing. Smoke seeped out from every engine, seeming to have fried them. The creature buckled over with a twitch at the impact, only to snap back upright with a ferocious hiss.

"I think I made it angry," Blaine glowered, seeing the beast extend its jaw. "Well, *angrier*, anyway."

"What were you *trying* to do?"

The Dark Mage cringed. "Honestly, that rune should've deep-fried its insides."

"Yeah, I don't think it worked," I barked, leaping back as the creature made continual lunges at the two of us.

Cruel, elongated yellow fingernails slashed at Blaine, and he swiftly ducked the creature's arms, springing up right in front of its face to throw an uppercut into the bottom of its jaw. The monster's head snapped back with a crack.

A low, guttural growl rumbled in its throat, the joints in its neck crackling as it instantly dropped its head back down. Strange sibilant hisses emanated from its mouth, as if it was speaking some alien language. One thing I did understand: "*Sitri*," Blaine's official name as Hell's High Prince. Running into this beast was no happy accident.

Blaine's arm lit up with a series of runes as he relinquished one attack after another into the creature. Again, none seemed to do any good, merely pissing off this thing more. It furiously thrashed its arms out at him, only to hit a car window instead as Blaine barely averted the swipe. The moment its nails hit the glass, the entire window shattered.

Blaine grabbed its arm, throwing the creature forward. It stumbled, allowing the Mage to drive his elbow down into its neck, rendering the creature into a face plant on the ground.

The beast swiped its razor-cut nails at Blaine's legs, slicing him right above the ankles. His knees buckled under him, but he never made it to the ground. The creature caught hold of him and yanked Blaine clear off his feet, squeezing its grip around the boy's throat until the veins in Blaine's face began to bulge as he gasped uselessly for air.

Well, shit.

He was definitely preoccupied, giving me ample time to run away. But if the ass-hat died...

I reluctantly took out the silver dagger Reese had given me, wielding it in my hand just as he'd taught me. With the creature's back turned toward me, I aimed the blade for the left side of its chest and positioned my arm accordingly. It hurtled with precision, but never *quite* met its target. Just as I released the blade from my grasp, the creature whirled around, yanking Blaine into its previous position. The knife cut through the air, only to plant itself right in the Mage's arm.

My hands instinctively shot to my mouth. "Sorry!"

Still breathless, Blaine seethed, and I couldn't blame him, seeing the tendrils of smoke arising from the wound.

Not only was a knife in the arm *extremely* painful by anyone's standards, but the blade itself was also made of silver. Something all demonic entities, including Dark Mages, were very much allergic to. It literally seared our skin just to hold it. And right now, it was apparently burning Blaine's insides...

The creature hissed, lobbing the Mage to the side. Appearances were definitely deceiving in this case, because its gangly limbs somehow catapulted the hale young man over the car beside them. Blaine skimmed the edge of the back hood, his body nailing the bumper before disappearing from sight.

"Motherf..." He glowered at me as he staggered back up to his feet, ripping the knife free from his bicep.

"I said I was sorry!" I yelped, seeing the monster jutting towards me.

"HEY!" Blaine let out an ear-aching whistle, effectively regaining the creature's attention. Silver sliced through the air in a blur, and the blade of the knife disappeared as the creature turned to face him.

Hot damn.

Blaine had landed it in the left side of its chest, right where the heart should have been.

Should have.

The pale creature didn't seem to take much notice, whirling back around to face me. "Sponsa of Sitri. Praeordino amasiunculus. Maledictionem prævaricator." Each syllable was hideous, dripping with such venom it made my blood run cold as the creature sneered and snickered. I could only assume it was speaking Latin, as many demonic figures did.

"Quid vis?"

I startled at the voice.

Blaine.

"Furantur tuus coniunx," the pale creature hissed in response.

Blaine growled. "Tange mate meum, et ego occident vos."

The creature snorted, its fingers wrapping around the tang of the knife. Even with the outside of its skin searing, it pried the cutlery free from its ribcage without so much as a twinge. There wasn't a smidgen of blood on the entire blade.

The fiend tossed the knife aside, sneering down at me with its gruesome wide grin on display. I pulled out the only other blade I had, a small pocketknife the length of my palm, and shakily aimed it at the creature. The beast lunged forward, its jaws snapping as it barreled down on me.

I stumbled back until I hit the wall of the building, finding no place left to go. The creature's grisly fingers were outstretched, seizing hold of my arms when a low *whoosh* accompanied an all too familiar metallic slice. The creature froze. Its razor-cut mouth lingered in front of me, and the beast seemed to sniff or gasp, I wasn't sure. The foulest odor batted me in the face as its jaw at last fell agape, revealing the spine of a blade jutting through the back of its throat. The creature's hold fell away, and it lifelessly toppled sideways to the pavement.

Blaine's words drowned under the roar of blood pounding in my ears. He'd embedded the blade *flawlessly* into the fiend's brain stem. As impressive as Reese proved to be with a knife, I'd never seen anything comparable to this...

Murderer.

Murderer.

Murderer.

Blaine had killed it.

Blaine had killed *me.*

Something he was evidently an expert at doing.

I couldn't do this.

I *couldn't* do this.

I couldn't do *any* of this.

I'd never be able to take him down, I'd never be able to outrun him, outsmart him, outmaneuver him. He was an assassin, a High Prince of Hell. And I was a meager pawn in the grand scheme of things. I was…trapped, condemned, damned.

"Kat?"

I snapped back to my senses, finding Blaine right in front of me, his fingers caressing my chin so that I met his eyes.

"Are you okay? Did it hurt you?"

I swiftly slapped his hand away, recoiling at the very thought of his touch. "Get away from me."

"Kat—" His hand instinctively reached out to me again, but he stopped himself, seeing me flinch. "I'm not going to hurt you."

"Get. Away. From. Me. You psychotic piece of shit."

Disappointment filled his icy gaze as he stepped back. "A simple 'thank you' would've sufficed."

"A 'thank you'? For what? Bringing that thing here to attack me?!"

"Again, do you really think I'd do that?" Blaine jeered, nodding down at his bloodied legs. "I'm not *that* much of a masochist."

"It doesn't matter if you sent it or not," I elucidated. "No one has come after me since I got away from you. For six weeks, I got to be normal again. And suddenly you turn up, bringing Hell in behind you!"

Blaine shook his head, exasperated. "Yes, because I'm the bane of your existence. Right?"

"Well, life wasn't too terrible before you entered the picture, so there's *that*," I snapped.

"All of this," he said, gesturing at the open air around us, "It's an elaborate illusion. You did the same thing in Mystic Harbor as you're still doing now. You keep telling yourself that if you play a little nicer, behave a little better, perhaps your folks might just change their mind and decide that you're worth more to them than their social status. Perhaps they'll come back from their Euro-trash vacation and promise to take you home. Maybe they'll give you a chance, see that you can repress your powers."

The lump in my throat expanded to the size of a softball, robbing me of a rebuttal.

"Maybe you can keep denying what's right beneath your skin." His words left a silent vibration coursing over the runes on my arms, making me shudder. "You can't ignore it, Kat. It's always there, roaring through your veins, the very same power that calls to you every minute of the day, begging for sweet release." He was too close.

Too close.

Too close.

Entirely too close.

There may have been four feet set between us, but it may as well have been four inches. It was as if he'd reached right into my chest and yanked out my heart, and the traitorous muscle forfeited all my secrets to him…

"You've tried being someone you're not for so long. What good has it done you?" He took a step closer. Then another. "You're never going to make those bastards happy. They'll never love you without condition. You've never been normal, and you never will be."

Tears burned behind my eyes, threatening to give me away. He may as well have stripped me naked. Blaine had just voiced every fear and hopeless wish and sense of resentment in my soul, exposing them to the world for the pathetic, puerile sentiments they were.

"It's time you stopped pretending to be something you're not." His voice was so deceptively gentle. "You have so much potential, so much power, if only you'd acquiesce to it."

"You mean 'to you,'" I finally bit back. "All you want is to *use* me!"

"You're my *mate*." I flinched at the word, and it only made the quiet rage in his eyes stir all the more. "I would *never* hurt you."

"No, you'd just *kill* me." Icy wrath crept its way into my arm. I prepared to level my fist into his face when the heavy metal door beside us flung open, the material slamming against the building's façade as a serviceman of some sort wheeled out a dolly.

Blaine's gaze still never left mine, even after the stranger said, "I'm sorry, but you're not supposed to be back here."

I looked to the other side of Blaine, down at the pavement. The creature's body still lay there, yet the worker carried on without so much as a glance. Blaine must have used a glamour of some sort to mask it from the guy's vision.

Grateful for the interruption, I sidestepped around the Dark Prince and caught the door before it closed.

"See you at home," Blaine crooned.

The words forced me to stop, but I refused to look back at him. With Hell behind me, I ran.

4

Wolf In Sheep's Clothing

"Y ou've gotta get out of there!"

This three-way phone call definitely wasn't going well. Twenty minutes in, and all there had been was copious amounts of yelling.

"No, I can't," I declared for the umpteenth time. "There may only be ten feet separating our respected living quarters, but Blaine still can't come into my house. Dr. Madsen's right. We need to take advantage of this."

Reese growled something inaudible on the other end of the call.

With nowhere else to go, I returned to my aunt's place and locked myself in the safety of my bedroom. Though, I really didn't have much of a choice in the matter either way. Because of Blaine's little trick, it wasn't like I could return to the coffee shop with a head full of spontaneous blonde hair. I had no choice but to ditch Hannah and Sam. They'd asked what happened, but I continued to ignore the texts until I came up with a plausible excuse. And as far as that bastard next door was concerned, so long as the window shades were drawn closed, this would remain as the only true safe haven I'd have.

"Hey, I don't like this anymore than you do. In fact, I *hate* it. But the doctor has a point," I said. "Blaine might have some intel we could use. He literally had truck-fulls of stuff delivered to his place. There's gotta be something in all those boxes that could help me. A codex, a spell book, something. *Anything.*"

"Precisely," affirmed Dr. Madsen. "Mr. Ryder learned how to cast the mating hex from somewhere, and I haven't been able to uncover this particular interpretation yet. If his version is logged like any other ritual, then the documented form will also contain the invocation to reverse it."

"*I* can drive down there and go check out the bastard's place," Reese interjected. "Kat needs to get the hell away from him though, while she still can."

"And what if Blaine just packs up and continues chasing me?" I asked. "We'll still have nothing, and I'll be on the run again—with nowhere to go. We need a plan on how to handle this, and we can't spook Blaine in the meantime. If he catches wind of you in town, there's no knowing what he'll do. I'm not gonna risk having him set his demonic cronies out on another murderous rampage."

"Also, if Ms. Montgomery can break the mating bond, then we won't have to hunt Mr. Ryder down. As she mentioned, he's right next door. We can take him out the very moment after we sever their connection," added Dr. Madsen.

"Well, I'm clearly outnumbered here," Reese huffed. "So, what do we do?"

"The moment I find an opening, I'm gonna sneak into his place and take a look around. If I come across anything, I'll let you guys know," I said, scratching my head. "I gotta get going. This stuff's burning my scalp."

I hung up and immediately hopped into the shower, rinsing out my newly purchased hair dye. As far as I knew, Reapers were still out there looking to kill me, so I needed to keep up my lame attempt at a disguise—no matter how much I may have hated the hair color.

And it only pissed me off further that Blaine knew it, too. If he was capable of knowing something as offhanded as my vanity, how easy would it be for him to figure out something big, like our recently hatched plan?

I finished washing up, wrapping my re-dyed brown locks into a makeshift towel turban to help wick the moisture out of it. I headed back to my room to slip on my pajamas when something caught my eye. At the end of my bed sat a smooth black and white apparel box adorned with red silk ribbons that tied into an elegant bow on the top.

Tucked beneath the bound ribbon was a simple white envelope with a single word written on the card inside.

I bolted for the hallway, almost tripping over my own feet as I raced downstairs. *"Jenna?"*

I found my aunt sitting on the couch with a cup of hot chocolate cradled in her hands. "What's wrong?" she asked.

"Did someone drop something off for me when I was in the shower?"

Her brows knitted together. "No."

"Did you invite Bl... I mean...*anyone* into the house?

Even Sam or Hanna?"

She shook her head. "Why?"

This made no sense…

Jenna took a closer look at me. "Did you dye your hair?"

"Uh…yeah." How did she know? I made sure to crack the bathroom window when I did it as to not let the chemicals permeate the house, and it was the exact same color it had been since before I moved here.

My aunt nodded to the side of my face, where a single loose tendril of hair had escaped from my towel wrap.

I froze.

Son of a b…!

Racing back up to my room, I tore the towel from my head in front of the vanity mirror.

Son. Of. A. Bitch!

There in front of me rested frosted blonde hair, again!

It had literally been BROWN not ten minutes ago, yet the color had…what? Up and vanished?

What the hell did Blaine do?

Whatever it was, it was still the least of my concerns. How did this box get into my room? Blaine wasn't allowed to enter, and Jenna hadn't let anyone in.

I stared at the one-word note, feeling vibrations raking across the top of my arm. A sharp, pale-blue light exploded from the ignited rune, overpowering even the strength of my lamp.

Was he serious?

Could he really be *that* delusional?

I fisted the note up into my palm, slamming the crumpled wad into the trash can beside my desk.

"Everything okay over there?"

My entire spine stiffened.

Blaine's voice.

It was in my head! I'd forgotten he could do that. Storming over to my side window, I yanked up the shade to see Blaine standing in the opposing view, one brow crooked at me. He nodded down to where the very same rune I had ignited was glowing faintly on his own arm. And to my disappointment, his other arm appeared to have already healed from the knife I'd inadvertently stabbed in his bicep.

Grabbing the unopened box, I yanked the window open and flung it outside, letting it smack against the siding of his house.

"Was that really necessary?"

Slamming my window back down, I gave him a smooth, unladylike gesture before yanking the shade and curtains over the locked glass.

There was one thing I hadn't taken into account. Sure, Blaine couldn't enter my home, but that also meant that *I* couldn't enter his. Without receiving an invitation first, there was no way I'd be able to sneak into his place when he wasn't around. I spent the next ten hours with my eyes peeled open, terrified by the prospect of falling asleep. Between my all-too-real-feeling nightmares and the unsolved mystery of how that blasted box made its way into my bedroom, I refused to doze off. But at least it gave me plenty of time to think this through…

As I stood on the porch come six o'clock the following morning, I was immediately regretting my decision. This was a horrible idea!

Footsteps trotted up as I proceeded to bang on the front

door again. I know, I know. I was totally nuts for considering this, but I was desperate.

Sure enough, Blaine opened the door, his face immediately lighting up with pleasant surprise to find me waiting on his porch. "Hey, stranger."

I took the crumpled wad of paper I'd pulled from my trash can and chucked it at him. "What the hell is this?"

He caught it after it smacked his chest, and he unfolded the note. "Uh...it's called paper, the last time I checked."

"I meant what's written on it."

"Can you not read?" His teasing smile only made me want to hit him more.

"*'Bygones?'* Seriously?"

"What? I was merely hoping we could make amends. You know: fresh start, clean slate, new beginnings. All that jazz."

"You seriously think I'd ever forgive you after what you've done? You *murdered* people!" I roared, intentionally catching the attention of Mrs. Rutledge as she came out to grab her morning paper.

A guilty smile tugged at Blaine's lips as he gave a polite wave to our neighbor, who rightly eyed him back with misgiving. "I doubt I'll be receiving an invitation for tea in the near future," he muttered under his breath with a laugh.

Obviously not wanting to carry on with this conversation in front of prying eyes, he stepped back from the door and gestured me inside. Yahtzee! It wasn't a verbal invitation, but the silent indication seemed to suffice, because I met no resistance as I regrettably crossed over the threshold.

When thinking of super villain evil lairs, one might picture the Death Star, or Dracula's Castle, or perhaps the

Hall of Doom. Not a traditionally styled two-story colonial abode with a cozy fire alit inside the hearth. Yet, there I was, standing in the foyer of a house as quaint and inviting as my aunt's. Oh, how deceptive appearances can be...

"Breakfast?"

I startled, returning my attention to Blaine only to find him far too close for comfort. *"What?"*

"Would you like breakfast?" he reiterated, closing the door behind him.

"No," I snapped, retreating back as he came onward.

"You sure?" He cocked a brow at me. "You haven't eaten in a while. And as they say, it's the most important meal of the day."

I glowered at him. Again, he was right. Because of my manic anxiety, eating wasn't exactly high on my list of priorities yesterday, resulting in me skipping dinner. "How would you know the last time I ate? Were you spying, or just molesting my mind again?"

Blaine simpered, but it lacked any real amusement. "I can hear your stomach from here."

"Oh..."

He didn't wait for my rebuttal, striding off down the hall towards the back of the house. I'd gotten the invitation I needed, so I could've just left. But this *did* give me a chance to poke around a little, get a general layout of the place. And maybe with any luck, I could get some answers.

The hallway leading back into the kitchen gave me a full view of the downstairs. The house was fully furnished, every room simple, yet elegant. No clutter, no paperwork, not even a piece of mail lay out in the open. Unless he had spell books shoved under the couch cushions, it was safe to assume Blaine had any of the real goods tucked away upstairs. Yippee...

When I entered the kitchen, Blaine already had a place setting for me at the table with a glass of orange juice, a napkin, and silverware prepared. He pulled the seat out for me, and I begrudgingly plopped myself down in it as Blaine returned to the stove to dish up what appeared to be eggs. There were little green leaves sprinkled in it, along with brownish onions, small clumps of pale cheese, and a strange dash of red powder.

"What is it?" I asked, getting an up-close view as he slid the plate in front of me.

"Scrambled eggs with caramelized onions and chèvre. It's quite good, I assure you."

"I didn't know you could cook."

A small smile tugged at his lips. "There's a lot you don't know about me."

That I didn't doubt. But I also had no interest in learning more.

Blaine planted himself in the seat across the way a moment later. Unfortunately, the table was small, so I only had about two feet of separation set between him and me. "So, how's your mission coming along?"

"Excuse me?"

"You know, the one to rid yourself of our bond?" Blaine emphasized the last word with particular mirth, making my insides turn cold.

What the...?

He looked at me over the brim of his coffee mug, obviously waiting for me to answer. When it was made clear I wouldn't, he shrugged. "Unlike natural magic," he said, tapping the rune on top of his hand, "wiccan spell casting leaves a trace. It's like catnip to demonic creatures. That's why people find themselves sometimes haunted after playing with Ouija Boards and whatnot. And you, my dear, are practically glowing in it."

This whole time I'd been doing everything magically possible to make sure he stayed away, and it had only led him right to my front door. "Is...is that how you found me?"

"No, our bond did that," he said, so matter-of-factly.

I couldn't believe this. Blaine knew...*everything.*

Despite my stomach's desperate plea for food, I set the fork aside.

"Something wrong?" Blaine took notice of me evidently scoping the food and drink with suspicion. He sighed. "I'd have nothing to gain by poisoning you. You know this better than anyone."

"I'm more wary of being *drugged*," I growled. "Thank you."

"I meant what I said yesterday. I want you to *want* this. I have no interest in stealing you away."

"Well, you're never going to get what *you* want, so how about we make a deal?"

He smiled back with evident amusement. "A deal?"

"Release me from this...*bond*, or whatever you want to call it," I scoffed, gesturing to the mating rune on my ring finger, "and leave town."

"A deal's a two-way street, love."

"There's an entire pack of Reapers dying to get their hands on you. If you break the bond, I won't report you to them."

"You won't do that anyway. As long as our lives are linked, you're not going to give me over to people who are guaranteed to kill me."

"I'm going to find a way out of this curse, whether you help me or not," I jeered. "Consider this a preemptive offer."

"I'm afraid I can't help you," he said smoothly, stabbing a healthy slice of egg.

"*Why?* What do you want from me? You could've chosen anyone to be your stupid 'mate'! Why did it have to be me?"

He leaned back in his seat, seeming to consider the thought. "And who should I have chosen?"

"You're a psychotic murderer with the face of an angel. If serial killers can get fan mail from adoring women, I trust you'll have no problem finding someone as demented as *you* are to replace me."

"Is the thought of being with me truly that repulsive?"

"You don't want me to answer that."

The muscles in his jaw tensed, muzzling an expression that flickered only for an instant across his eyes. The faint scent of rose pedals lingered in its wake, and I had no idea what that implied. But it seemed safe to assume he was displeased, to say the least.

And just like that, it vanished, bringing a sardonic twist to his lips. "So, you think I have 'the face of an angel'?"

Now *I* was the one scowling, or at least, more than I already had been. "You never answered my question. What do you want from me?"

"Isn't it obvious?"

"I'm not going to sleep with you just so you can unleash your wrath on mankind," I scoffed.

He actually laughed. "Come again?"

"I'm not stupid. You want to throw the world into death and destruction, bringing about the apocalypse! And I know I'm the key to getting your satanic powers topside. You and your so-called 'mate' have to consummate your relationship in order to break the remaining seal trapping your powers in Hell."

Blaine smirked. "And who told you this?"

"I read it."

"Where?"

"It was in one of the old journals Reese's father left behind."

"And who might Blackburn's father be?"

"A Light Mage." At least, I was pretty sure...

"His name?"

"I...I don't know. He abandoned Reese when he was still a baby. I never met the man."

"So you'd take the word of a total stranger as gospel rather than hear me out?" He chuckled to himself, leaning back with a sigh. "Tell me, if this random person wrote that Chihuahuas had laser beams in their eyes and were secretly plotting world domination, would you believe that, too?"

I shot him a dirty look.

"Well, I have to ask, seeing as how it seems you'll believe anything."

Bastard.

"Okay, Obi-Wan Kenobi," I jabbed, "Enlighten me. What's your 'true' objective?"

"I think I've made myself pretty clear as to my intentions regarding you. As for the rest, I suspect you'll discover that soon enough." His vibrant, icy eyes took in the sight of me, making my fingers curl into my palms as he surveyed me intently. "You look well."

"Better than when you first bit me," I countered.

"You're welcome."

At first, I couldn't figure out why my jaw wasn't in my lap, because I gawked at him, openmouthed and dumbfounded, in utter disbelief. He...he was serious. That bastard honestly thought what he had done to me was a favor—*a favor!*

Before my brain could catch up to my actions, I snatched up my fork and hurled it at him. Despite my hopes that the prongs would stab him, the utensil sadly hit him vertically, making it bounce off his beaten shoulder.

"Owww," he remarked flatly, setting down his coffee mug.

I was on my feet in an instant, my hands suddenly clasped on the front of his shirt. I hauled him right up out of his seat, slamming Blaine into the wall behind him so hard the nearby hanging picture frames rattled from the impact. "You made my life a living hell!"

"I *saved* your life."

I yanked him off the wall, only to hammer him back into it. Harder. "I lost my family because of you!"

His cool demeanor slipped away, replaced by antipathy. "They weren't your family."

"Those people raised me! Whether they were my biological parents or not, it doesn't change that!"

"Anyone who abandons their child has no right to call themselves a parent. They were chickenshit, just like mine."

Unadulterated rage boiled my blood, and I awaited the sweet release of my runes igniting. I didn't want to slam him into the wall. I wanted to put him *through* the wall.

The faintest hum tickled the skin over my forearm, but died out just as quickly. My fists only balled up tighter into the fabric of Blaine's shirt. Why weren't they igniting?

"Sorry, love, but I'd rather prefer you *not* try to break every bone in my body."

Just as he'd done on the night he'd bitten me, Blaine managed to turn off the use of my runes with a mere touch.

"I *hate* you."

His eyes locked with mine, merciless, as he said so softly, "No you don't."

"I *HATE* YOU."

His fingers were suddenly wrapped around my wrists. With next to no effort, Blaine pulled my hands away, holding them down at my sides. Panic hit me like a raging river. Wave upon agonizing wave crashed against every cell in my body, begging me to break free, to run out. But I couldn't move.

One moment, I had him pinned against the wall. The next, Blaine was guiding me backward until my hip met the kitchen table. I was trapped under his hold.

"You don't hate me."

"You really are psychotic if you actually believe that," I seethed.

"It's not what I believe; it's what I've *seen*." His voice only lowered as he moved in closer. "The night of your Rite, when you came to visit me in the basement of the compound…"

My whole body shuddered at the very thought, and he was too close to not feel it.

"As much as you wanted to hate me, as much as you told yourself you'd be happy to see me tortured by Reynolds's men, you were repulsed at the sight of what they'd done to me. Deep down, you knew I was still the man you first met. You cared about him. I still *am* that man."

"*He* was never real," I growled. "You're a sociopath. You even admitted to it after Daniel kidnapped me!"

"That was for the benefit of our audience, not you."

"Meaning what?"

"Meaning I have a reputation to uphold. Cruelty is the only thing that drives fear in people like Mr. Reynolds, or Daniel, or my bosses. For appearances' sake, I have to be malicious—"

"And you're not?" I scoffed.

His gaze hardened. "When have I ever been cruel to you?"

"You bit me!"

"To protect you the only way I could."

"You *kissed* me. You knew I was disgusted by you, and still, you had your hands all over my body!"

"Is that right?" He closed the distance further. "You were disgusted?"

To my horror, he knelt down. As if plucked right out of one of my worst nightmares, Blaine grinded his hips into mine, leaning in until no space was left between us. His mouth was so close, the warmth of his breath stirred against my own lips.

I stood paralyzed, anticipating the horrible moment when his lips would meet mine.

Instead, he whispered, "Am I giving the impression I want to kiss you?"

His hands loosened their hold on me, gently grazing over the skin on my wrists. Images crashed back into my mind, almost knocking me backward as I startled. The old weightlifting room. When I'd been handcuffed to one of the pull-up bars. The night Blaine had bitten me.

I had nowhere else to go, no other plan to get out of there. It was just him and me. Alone. I knew I needed to earn Blaine's trust to get me out of my restraints. He had kissed me first, but...I was the one who leaned into him, who grinded my hips against his, who made him think I wanted him...

As if the air was punched from my lungs, I finally exhaled, my vision snapping back into focus. *"What?"*

He patiently repeated the question, and the tremble coursing through my entire body served as answer enough. His hands slipped from my wrists before he stepped back. "Now you know how it feels."

I was literally shaking.

Is that why he was here? To torment me? All because I lied about wanting to be with him? He'd sent his goon of Hellhounds to murder our fellow classmates. Had that bus of students attacked. He'd held me captive. He was clearly *insane.* Being honest with him hadn't exactly seemed like the best idea at the time...

"You should probably eat a little something before we leave," he offered.

"We?" I managed to utter.

"It's Monday morning. And in America, that means that we're required to attend high school," Blaine affirmed, flashing me a set of papers he pulled out of his back pocket. "It's my first day."

My eyes widened to the size of saucers. "Please tell me you're kidding."

Everybody Wants To Rule
The World

laine wasn't kidding. The Dark Mage would officially be attending John Addams High, under the alias Remy LeBeau, as in "Gambit" from the *Marvel* comics. Personally, I thought he seemed more like a Loki/Kilgrave type, but I could only assume either name would be too on-the-nose. Though I couldn't really talk. After speaking with the school about my predicament concerning my stalker ex, my teachers allowed me to use my aunt's last name, Shaw, so none of my classmates were the wiser as to who I really was. Last thing I wanted was for my actual name and face to be tagged on social media for the world to see.

And Blaine had taken the initiative to tell Jenna that he would be driving me to school. I wanted to protest, but found Officer Hernandez pulling his squad car into my aunt's driveway just as we were leaving, effectively blocking my own vehicle in the garage. Considering how peculiar I'd been acting since Blaine's arrival yesterday, I really didn't want to make matters worse by drawing more attention to the issue, seeing Jenna's obvious concern towards me.

Even worse, Blaine walked me down to the curb where a pristine black 1972 Oldsmobile Cutlass SS was parked. With white stripes running up the hood, it looked just like a model I'd seen before... It was a beautiful car, and he knew it.

"HOTTIE ALERT!" announced Hannah's text message as Blaine pulled into the school's parking lot. She obviously hadn't gotten a good look at who was sitting in the passenger seat, because her jaw dropped the moment she saw me exit the vehicle with him. Even Sam was grinning like a fool.

"Holy Crab Cakes! We were wondering where you guys ran off to yesterday," Hannah declared, wrapping a lock of my naturally frosted blonde hair around her fingers. "Did our new neighbor whisk you away to a salon? Because I most definitely approve of the new-fangled hair color!"

A smile pulled at Blaine's lips that he did very little to hold back.

I snatched up my bag and turned to Sam instead, praying he'd give me an out.

"Seems someone's thawed out the Ice Princess," he teased me quietly with a nudge. "Did his shirtless escapades next door finally get to you?"

Or not...

"Oh, he got me, all right," I murmured. *'If only he'd lose me'* is what I didn't say. Instead, I was forced to give Blaine a polite, "Thank you," before heading inside the building. It was the first thing I'd said to him since leaving his house, and I had no intention of adding to it.

My entire arm ached as vibrations danced across my skin. Anger, despair, confusion; every emotion roared through me as I desperately tried to calm down. But I couldn't. My life had finally found some semblance of normalcy again, and it got blasted all to Hell the moment he strolled back in. I'd made it ten minutes through History class before a flex of my fingers sent a stack of textbooks shooting off Mr. Hennessey's desk into the chalkboard. Everyone yelped, especially our teacher who had been standing not a foot away from the spot of impact. Unable to contain it anymore, I asked if I could be excused. Even with my leather jacket on, it barely contained the pale blue light humming beneath the fabric. As I approached the bathroom, I could hear voices inside, making me slam on the brakes. I needed somewhere empty. And fast.

Hurrying down the hall, I yanked on the side exit to the locker room, only to find it locked. Everyone was already running drills in the gym, so I slinked past Coach Niles and ducked into the main door of the locker room, thankful to find it vacant. Heading to the far back, I slid down to the floor. My chest heaved, my heartbeat pounded in my ears, my entire body damn near convulsed. I crumpled forward, my hands clutching to the sides of my head. I'd never felt this before. Not to this extent. Every cell in my body was brimming with this barely contained power, begging to be unleashed. One silent scream, and everything shattered.

Even with my eyes pinched shut, light exploded behind my lids from the sheer intensity. Relief was immediate, the power uncoiling itself from around my bones, as the air rippled and expanded out. In an instant, my head snapped upright as the laundry bin beside me disappeared from my peripheral vision and slammed into the opposing wall. And it wasn't the only casualty left in my wake. Every locker door in sight flung open, the combination locks snapping right off as an assortment of clothes, purses, perfumes, and cosmetics launched out across the space.

"Shit!"

I scrambled to my feet at the sound of the intruder, finding Blaine standing at the entrance with his hands shielded over his face as the debris finally met with gravity and rained down to the floor.

"What're you doing here?" I demanded, furiously wiping the tears from my face.

"I thought something was wrong. You ignited half the runes on your arm," he panted, hinting he'd been running.

The heavy main door swung open behind him. Coach Niles poked her head inside, taking in the catastrophe that was now the locker room. *"What happened?"*

"Everything's fine," Blaine said, motioning her out with a dismissive hand.

Our P.E. teacher was a total hard-ass when it came to following rules. Seeing the entire girls' locker room destroyed would have made her blow a gasket. To find a boy in there as well... Oh, Hell hath no fury. So imagine my shock to find her walk out, closing the door behind her without protest.

"What *did* happen?" Blaine asked, looking about the destroyed space.

The side exit was usually unlocked—from the inside—

so I rounded the closest set of lockers and headed for the door.

"Kat?" he pleaded.

"Just stay away from me," I bit back, charging out into the hall.

"I can't do this." I was practically wearing a hole through the tiles as I continued to pace the short length of the bathroom with my cell to my ear, grateful to find the space finally empty.

"Reese just informed me," confirmed Dr. Madsen. "It's important right now that you try and stay calm."

"You should've seen it; I had no control! Someone's going to get hurt, and I highly doubt it'll be the person I want to."

"Where's Blaine right now?"

"Probably drinking the blood of the innocent or telling children there's no such thing as Santa Claus. Who the hell knows?"

"Do you think you'd be able to get out of town for a short while, without Mr. Ryder knowing about it, I mean?"

"Why?"

"Are you familiar with the Bridgewater Triangle?"

"The what-what-what?"

He sighed. "Bridgewater. Otherwise referred to as the Bermuda Triangle of Massachusetts. It's something of a hotbed for paranormal activity, particularly in the forests. Ghosts, aliens, Indian curses and whatnot. There's someone there I think you should see."

"Who? Bigfoot?" I mocked, throwing myself against the wall.

"I wouldn't be too quick to laugh," said Madsen. "There have in fact been sightings of that as well."

"*Seriously?*"

"But thankfully, you won't have to contend with Chewbacca's cousin today. You'd only be visiting Freetown, not the State Park."

"And who might I be 'visiting,' exactly?"

Due to me arriving in the middle of the semester, my schedule was a bit screwy, which right now played out in my favor. Each class was ninety minutes long, with a ten minute break between each subject, and Freetown was a half-hour drive each way. Given that Study Hall didn't require attendance, I essentially had a free period. So long as I hauled ass, I'd be able to make it there and back again before Lunch, where Blaine would surely notice my absence. And thanks to Hannah lending me her Prius, I wouldn't have to resort to magical grand theft auto for a ride. So long as I could keep my runes in check, I stood a chance of Blaine not monitoring me.

And I'd made better timing than I thought, entering Freetown almost ten minutes ahead of schedule. What Madsen failed to mention was that the town happened to be divided into two villages: Assonet and East Freetown. I wasn't sure which one the shop was located in, and Hannah had already warned me about not using the GPS in the car. Last time she tried, she ended up three towns over for a trip that was supposed to be only about ten blocks down the street. Plus, Google Maps kept trying to take me down the same dead-end road for the fifth time. As it turned out, Lucinda Palatine, the woman Madsen sent me to meet, had closed down her shop and relocated to another storefront in Bristol County that took another fifteen minutes to find. So much for good timing...

On arrival, I found that the fortunetelling shop wasn't exactly what I'd been expecting. I'd never been in one of these places before, but I'd seen some from the street when I was in New York. Tacky neon signs, depictions of creepy eyeballs and palm readings, weird talisman symbols hanging in the windows, the whole nine yards.

This shop, however, had nothing but a clear glass door with elegant writing that simply read, "Mystic Tarot." A sign out front also advertised $10 Specials on Crystals and Love Stones, promising to "Reunite Lovers." What mattered most to me though: "Walk-ins Welcome."

The pleasant aroma of lavender, rose, and other essential oils greeted me as I opened the front door. And I laughed to myself, hearing Calvin Harris's "Feel So Close" playing quietly in the small foyer. Again, some part of me had expected the weird mood music from *The Legend of Zelda* or something.

The corner shop was small enough to see it in its entirety from the front door. To my right, a couple customers meandered about the sales counters, checking out the variety of "magical" crystals and tarot cards. With the chic display cases and classic furnishings, the place looked more like it sold upscale cosmetics rather than cheesy charms and false hopes.

"Can I help you?" asked a woman, emerging from the back room to my left. She was maybe thirty at best, her light brown hair pinned up in a trendy bun. A simple long-sleeved black dress and killer knee-high boots solidified the perfect balance between casual and classy. Behind her was a fogged-glassed, black paneled door with

"Private Reading Room" labeled across it.

"Hi, is Lucinda here by any chance?"

She smiled. "That depends. Why are you looking for her?"

"I was wondering if she could give me a reading."

"Then it's a pleasure to meet you," she chuckled, shaking my hand before escorting me to the room she'd just emerged from.

The space was simple enough. No traditional lamps or light fixtures. Just a few candle sconces that were dialed down to give the beige walls a peaceful, warm glow. A small table sat in the middle of the room, draped with a champagne chiffon overlay, and apart from a few plants, nothing else occupied the space.

"It's always nice to know you've left a positive impression with a client. Who recommended you see me?"

"Doctor...Madsen," I muttered.

"Madsen?" She seemed to consider the name, but clearly came up empty-handed as she closed the door behind us.

"He came to see you, about eight years ago," I said sheepishly, nodding to her left hand.

At the very cusp of her sleeve I could see the edge of a metallic tattoo entangling her wrist. She immediately recoiled, frantically reaching for the door handle as if my head had just done a full 360 *Exorcist* rotation.

"I'm not here to cause you any trouble. All I'm looking for are some answers," I said, pinning my hand against the door before she had the chance to pull it open. "Please."

Her grip on the handle loosened as she noted the runes on my own hand. "I already told your friend years ago, I want nothing to do with your world. Being what we are...it cost me everything. I just want to be left alone."

"And no one understands that better than me."

"I seriously doubt that."

I removed my hand from the door, only to hold it in front of her face.

She studied the metallic runes imprinted on my skin, only looking more confused. "Are...are those Enochian?"

"Yeah, and they were gifted by a High Prince of Hell after he put a binding hex on me," I affirmed, tapping the intricate inked band tethered around my ring finger.

Her already-pale face only grew whiter. "What do you expect me to do?"

"Madsen told me you were prophetic, that you could see glimpses into the past and future. I need to know if there's any chance that your visions could somehow give me a clue on how to break the spell."

"I don't dabble in casting—"

"And I'm not asking you to. I just want to know if there's a way that you could maybe see how the spell was performed, or maybe even see how I eventually break it. Hell, even if you could tell me whether or not I still have the branding in the future... I'll take anything I can get."

She at last sighed. "I can't control what I see."

"And I understand that."

Lucinda nodded, gesturing me to the reading table. We both took a seat on opposite sides, and she fanned out what I assumed were tarot cards.

"Run your hand over the deck," she instructed. "It'll help connect me with your energy."

I did as she said, letting my palm hover just above each card as I drew my hand across the entire deck.

"Good." The woman ushered my hand away, sliding out three cards at random from the pile. She flipped the first, revealing the depiction of a reaping skeleton. It was labeled Death.

Not a promising start…

The next, a picture of a man being strung up by one leg, labeled The Hangman. Though, the image was upside-down.

Lastly, a card titled The Three of Swords, where a trio of blades pierced a bleeding heart. It too was upside-down.

"Interesting," the woman murmured, more to herself.

"What?"

"Each card represents a stage in your life. Past, present, and future."

Well, Death definitely seemed accurate, being as how Blaine had already killed me and all. But the rest…? "So I died, only to come back and be hanged before getting stabbed in the chest? Very encouraging," I huffed.

"It's not always so literal. In fact, it's quite rare." She gestured for me to give her my hand again. Turning it over, her fingertips softly grazed over the lines inside my palm, making the skin tickle ever so slightly.

Lucinda closed her eyes and hummed quietly, focusing her touch on the mating rune. A good minute or so passed before she gasped. Her spine stiffened in an instant as her grip on my hand tightened. I panicked, trying to pull away. It was no use. The woman's eyes flew open, only to roll back into her head until there was nothing showing but white.

Her voice came out ragged, as if strangled. It didn't even sound like her. Each syllable dragged out in a low, vicious hiss. "Mors venit ad vos."

Suddenly, against all my willpower, my eyelids grew heavy. Unable to rip free from the woman's grasp, rapid imagery ran through my mind like a film reel gone awry. I couldn't make much out, but a glimpse of woodlands and an open field... Something blasted through the air. A gunshot! A sharp pain instantly tore into my shoulder. But it paled in comparison to the slow, deliberate drag of steel plunging into the left side of my chest not a moment later!

"Sanguis quia sanguis."

I reeled back, nearly falling out of my chair as I at last managed to yank my hand free from Lucinda's hold. My eyes flung open, the pain disappearing in an instant. Lucinda startled away too, seeming to also regain consciousness.

I mindlessly examined myself, finding no wound where the momentary agony promised there'd be. I knocked my chair over as I scrambled back. *"What the hell was that?"*

"Your...your death," she muttered.

Praying that perhaps we saw different things, I asked, "Was it a car accident, by any chance? That's how I first—"

She shook her head, her hand involuntarily covering her mouth as she looked down at the last tarot card. At the image of the swords piercing a heart.

To say the news put a damper on things would have been putting it kindly. Not only had I learned nothing helpful from the trip, but I was officially freaked. From what Lucinda could see, her vision had been from the vantage point of my killer, so she couldn't help in identifying the culprit. I'd relayed the session to Dr. Madsen, who confirmed the fortuneteller's suspicions. Something about the mating bond had triggered the vision.

Somehow, someway, I was going to die—because of Blaine. Only this time, there would be no coming back.

But when? And why?

Attempting to pay attention during my remaining classes for the day was the last thing on my mind. Amid the constant yammering from my teachers, I tried desperately to fend off the darkness behind my sinking eyelids. Every time I'd begin to doze off, my mind continued to replay snippets of the vision, particularly the painful parts.

"I didn't know you could draw."

Hannah's voice snapped me out of my mini-nap, and my eyes shot to the open notebook sitting on my desk. The pencil immediately rolled out of my hand. "What the hell?"

"It's really cool. I mean, don't get me wrong. It's kinda creepy, but still..." She sighed, doodling something of her own on the corner of her Literature homework. A simple smiley face.

It wasn't that I couldn't draw; it was the fact that I didn't know I had been. I'd closed my eyes a good ten minutes ago, when the only thing in front of me had been a blank sheet of notebook paper. Now, the entire page was filled with an intricate design I'd never seen before. Two swords were crossed together, making what looked like an upside-down crucifix. And there was a gigantic snake wrapped around the blades, seeming to consume fire. I looked down at my drawing hand, seeing my fingertips completely gray from the shading I hadn't realized I'd been doing.

Staring back at the illustration, my eyelids drew heavy again. Something flashed behind my closed eyes, and the sound of a gunshot blasted again. Gasping at the searing pain, I startled awake with a stifled yelp.

Just as before, I was okay. The instant I opened my eyes,

the pain vanished.

"Kat, you okay?" Hannah muttered, looking at me in concern, along with the rest of the class.

Um...no.

6

Sweet Dreams

Today was not my day. Things continued to get weirder, and by Math, something just didn't feel right. Electricity clung to the air as the skies continued to darken to the point that it looked like it was nighttime. The windows lining the side of the classroom continued to emit a low howl as devastating gusts of wind battered the building, and the bare branch tips to the birch tree right next to the school scraped shrilly across the glass pane. Mr. Kroeger tried his best to earn our attention, but as soon as the lights began to flicker, we all lost interest in the lesson plan. Though most of the students were praying that the electricity would go out, forcing the school to call an early dismissal, I found myself unable to shake off the sensation of a looming threat. One unassociated with the weather. My heart was suddenly racing, my inner core felt oddly cold, my palms were sweating, my chest was tightening, and a faintness had washed over me.

Trying to rid the bleariness from my vision, I rubbed

my eyes, only to find the text from my book blurring and the letters jumbling about on the page. I immediately raised my hand, cutting Mr. Kroeger off mid-sentence.

"Yes?" he said.

"Could I be excused?" I asked weakly, my voice barely managing to reach the front of the room.

"Uh, sure." He motioned to the lavatory pass. "Are you alright?"

"I'm okay," I muttered as I walked woozily to the door.

Muffled voices could be heard through the closed classrooms down the corridor as I continued in my trek to the bathroom down the deserted hallways. The lights continued to flicker, and accompanying a loud, thunderous *BOOM!* came my greatest fear. All the lights went out, and I instinctively jumped at the screams emitting from the nearest classroom.

"Everybody, settle down," ordered Mrs. Branford from the other side of the closed door.

Two soft taps echoed in the distance behind me in the corridor, and my heart throbbed as I cowered over to the side of the hall. The only thing worse than being left alone in the dark was coming to the realization that you weren't *really* alone, and that dread overwhelmed every fiber of my being.

Then those two taps resonated again.

And again.

And again.

Someone was heading down towards me.

I quietly crouched down, my back pinned against a locker, as the footsteps galloped in my direction. The shoes froze the instant they reached me, and all the hair on my arms prickled up as my skin ached from the goose bumps that suddenly formed. The lights crackled back on for just an instant, and I nearly screamed.

But it wasn't from what or who I saw. It was from what I didn't see. I didn't see *anything*. The hallway was completely empty.

I expelled a stifled breath, seeing it vaporized from the bitter cold that suddenly invaded the air in the last second just before the darkness swallowed up the surroundings once more.

I scrambled to my feet, uncertain as to which direction I should run. With fifty-fifty odds, I shot off to the right, only to hear footsteps meeting up with me at the corner of the adjoining hallway. Slamming on the brakes, I whirled around in anticipation to run like a bat out of hell. Only, I crashed into the heavy, unmoving figure that suddenly manifested directly in my path just as the lights flickered back on. Scuttling back upright from the cold tile floor, my eyes traveled to the brute's knee-high black leather steel toed boots and up to the long leather duster whose deep-set hood hid this stranger's features.

Raising a leather-gloved hand, this figure unsheathed a long filigree sword from the scabbard resting across his back. The frightening markings gleamed under the florescent tube light bulbs lining the hallway. It was most definitely an Angelorum blade.

I outright screamed as I ducked and sidestepped the first attempted strike that connected with the front of the locker closest to where I had just been standing, the steel carving clean through the painted sheet metal of the door like it was made out of tinfoil. Bolting back in the direction I had originally chosen to flee from, I wound up colliding with someone else the instant I rounded the corner into the next hall, my body ricocheting off them before smashing into the wall as I hit the floor.

Sprawled out and dazed, I stumblingly climbed back up to my feet in desperation, but my disorientation sent me crumpling back down to my knees as my vision swayed and my body stung.

"Kat?"

I bewilderedly looked up to see Mr. Warski, my teacher, readjusting the glasses on his face as he got back up to his feet as well following my impact.

"Miss Shaw, you cannot just go flying down the hallways like that," he snapped angrily, rubbing his beaten shoulder. "Someone could get seriously hurt."

"But he-" I muttered, pointing back down the hallway where I came from. I was dizzy with fear-induced adrenaline, preparing to continue in my escape attempt when Mr. Warski poked his head around the corner of the hall.

"Don't!" I screamed, stumbling backward.

"Kat, there's no one else out here," he said, looking both ways down the hallway. "What were you doing?"

He was completely calm, so I stole a look as well. Sure enough, it was deserted, and the damaged locker was now perfectly intact.

"Miss Shaw, are you all right?"

Vertigo had taken me over and I was shaking violently as cold sweat ran its way down my neck. "N-no, I…I think I have to go to the nurse," I stammered, clumsily going down the hall away from him. "I'm really not feeling well. I'm-I'm sorry."

I wasn't sure what it was with the local medical practices' insistency to leave burnt purple spots in their patients' vision, but I spent the whole next period in Nurse Patty's office with her shining a small flashlight into my eyes about a thousand times. It came as no surprise that she suggested I had suffered a panic attack, given that my heart still pounded furiously a good ten minutes after I came in to see her. I obviously left out the part about the phantom attacker. As soon as the manic anxiety subsided, I was sent back to class. I told myself I could handle the wait until the end of the day to talk to Blaine, but my body didn't seem to agree.

I sent him a handful of texts that went unanswered, and in my state of desperation, I did the unthinkable…for me anyway. I snuck out of class. Thankfully, Mr. Foster had his classroom door open, and I immediately spotted Blaine sitting right by the entrance upon arrival.

"Pssst."

With an arm perched up on the desk, Blaine had his head resting against his hand as he was clearly sleeping.

Perfect.

I wound up waving my arms to catch someone else's attention around him and motioned for them to nudge him.

The guy behind Blaine gave him a soft poke with the top of his pen, and Blaine snapped awake. He looked around, immediately spotting me by the door.

"We need to talk," I mouthed, motioning for him to join me in the hall.

"A little busy," he mouthed back with a yawn, nodding to the front of the room.

Bastard. The second Mr. Foster turned his back to the class, I raced over to Blaine and dragged him clear out of his seat and into the hallway. "I have a problem."

"I'd say," Blaine cracked, straightening himself out after I released my hold on his arm.

"I'm serious."

"What? Did Little Miss Overachiever fail an exam, or something?" he jabbed, and I all-out hit him. "Owww!"

"This isn't funny!"

"Well, I'm sorry, but was it not *you* who ordered that I leave you alone?" Blaine drawled. I continued to glare at him, and he finally huffed. "What kind of problem are we talking about here? 'Dagnabbit, there's no milk at home,' or 'Holy Swiss cheese! There's a meteorite plummeting from the sky right for us!'?"

"Consider the fact that I chose to sneak out of class to come and talk to *you* of all people," I countered. "I'll let you be the judge."

"Point taken." He bowed. "What troubles you, Majesty, to come and grace a commoner such as myself with your divine presence?"

My teeth gritted as I tried to refrain from going off on him. He knew I needed his help, so the ass-hat was going to take as much pleasure from the scenario as possible. "Someone attacked me in the hallway," I whispered.

"Come again?"

"I was on my way to the bathroom when some hooded *Assassin's Creed* wannabe suddenly showed up and went after me!"

"Did your Omen rune ignite?"

"Yeah."

By the look on his face, it was obvious Blaine was far more doubtful than alarmed.

"*What?*"

"Our runes are linked; as your Maker, if any of yours go off, those same ones will light up on my own arm. Granted, mine won't *ignite*. It's more like a subtle glow, but with some serious vibrations," he drawled casually. "Hence, my disbelief, given that there's been inactivity on the runes-front all afternoon."

"Well, maybe if you weren't *sleeping*—"

"Trust me, *that* would wake anyone up."

"Well, I'm sorry," I scoffed, "but I know what I saw."

"And pray tell, how did you fend off this guy?"

"I-I didn't... He just disappeared."

Blaine sighed. "Kat—"

"I wasn't imagining it!" I sneered, trying to keep my voice under nothing but a low snarl.

"How have you been sleeping lately?"

I looked away, guilty.

"Okay, let me rephrase that, how much sleep have you been getting?"

"I plead the fifth."

"Montgomery?"

"Okay, so I really haven't gotten a lot of rest the past few nights," I admitted. "That still doesn't justify full-blown hallucinations."

To my surprise, he winced. "Actually..."

I all-out growled. "What aren't you telling me?"

"As the Prince of Lust, I'm blessed with the gift of prescience. You know, visions and omens and whatnot," he said, tapping the literal Omen rune on my arm. "And since your powers are also an extension of me, you have the ability of foresight as well. But you'll find the gift to be a little temperamental when you're tired. You may just catch glimpses of some things, or you can go as far as experiencing waking night terrors."

"What does that mean? That I'm gonna start trying to lick the grapes off the wallpaper soon?" I bellowed.

He chuckled.

"I'm serious!"

"No, you're not going crazy, nor will you. Okay?"

"Something else is wrong…"

"You're not gonna tell me you see dead people now, are you?"

"No, smartass." I was about five seconds from kicking him in his jewels! "This guy had the same kind of sword Russell tried to kill us with."

Blaine immediately paled, the amusement slipping from his face. "Are you sure?"

"Positive. It was Angelorum, and it had the *exact* same markings." Before I could protest, Blaine was towing me down the hallway toward the east end of the building. I tried pulling out of his hold, but he refused to let go as his pace quickened. "Where are we going?"

"I'm dropping you off at my place," he said, shoving a key into my hand.

"Why?"

"Because there're wards set up around the entire house. No one apart from you or I is allowed to enter. It's the only place I know you'll be safe."

"Safe from what?" I snapped, ripping my arm free. *"Who attacked me?"*

"The Angel of Death."

7

Killing Strangers

I'm sorry, the *what*?"

We were practically running down the hallway now. Blaine paid no mind to the parking lot attendant as she hustled out after us through the side exit.

"Excuse me, young man, but where do you think you two are going?" the old woman barked.

Blaine came to a stop, turning to address the busybody for the briefest second. "You never saw us." He pulled me back along as her uptight expression was suddenly wiped vacant.

"I never saw you," she muttered absentmindedly, turning and heading back inside without further protest.

"What did you just do to her?" I demanded.

"We have far more pressing matters here, love," said Blaine, ushering me inside the parked Cutlass.

The part of me that wanted to argue—which was a very, very large part—was silenced as I looked back at him. I could see the tension in his jaw, the worry wreaking havoc inside his eyes. This wasn't a trick or some sick little game he was playing. Something was *really* wrong.

Tires squealed as the Cutlass floored it into Blaine's driveway. My neck snapped like that of a crash test dummy as the Dark Prince slammed on the brakes.

"Don't invite anyone inside," he ordered. "Not your friends, not your aunt. Understand? No one."

"I can stay at *my* place," I said, pointing right next door.

Blaine's gaze hardened.

"Fine," I conceded, rolling my eyes for effect. "Your house it is." I knew he wouldn't give in to the suggestion, and I had to suppress the grin threatening to expose myself. I couldn't afford to seem *too* eager at the prospect of staying at his place.

"I'll be back as soon as I can."

"If the Angel of Death really was out to get me, why didn't he just finish the job? I doubt Mr. Warski posed *that* much of a threat," I said disbelievingly.

"Firstly, unless they've fallen, angels aren't allowed to be seen by humans. Secondly, that wasn't actually Death that attacked you. What you experienced was a waking omen, meaning he's on the hunt."

I gave him my best "uh-huh, sure" face.

"Trust me, if he had found you, he wouldn't be so sloppy as to do it in the middle of a public venue." I rolled my eyes, reaching for the door handle when his hand claimed mine. His hardened gaze could have cut through steel, making my insides go still. "Please, just do as I ask, and stay inside."

Swallowing down the lump suddenly caught in my throat, I nodded and climbed out of the car. The glorious purr of the classic engine ignited once more as I headed in the house. Blaine pulled the car back around and floored it off down the street. Wherever he was going, he couldn't seem to get there fast enough.

Well, this was something.

There I stood, alone and welcomed inside the Dark Prince's home, allowed to venture freely. Unsupervised. Prying the boots off my feet, I kicked the front door closed and threw all the locks into place. After tossing my coat onto the rack, I yanked every last window shade down and began my search.

If I was highly classified information, where would I be hiding?

Despite my initial assumption of the downstairs, I decided it would be best to not leave any stone unturned. I wasn't the type of person to rifle through other people's personal belongings, but I happily made an exception in this case. Sadly, all the cabinets and drawers were either empty or filled with nothing of consequence.

Making my way upstairs, I was met with further disappointment to see the first two bedrooms were literally bare. Not so much as a moving box inhabited the space. I could see the door to the Master Bedroom cracked at the end of the hall, but any interest vanished as I snuck a peek into the only other room.

An office.

Rich mahogany furnishings occupied the space, the scent of coastal beach soap lingering in the air. Blaine always smelled of it, hinting he'd spent a great deal of time in here to leave a signature like this so quickly after moving in. I took a seat at the desk, nearly jumping out of my skin at the sound of my cell phone going off.

"Hey," I sighed.

"I got your texts. What the hell's going on?" demanded Reese.

I relayed everything—or at least, *almost* everything—to him, from the fortunetelling place to the attempted murder in the hallway.

"But you're okay?"

"I'm fine. I left school," I assured. "Right now I'm at Blaine's place."

"...Come again?"

I half-laughed at the ridiculousness of the situation. "Yeah, I know. He said the place was protected by wards and stuff to keep anyone else from getting inside here, so I'm safe—at least, for now. Blaine thinks it was the Angel of Death who attacked me at school. Do you know anything about him?"

"Is he there?"

"Death?"

Reese sighed. *"Blaine."*

I chuckled, continuing to scour through the desk drawers. "Sorry, blonde moment. No, he ran off to go investigate his theory. I'm just in here doing a little reconnaissance work." Any amusement died as I finally brought myself to ask what I'd been dreading to even articulate. "Did you ever read anything about Blaine being able to control people? Like, have power over their minds?"

Only silence answered.

"Reese? You still there?"

"...You talked to Madsen." It wasn't a question.

"Earlier, about visiting Lucinda. Why?"

"Oh…" The sudden awkwardness was goddamn palpable.

"Reese, what aren't you telling me? Did Madsen find something?"

He exhaled roughly. *"Remember what my father's journal said, about Blaine?"*

"Vaguely."

"It talked about his powers of persuasion."

'His influence is nearly impossible to resist, thus turning anyone he captivates into his unwitting servant.'

"Yeah, so?"

"I lent the book to Madsen for him to cross-reference," Reese muttered. *"Blaine's rune, the Mark of Sitri, it's recognized as the primary sigil utilized in accordance with his specific powers of persuasion. It's part of a ritual… A hex, more specifically."*

"Like, for a mating bond?" This should've been good news, great even. So why did Reese sound like someone just ran over a basket of puppies?

"Madsen still can't find the full details on the ritual, so he won't be able to backtrack in order to find a cure." Reese cursed under his breath.

"What aren't you saying?"

"The hex…it works like a slow-acting virus. It infects the victim, but it can incubate in the person's system for days, weeks, even months before symptoms manifest."

"Symptoms?"

"When the Crown Prince of Lust chooses a mate, his Mark is the source of their bond. And it's the same sigil used for his persuasion. It slowly infects the mind, gradually brainwashing the victim to the caster's will. Eventually, the hex—"

"Turns you into his unwitting servant."

"I mean, we can't say for sure if this is the hex Blaine used on

you or not," Reese tried to assure.

Blaine's last words to me before I fled Mystic Harbor hit me like a bullet train. *"'I know you hate me. But you **will** change your mind, someday.'"*

Is that why Blaine hadn't come for me sooner? Because he had to wait for his hex to fully go into effect? If he was here now, did that mean…? How much time did I have left? The grandfather clock chimed at a quarter after six, and I still hadn't heard a peep from my arch nemesis. Fine by me. What wasn't so fine: I hadn't found anything in my entire search of the house. Calling it quits for the time being, I grabbed a can of soda from the fridge and an apple from the counter, heading into the family room. Seeing as how I wasn't sure how long I'd have to wait in here, I shot Hannah a quick text, asking her if she could cover for me. The last thing I wanted was to worry my aunt, so if I wouldn't be coming home tonight, I knew it would make her feel better thinking that I was just crashing at Hannah's place for a sleepover.

With all my bases covered, I plopped down on the loveseat in the corner, nuzzling up with a fleece blanket and a plush pillow. Despite being psychotic, Blaine *did* have good taste. The couch was comfy, the blanket was warm, and he had a killer music collection. A record player sat beside me, along with an impressive catalog of vinyls. Putting on Joe Bonamassa's Dust Bowl, I cracked open my soda can and angled the reading lamp behind my head, trying to let the sounds of "Slow Train" drown out my thoughts.

Was it really going to happen? Would I really wake up one

morning and be evil? Would I suddenly be throwing myself at Blaine? Was I going to become some brainwashed sex slave, convinced that I loved him? My mind involuntarily conjured up an array of disturbing images. Was I really going to become a Princess of Hell?

Resolute in my decision to stay awake, I picked up the novel resting on the coffee table and started reading, taking in a healthy swig of caffeine to boot. The effort apparently wasn't enough though, because I couldn't remember anything that happened after page ten before my eyelids sank shut.

A wood paneled wall materialized before my very eyes as my insides danced and churned in anxious anticipation. I flinched at the touch, feeling familiar hands graze the skin along my arms. I turned just enough to catch a glimpse behind me of his natural, raven-black mane and gleaming icy eyes in the candlelight. Goose bumps raked across my bare legs from the cold, but every inch of me went flush as Blaine pulled me against him. He swept the hair away from the right side of my neck and tugged down the collar to my linen gown past my shoulders, baring my entire neckline. His lips pressed to the back of my shoulder blade, slowly moving their way up my neck as his hands caressed my waist.

"I love you," he whispered tenderly into my ear. His breath cascaded down my jaw, and any apprehension inside me vanished. I angled my head and raked a hand through his tousled mane as our mouths met. His hair was nearly to his shoulders, revealing a natural wave to it that wasn't noticeable when shorter. He was so beautiful.

A gasp escaped my lips, inciting a mania within him at the very sound, and that passion enveloped every fiber of my being as his kiss deepened. He whirled me around to face him, simultaneously tearing the shirt off his very frame. Blaine drove me back against the wooden wall, and I outright moaned from the ecstasy his mere taste gave me as his hands dropped down to my thighs.

Sweeping me up in his arms, he carried me across the unfamiliar room, setting me down on an equally unfamiliar bed. Such unspeakable delight lit up his face, his eyes, as he took in the sight of me. I gripped his shoulders, silently demanding his lips as he lay over me, but Blaine suddenly pulled away. The bright smile decorating his mouth curved into an immodest grin as he slowly eased himself down the bed, down the length of my body.

"You belong to me now," he purred, pulling my legs apart to accommodate him. He rested back on his knees, and shivers shot up into my core as he took his time sliding up the skirt of my nightgown over my thighs. I had to bite back the impulse to cry out. Inconceivable pleasure poured into every last inch of my body, feeling his lips bear down on my exposed thigh.

My entire body jerked, wrenching me right out of my dream and landing me face-first onto the floor as I toppled clear off the couch with a scream. I tried to breathe, but my heart was thundering inside my ribcage so fervently, it seemed to rob my lungs of the required space.

What the hell was that?

Recognition hit me harder than the hardwood floor beneath me as I realized that wasn't the first time I'd dreamt that. The night of my Rite, after Blaine had bitten me. Fighting the demonic fever, I'd fallen unconscious, sharing in the exact same nightmare. Only now, it had gone on for even longer, and had felt even more real.

Still lightheaded and flushed, I towed myself back up on the couch. It was just then that I noticed the light bulb flicker in the reflection of the mirror across the room, immediately followed by an unexplainable tug from within my chest. It practically threw my unsuspecting frame off the couch again, desperate to pull me towards the front door. *Had that been what forced me out of the dream?*

As soon as I entered the foyer, I was yanked to the side window. I immediately spotted Hannah's Prius rolling up into her driveway across the street. She and Sam climbed out, and to my horror, Hannah started heading towards my house.

Hadn't she received my text?

I yanked out my cell to see *"Failed"* labeled beneath the message.

Double crap on a cracker!

The last thing I needed was to arouse suspicion with my aunt, and lying about where I was sleeping at night definitely looked like a cause for concern. The moment Hannah knocked on my door and asked Jenna where I was, I would officially be screwed. Dialing her number, I cursed under my breath when Sam answered instead.

"Well, if that ain't a fine how-do-you-do," he laughed.

"Can you give the phone to Hannah?" I pleaded.

"She's heading over to your place right now—"

No kidding! She was already halfway up the driveway, leaving me no choice. I ducked back into the kitchen and slinked out the side entrance. I leapt over the bushes dividing Blaine's house from mine, scaring the wits out of the poor girl as she came up the walkway to the front door. Hannah shrieked.

"It's just me," I whispered, yanking her over to the side

of the house when my aunt's shadow cast in the front window.

"What the hell?" Hannah sneered, holding a hand over her thundering heart.

I explained how I lied and used her as an alibi, but it didn't seem to clear anything up on her end.

"You told Jenna that you'd be sleeping across the street, when in reality you're, what? Lurking in the front bushes?"

"What? No! I'm staying next..." Oh crap.

Hannah's eyes expanded, looking at the house I'd unintentionally motioned to. "You're staying next *door*?" She squealed, practically bouncing with delight. "Are you seriously hooking up with the new guy?"

I buried my face into my hands.

"Awww, come on now. Don't be stingy with the details, girl. What are you two doing?"

"He's not even home," I confirmed.

"He's *what*?"

Yeah, come to think of it, the Angel of Death would've been easier to deal with...

"He just ran out quickly to go...grab some stuff," I clumsily countered.

"What? Like more 'protection'?" She teased. "Did you guys already use up his supply?"

"I'll talk to you later," I sighed. "Just, please, please, don't say anything to my aunt."

"Only if you tell me what he's wearing."

I shook my head.

"Is he even wearing *anything*?" She snickered.

Just as we shared in a laugh, headlights blinded us as a vehicle pulled up into Blaine's driveway. Without even looking, I knew it wasn't him. The Cutlass had a very distinct, and much louder, engine. This vehicle only let out a gentle purr as it rolled up to us.

"That's not Kat, is it?"

Hannah and I stepped aside to see a handsome face staring at us from behind the wheel.

The stranger beamed an irresistible smile as he rolled the window all the way down to get a better look at me. "Indeed it is."

"I'm sorry. Do I know you?" I asked. Nothing about him looked remotely familiar, and he most definitely had a face worth committing to memory. His bright porcelain teeth gleamed with boyish mischief, only offset by eyes that appeared nearly black in the limited light. His hair was dark, the sides closely shaved to the scalp while the top was a bit longer, slicked back pompadour-style. The slightly cultivated five o'clock shadow added a rugged quality to the appealing '50s Americana vibe he radiated to perfection. I would have guessed he was probably a couple years older than me. And though he wasn't bulky by any means, his black and white leather racing jacket did little to hide the taut muscles of his arms and chest concealed beneath the fabric.

"Oh, I met you briefly," he confirmed, "but I doubt you'd remember." That charming smile did little to wane the chill raking up my spine as I took notice to his hand draped over the top of the steering wheel. And he didn't miss a beat, winking at me as my eyes snapped back up to meet his. "Blaine has told me so much about you though."

My stomach hollowed out.

"I just swung by to pay him a visit, in fact."

"Well, he's not here right now," I attested.

"That much I inferred." He chuckled, taking another long look up and down my body. "How about I take you for a ride?"

"*What?*"

He just gave me a knowing stare, accompanied by a pirated grin.

I grabbed Hannah's arm, taking her with me as I backed away. "No, thank you."

"But your friend wants to," sighed the stranger, looking to Hannah next. "Don't you?"

An all too familiar vacancy suddenly washed over her face as Hannah nodded with a dopy smile. "I wanna go for a ride."

I continued pulling her away, but she suddenly started batting her hands at me. The harder I tried, the more aggressive she became, nearly pounding her fist into my cheek that I narrowly dodged.

"Will you *stop*?" I growled to the stranger as Hannah continued wrestling against me, desperate to reach the vehicle.

He popped the locks up on the passenger door. "Then get in."

I reluctantly nodded, and just like that, he told Hannah to return home. She suddenly shrugged and happily went on with her business, skipping down the driveway back to her own house across the way as if nothing had happened.

"I can always order her back here," the driver taunted, seeing me make no effort to join him. "And I have a feeling she'll be far more cooperative, too."

The fact that my Omen rune hadn't ignited was the only ounce of comfort I could take from the situation. "Where might you be taking me?"

"To pay your boyfriend a visit." The stranger stole a look across the street to where Sam and Hannah were still hanging out in her driveway. "Should I invite *them* instead?"

That strange tug in my chest continued beckoning me toward the car, clearly wanting me to get in. Against all better judgment, I did. Whatever this stranger was up to, I had a far better chance of defending myself against him than Sam or Hannah ever could. Now I knew why Reese refused to have friends. When you had a supernatural target on your back, everyone you cared about had one too. They'd always be at risk so long as I was in their lives.

I kept my right foot drawn up as I settled in the passenger seat, ready to snatch out the blade strapped around my ankle.

Ten minutes into the drive, and all I knew was that we were heading north.

The stranger finally laughed, breaking the silence that had settled between us. The sudden outburst sent my fingers wrapping around the knife's handle, prepared to pluck it out at the slightest movement.

"Anyone ever teach you it's not polite to stare?" the stranger chuckled.

It wasn't like I could help myself. My eyes kept drifting back to the tattooed rune on top of his hand. "You're a Mage," I said softly.

"Well, aren't you clever. What gave me away?"

I shot him a dirty look, but the devil in his smile had my body pressed against the passenger door, as if those two extra inches placed between us would make any difference. "How about you keep your own eyes to yourself?" I countered. It wasn't like subtlety was *his* strong suit, either. He'd spent the better half of our ride so far staring at *me* rather than the road.

"What can I say? I appreciate beauty when I see it," he simpered. "I like the whole look. You have a Taylor

Momsen vibe about you. Very rocker chic. Can you sing as well?"

"My concerts are limited to the inside of my shower," I admitted.

"Well, then I definitely want to see *that* performance." I could only imagine what kind of mental image he'd drawn up for himself as his eyes roamed over me again, his blatant immodesty making me cower so close against the passenger door I was practically sitting on the handle.

"Relax," he laughed. "I'm not in the habit of messing with someone else's mate. Especially my brother's."

Wait...

What?

8
Addicted

laine had a brother?

I knew he was the only child in his adopted family back in Mystic Harbor, but I never considered what his real lineage might be. I went from gawking at the man's runes to studying his face, trying to find a familial resemblance. I wasn't really seeing it. Blaine's cheekbones were sharp, high, angular, and his serpentine eyes were so pale they looked like that of a young wolf. His brother's face was more oval, accompanied by hooded bedroom eyes darker than his hair. The man beside me may have been more rugged, but Blaine was still unquestionably more handsome.

And I had plenty of time to make further comparisons. A good hour passed before we finally pulled off some remote back road into a gravel parking lot. I honestly wasn't sure what state we were even in anymore. An inky blue farmhouse rested up ahead where muffled melodies greeted us as we stepped out of the beaming new Cadillac. The stranger gestured for me to follow, and we passed by a few old-fashioned whiskey barrels at the entrance, seeing a sign that read, "Nucky's Hideaway."

"Val!" greeted the hostess as my traveling companion and I approached her at the end of the front hall. Based on the dozens of 1920s jazz photographs lining the walls, it was safe to assume this place was a speakeasy. "How lovely to see you again! Table for two? We're a bit full tonight, so it'll be a wait."

"That's alright," said the stranger—Val. "We're just here to find someone."

The woman nodded with a smile as she motioned us on, but then paused, taking another look at me, at the tattooed band wrapped around my left ring finger. "You're…? Oh, well now…" The hostess took her time admiring me from head to toe. "Aren't you just delicious."

She bared her teeth, revealing pointed canines as her eyes flashed a golden yellow.

Hellhound.

"Ah…thank you," I muttered, my nerves clearly getting the better of me.

Val chuckled, wrapping his arm around me as he guided me into the bar. "Don't mind her. It's just that your reputation precedes you with a few folks of the demonic persuasion."

"Reputation?"

"You know. You and my brother, a.k.a. Hell's cutest couple," he affirmed.

I attempted a smile, but it was shaky at best before I suddenly gasped, pinching my eyes shut as I instinctively covered my lips. The tantalizing sweet scent hit me hard, compelling my fangs to jut out from the roof of my mouth. This very reason was why I refused to attend high school parties anymore. Hormones and alcohol were a surefire combination of lustful behavior. But even the most sexed-up high school rave couldn't compete with this place. The overwhelming scent left my body buzzing with a high I could only imagine cocaine addicts would understand.

"Hey." Fingers brushed my chin, forcing my head up. "Open your eyes."

"I can't," I murmured.

Val let out a low laugh. "Open your eyes."

"I. Can't." I couldn't risk a crowded lounge seeing my eyes like this.

To my complete and utter horror, Val ripped my hand away from my lips. With my fangs completely jutted out, I couldn't close my mouth, leaving the pointed incisors on full display for anyone to see.

"What are you doing?" I shrieked, forcing my eyes open. I'd been prepared to bolt for the door, but the sight in front of me glued me in place.

Val's towering frame lingered right above me, his eyes as red as blood and his fangs as sharp as razor blades. "Look around."

Still petrified to be seen like this—like a monster—I stole a quick glance at the other patrons. Wait…

All their eyes were completely black or glowing yellow. Every last person in here. They were all either demons or hellhounds.

Val smiled. "This is the one place where our kind never has to hide our true nature."

And he was right. People glanced at us, with our fangs and red eyes on display, and they all simply nodded or smiled.

"Freeing, isn't it?" Val purred into my ear. "We put wards up all around the joint, making it impossible for anyone who isn't demonic to find this place. No humans, angels, or Reapers allowed." I sighed, only inciting his smile to grow. "It's a shame my brother didn't take you here sooner. Seems you could've used it."

This felt…amazing.

I'd spent how much time trying to rein myself in, to not allow myself a slipup. And yet here I was, in full exposure to everyone, and nobody cared. Nobody was scared. Nobody was running away, screaming, "freak!" Nobody had a gun aimed at my chest. Nobody judged me.

And the ugly truth that I needed to be in a room surrounded by Hell's Finest in order to feel normal quickly killed my buzz.

Val unreservedly hooked his arm around my waist, guiding me inside a dimly lit dining hall full of rich leather furnishings, elegant red velvet couches, and gleaming hardwood floors as everyone chatted loudly over the live jazz band.

"I'm gonna grab us some drinks," remarked Val over the clamor. "Wait here."

I turned to protest, but he'd already disappeared into the throng of people as he headed to the bar. I caught the growing number of eyes suddenly taking notice to me. Whispers were bountiful, and certain words clung to my skin like cellophane. *'Marked,' 'mate,'* some… seriously graphic profanity.

"Think it's legit? I mean, mates are supposed to be all over each other. Sitri would've presented her to the Master by now if they were together. Right?" remarked someone to my left.

The person beside the commentator cast me an

enigmatic grin, nudging their friend. "It seems we'll just have to wait and see for ourselves." Both men took notice to the rune wrapped around my ring finger, inciting dangerous smiles.

I was officially going to vomit.

I took a step back, only to knock shoulders with another patron. "Oh, sorry," I muttered. Then I looked up. And I was anything *but* sorry.

"Well, well, well. If it isn't Little Miss Goodie Two Shoes Gone Bad."

He looked so much more imposing than I last remembered. Although, most of my memories of Daniel were nice ones, back during a time when he wasn't pure evil and trying to kill my best friend—a.k.a. *his* own girlfriend. But there my former classmate stood, his wavy brown locks falling into his eyes, just above a shit-eating grin. He'd once been so sweet, so caring, and completely in love with Carly. That man was long dead, replaced by a merciless killer who still wore his face.

"Oh, how the Mighty have fallen," the Hellhound mocked, invading every inch of my personal space as he hovered over me. His interest immediately homed in on the fangs I hadn't managed to retract yet. "Diggin' the new accessories, Princess."

I shuddered at the nickname. Only Reese called me that, and it was a playful reference to Princess Leia from *Star Wars*. Not because Blaine, the Crown Prince of Lust, had apparently damned me into becoming his eternal mate, and therefore his *Princess*.

"How's my girl doing?"

"*Your* girl?"

"You can't tell me Carly hasn't been pining for me," Daniel crooned. "That little spitfire needs a real man to get her pilot lit, and boy, does she have an appetite."

I scoffed.

He didn't seem to appreciate the gesture, because his grin quickly turned venomous. "Perhaps I should go pay little Car-Car a visit. Remind her of what she's been missing." He bared his teeth with a growl, revealing vicious canines of his own as the yellow in his eyes turned to gold. "Oh, when I get my hands on her—"

My arm grew hot, and before I could think, I slammed Daniel facedown onto the nearest table, sending the shot glasses and beer bottles occupying the space to shatter on the floor. The demons seated at the table didn't seem keen on getting involved, ditching their remaining drinks as I pinned Daniel in place. They all stood and backed away without objection.

Daniel merely snickered, his cheek still mashed against the resin wood table top. "You forget, Princess, I don't feel pain."

"Oh, I remember," I sneered, wrenching both his arms behind his back. "I'd just like to see how you're gonna get your hands on Carly when you have *no arms*." The runes on my skin roared as I twisted his forearms, taking pleasure in hearing bones break.

Despite his considerable strength, Daniel couldn't wiggle out from under my hold. My runes only grew hotter the harder he tried, seeping their potency into my limbs. Panic finally seemed to settle in, because Daniel began thrashing, hearing a loud *crack!* as I twisted harder.

Warmth spread over my chest. My eyes immediately snapped up, spotting him instantly across the dance floor. He seemed to share the sensation, because his spine stiffened. Slowly, he turned around, his own eyes as wide as the sky as they settled on me.

"What...?" Even his voice in my mind couldn't find the words.

"Get off me!" Daniel barked. He threw his weight up, attempting to break free. I teased him, letting him up just enough so I could relish in knocking him back into the table. I looked back up at where Blaine had been, but he was gone.

Daniel was suddenly wrenched out of my hold, his body slamming against the pillar beside me with a gloved hand clamped around his neck.

"What did you do to her?" Blaine growled, tightening his grip.

"Nothing," Daniel choked out. *"She* attacked *me.* Put your bitch on a leash!"

Blaine pried the Hellhound off the pillar, slamming him back into the table, this time with Daniel facing upward. The Dark Mage pulled out what appeared to be a flask from his back pocket, dangling it above the Hound's face. A malicious grin spread across his lips until it stretched into a cruel smile.

Something about the flask made Daniel suddenly go still. "Come on, man. Take it easy. I didn't break your order. I never laid a hand on her."

"What did you just call her?"

Daniel squirmed, knowing full well he was in trouble, and that glimmer of fear only made Blaine laugh. Everything about the Prince made him appear thrilled by the present situation, but the scent in the air betrayed his veneer. It should have been floral. Instead, the sweetness that had ignited my fangs was overwhelmed by a bitter tang. Blaine was *livid.*

Keeping one hand pinned to the Hellhound's throat, he flicked open the lid to the flask and began pouring its contents out onto Daniel's face. The liquid was clear, like water, but smoke rose up from the flesh upon contact. The skin sizzled and blistered, turning a painful, beaten red. Hellhounds weren't supposed to feel any pain, but this… Oh, Daniel felt it. Throwing his limp, broken arms up in a pathetic attempt at defense, he howled and screamed and begged for the Mage to stop, his body crumpling onto the floor as Blaine finally released his hold.

"Next time you so much as look at her in a way that displeases me," Blaine growled, "you're gonna be taking a bath in this shit. Understood?"

Daniel's entire face was scorched with what looked like second-degree burns, his body trembling from the agony he was trying to suppress. He barely managed to nod.

"Good boy." Blaine patted a gloved hand against the Hound's seared cheek. Daniel shuddered painfully at the contact, seeming to only please Blaine more. He laughed as he removed his gloves, tossing them aside with indifference. "Now, get out of my sight."

A couple of nearby patrons helped pull Daniel up to his feet, careful not to touch any of the liquid dampening him.

The haltered graphic tee I wore was completely bare down the length of my back, and Blaine's bravado didn't wane as he rested his hand on the small of my back, pulling me into him. "Well, it appears even angels can be naughty, because you look like the Devil tonight. Killer bite." He, too, admired my fangs, cupping my chin with his free hand. I wanted to slap it away and push him off me, but I knew better in a place like this. We had an audience.

"Oh, that's not the only thing about me that's lethal," I gritted quietly through a forced smile, feeling every last eye in the joint focused on the pair of us. "If your hand manages to venture any lower, my knee is going to find its way somewhere very specific below the front of your beltline."

"You are positively exquisite," he practically purred. His own smile didn't falter as he turned me around, guiding me toward the opening of a dark hallway across the room. "Dare I ask what you're doing here?"

Reveling in the fact I was out of sight from prying eyes with his back to the crowds, I finally slapped his hands away. "Ask your brother."

That smug smile dissipated. *"Come again?"*

"That's right." I crossed my arms over my chest, hoping to wedge some much needed space between us. "He dropped by your place, and let's just say he was rather...*persuasive* that I come with him."

If Blaine came any closer, his entire body would've been fused to mine. "Did he threaten you?"

"Not exactly."

This didn't help the tension knitting into his brows. "There's a killer angel on the loose, and I asked you to stay put at the one place you'd be *safe*. So, naturally, you...*what*? Got in the car with the first stranger who came to the front door?"

"It wasn't like that," I spat.

"Did you invite *him* inside?" The very way he struggled to even acknowledge Val by name told me everything I needed to know about their relationship. I rolled my eyes, but yelped as his hands seized my arms. "I'm serious, Kat. Did you invite him in my house?"

The edge in his voice set my spine stiff. "No."

He sighed. "Then how did he get to you?"

"I was...outside," I admitted, seeing his frustration. "And I had my reasons, so don't even start. You can't expect me to be held up in your house like some kind of prisoner. I didn't even know *if* or *when* you'd be coming back."

The slightest hint of his pirated grin returned to his lips. "You didn't think I'd return to my own house, with *you* in it no less?"

I ignored the dalliance. "If you didn't want your brother coming around, then why did you even tell him that you bought the house?"

"I didn't."

Oh...

"I'm gone for two minutes, and you start a bar brawl?" Val drawled, appearing over Blaine's right shoulder. He extended a shot glass to me, which Blaine slapped away before I could even accept or decline it. "How uncouth of you, brother, when I come bearing a peace offering."

Blaine grabbed hold of Val's collar, throwing his body against the wall of the corridor. "Forgive me, but after your last 'peace offering,' my faith in you is a bit askew," he said, pinning the silver edge of a pocketknife against the man's throat.

Val flinched as a subtle cloud of steam rose from the scarce contact. He nevertheless laughed. "What? You gonna fight everyone in here tonight?"

"A fight implies the other party will actually be participating. I'm a hundred times stronger than you on my worst day. You'd be dead before you hit the floor." Blaine dragged the tool across his windpipe. A small slit, the size of an elongated paper cut, bled from the tow of the knife. "Now, tell me, brother, why did you bring her here?"

Val threw his hands up in mock surrender. "Hey, don't ask me. I was just following orders."

"Whose?"

"Mine," announced a lilted voice beside us.

We all looked to the far end of the hallway, finding a hale figure leaning contentedly against the wall. Scarce lights lined the corridor, and it only got darker the further along it went.

A subtle glow highlighted the individual's mouth as the flame to a lighter lingered in front of his face. The cigarette resting between his lips burned as he took a drag, making his way towards us. "You know I don't like roughhousing in any of my establishments," he drawled, showcasing a conclusive English accent. "But I certainly appreciate the passion, especially concerning one's mate."

Blaine lowered the blade from Val's throat and quickly stepped in front of me, obstructing my view of the stranger. It didn't hide the sight of him for long, because he just as quickly emerged from the darkness. On the surface, he didn't look particularly imposing. His hair was ash blonde, neatly slicked back at a medium cut, and his eyes were platinum gray, emphasized by alabaster skin. His clothes, too, were elegant yet simple; a short cotton trench coat, gray cashmere sweater, and black slacks. The cleft in his chin made his features appear softer, until he smiled. His teeth were startlingly white, and the natural tilt of his lips seemed to be pulled into an eternal leer.

"What a pleasure to see you again, Sitri. It's been far too long." His gaze drifted from Blaine down to me. "And this must be the illustrious Katrina I keep hearing about."

What the hell?

Seriously, did *everyone* know who I was?

"My, my, my. Just look at you," he purred, surveying me from head to toe. "Mr. Ryder here is a very lucky man, because you, my dear, are absolutely stunning."

My befuddled expression must have said enough, because he chuckled.

"My apologies. I've let my manners escape me." He extended his hand. "I have many names, but you may call me Raelynd."

My skin crawled as I shook his hand, but I still managed an uneasy smile.

The stranger's eyes gleamed with wicked delight, casting my insides cold as he released my hand back to me. "Why don't you boys run along and fetch us some drinks? I'd like a moment alone with the lady."

Blaine opened his mouth in evident protest, but the Englishman simply added, "I insist." And just like that, Blaine regrettably retreated back to the bar as Val forced an arm around him and dragged him away. He shoved his brother off, his face as sickly white as snow blossoms. Definitely not a good sign.

"How can they buy drinks?" I asked, following Raelynd as he directed us to a nearby booth. "Blaine's only eighteen, and his brother doesn't look much older."

The occupied table in front of us emptied out with a wave of the Englishman's hand. Every member of the exiting party nodded to the man, silently affirming his authority over them as well. He didn't have any runes covering his hand or wrist, so he couldn't be a Mage, and Hellhounds were considered to be minions of the Underworld, leaving only one other alternative. Demon. And if he held dominion over a Crown Prince like Blaine, then he had to be frighteningly high up on the totem pole.

"Sit," he ordered.

I didn't argue.

"We don't concern ourselves with technicalities such as age in these parts," said Raelynd. "Some people in this joint are a lot older than they look, and the rest don't let menial details get in the way of their fun."

"I see." I gave him another polite smile and returned my attention to the crowd, hoping he couldn't sense my repulsion as he slid closer to me in the rounded booth. The back of his pointer finger teased down my arm, and it took everything in me to not flinch.

"I like what *I* see."

I finally faced him again to observe a smile that was surprisingly softer than it had previously been. "And what do you see?"

"Darkness." His touch traced its way back up my arm, but his eyes never left my face. "I've been watching you since you came in, and I'm quite pleased. You have his darkness inside you. Not only do you bear his mark, but you have kindred souls. Such passion and malice. It's no wonder you're his mate."

Mate.

Every time I heard the word, it twisted my stomach up like a wet dishrag. I wasn't Blaine's mate. The old texts Dr. Madsen had lent me spoke of a true mating bond. *"Equals in heart and mind."* Blaine's bond, however, had been forged from black magic, a hex that infected its host like a merciless parasite, taking its time as it slowly warped the poor person's mind until they became nothing but an unwitting servant to its evil. If Raelynd sensed darkness in me, *Blaine* had put it there.

"Together, the pair of you will be unstoppable," he said, his hand suddenly dipping down to my stomach. "And your heirs…"

My body betrayed me, jolting far enough away to get out of his reach as I instinctively crossed my arms over my navel. My heirs? Our heirs?

Was he crazy?

His soft smile melted into a wicked grin once again. "Are we already expecting?"

"What? No!"

"Are you positive?"

"Yes," I growled. With this stupid mating bond, Reese and I couldn't so much as pass second base out of fear that my runes might alert Blaine, and I would sooner douse myself in boiling tar than share a bed with that bleached-blonde bastard.

Raelynd took another long drag from his cigarette, and I tried not to gag as the noxious cloud engulfed me. "Clearly, you don't trust our kind. So, I have to ask, what could have possibly swayed you to commit to our dashing Prince of Lust?"

And there it was. The true motive for bringing me here. Everyone seemed to be under the impression that Blaine and I were hot-and-heavy, but there was clearly some skepticism from a few. This whole scene, it was a test.

"Well, he's not exactly what you'd call hard on the eyes," I remarked, trying to regain my composure as I struggled not to choke on the building smoke. "Not to mention, he's saved my life on a number of occasions."

"Ah, yes, I heard about your encounter with a certain Angelorum blade. Admittedly, most of our kind would have fled from that scene faster than any poor soul trying to escape a Yoko Ono concert."

I couldn't help but laugh. "You don't seem to have much confidence in your workforce."

"Oh, there isn't a doubt in my mind of Mr. Ryder's capabilities, but we Underworlders are beings of self-interest. The fact he would risk getting his very soul claimed is a true testament to his character."

Claimed?

What did that even mean?

God, I was so far out of my depths with all this demonology stuff. It seemed even with all of Reese's research, I still hadn't scratched the surface of what I needed to know.

"Then why would he risk it?" I asked, hoping Raelynd would shed a little more light on the matter.

The Englishman slackened his arm on the top of the booth's backrest behind my head as he once again proceeded to move closer. "I'm looking at her."

"You give me too much credit."

The tips of his fingers suddenly traced the top of my shoulder, and I couldn't help but shudder ever so slightly under his touch. "Oh, I fear I still don't give you enough."

"Why?"

"Because, darling, as Charles Spurgeon so eloquently once said, 'A lie can travel halfway around the world while the truth is putting on its shoes.'"

I didn't have to feign my obvious look of confusion.

"You're a magnificent actress. What I have yet to determine is, who are you really performing with?" His eyes suddenly sharpened, forcing a knot to form in the bottom of my throat. "Which is it? The Prince, or the magician?"

It was as if someone had sucker-punched me in the gut. I tried to maintain my composure, but the words still didn't come out evenly. "I-I'm sorry?"

"You honestly think I haven't done my research? I know of the boy-toy you've been stealing kisses with. Tell me, how does he fit into all this?" Raelynd queried, pulling out his cell. A quick search into its contents, and he slid the device over to me with a picture on display. It was a photo of Reese and me, on the back porch of my aunt's house, in the middle of a lip lock! "Because you two seem genuinely chummy."

Now I knew how celebrities felt. Violated. My heart throbbed in my chest, and I did everything I could to keep my breathing steady. "Uh..." *Say something. Anything!* "Um, well, it's just that... ah... Every Reaper out there is looking for Blaine and me as a couple, so he and I just thought that having a red herring in my love life would be smart. Make them think that they just mistook me for...uh...me."

God, it sounded even stupider out loud than it did in my head! And that was saying something. But what other excuse was there?

"Is this young man aware of you using him?"

"Do you honestly think he poses a threat to Blaine?" I tried to sound flippant in regard to Reese, but I wasn't sure how the words came out. I casually extended my arms outward, hiding the trembling that had coursed its way into my hands. I needed to get out of here!

"Tell me, how do you feel about Mr. Ryder?"

That wasn't exactly the question I had anticipated. "He's a real pain in my ass. His wise remarks make me want to hit him where it hurts. And he can't seem to convey affection without turning it into an innuendo," I admitted. Raelynd still stared at me pointedly, proving that I needed to actually answer the question. "But...all that aside, I do care about him, and I believe he feels the same."

"Not quite." Raelynd spoke so matter-of-factly, and I could feel the contents in my stomach threatening to make their way back up.

Of course he wasn't buying this. Saying that I cared

about the man who had killed me and ruined my life was about as convincing as my Uncle Frank's toupee.

The Englishman pointed over to the bar at Blaine. "You know, not too long ago, our dear boy there enjoyed the destruction he implemented on others. The world has not been kind to him, and he relished in returning the favor. He'd have a tornado rip right through the middle of a crowded church during Sunday mass if he could." Raelynd sighed at the thought. "Now look at him. He's domesticated. Mr. Ryder hasn't taken his eyes off you since we sat, in the midst of some rather lovely ladies trying to earn his attention."

I turned, and sure enough, he was right. Despite the small congregation of women flocking around Blaine with batting eyelashes, he didn't pay mind to any of them.

"Question is, are *you* as committed?"

"Clearly, my saying so won't satisfy your interest." My words suddenly cut sharp, almost critically, earning a vicious grin from my counterpart. "But I still have to ask, why are my affections any concern to you?"

"I'm a businessman, Katrina. And you, my dear, as a Princess of Hell, are an invested asset."

"What do you expect from me?"

"Right now?" Raelynd gave me a good, long look. "I'd like to see a little demonstration of your affection."

My poker face vanished in an instant as I gawked back at him, blatantly appalled.

The Englishman threw his head back and laughed. "Not with me, sweetheart." Raelynd motioned over to the bar.

My expression didn't wane. *"Blaine?"*

He smiled a snake-like, tightlipped grin. "Your magician friend isn't going to mind now, is he? Because I would hate to have to remove a handsome young man such as Mr. Blackburn from the equation."

I...I didn't have any other choice. He knew about Reese! One thing was for sure: I was going to murder Blaine, or at least come as close as I could without actually doing so.

"I'm not a particular fan of the PDA," I choked out.

"With a stud like him? I find that hard to believe." He blew a puff of smoke directly into my face this time, and I bit back a cough.

Oh, Blaine was a dead man…

"Will that be all?" I asked, preparing to slide out of the booth.

"Until next time." His bloodcurdling grin somehow managed to tighten even further as he waved me away.

Don't panic, Kat. Don't panic.

I weaved between the crowds of people, heading over to the stools at the bar. Every step was too fast. Too fast. Too fast. But I couldn't stop. If I so much as hesitated for a second, I'd find myself bolting for the doors, puking my guts out. Between Raelynd's not-so-veiled threat towards Reese and what he was forcing me to do now, my stomach roiled, making me feel like I'd just ingested a softball. It was all the more unbearable seeing Blaine's eyes on me out of his peripherals. I was going to Hell for sure.

As I approached, he started to turn, forcing me to grab him by the back of his hair before he could speak. There was no use in suspending the inevitable. Crushing my mouth against his, I drank up his intoxicating taste, along with the bitter sting of whiskey on his lips. The anger and terror brewing inside me provoked such aggression that it had my arm vibrating as a rune ignited.

Blaine suddenly jerked away from me, as if I'd burned him. "What are you—"

My hands remained in his hair, desperately pulling his face back down to mine. He tried speaking again, but I didn't give him the chance. I bit his lower lip, silently commanding him to keep up. Raelynd was sure to be watching.

The bite wasn't hard by any means, but the simple gesture had Blaine's hands wrapping around my own forearms. The silent quiver on his left palm danced across my skin. His own rune had ignited, but it was a very, very different one.

It took Blaine not more than two seconds to respond to it with an equal ferocity. He rose up from his chair, embracing his hands now on each side of my hips. I moved between the stools, instinctively trying to find more room after blindly bumping into another patron. Blaine immediately drove my back into the bar counter, pressing me into the curve of his body. I barely had time to gasp before his mouth reclaimed mine, each kiss feverish, hungry, desperate.

His lips molded to mine, only to find their way to the side of my neck, to my throat, to my collarbone. And every inch of my skin could feel just how badly he craved it as he breathlessly moaned my name. Blaine wasn't just kissing me. He was tasting me, devouring me, claiming me. To only make matters worse, the rune on top of my hand gently hummed, making my whole body go flush with what would best be described as a hot chemical rush. And I couldn't quite determine if it was adrenaline caused by fear, or dopamine caused by…something else.

What was I doing? My hand wasn't just in his hair. Both hands were, and they were raking my fingers through his mane, desperate to cling to him, to pull him closer. I wanted to murder him, and yet blood pounded in my ears from something I knew wasn't rage.

A bright flash exploded overhead, followed by a loud crackle, startling us both enough that I managed to pull away. Of all things, the patrons around the bar gave us a round of applause, thoughtlessly wiping away flecks of what appeared to be broken glass. We looked up, seeing every last light bulb above the bar had burst! Managing to catch my breath, I took hold of Blaine's hands, interlocking my fingers with his as his lips lingered intimately in front of mine. "I think it's time we got out of here."

He nodded, hovering over me for a moment, his eyes still ablaze as his breathing remained jagged.

"Please."

Blaine finally retracted, keeping hold of one of my hands. I led him back to the front entrance, trying to keep calm as I headed up the steps to the main hallway. Our path was blocked just as we reached the top.

"Well, I stand corrected. It appears my brother here has found himself someone even more wayward than he is." Such peculiarly wicked pleasantries caused my heated insides to turn cold again as Val peered down at me. "Just keep a good eye on her, brother. Mavericks like her rarely keep their heart open for just one man."

I wasn't sure if it was *my* emotions or Blaine's that had ignited the Wrath rune on my arm, and I didn't care. Pinning a hand to his chest, I threw Val back. He barely managed to keep his footing as I shoved past him, taking Blaine with me.

"Have a good one, you two," Val called out behind us with a snicker.

As we approached the parked Cutlass outside, Blaine stepped ahead of me and opened the passenger door. Climbing in, I ignored the gesture and looked back at the entrance to the Hideaway, seeing Val leaning against the open doorway with his shit-eating grin still plastered in place. The weight of the car shifted as Blaine climbed into the driver's seat, and I did everything I could to not pay mind to him. My body was shuddering with the dying effects of several ignited runes, making my nerves all the more heightened. It was the most horrifying high…

Blaine leaned in. "Kat—"

"Don't," I snapped.

9

The Bird and the Worm

"Kat—" Blaine tried again.

"Say another word, and I swear to God, I will punch you in the mouth."

He pinched his lips shut, seeming to consider the option. One look at me, and he knew better, silently turning over the engine.

After the longest, most awkward silent car ride home, Blaine finally pulled into his driveway. Before the car even came to a complete stop, I leapt out, racing up the front walk to my aunt's porch.

"Hold up!"

I stopped midway on the steps, hearing him head over.

"Why are you mad at *me*?"

I whirled around. "You're kidding, right?"

"No," he said, crossing his arms over his chest. "I didn't make you go outside, and I'm not the one who dragged you to the club. I asked you to stay put. I did everything I could to *protect* you—"

"Is anyone watching us?"

"What?"

"Are any of your boss's cronies watching us right now?"

"Ah... No," he said, clearly baffled. "Not that I know of."

"Good." I climbed back down a couple steps, looking him square in the eyes. He didn't even have the chance to notice the blue light emanating from my arm. The air resounded with the wallop from my hand as I smacked him across the face. With my rune ignited, the simple slap had outright wrenched Blaine's head to the side.

"Ahh!" He staggered back a step, tenderly rubbing the spot of impact as his eyes shot back up at me. *"What the hell was that for?"*

"You selfish, egotistical asshole!" I sneered, proceeding to pound my fists into his chest.

"Hey, hey!" Blaine finally grabbed hold of my wrists before I could strike him again. Despite my rune giving me a little extra strength, he still managed to pin my hands down. "Take it easy there, Rocky."

"What the hell is your problem?"

"Might I ask you the same?" he challenged as I ripped free from his grip.

"What the hell have you gotten me involved in here?"

Understanding seemed to slam into him, because I watched as his beaten face phased through fifty layers of confusion...and realization.

"What? You thought I wanted *that*?" I actually laughed out of my own disbelief. "I fled across the country to get away from you! What would ever make you think that I'd ever want anything to do with the man who killed me?!"

He did little to suppress the crooked grin that suddenly pulled at his lips. "I brought you back."

My jaw dropped. "Are you serious? You ruined my life—turned me into this...monster, and that's all you have to say for yourself?"

Biting his bottom lip, he climbed the remaining step separating us. "Well, if memory serves me correctly, I've saved your life more times than you claim that I've 'ruined' it. I'd think a little gratitude was in order."

I slammed my hands against his chest, disappointed to find the effort was useless. My rune had faded, making the unaided action futile.

"Oh, come on," Blaine teased, hooking his hands on my hips. "You can't deny you enjoyed that back there."

"You. Disgust. Me." I ripped his hands off, but he grabbed my left wrist, showing me the rune stamped on top of my hand.

"Your body says otherwise."

That rune. It was the symbol for Lust. And it was still glowing ever so slightly.

"It's ignited, because of *you*," I snapped, taking notice to the same symbol alit on his hand. "You can control my runes. Turn them *on*, just as you can turn them off."

"Is that what you think?" He smirked. "You really have no idea how any of this works, do you?"

"Well, if you're such a know-it-all, enlighten me then," I growled.

"As your mate, my omen rune *will* glow to warn me if you're in danger, and I can shut down your runes if need be. But I don't have any power over which ones you ignite."

I staggered back a step, nearly tripping over the next

stair. "You're lying."

"Is that so?" That teasing grin turned into an all-out vulpine smile. "Tell me, did any of your runes go off in the past eight weeks since you ran away—that *you* didn't ignite?"

He already knew the answer, so I merely scowled at him, hoping my anger would overwhelm the sheer panic boiling in my gut.

"Do you *really* think I didn't use any of my own runes while you were away?"

Panic.

Panic.

Panic.

If my accusation was right, then anytime he'd ignite one, my arm should have lit up as well. But it hadn't. Not once.

Oh God.

Was it already happening? Was... Was my body betraying me? Was this how the hex started? On some creepy subconscious level?

"Screw you," I bit back, turning to head up the porch.

A shadow cast across the inside of the front window as someone approached the door.

"Good night," Blaine called out in an irritatingly sugary tone, "neighbor."

Flipping him the bird, I marched up the steps and yanked the door open, finding Officer Hernandez standing on the other side of the threshold.

He caught sight of Blaine and even prepared to address him, but I slammed the door shut before either could so much as make a pleasantry to the other.

"Your girl friend looks a little different from what I imagined," he laughed, gesturing outside as I locked the door behind me.

"What?"

"Jenna said you were sleeping over at a girl friend's house tonight. Gotta say, 'she' looks a little manly."

I cringed.

How could I have totally forgotten about my lie to Jenna?

I decided against taking off my coat, since I could feel a rune, most likely Rage, vibrating beneath my sleeve, and I really wasn't in the mood to explain a glowing tattoo. And like that, it hit me. With all the craziness going on, it only now just occurred to me that I was walking in at midnight—on a school night! Oh boy, was I in trouble. Antonio had the tendency to be rather fatherly, not sparing Hanna or me a lecture on appropriate teenage behavior. I took one last look at Blaine through the window beside the door, seeing him still at the bottom of the steps. That infuriating grin of his had at least subsided.

"Is Jenna asleep?" I asked nervously.

Hernandez shook his head, taking a drink from the beer bottle in his hand. "Nah, she got called back into work to cover for another bartender. Shouldn't be back for at least another hour or so."

"Any chance you won't tell her about this?" I asked, desperately hopeful as I nodded to the clock beside me.

"Silent as the grave," he chuckled.

"Really?" Well, this was new. I laughed. "You feelin' okay?"

"Great!" he affirmed, stretching his arms out above his head blithely.

"That's good to hear," I sighed, both relieved and taken aback by his chipper demeanor. Then I looked over by the refrigerator, seeing a hefty number of beer bottles that had collected at the counter next to it. "Geez...well, that explains it."

"What? One of Evermore's finest isn't allowed to unwind?"

"Uh, no, this just isn't like you, that's all." I pulled the fridge open and took out a bottle of water.

"Pity I can't stay like this. I'm kind of enjoying it."

"What? Being drunk?"

He nodded merrily.

I looked back at him crossly. "You know who else says that? Alcoholics."

"I know. Aren't they the best?"

"Wow, oookay... Someone really needs to get some sleep." I turned to head out of the kitchen, and that's when I realized it.

The rune on my arm. It wasn't from rage.

It was Naudiz. The omen rune.

My voice cracked as I added weakly, "I forgot my phone at Hannah's. I'll be right back." I started backtracking towards the front door again when the officer laughed, cutting in front of me.

"Oh, what's the rush, sweetheart? Don't you want to spend time with your aunt's beau?" he sneered.

I whirled around, bolting back through the kitchen to the side door.

A firm grip caught hold of my collar, and it sent me hurling backwards just as I reached for the knob. "Where do you think you're going, dearie?"

I began pulling myself off the floor, looking up at Hernandez. He was now blocking the doorway. The officer cast me a cruel smile, blinking on cue to reveal exactly what I had suspected. Black orbs covered his eyes. He was possessed! Trying to run for either the front or patio doors would have been pointless given my heels, so I raced up the steps beside me to the second floor. Halfway up, my left foot jerked down with a violent wrench. I crashed into the stairs as Hernandez's grip around my ankle tightened.

I kicked my free heel into his arm, and he released his grasp on me, but not a second later did he lunge forward, grabbing hold of my waist. My hands clenched onto the posts of the banister beside me, clinging on for dear life as he heaved all his weight downward. It was no use. My fingers bit into the corners of the railings, and the force proved to be too much. Hitting each step on the way down, I fell back onto the landing and was immediately pried off the floor.

"Kat!" The front door pounded with what I guessed was Blaine throwing his weight into it.

"Side door!" I managed to scream just as Hernandez yanked my disoriented frame back into the kitchen. He snatched a steak knife out from the countertop holder and pressed the blade firmly against my throat, throwing himself behind me to provide coverage.

Blaine kicked the side door open not ten seconds later.

"Well, well, well. Look who we have here," hissed the officer. "Prince Charming."

"You would've killed her already if that's what you wanted. You *need* her," said Blaine, his voice notably losing his distinguishable air of assurance as he stood on the threshold of the doorway. He couldn't come in… "She's no use to you dead."

"You bring up a good point." He slid the knife firmly up to my face, pressing the serrated steel against my cheek. "My boss *does* need her alive. That doesn't mean she has to still be in one piece though. What do you think? Is a bit of maiming required?"

Blaine's ire set his entire sleeve ablaze with every last rune as he lowered himself, his feet pivoting into a stance.

The demon clicked his tongue. "Take one step, and I carve her eye out. I've never done it to one of your kind, but I have a feeling even your healing properties won't help it grow back." His hold tightened around me. "Wouldn't want to spoil this pretty little face now, would we?"

"I'd be more worried about your own face." Slamming the heel of my boot into the top of the Officer's foot, I simultaneously threw my head back, nailing the base of it in the demon's nose. I cursed, feeling the blade drag across my cheek. "Move!" I ordered.

Blaine sidestepped from the doorway just in time as I snatched the demon by the collar, throwing him outside. The runes on my arm helped catapult him—a little farther than I intended. His body crashed against the siding of Blaine's house, and I just as quickly reclaimed my hold on him. With my grip tightened on the front of his jacket, I used all my strength to force him right into the wall beside *my* door. His body nailed the brick siding, and I leapt away.

The officer looked at me, baffled, and prepared to bolt. He made it not one step before being forced to a halt. "What the hell?" He lunged again, expecting to break free, only to be knocked back on his ass. The demon sneered, dropping his gaze to the long area mat resting beneath him.

"You've got to be kidding me," he groaned. "He said you were clever, but I've got to hand it to you; you've certainly outdone yourself here."

"*He* who?"

"Why would I tell you?"

Blaine made a move towards him, but I immediately shoved him back. "Don't," I warned. "One step, and you'll be stuck in there with him."

The Mage crooked a brow at me, kneeling down to peel back a corner of the rug. It was a ratty old thing, only used to wipe off shoes if they were *really* dirty. Blaine laughed, observing the edge of the symbol I'd spray-painted on the underside of the mat. "Containment sigil?"

It was a trick I'd picked up from Doctor Madsen. The moment anything demonic stepped into the threshold of this painted symbol, they became trapped inside it, which sadly meant *I* also would get stuck. I marked areas around the house with them, just in case Blaine or one of his little friends decided to snoop around.

"Nice touch." Blaine's smile was of pure adoration as he rose back to his feet, but it quickly turned devious as I came up and wrapped my arms around his waist.

"Take it easy there, Romeo." I pulled out the flask from his back pocket. "Holy water?"

Blaine nodded, seeing the demon pale just as Daniel had.

"Let's try this again," I said, returning my attention to the officer. "And I'd be very careful with your next choice of words if I were you, because if you don't tell me what I want to know, I'm gonna pour this entire thing down your throat before you even so much as get out another syllable. Are we clear?"

"You think I'm scared of *you*? Anything you'd do to me pales in comparison to what my boss is offering," the demon spat. "Torture me all you want. I'm not telling you a thing, Blood Whore."

"Wrong answer."

"That's not gonna hurt him, is it?" Blaine whispered. "I

mean, the *real* guy? When he wakes up?"

"You don't know?"

He almost laughed. "It's not like I make it a habit of attacking demons. And if I do, I'm not hanging around to do a Q&A with the person after they wake up."

I cocked a brow at him. "That almost sounds like you care."

He shrugged. "Just curious."

"No, it won't hurt Hernandez a bit. But it'll hurt like hell for *him*," I confirmed, looking at the demon crumpled down on the area mat. I splashed some of the water into his eyes, causing him to scream out as I ripped the rug out from beneath him. Prying the officer's mouth open, I dumped the entirety of the flask down his throat. The demon thrashed and shuddered about violently as I chanted the prayer Madsen had taught me. Eventually, black tendrils of smoke escaped from the Officer's mouth and busted nose, and he stopped moving. He lay unconscious on the ground, and I pressed my fingers to his neck, checking his vitals. He was fine.

"Okay, I don't know about you, but I'm admittedly turned on," remarked Blaine, leaning contentedly against the opened doorway.

I shot him a look. "You wanna take a turn on the mat next?"

His soft chuckle stirred my hair as he knelt down beside me. I flinched, feeling his fingers cup my jaw as he inspected the gash on my cheek. Blaine caught a hold of my hand before I could hit him. "You're bleeding."

"I'm fine." I brushed him off, grabbing Hernandez's unconscious frame from under his arms. My runes were still lit, letting me drag his body with next to no effort inside to the loveseat not far from the doorway. Heading back out, I repositioned the old mat, only to find Blaine blocking the door as I turned to go inside again.

"What're you doing?"

"What does it look like?" I tried sidestepping him, but he quickly countered.

"A demon just tried to *kidnap* you, and you're going back in there?"

"It's *my* house—"

"No, it's your aunt's house, which means she could have let anybody in there. Clearly, that demon already had an invitation if he was able to get inside. There's no knowing who else could come in. Electricians, cable repair men, plumbers, your aunt's book club; they're all possible risks."

I knew exactly where this was going. "And let me take a wild guess where you think I should stay…"

"Just give me a couple hours to put up a few wards around the house," said Blaine. "I can't make it impenetrable like my place, seeing as how your *aunt* owns the property, but I can at least make it a little more challenging for any lowlife demon to come sauntering inside."

"I don't get it. Why would a demon even want me?"

"Your blood."

"My…what?"

Blaine leaned against the doorway, keeping an arm pinned across the threshold, barring me passage. "You come from a powerful bloodline. Even though the fullest extent of your abilities hasn't been unlocked yet, the power is still there nonetheless. And it gets passed down from generation to generation. Any Duke or High Lord in Hell would love to get their hands on you, even by means of kidnapping, so long as they can use you to…"

"Give them heirs?" I spat, remembering what Raelynd had mentioned in the Hideaway. But...wait. My bloodline? Not Blaine's. *Mine.* "Do...Do you know who my parents are? My *real* parents?"

His jaw tensed.

"Are my parents..." *Not human?* I couldn't bring myself to finish the question out loud, but Blaine nevertheless nodded. "Is that why you targeted me? Because of my bloodline?"

"I didn't 'target' you," he said, his lips pulling into a teasing grin. "And your heritage is hardly your finest selling point."

Trying to ignore the innuendo, I growled, "Who are they?"

"This really isn't the time or place for that conversation, love," he said, hooking his fingers into the front pockets of my pants. I tried yanking back, but he only pulled me closer, plucking out his house key that I had tucked in the right side, pressing it into my palm. "Go, try to get some sleep. When I'm done over here putting up the wards, I'll come and get you."

"Who. Are. They?" I demanded again.

"My bed's particularly comfortable, so don't feel shy about getting under the covers." It didn't take a genius to figure out he was purposely trying to annoy me—anything to get me to drop the subject.

"Don't do that! Just tell me—"

"Trust me, you're better off not knowing," he said, suddenly serious. "Hell knows I was."

"What is *that* supposed to mean?"

"Another night."

I opened my mouth to further protest when the next thing I knew, Blaine's hands had snatched me up. In one swift motion, he had me slung over his right shoulder with my upper body dangling behind him as he held me by the waist and thighs.

"Are you kidding me?" I fussed about, hitting my fists into the middle of his back. "You son of a b—"

"Watch your language, love." He purposely jostled me enough to make me shriek as he led us across the way to the side entrance of his place. Without even touching the door, the lock unlatched with a wave of his hand, the door swinging open a second later.

Okay, even I had to admit, it was impressive. My attempt at homing in my magic skills was like an angry gorilla throwing a temper tantrum. While Blaine's handiwork was precise, my endeavors usually ended with something smashing, breaking, or exploding.

Carrying me to the base of the stairs, he swung me back over his shoulder, planting me on my feet. "Sleep tight."

"I am not sleeping in *your* bed!" I barked.

Without another word, he turned on his heels and headed for the door.

"Blaine!"

He suddenly stopped in mid-step, looking back over at me with his lips pulled in, as if trying to hide the most curious smile.

It only pissed me off more. *"What is so funny?"*

He just shook his head.

"What?"

"Nothing. It's just," he sighed, ruffling a hand through his hair, "that's the first time you've called me by my name since…"

Since he'd bitten me.

Resigning myself to the family room couch, I grabbed the blanket I'd left there earlier and curled back up into the lush cushions. Only, between the lack of sleep and being stuck in skinny jeans all day, I wanted nothing more than to change out of my clothes. I sat restlessly for over an hour, unable to relax. Worse yet, my aunt's house could be seen right outside through the kitchen window.

I *could* run across the way and just grab some fresh clothes. It would only take a minute, if that. What would be the harm?

My hand reached for the door knob, but I quickly pulled it back to my side. I'd already had enough misfortunes today. And with how rotten my luck was, I'd be stupid to take a chance on something so trivial. But how much longer would I have to wait for Blaine to finish up? I unbuttoned my jeans and pulled them down my thighs, seeing the impressions the stiff fabric had imbedded into the skin. Twenty minutes later, and I surrendered.

No, I didn't go outside.

I headed into the laundry room where I'd remembered seeing newly cleaned clothes folded on the dryer. Amongst the set was a long-sleeved tee that on my small frame fell down past my butt as I slipped it on. Contentedly discarding my top and pants, I headed into the family room and plopped down on the loveseat in the corner, nuzzling up with the fleece blanket once more. I told myself to merely rest my eyes. I was not going to fall asleep here. No way in hell would I ever leave myself unconscious and wholly vulnerable, knowing you-know-who could come in at any moment.

The effort apparently didn't work though, because the

next thing I knew, sunlight was pouring into my bleary eyes as the low drone of Mr. Welling's lawnmower rumbled outside. I groaned, nestling into the cushion beneath my head.

I'd slept the entire night?!

"Rise and shine, lovely," cooed a soft voice.

My eyes snapped back open, finding my cheek resting on what I quickly realized was *not* a pillow, but a warm, muscled chest that rose and fell with every breath.

"You're adorable when you sleep," Blaine chuckled, coaxing his fingers through the ends of my hair as he lay laxly beside me.

I outright screamed, trying to disentangle myself from the bed sheets.

Wait...bed sheets?

I wasn't on the couch.

I was in a bed.

My bed.

With my legs still wrapped up, I wound up falling out onto the area rug.

I was in my room.

And so was Blaine!

10
Tornado

laine was in my room. In *my* bed!

"*What the hell are you doing here?*" I bellowed.

"Just making sure you slept well." Blaine's eyes traveled freely down my frame as I finally managed to free myself from the covers that I'd pulled right off the bed. That's when I realized I was still in his shirt, and nothing else apart from my socks and panties.

I snatched up a pillow and chucked it at his face. "Bastard!"

"I'd keep your voice down if I were you," he advised with a devilish grin. "Wouldn't want your aunt walking in here now, would we?"

I gritted my teeth. A strange boy in my bed, and me dressed in nothing but *his* shirt? Yeah, not ideal. "How did you even get in here?"

"The house key was in your purse."

"But you were never invited in."

His brows furrowed. "So…?"

"You're not allowed inside someone's home without an invitation," I gritted, trying to keep my voice as low as possible.

This didn't seem to clear up his confusion any. "You're my mate."

"So…?" I mocked right back.

"So," he emphasized, propping himself up on his elbows. "What's yours is mine, and what's mine is yours. That extends to invitations."

My stomach hollowed out.

"I assumed you knew."

Blaine hadn't given me a verbal invitation into his home yesterday…because he didn't need to. With our bond, there was nowhere I'd be able to go to truly get away from him. He'd always know what I was thinking and feeling and he'd always be able to find me. And get to me.

I was going to be sick.

"Now, hop to it, missy," he declared, rising to his feet. "We need to get a move-on."

"I'm sorry, *what?*"

"We. Need. To. Leave. Preferably sooner rather than later."

"I'm not going anywhere with you!" I barked, noise-control be damned.

He shrugged, sauntering towards the door. "Fine, stay in town with the big bad demons and killer angel."

"Wait, what?"

"I have it on good authority that several more of Hell's Finest will be making an appearance in your quaint little

Evermore, and I don't suspect their interest is in taking the historic bus tour."

"*Why would you do that?*"

He gave me another confounded look. "Do what?"

"Invite them here!"

"Hey, don't look at me."

"Right, because they'd so conveniently show up right after *you* would," I scoffed. "Go sell your bullshit someplace else, 'cause I'm not buying. And get the hell out of my house."

Blaine rolled his eyes, exasperated. "Such gratitude, as always."

"Gratitude for what? You inviting yourself into *my* bed?" I snapped. "How did I even get here? I was on your couch."

"I figured you didn't want your aunt seeing you leaving my house come morning, so I tried waking you up. But you were out like a light, so I carried you back over here before Jenna came home."

"That still doesn't explain why *you* were in my bed."

He pointed around the room. I just looked at him confusedly, until I realized it. Everything was a mess. All the picture frames on my dresser had toppled over, books and papers were scattered about the room, and posters that had been tacked to the wall were now tossed to the ground. It looked like a tornado had torn through here!

"You must've had one hell of a nightmare last night, because you ignited several of your runes in your sleep. I was going to leave, but the moment I stepped out of the room, Hurricane Kat started wreaking havoc," he said, kicking my fallen wastepaper basket back upright with his boot. "I didn't know what else to do. The only thing that can shut down your runes is my touch, so unless you wanted to destroy your room..."

"So we *slept* together?" The sudden urge to bathe myself in bleach overwhelmed me as I forced out the words.

"You don't have to say that like you're going to vomit," he muttered, leaning back against my dresser.

"Well, I can't help my body's natural sense of revulsion to you," I scoffed, grabbing a pair of pants from the closet.

"Keep telling yourself that." There wasn't a hint of mockery or conceit to his words, even as he plucked up a picture I had of Reese sitting beside my vanity mirror. Blaine tossed the photograph aside, feeling my gaze on him. "This isn't a one-way street here, and we both know it."

"You actually think something's going to happen here, between you and me?" I laughed, but it wasn't from amusement. Far from it. "Wow, I knew you were crazy, but I didn't think you were *this* delusional."

He just rolled his eyes.

"Seriously, what the hell's the matter with you? I told you how much I hated you, nearly killed you, and then ran away as far as I could get! Yet, you didn't take any of that as a hint?" I further prodded. "Why did you hunt me down? *What do you want?*"

"You." The room suddenly felt too small. The walls had to be moving in on me, because my back was against my closet door, and he was only getting closer. "I want you to live up to your potential. I want you to fight back, to takedown the people who've hurt you. I want you by my side when I make every last one of them pay for what they've done."

"You want me to help you *kill* people?"

"Some, yes. Others..." He seemed to consider this.

"Death may be too good for them."

My stomach was no longer in my body. It had to have been replaced by a volcano, because the bile rising in my throat was searing my insides. "I'm not going to be your monster!" I only pressed myself deeper against the closet door as he approached. "And I'm not afraid of you!"

"I don't want you to be, either of those things." His hands pressed against the door on either side of my hips as he lowered himself to meet my eyes.

"Then what *do* you want from me?"

"Everything." *Mind, body, and soul*, whispered his voice inside my head.

"You mean, *half* a mind," I sneered in return.

His eyes narrowed. "What's that supposed to mean?"

"I'm not an idiot—"

"I never said you were." His voice was low and easy as his arms closed in around my waist, pinning me in his embrace. "In time you'll find I make a far better ally than an enemy."

"I think your enemies would disagree," I sneered.

"You could always ask them, but it may take awhile to find one that can still talk." The lazy amusement laced in his tone sent chills up my spine.

"Kat?" My aunt's voice made us both whip around. "Kat, is that you?"

I wanted to DIE as she nudged the door open.

Jenna froze, taking in the sight of Blaine, not to mention me blocked in between his arms. "Oh, sorry… You said you were at Hannah's, but I heard your voice…"

She kept looking between us, drawing the obvious conclusion.

"It's not what it looks like," I growled, shoving past the bleached-blonde jackass still blocking my way.

"Sadly, I can attest," Blaine drawled. That charismatic mask of his slid right back into place the moment he turned to face Jenna.

My aunt, clearly not convinced, still stepped out of the doorway as I snatched up my bag and headed out. "Forgetting something?" she whispered under her breath.

My baffled look spoke for itself, forcing her to tug at the hem of her shirt.

"*What?*"

She rolled her eyes, nodding down at my outfit.

Crap. I was still wearing Blaine's shirt.

I whirled back around, prepared to grab the first available top I could find. The only thing I wanted was to get out of this room, to get away from *him*. The instant I turned around though, I was met with immediate resistance, colliding into a solid wall of defined muscles.

Blaine.

With that punch-inducing smirk pulling at his lips, he dangled a black shirt between his fingers. A silent peace offering. Ignoring the victorious glint in his eyes, I snatched it from him and stormed out the door.

The moment I hit the bottom of the landing, I ducked inside the coat closet and swapped shirts at Superman speed. It was a strange sort of talent, really. After going to gym class all these years, this skill became a necessity, if you wished to escape the perfume overload brought on by the girls' locker room. Within seconds, I reemerged from the closet and threw the shirt at Blaine's face as he reached the bottom of the stairs.

"So it's safe to say you're *not* a morning person?" He chuckled, pulling the fabric off his head. It only further added to the tousled, bed-head look he was sporting, and good God, it was nauseating how gorgeous he was. Why did assholes like him always have to be so handsome? It felt like some unspoken law of the land. If your insides were truly ugly, then your outsides had to make up for it. How else were you going to lure in your victims?

Thank the Lord, Hannah's Prius was still in the driveway when I bolted outside.

"Could I have a lift?" I asked, finding her in the garage swiping a stash of energy drinks from the backup refrigerator. I had my own car, but with Blaine still talking to my aunt on the front porch, I wasn't about to take the chance of him asking for a ride.

"Sure." She stole a look over her shoulder, catching the spectacle on display across the street. "But wouldn't you rather ask Romeo?"

"I'd rather you hit me with your car."

This day couldn't end fast enough. John Addams High's curriculum rotated every other day, and I came to the horrifying realization that Blaine shared every single class with me on this rotation. I didn't so much as look in his direction, but that inescapable heat in my chest refused to dissipate, leaving me flushed and flustered.

With an AP Psychology paper due immediately following Winter Break, I used it as an excuse to escape from Study Hall. All I wanted was to disappear, so I went to the one place where that was possible: the library. Perusing the shelves, I grabbed as many of the recommended reads Mr. Dennings had suggested. God knows I needed the help. I still had no idea what my topic was even going to be. With the threat of the apocalypse, thinking about Freud's psychoanalytic theories hadn't seemed like a priority.

Grabbing the final book I needed, I started making my way toward the counter when that familiar heat spread across my chest. *For the love of God, could I catch a break?* A pair of hands snatched hold of my waist from behind, yanking me back into the aisle. I choked on a stifled scream just as it reached the top of my throat.

"Surprise," he whispered into my ear.

I immediately froze. "Are you stalking me?"

A soft chuckle warmed my ear. "I wouldn't be the first guy."

"That's not a consolation. Two wrongs don't make a right," I said, turning on my heels to face him. That brilliant dimpled smile of his beamed from ear to ear, only inciting an even bigger smile from me.

"Hey, Princess."

Mindlessly lobbing my collection of books on the nearest shelf, I practically tackled Reese, wrapping my arms around his neck. He welcomed the embrace with a laugh, managing to steady his balance before I toppled him into the bookcase. Returning the gesture, his hands cradled the small of my back.

"What are you doing here?" I whispered, still unable to wipe the massive smile from my face. "If Blaine sees you —"

He dipped down, capturing my lips. "Then I suppose we should go somewhere a bit more private then."

I opened my mouth in protest, but he laid his finger against my lips and took possession of my hand. Guiding me through the library aisles all the way to the abandoned back corner of the German Philosophy section, he wasted no time. I squealed as he spun me around, pinning me against the bookshelf beside us. His mouth teased in front of me, our faces so close that our noses brushed together. I leaned in, but he recoiled, taunting me in the cruelest fashion.

"Tell me you're happy to see me," he chuckled, biting his bottom lip.

God, I wanted that lip, and everything else attached to it. That layered chestnut hair, those soulful amber eyes, those adorable dimples. All of it. "I *am* happy."

Those three little words barely escaped my lips before he reclaimed them, kissing me so heatedly I couldn't even breathe. Tiny shivers danced up my spine as a low moan resonated deep in his throat. The fervent quality to it had me pushing off the bookshelf, erasing what little space was left between our bodies.

Whispers sounded towards the front of the aisle, and before I could push him away, Reese picked me right up off my feet and carried me to the other end, effectively hiding us from anymore prying eyes.

"Reese," I hushed. "Mr. Stover and Mrs. Artfield are right in the office over there. What if someone catches us?"

"I can always make myself invisible. They can't accuse you of making out with yourself," he laughed. "Can they?"

"No, I'll just look totally certifiable," I chuckled, giving him a playful shove. It wasn't enough to deter him though as his lips pressed a soft kiss to my chin.

"Then we'd be perfect for each other," he whispered, breathless.

"And why's that?"

Reese caught hold of my waist, reeling me into him until our hips met. "Because you drive me crazy."

Heat and ice simultaneously shot through me as his mouth trailed down the left side of my neck. I learned quite quickly that the scars on the other side left by Blaine's bite didn't seem to like anyone touching the skin. An unspeakable revulsion would roar through me, leaving me shaken and unnerved. But Reese knew better than to go there, and it was a relief that I didn't have to explain it. He knew me, better than anyone else.

I still laughed inwardly at the idea. Reese Blackburn, the same guy who I thought just a couple months ago *loathed* me with every fiber of his being, was kissing me. And God help me, he felt so good. After everything that happened, he was still the one person—who knew my dark secret—that wasn't afraid of me. Well, apart from Blaine. But the latter wasn't saying much. That would've been like Hannibal Lector being put off by you becoming a cannibal, only after he forced you to eat his other dinner guests.

I shook my head, wiping the image of both *that* and Blaine away. All I wanted was to live in this moment. I would have smashed every clock and hourglass and watch in the world just to hold onto it. I slid my arms up his chest, wrapping them around his neck. Reese hoisted me up by the hips, and it only made my pulse pound harder. Even the heat in my chest had grown hotter. I wanted to tear away every last layer of clothes keeping me from him.

Just as I crushed my mouth against his, a soft, "*Ahem*," rattled us both out of our frenzy.

To my absolute horror, I looked over to the single leather chair pushed against the corner of the wall not two aisles down, seeing the all-too-familiar icy gaze focused on me. Those eyes almost looked like two slices of silver in the low lighting of the library. Every muscle in Reese's body went taut as he glanced over at what had so adamantly stolen my attention.

Blaine merely crooked a brow, eyeing the magician up and down in appraisal, clearly not finding anything to his liking. "Blackburn," he droned.

"Well, if it isn't the Dark Prince of Peroxide," Reese retorted with equal crass as Blaine ran a hand through his bleached hair.

"What are you doing here?" I scoffed.

"What am I doing here? A student? In the library? With a book?" Blaine mocked, flashing us the back cover of some leather-bound volume in his hands. "Gee, I don't know. You might need to call Angela Lansbury in to solve this one."

I deflated, feeling the fleeting euphoria from just a moment before dwindle to nothing.

Reese released his hold on me, shaking his head. "Come on."

He started leading me toward the aisle we'd come from when Blaine suddenly appeared at my side.

"Do you really care that little about his wellbeing?" the prince remarked, nodding to Blackburn.

"Excuse me?"

"Well, I have to ask, seeing how that seems to be the only logical explanation for why you two would be flaunting your affections out in public." The whimsy in his voice still couldn't conceal the metallic aroma radiating off him. Yep, he was not a happy camper, and that would've delighted me, if not for the clear undertone Blaine had just laid.

"Are you threatening him?" I growled.

"Me?" He batted his lashes, the perfect façade of innocence. "Why, never. I just thought that you'd exercise a shred of common sense, being that *our* boss already made it clear he'd be keeping a close eye on us."

Raelynd's words hit me like a ton of bricks. *"I would hate to have to remove a handsome young man such as Mr. Blackburn from the equation."*

Vibrations coursed up my arm, tickling the heated skin as my hand suddenly clasped around Blaine's throat. In one fluid motion, I threw him into the end of the bookshelf, my fingers only squeezing harder against his airways. He grabbed hold of me, immediately cutting off the energy from my runes, but panic slammed into him when he realized I hadn't let up.

I didn't need magic to give me power. My fury alone supplemented me with plenty enough. "If anything, and I mean *anything*, happens to him because of you or *your* boss, I will end you," I seethed. "I don't care how long it takes to break this bond. You hurt Reese, and I'll become your worst goddamn nightmare."

The veins in Blaine's face began to bulge as he rasped uselessly for air, giving me a perverted pleasure as I pressed harder. I'd expected him to fight back, but his hands grappled at a spot near the center of his chest. He tried to speak, but the pressure on his larynx only let a strangled gasp escape.

"By the time I'm done with you," I whispered, leaning into him, "you'll be begging me to put you out of your misery. And I will take pleasure in giving it to you."

I finally released my hold, and he choked on the abundance of oxygen as he sank to the floor. His hands remained pinned to his chest, his body involuntarily shuddering. Even as he gasped at the newly reclaimed air, the panic still hadn't left Blaine's face, paralyzing him in place. He pinched his eyes shut, and I startled back at the blaring succession of sharp blasts that sounded inside my head.

"Kat?"

I flinched, feeling fingers grip my shoulder.

"You okay?" Reese whispered behind me.

Without looking back at him, I took hold of Reese's hand and ran.

Battlefield

ll right, what's going on in that beautifully chaotic mind of yours?" asked Reese, observing me out of his peripherals as he drove his truck back to my aunt's house.

I just shook my head, as if that passed for an answer.

"Just forget about him. At least for the afternoon, anyway. He's out of sight, so let him be out of mind." Reese put the truck into park as we rolled up to the front of the house.

"I don't know what happened back there. I just...lost it," I murmured, taking notice to the Nissan's absence as I climbed out.

"Hey, cheer up," demanded Reese, coming up behind

me and ensnaring me into a hug as we headed to the front porch. "You didn't try strangling a puppy, okay? The guy deserved a lot worse."

"True."

"Not to mention," he chuckled, kissing my neck as I let us inside, "it was kinda sexy seeing you kick ass like that."

"You don't say?"

"You were ravishing."

"More like ravenous," I muttered.

"Yes, you are." He couldn't help but grin, hauling me right back into his embrace. "So, what would you like to do with our few stolen hours? Watch a movie, play a game—"

I pulled him back down to me, cutting off his thought as I crushed my mouth against his.

"...Or we could just pick up where we left off," he finished breathlessly.

"I like the last option."

"Me too." Those infectious dimples never ceased, even as Reese pulled away. "Just for the record, your aunt's not home, right?"

At last, I smiled. "No, her car's gone."

"Okay, just making sure," he chuckled, kissing me once again.

"What? Are you afraid of her?" I teased.

"Me? No." He lowered his voice to nothing more than a whisper. "I just don't want her to see what I'm going to do to you."

My heart soared at the idea, but reality sent me plummeting back to the ground just as quickly. "Reese, you know we can't—"

"Can't we?" His lips teased along my jaw. "Blaine's already here."

I shuddered at the thought, but quickly realized what he was *really* saying. The only thing stopping us from going farther than some watered-downed kissing was my fear that the rune for Lust would ignite, signaling to Blaine where I was. But he was already here. What could be the harm now?

"Sure you can handle it?" I teased.

"The only people who would question that are those who don't understand just how incredibly sexy I really am."

"Is that so?" I laughed.

"Yes. That's why you should be thankful that you can see and appreciate what a catch I really am, all six feet and a hundred and sixty pounds of my glorious slightness." He couldn't help but snicker as I shut and locked the front door.

"I must say, you talk an awfully big game," I remarked grinningly, removing my jacket.

"And I've got the performance to match," he grinned back.

"Oh, really?" I went up and unbuttoned his embroidered black tailcoat, sliding it off his shoulders.

Reese wasted no time, picking me up and carrying me through the kitchen to the upstairs. At the end of the hall, he laid me down on my bed and removed his waistcoat, unbuttoning his dress shirt as well.

He suddenly paused as another one of my dangling posters fell to the floor behind him. Reese turned, taking a better look around the room. "Ah...did you do a little redecorating since my last visit?"

I sat up, seeing Reese gently brush a stray piece of notebook paper away from the bedside. My room was still a total disaster zone from my apparent nightmare-induced tornado.

As if on cue, a lopsided frame toppled on the dresser, taking the remaining photos down like a row of dominos. Reese, with his lightning fast reflexes, managed to catch the frame at the front of the stand before it crashed to the floor. He looked at the image inside and inwardly cringed. It was a picture of my parents.

"You hear from them at all?" he asked, nervous.

I shook my head. "They said they were going for marriage counseling in Phoenix, but from what Blaine inferred, they're most likely gallivanting around Europe." I felt sick just thinking about it. And it wasn't even because Blaine had been spying on them in his quest to hunt me down. It was the fact that he knew more about them than I did. Their own daughter.

I really had been abandoned.

Trying to hide the hot tears creeping into my vision, I climbed off the mattress and started collecting the discarded items scattered across the floor, but froze at the sight of the white apparel box resting on top of my nightstand. With its red silk ribbons, it was indeed the same box Blaine had left before. The corner had a small dent in it, presumably from where I'd thrown it against his house.

Once again, there was a card tucked in the trimming. Since it seemed like fresh paper, I could only assume it was a new note. Part of me felt the temptation to open it, but I muzzled it down. Just having to look at that box made me only want to cry harder. All of this was *his* fault.

And he thought he could make amends for everything with a gift? Like I could be bought off.

Vibrations coursed up my arm and I immediately snatched up the box, chucking it under my bed before the runes could ignite. If I let them light up, who knows what they'd do? I turned my room to rubble when I was simply sleeping. I'd probably level the whole house if I wasn't careful.

"Hey." Reese came up behind me, placing gentle hands on my hips as I stood upright. I still couldn't bring myself to look at him, not when I had tears blurring my vision. I didn't want him to see me like this. I was a mess, inside and out. "They'll come around," he murmured.

It took me a moment to regain my thoughts, realizing he was talking about my parents. I shook my head, feeling wet streaks stream down my face. Blaine had been right about them from the very beginning. Before my parents discovered what had happened to me, Blaine said that they'd desert me, first chance they got. And they did.

If my friends saw me for what I was, they'd leave too. So would my aunt. To Raelynd and Blaine, I was nothing more than a plaything. To the world, I was an abomination, something that needed to be put out of its misery. Mr. Reynolds, the man who had been more of a father to me than my actual dad, had sent a thug out to exterminate me. And that was *without* the knowledge that Blaine had already bitten me.

Reese took hold of my arms, urging me to turn around. When I wouldn't, he stepped in front of me, forcing me to look him in the eyes. Of all things, the tears had dissolved into bitterness, to anger. My skin vibrated again, but it was from a different rune. Wrath.

If Blaine wanted me to fight back, then fine. He would get exactly what he hoped for. My hit list had just been forged, and Mr. Blaine Ryder had the distinguished honor of top billing.

Reese helped me tidy up my room before taking me back over to the bed. We didn't say anything as we lay side by side. With my back to him, he pulled me against his body, wrapping his arms around my tiny frame. I shivered at the gentle caress as his thumb stroked up and down the length of my forearm. The touch sent electricity crackling over the skin, leaving little sparks to dance between my flesh and his fingertip.

I couldn't help but giggle at the tickling sensation, and it seemed to have the desired effect Reese had been hoping for. I sighed, feeling the humming Wrath rune still threatening to ignite suddenly peter out.

"It appears I've got the magic touch," he chuckled, planting a kiss to the back of my neck.

I traced the tattooed sigils running along the length of Reese's forearm. "It appears you do. And it must be nice, having control of it." As a Light Mage, all it took was simple concentration to ignite or disarm his runes. Being angry or upset or too happy didn't risk things blowing up or going haywire. Yet, here *I* was, the five-foot-three demonic Hulk.

"You'll learn how to harness your magic," he assured, rolling me over to face him. "Don't let him get under your skin. It's what he wants."

"He's already under my skin, and *on* it." I leered at the tattoos sullying my arm, at the band on my ring finger. It gleamed in the light with its permanent metallic ink, mocking me as an everlasting reminder that I now 'belonged' to the one person I hated most.

Reese took hold of my arm, pulling it up to his lips. "How about you let someone else *on* it?"

Soft kisses pressed to each of the brands, triggering goose bumps across my skin as the cool electricity stirred with the heat of his breath. His mouth trailed further up my arm, to my shoulder, when I suddenly found him laying over me. All the pain and hurt and self-loathing flitted away, bit by bit, with every kiss.

The world around us dissolved to nothing more than static. Our mouths met one another's, only to find their way to someplace else. Our shoulders, our necks… I was sure to end up with a hickey, and the thought only excited me more. I'd be branded, all right. By whom *I* chose.

A sweet, sugary scent prickled at my nose, and Reese's lips impulsively traveled to the one place I dreaded most. The right side of my neck.

It was too much.

Nausea, revulsion, fear. It all hit me so hard, so fast, I couldn't control my own instincts. Red filled my vision as my gums ripped apart to accommodate the elongated pearly white incisors. All my instincts could see was a threat. My hands suddenly gripped Reese's neck, and his pulse thrummed in my ears. I could see the artery throbbing beside his windpipe.

He stiffened at the realization of what he'd done, feeling my body go taut beneath him. Reese shifted his head, despite my firm grip still held around his nape. My jaw suddenly snapped up at him, begging to tear into his neck.

"Shit!" He barely managed to pull free as he scrambled upright, nearly falling off the end of the bed. I hadn't actually managed to bite him, but his hands still mindlessly grappled at his throat in blind panic.

The terror in his eyes as he beheld me…

Mortification and disgust riddled every inch of my

body. I... I was beyond repulsive; I was a *monster*.

I covered my mouth and lunged for the door, desperate to get as far away from him as possible.

"*Kat?*" Blaine's voice whispered to my thoughts, and I screamed, clawing my hands over my ears as if it could somehow drown him out. It only made the rest of the world go quiet, leaving the reverberating echoes of his voice to carry into the corners of my mind.

I heard my name being called again, but it was out loud.

Reese.

I could hear his pleas, the desperation in his words as he tried racing after me down the stairs, begging me to come back.

I couldn't. I snatched my purse off the floor where I had blindly tossed it, and I darted through the kitchen to the garage. Reese caught up to me, but it was too late. I had already locked the doors behind me after jumping into my car. His palms hit the window, begging me to look at him.

"Stay away from me." I had practically mouthed the words as I choked on them, but he'd heard them all the same.

His shoulders slumped, his face consumed in hurt, desperation, disbelief. "Don't do this..."

Blinking away the tears, I floored the car backward, barreling it down the driveway. Reese's truck was still parked out front, blocking me in, but I didn't stop. I swerved the steering wheel and drove my hatchback over the lawn until I was in the clear.

"*Kat, what happened?*" Blaine's voice demanded inside my head.

My fingers practically pummeled in the buttons as I slammed my hand into the radio. Finding the loudest song possible, I twisted the volume dial up until I couldn't even hear my own thoughts as I floored it down the street.

What had I done?

What had I done?

What had I done?

Dangerous Woman

riving on instinct alone, I eventually found myself pulling into the gravel parking lot of a familiar inky blue farm house. Knocking back another shot of tequila, I reveled in the warm, tingling buzz. I could feel the anxiety and humiliation slipping away. A couple more shots, and I probably wouldn't have cared even if someone came up and punched me in the face. And nothing was going to stop me from achieving that level of blissful intoxication.

"Of all the gin joints in the world."

I out-and-out whimpered, thumping my head on the counter. "Can't a girl get a moment's peace?"

"Oh, I think you've had more than a moment. Or, at least I *hope* you have, judging by your rising alcohol level," laughed Val, picking up my empty shot glass as he took the vacant seat beside me at the bar. "What number you on?"

I held up my hand.

"Three?"

I scrunched up my nose, taking inventory of my fingers. "Oops." I flicked up another.

The ruffian chuckled. "You drink often?"

"Never," I grumbled, folding my arms on the bar so I could rest my head on them for comfort. "What're you even doing here? Aren't you supposed to be out with your brother wreaking havoc and destruction on mankind?"

"Uh-oh. Trouble in paradise?" he teased.

I simpered.

"Oh, come on. It can't be *that* bad."

"Easy for you to say. You didn't nearly rip out your almost-boyfriend's throat during a make-out session—with these stupid things." I ran my tongue over my teeth, feeling my fangs still jutted out. The moment I entered the Hideaway, they sprang free and refused to retract. And at this point, I didn't mind. Between my runes and my bite, the male patrons here had the commonsense to leave me alone. One look at the tattooed band on my ring finger, they knew I was taken. And my fangs drove the message home, for those who weren't yet dissuaded. Except for Val.

"So, you almost tore out my brother's windpipe, aye?" The Mage nodded, almost appreciatively.

I cringed, apparently giving him an "Ewww" face at the very thought. As if I'd make out with that cretin...again.

Val smirked. "Ah-ha, the plot thickens."

Crap.

My blood alcohol level had apparently thrown out my mental filter, along with my poker face. "N-no, it doesn't,"

I clumsily countered.

"Don't be coy." He gave my arm a playful nudge, running a finger over my mating rune. "We're practically sibling-in-laws."

And on that note, I signaled to the bartender for another shot. "Don't make me vomit."

"Let me guess." The Mage stroked his chin in mock deliberation. "The magician?"

"No," I blurted.

Gee, nice one, Kat.

That was about as smooth as sandpaper to the face...

It only made Val's smile grow. "What? Having your 'one true mate' isn't all it's cracked up to be?"

"Mate." I scoffed at the word. "What the hell does that even mean? What am I supposed to do as his 'mate'?"

He shrugged. "The usual, I guess. Keep his bed warm, punch out a few of his pups—"

Now, I literally *could* feel bile rising in my throat. "Ugh! Hell no!"

"To what part? You have to give him at least *one* heir. That's kind of what our boss is counting on." The bartender slid a shot glass my way, but Val knocked it back before I could so much as reach for it. He coughed on the burn as the ethanol made its way down his throat. Served him right. "How else do you think family legacies stay alive?"

"Aren't you the eldest brother?"

"That I am."

"Then by logic, shouldn't *you* be the first in line to Blaine's title? How did he get it? Is it like some kind of contest? Only the sexiest brother can be the Prince of Lust," I mocked.

Val's smile only widened. "Are you saying I'm not sexy

enough?"

I rolled my eyes. "Yeah, you're a total eyesore."

"Ah, okay, so I *am* sexy. I'm just not as much as my brother."

"Precisely." The word slipped out before my brain seemed to process the thought, and I immediately reddened.

He laughed. "Ooooh, you really are in a tough place, aren't you. You hate his guts, and yet you still find him attractive. You naughty little minx."

"That is *not* what I meant." I tried shoving him, but it ended up being more of a nudge as I swiveled on the bar stool.

"Oh, come on. There's no shame in admitting it." He turned in his seat to face me directly as I snorted at the idea. "You met him before you found out about...what he was, right?"

"You mean...?" I held up a finger on each side of my head to imitate horns as I gave an animated hiss.

Val doubled over in his seat, sharing in my drunken mirth. "Well, if you're going to put it that way, yes."

"Yeah, we kind of became friends, actually."

"And are you really gonna tell me you weren't even the teeny, tiniest bit attracted to him?"

I grumbled, unable to find the will to deny it.

"What was your first impression of him?"

Maybe it was the alcohol talking, but something about those soft charcoal eyes had my defenses down. "I thought... I thought he was one of the most gorgeous men I'd ever seen," I admitted. "So, of course, he'd have to be a raving, demonic lunatic." I blew away the loose strand of hair that toppled over my face. "My taste in guys sucks."

To my surprise, the Mage's smile seemed genuine.

"You having any fantasies about him yet?" I could only imagine the look on my face, because his smile was all fox. "I may not have marked a mate of my own, but I've heard all about how it works with our kind."

"The only fantasies I want are ones where I get to murder him," I grumbled.

"Well, well, well. Now we're getting somewhere." He was practically giddy, downing what was left in his own Scotch glass. "What did you have in mind?"

"Wood chipper. Or steamroller, perhaps. Maybe full-on *Wicker Man*. Death by a thousand bees, Nicolas-Cage-style." My eyes brightened at the very idea.

"My, my. Aren't we wicked? You may not want to admit it, but you are just who my brother needs."

"I am not! I'm a good person—"

"'Good' people don't fantasize about murder."

"Well, blame Blaine." I giggled at the tongue twister. Try saying that five times fast. "He's the one who went all Dracula on me," I said, absentmindedly rubbing the faded fang marks on my neck. "I didn't choose to turn to the dark side."

"Perhaps not, but we're infinitely more fun than the folks upstairs," he said, pointing to the ceiling.

"There's a second floor here?" I slurred, looking up drunkenly at the rafters overhead.

"Yeeeeah, you definitely don't need any more of this," Val chuckled, snatching away my next shot glass.

"Yes, I do." I practically tackled him into the bar as I tried to wrestle the drink from his hands. With his height, he managed to hold it up well out of my reach the moment he rose to his feet. If he wanted to play games, then who was I to put a damper on his plans? I leaned into him, stroking a finger up his chest until I flicked it beneath his chin. "What do you want for it?" I purred.

Val beamed down at me, fascinated. "Like mother, like daughter, I see."

"Meaning?"

"It's only natural that you'd use your sexual prowess, being the offspring of a succubus," he crooned.

My mother? A succubus? I'd never heard of it before, but it didn't sound pleasant.

"The Prince of Lust and a daughter of seduction. No wonder my brother's so infatuated. It's kismet."

Any playfulness I had petered out at the mention. "Don't say that."

"He's a very lucky man." An unspoken softness met his gaze, depleting his smirk of its intended infliction. It was the first honest face I'd seen in so long from someone who knew the truth about me. Blaine had an assortment of masks he chose to hide behind, never hinting to which one alluded to the *real* him. And even Reese, despite his best intentions, had been lying these past two months. To himself. He was so determined to prove I hadn't turned into a monster, to prove that he could save me from myself, only to show his true colors the moment he saw me for what I *could* become. I had horrified Reese back there. And I couldn't blame him. He shouldn't ever feel guilty for fearing me. He had every right. All I wanted for him was to be happy, and safe. Two things I couldn't promise him anymore.

But Val? I could have cared less about his safety or his feelings, and he'd just told me more than Blaine and Raelynd combined.

"Why aren't you the Crown Prince?" I asked softly, leaning closer into him.

"I'm damaged goods, Doll Face."

"Aren't we all?"

He raised his arm, letting the fabric of his jacket ride up enough to flash me some skin. His runes... Two separate designs covered his flesh just above the wrist, but unlike the sigil on top of his hand, the ink wasn't black. It was silver, the flawless metallic shimmer almost ethereal, with the exception of the ghastly lines sliced down the middle of each symbol. Scars. They weren't large, but for some reason I shuddered just having to look at them. The skin was a sickly purple and raised, like it had been seared opened.

I didn't know what else to do but gawk.

The healing process for Mages was freakishly fast. Injuries that would take regular humans days, if not weeks, to heal from took us mere hours. And even after all the hits I'd taken, I still didn't have one scar to prove it, save for the fang marks. Our power was *that* effective. So what could have done that to his skin? How come it hadn't healed?

"Dance with me." Val didn't wait for me to answer as he directed me through the crowds to the dance floor, and I wasn't about to object. A million questions raced through my head, but I couldn't bring myself to ask him. My happy helping of tequila had made my mouth looser than a wizard's sleeves. I didn't want to take the risk of sounding too eager to learn what happened. Not until I could bring a better poker face to the table.

Despite the 1920's esthetic, the Hideaway wasn't playing the same jazz melodies they had the other night. Contemporary R&B filled the room under the warm glow of red mood lights. A mid tempo slow-jam began, only adding to the sensual atmosphere. With my hand in his, Val whirled me around in a tango-esque fashion, securing me in his arms as I spun into him.

"Well, look at Johnny Castle here," I laughed.

"Does that make you my Baby?"

"You wish." I pulled away, but kept hold of his jacket, drawing him back in. The percussive beat controlled my hips as I let the rhythm take over. Val took hold of my waist, moving harmoniously with me to the music. He released me into a dip and we both laughed as he pulled me back up.

"Feeling any better?"

I nodded.

Because I meant it.

Apparently, once the liquor hit my bloodstream, I was a happy drunk.

For the first time tonight, I couldn't feel the weight of everything bearing down on my shoulders. Everything turned into a blur of bodies and beats as I got lost in the music, dancing with anyone and everyone. My buzz had every inch of my body smoldering in a delicious warmth that left me vibrating. Even with the sweet, lustful scent still engulfing me, I'd become so relaxed that my fangs had retracted on their own.

Another pair of hands took claim of my waist from behind. Continuing to sway to the rhythm, I threw my arms up, draping them over tall, taut shoulders. I sighed, feeling the heat only intensify as I dipped down. My back grinded against hardened muscles, all the way from his chest to his chiseled abs. My hands teased through silky strands of hair as I came back up, and curiosity got the better of me. I turned to face my new dancing partner.

"Enjoying yourself?" Despite his hands on my waist, I realized he wasn't dancing. And he didn't look particularly pleased either.

Oh. My. God...

If my buzz had allowed me to comprehend such shame and abhorrence, I probably would've been reddened to the point that I could have blended seamlessly in with the mood lighting.

"This is *your* doing, I take it?" Blaine remarked, looking over my shoulder.

I turned to see Val not three feet away, dancing with a redhead. He raised his palms up, the universal "don't-look-at-me" gesture.

"I came here on my own," I declared.

"Did you, now?" Blaine hardly seemed convinced. "You're telling me you triggered your Distress rune and took off so fast that I couldn't track you, just to get drunk off cheap liquor?"

"Yeah, what's your point?" I cooed, still swaying to the music.

"Nuns have a higher alcohol tolerance than you."

I just laughed. "So?"

"Seriously, did Val abduct you? Force you to take something? A drink? Some kind of drug?"

I snorted. "Will you relax, Tarzan? Jane. Fine," I mocked, attempting my best impression of the feral orphan. It sounded more like a caveman, only making me laugh harder. "You really need to lighten up. You're gonna get frown lines."

His hold on me tightened, hauling me right up against him. A peculiar flutter ignited in my chest. I found myself inclining my head up to meet his gaze, at those wolfish eyes, those sensuous lips.

His eyes cut away from mine, taking interest in my hand. "Wow, you are *really* drunk."

I looked to see the rune on top of my hand burning

bright blue. Before I could meet his eyes again, I was suddenly slung over his shoulder. The new position made my stomach flip and my head spin. "Put me down, you Neanderthal!"

"Come on, man. She just wants to unwind. Let her live a little," laughed Val, coming to our side as Blaine began plowing through the crowds with me in tow.

His brother turned to him, and a loud *pop!* sounded over the music. As Blaine continued to the door, I caught sight of Val, who was now sprawled out on the floor, his nose evidently broken as blood trailed from it.

"What the hell's your problem?" I snapped, beating a fist against Blaine's back. "He was just being nice."

Blaine scoffed as he carried me out into the parking lot. "My brother doesn't do 'nice.'"

"A familial trait, then, no doubt," I jeered. "And yet, he's still better company than you. I'm beginning to think your boss set me up with the wrong brother."

Of all things, he laughed.

"Why is that funny?"

"'Not knowing anything is the sweetest life.' Is it not?"

"Is that supposed to be your excuse for trying to keep me in the dark? Some stupid Pinterest quote?" I scoffed. "At least Val's not playing dirty."

Blaine finally set me down beside the Cutlass's passenger door. I pulled at the handle to open it, but his hand pressed against the frame, securing the door shut. I rolled my eyes as I turned to face him, an insult already loaded on the tip of my tongue. It tumbled back down my throat, and I choked on the lump, finding Blaine standing mere inches before me. It took everything I had not to cower back at the predatory gaze as he lowered himself to meet my eyes.

"I may be dirty, love, but I am not 'playing,'" he purred, his voice low and intimate as his lips lingered in front of mine. "If you wish to challenge me in a game, you *will* lose."

My breath caught at the soft caress of his fingers suddenly on the nape of my neck as his mouth moved to my ear.

"But I can guarantee you won't be mourning the loss for long."

Goose bumps shot up my spine, my arms, and everywhere else as his teeth gifted my earlobe with a teasing nibble, simultaneously stroking gentle fingers down my neck. I gasped at the sensation, at the satisfaction it gave to the dark energy rooted deep within me. It practically purred at the contact, leaving me equally euphoric and horrified.

"Take me home." The words barely escaped my lips as he pulled away.

Embers crackled in the fireplace as flames pressed their gentle heat against my cheeks. I stirred in the downy mass of cotton and fleece, finding myself nuzzled up in blankets on a couch. Blaine's couch. I was in his family room. My last words reverberated in my head, and panic hit me like a punch to the stomach.

What happened? Had he misunderstood what I meant? My thoughts were a muddled mess, and it didn't help any that the room spun as I shot upright. I peeled the blankets away, relieved to at least see I was still fully clothed.

"How bad is it?" Though his voice was soft, it still had me recoiling to the far end of the couch as Blaine entered the room.

The sudden action sent a stabbing pain into my temples. The room tilted, and I collapsed back into the cushions despite myself.

"Here." Blaine came up to the side of the sofa, offering me a glass of water, along with a couple of aspirin.

"What happened?" I asked, even though I was terrified of the potential truth.

"You drank your weight in cheap tequila, cursed me out in a drunken tirade in the car, passed out, and now, by the looks of it, you have a pretty awful hangover."

I had no recollection of the third part, but it didn't surprise me. And relief eased back into my thrumming pulse. I hadn't done anything I would've regretted. But…

Hangover? "How long have I been here?"

"About an hour."

I may have been new to the whole drinking scene, but weren't you supposed to get those the morning *after*? Between the car ride and time spent here, only a couple hours had passed. Three at the very most.

Blaine offered a small smile. "Since our bodies regenerate so quickly, substances like liquor don't really stay in our systems for very long. You'll still feel like shit, but the hangover won't last for more than an hour or so."

"Sorry about earlier," I mumbled, gesturing at his throat.

Surprise filled those pale eyes.

"Don't get me wrong. You still deserved it, but…I shouldn't have done it." I was better than that, or at least, I *thought* I was. Seeing that side, what I was capable of, it scared me.

"Devotion for the people you love is never something to apologize for. It's one of the things I admire most about you." His eyes roamed over my hand, to the rune wrapped around my ring finger. "Perhaps, one day, you might extend that fervor to me."

I inwardly cringed. I could only imagine what kind of 'fervor' I'd have for him after his hex went into effect.

"You're crazy," I muttered.

"So I've been told." He took the empty glass from my hands and pulled the blankets back over me. "Just try to get some rest."

My eyelids were already drawing closed as he turned to leave.

"Why did you do it?" I murmured.

"Do what?" his voice asked softly in the darkness.

"Kill me, the night of the bonfire?" When he didn't say anything, I forced my eyes back open, believing he had perhaps left the room. But there he stood, staring at me, still. "I...I liked you. And you knew that. Why didn't you let me get to know you first, to *really* care about you?"

Something flickered in those icy eyes. Sadness.

He opened his mouth, as if to respond, but decided against it. "Get some sleep," was all he said, before disappearing into the darkness of the hallway.

Slow Dancing In a Burning Room

Blaine had been right. When I awoke, it was still dark outside, but the clock told me it was a quarter after five. Almost sunrise. The world was no longer spinning, and my head felt okay for the most part. Only a dull ache rested behind my eyes. The fire inside the hearth had died hours ago, leaving the crisp winter air to bite at my skin as I tugged off the blankets. My ears strained to hear something in the silence, but alas the house remained quiet with the exception of the soft ticking from the grandfather clock.

Without the glow of the fireplace, I found the room still bathed in a warm orange light. I craned my head behind me, expecting to see some kind of nightlight. Instead, I beheld the strange pinkish-orange rock placed on the corner table I'd noticed during my investigation of the house. It appeared translucent, like fogged crystal, as a glowing light rested in the center of its base. Up close it looked less like a crystal and more like a giant piece of orange rock candy.

A Himalayan salt lamp. I'd never seen one in person, but I remembered my aunt talking about wanting to get one. They supposedly helped balance positive and negative ions, which in turn improved energy levels. I wasn't sure if any of that was true, but I had to admit, it certainly looked interesting, almost magical.

Something stirred in the opposite side of the room. I snapped upright, straining to see in the limited light. A dark silhouette filled the corner chair with a crown of blonde hair catching my eye. Blaine. I hadn't noticed him when I awoke, his figure unmoving in the dark leather chair as his feet rested up on the matching cushioned ottoman.

His head was propped up on his bent arm, his cheek resting on a closed fist. I inched closer, waiting for him to move or say something, but he remained still. It wasn't until I was a few feet away that I realized he was asleep. It seemed odd, really. I mean, even Mages required sleep, but I would never imagine seeing him like this.

So peaceful.

So vulnerable.

Without those startling pale eyes boring into me, the smooth planes of his face made him appear almost...lovely. Sleep stripped us all of our masks, and in this light, he was beautiful. Delicate. Beautifully broken. I'd seen glimpses of his kindness, of his affection, felt it the very first time he'd kissed me. But everything else I witnessed, everything he put me through, it painted a much uglier portrait.

Why did you do it?

That question had haunted me these past months. Whether I had been singled out because of my bloodline or even just by happenstance, I still couldn't figure out why Blaine had gone about all of this the way he had. If he wanted me to become his 'mate,' then why had he killed me the night of the bonfire?

Blaine wasn't impulsive. Everything he did was calculated, mapped out ten steps in advance. When he had tracked me down, he could just as easily have shown up on my aunt's front porch one morning, taken me hostage, and simply bided his time till the hex kicked in. Instead, he bought the house next door. Why? Because he knew I couldn't run away from him, not again. It allowed him to meddle in my life, allowed him to keep a watchful eye on me, all without having to put in the added effort. So why hadn't he tried to seduce me *before* choosing to kill and resurrect me?

I liked him the moment we first met, and Blaine knew that. But we hadn't even gone out on an actual date yet. All he had to do was wait for things to progress on their own. With him being nothing more than a relative stranger, Blaine would have known I'd be afraid of him, of the Crown Prince of Hell. So why? Why expose me to this world, to this madness, without any assurance that I would succumb to him? Using some hex to brainwash me seemed like it should have been a last resort, not Plan A.

Was that all he wanted from me? To be a witless, indoctrinated servant?

He stirred for a moment, and I leapt back, nearly knocking over a floor lamp in the process as I bumped into it. Catching it before it toppled over, I stole a look back at him, seeing him still fast asleep. And in his hands rested the same old leather-bound book he had been reading in the library.

The new perspective gave me a clear view of Blaine's right forearm. My eyes widened. The buttons lining the cuffs of his sleeves were undone, exposing the inside of his arm. Curiosity got the better of me as I knelt down to get a better look. A long ghastly line maimed his otherwise perfect skin, so extensive that it continued on well beneath the remaining fabric of his sleeve. Why had I not noticed this before?

I was a hot mess. With all the smeared mascara and smudged eye shadow around my eyes, I looked as if I took make-up tips from the Joker. I didn't have my purse, so I couldn't even attempt to clean it up, leaving me with no choice but to just wash my face when I ducked into the bathroom. All I needed was to look presentable. I wasn't sure if Jenna was awake yet, and I didn't want to risk waltzing in the house at dawn, looking like the poster girl for the Walk of Shame. I still didn't know how to explain my absence last night or what had happened with Blaine in my bedroom yesterday morning. If things didn't return to normal, and soon, I suspected my aunt's goodwill would run out as well.

I needed to get the hell out of here.

Bolting from the bathroom, I went to close the door behind me. It wasn't until I grabbed the handle that I noticed the vibration dancing up my arm, and by then, it was too late. I'd ripped the doorknob right out of the wood.

Seriously?

I'd managed to go a whole month without one of these mishaps.

My emotions were all over the place, and my runes couldn't seem to decide what to do with them. I wanted to cry, I wanted to scream, I wanted to punch something in... Every last sentiment had my arm illuminated like a kaleidoscope lightshow.

I prepared to slam the stupid handle on the counter as I cut through the kitchen to the side entrance, but decided against it. Without my emotions in check, I'd probably end up smashing my fist through the marble countertop. I turned the corner to find Blaine leaning against the table, eyeing the colonial handle still wielded in my grasp.

"Sorry," I murmured, attempting to set down the device as gently as I could.

He smiled, pressing back a laugh. "It takes some getting used to. Our power, I mean."

Power?

I scoffed. "It's a *curse.*"

Of all things, he glared at me. "It's a gift. You'd see that if you'd open yourself up to its potential."

I wanted to laugh. It was the only thing I could think to do to fend off the tears building behind my eyes. I threw the handle to the floor, letting my unruly magic obliterate the porcelain into tiny pieces across the hardwood. "You call *that* potential?" I snapped. "How about me nearly tearing Reese's neck out? *Is that your idea of a fucking 'gift'?*"

"Is *that* what happened yesterday?" His face, his tone, everything was so extraordinarily detached.

I wasn't sure why I had expected more. It wasn't like I was anticipating an apology, but maybe, just maybe...a little remorse? A glimmer of regret, perhaps? But there was nothing. Nothing except a hint of mild curiosity.

"Why are you here?" I growled.

His shoulders stiffened. "You know why—"

"No, I don't. You don't give a shit about me. I'm nothing more than a plaything to you, so cut the bullshit and just tell me what you want! Tell me what you want, so I can get you out of my life."

"Well, that's unfortunate—for *you*," he mused. "Because I'm not going anywhere."

"What did I do to deserve this? *Huh?*" I slammed my hands into his chest, knocking him back with enough momentum that it thrust the entire kitchen table behind him across the hardwood as well. "*Why are you torturing me?*"

I couldn't stop it, couldn't stop the tears from pouring down my cheeks as I sobbed. "I cared about you. I cried over you when I thought you were dead. I cried at your goddamn funeral!"

He flinched.

"And you were there all along, alive and well," I bawled. "You let me believe for weeks that I was responsible! You let me torture myself, thinking that I had inadvertently killed you!"

"I never meant to hurt you—"

"Bullshit!" Those icy eyes sharpened, and the quiet rage behind them should have made me recoil, but fury had taken me over. "I never did anything to ever hurt you, or anybody else, and you do *this* to me?" My fingers furiously dug into the ink on my arm until I nearly drew blood.

"Stop!" He snatched me by the wrist, prying my hand away. A metallic scent engulfed me as his voice fell ragged. "Don't do that."

Pain. That was…pain in his eyes.

His voice was nearly a whisper as he said, "You have no idea what I've done to protect you."

That strange essence living beneath my skin—that essence buried deep into my bones, into my core—it tugged inside my chest. A silent plea. A plea to make me stop, to not say what was resting on the tip of my tongue.

"I don't care," I bit back, merciless, as I ripped my hand free from him. "Your own mother didn't even cry at your funeral. It doesn't matter how many of my dreams you invade, or how many hexes you put on me. I don't ever want you to touch me. You will never find me in your bed. And I will *never* be yours. All you are is a pretty face with a black heart. *No one* could ever love you."

Words were a funny thing. They couldn't be taken back, and their damage festered longer than any physical wound. I could have literally stabbed him in the chest, and it would have hurt less.

He did feel pain. *True* pain.

His jaw was set, forcing his features into neutrality, but he couldn't hide the anguish in his eyes, couldn't hide the fact that he wasn't breathing.

After everything he'd put me through, I had every right in the world to be cruel. But looking at him in that moment, I felt as monstrous as how Reese looked at me yesterday.

Without another word, I turned and headed out the side entrance. It took four steps to reach my aunt's house. I froze as I reached for the doorknob, but not because I was afraid of tearing it off. It was from what had caught my attention. *How could that be?* Blaine had driven me back last night in *his* car, yet my little red Civic was parked out by the curb. I started making my way towards the front yard when another vehicle caught my attention. I hurled myself against the side of the house, praying he hadn't seen me.

Reese.

I did the only thing I could think of.

I ran.

Darting inside the house, I cringed as the floorboards creaked overhead. Yep, my aunt was up, alright. And I was totally busted.

But the floorboards kept squeaking, in the exact same place. Rhythmically. Right around where I'd estimate Jenna's bed to be positioned in her room.

Can you say *awkward*?

I still tiptoed up the steps, but even as a loose floorboard creaked beneath my feet, no one seemed the least bit interested enough to investigate. Especially as what I could only assume was the headboard pounding against the wall. At least someone's love life was faring better than mine.

I took a quick shower and changed my clothes, clinging to the hope that Reese wouldn't still be waiting outside when I finished up in the bathroom. Since I hadn't taken my phone when I ran off yesterday, all his texts and phone calls went unanswered. Why was he still here?

I already knew the answer, but I didn't want it to be true. I didn't want to face him.

My inner coward pleaded with me to sneak out the side door again, run to the car, and burn rubber as I floored it out of there. Yet, I opened the front door, finding Reese slouched on the porch swing. His clothes were rumpled, and his hair was equally disheveled. He still donned the same outfit as yesterday.

Had he stayed here the whole night? Had he seen Blaine carry me inside his house?

The moment I stepped out on the porch, his amber eyes met mine as he sat upright, smoothing a hand over his hair as if to make himself more presentable.

"Hey." He rose up from the swing and made his way over to me, but I quickly countered it with clumsy backward steps.

"Please, don't...." I barely managed to mutter, desperate to keep what little space was left between us. I couldn't bear to see him afraid of me again, but I also didn't want him to pretend everything was okay either.

He stopped, noting the unmistakable panic in my eyes, and I at last breathed a sigh of relief, convinced he'd stay away. But before I knew it, he advanced on me, so fast I barely detected the movement until his hands suddenly cradled my neck. His lips crashed against mine, and I staggered back. Only, he didn't let me go.

"I'm sorry," he whispered against my lips as he broke the kiss. The words rattled through me, and I couldn't fend off the tears. After I had nearly bitten him, *Reese* was the one asking for forgiveness.

I choked on a sob, trying to pull away from him. "You need to leave."

His hands clamped around my forearms. "No."

"Reese, please!" I shoved at his chest, but he only hauled me closer until my face buried in his shoulder. "I'm going to hurt you!"

"And I'm going to help you."

I kept shaking my head, even as Reese lifted my chin.

"This is what he wants, to isolate you, to make you feel helpless," he said. "If you push me away, you'll be playing right into his hands. We'll find a way out of this, I promise, but we have to stick together."

Something slammed behind me, and I felt that invisible

leash tug against my bones, forcing me to turn around. Blaine locked his front door and headed down the porch to the driveway, stealing only a glance at the two of us—locked in each other's embraces—before climbing in his car. His face was a perfect mask of indifference, and I couldn't catch any scent from this distance, but something ached in my gut.

Reese growled, and a bitter metallic tang wafted in the air. "How can you stand seeing him?"

My stomach twisted tighter. "It's not like I have much of a choice."

"You will, if I have anything to say about it."

It didn't matter what I said; Reese wasn't leaving town. He wasn't leaving *me*. And that was the only thing I could take comfort in as I walked into school. That deep ache within me never subsided. Every corner I turned in the hallways, I ran into Blaine, but he never taunted me. In fact, the moment he so much as sensed me, he disappeared just as fast. We hadn't spoken a word the entire day, even when we both arrived at the same time to AP Chemistry come final hour. Without meeting my eyes, he gestured me inside before slinking in after me to the other side of the classroom.

"Okay, class. Open your textbooks to page 258," announced Mrs. Woodard. "We'll be continuing our studies on Thermodynamics."

That alien energy inside me compelled my head to turn, and before I could find the will to resist, I found myself staring at Blaine. Thank God he wasn't looking back. His attention was wholly fixated on the textbook in front of him.

Who knew he found entropy to be so fascinating?

He flipped the page, exposing the paper for what it really was. Parchment. Ooookay, so maybe he wasn't reading our chemistry textbook after all. Big deal. I tried to turn my head back to my own desktop, but that force inside me wouldn't relent.

"What the hell do you want?" I wanted to scream at it.

When Blaine prepared to flip to the next page, he found the aged sheets sticking together. Upon separating them, he lifted up the book just enough to reveal the familiar leather-bound brown cover. But that's not what earned my attention. It was the design on the page he'd just turned to. I nearly gasped, instinctively leaning in as close as I could get.

Two swords crossed together, making an upside-down crucifix, with a gigantic snake wrapped around the blades, appearing to consume fire.

"Ms. Shaw?" announced Mrs. Woodard sharply.

Her voice startled me enough that I actually jumped. Since I had literally been on the edge of my seat, the scare sent me falling off onto the floor. A chorus of giggles and snickers inevitably followed as I pulled myself back up into my chair.

"Would you mind terribly if I continue in my lesson, or do you wish to further ogle over Mr. LeBeau?" the elder woman huffed, nodding over to Blaine.

I surprised even myself as I jokily replied, "Nah, I'm good. I can see him just fine from here." I added in a whimsical smile that only had Mrs. Woodard crossing her arms over her chest as the same group of students laughed again.

My cheery brush-off seemed to convince my fellow

classmates that perhaps Mrs. Woodard was mistaken in her assessment of me and Blaine, but I knew all too well what I would find when I looked back over at the Prince of Darkness.

As certain as death and taxes, I wholly expected to see a massive smirk beneath a victorious pair of gleaming icy eyes. So it came as one hell of a surprise to find Blaine staring back at me, looking particularly...unnerved. His gaze swept back to the book, then to me, and he only became paler. I shot him a competitive smirk, but even then, he failed to return it, hunkering down in his seat.

His breathing hitched as his fingers clawed into the book's cover. He suddenly shot up from his desk, taking his belongings with him.

Mrs. Woodard didn't even have time to say his name, let alone reprimand him, as he took one look at her and said, "You have no problem with me leaving."

Like all his other victims, the hypnotized teacher simply shrugged her shoulders and returned to the lesson plan without another thought.

Something had definitely just rattled him, and I had a pretty good feeling it had to do with that book.

I pulled out my phone, hiding it beneath the bulk of the desk as I texted Reese. *"You near the school?"*

The phone buzzed not a moment later. *"I'm at the corner café just down the street. Everything okay?"*

"I need you to follow Blaine."

"Dare I ask why you have me stalking your stalker?" Reese queried the moment I called him after class let out.

"Do you see him?"

"You mean Tall, Blonde, and Creepy? Yeah, I have him in my sights," he answered flatly.

"Where is he? What's he doing?"

"He's sitting on a rock."

"He's what?"

Reese gave a noisy exhale, evidently bored. My phone buzzed a few seconds later, showing me a picture of Blaine indeed resting on top of a massive boulder beside a lakefront of some sort. His legs hung over the ledge that jutted out into the water, his toes mere inches above the calm surface. Surprise, surprise. He was looking at that same leather-bound book.

"I have to admit, when you sent me out to spy on a Dark Lord of the Underworld, I kinda anticipated a bit more excitement. You know, like me hiding in the bushes as he makes shady transactions, or entering into a high-speed chase to escape his evil cronies. Spending the last forty-three minutes watching him read isn't exactly adrenaline pinching."

I couldn't fight off the wicked smile pulling at my lips. "Are you really up for a little excitement?"

"At this point? Watching grass grow would be more stimulating," Reese laughed.

"I want you to swipe the book he's reading."

"Why? Did he check out the last copy at the library?" he mocked.

"Remember that image I sent you and Madsen the other day? Of the drawing I sketched when I fell asleep in class?

"Yeah."

"I just saw the exact same thing printed inside that book Blaine's been carrying around. I think he's up to something, something *bad.*"

The hot, buttery aroma of baking dough engulfed me as I stepped up to the soft pretzel stand. Reese handed me my very own gigantic, salty treat, and I thanked him between delicious mouthfuls before we took a seat in the back corner booth of the eatery. Between my overactive metabolism and the fact I was wired, my appetite was insatiable.

"I don't know how much time we have," remarked Reese under his breath as he slid the book my way.

"How'd you get it?"

"Blondie made a pit stop across the way, over at the bar and grill. And let's just say there's perks to him driving an old car," he sassed, flashing me a long, flat piece of plastic.

"Is that a car window regulator?"

"Among many things." Reese smiled guiltily. There wasn't a doubt in my mind that he'd used it to lift the interior latch on the lock. Without the hi-tech security that modern vehicles were equipped with, classic muscle cars were much easier targets for break-ins. "Putting my vehicular transgressions aside, would you mind filling me in, Nancy Drew? I have to get that book back inside his car before he realizes we were snooping around in it."

Cracking open the spine, I began my investigation. The cover may have been blank, but the insides...they were brimming with sigils. And not just any sigils. Enochian runes.

Black Magic.

Page after page spoke of curses, and divinations, and necromancy, and...hexes. If my heart had fists, it would have punched itself free from my chest and flown away; I couldn't contain the hope rising inside of me. It was too much. I didn't know what any of these sigils were exactly, and I couldn't read any of the spells, as they were scribed in Latin, but this had to be it! This had to be the grimoire Blaine consulted to perform the mating hex.

I skimmed through the pages, trying to soak in as much information as I could, until I finally found it. Halfway through the book, the familiar symbol practically screamed at me, the black ink so heavy and thick, it seemed to weigh down the parchment. The next five pages appeared to be dedicated to this sigil's history, so I turned the book back to Reese in the hopes that he could make sense of it.

"I haven't seen this symbol before in any of my research, but I've heard about *this*." He tapped the title written beneath the illustration. "*Potestas Binding*, also known as Power Binding. It's typically accompanied with *Sanguis Bindings*, used for summonings and proscribing."

"I have no idea what you just said."

"Blood Bindings. Certain blood has magical properties, so it can be used in rituals to build or break seals," Reese attempted to clarify. "Remember the vision you had a couple months ago, about the girl in the woods?"

I shuddered at the recollection. One of the cheerleaders attacked on the Hersey bus had been taken by Hellhounds and held captive for over two weeks, only then for Raelynd's cronies to drag the poor girl out into the forest and slash her throat. Then I remembered the strange symbol they'd created with rocks and loose tree branches inside a makeshift pentagram. It wasn't the same as the one on the page, but the very thought of it sent ice into my veins.

"Why would I draw this?"

Reese shook his head, unable to answer, when a low hiss crept its way back into my mind.

"Sanguis quia sanguis."

His eyebrows furrowed in an instant. "What?"

"When I was in the fortunetelling shop," I gasped. "That's what Lucinda said to me when I saw that vision. 'Sanguis quia sanguis.'"

"'Blood for blood'?" Reese pulled the book closer, combing over each word more intently, as if the proximity would make something magically jump out at him. "Did she say anything else?"

"Uhhh…" She had, at the very beginning of the session, but what was it? "'Moss…venti…queen avose'…" By the look on Reese's face, I only assumed I'd spoken pure and utter gibberish. I mean, seriously? Did I just say 'venti'? I highly doubted an omen about my untimely demise had anything to do with freaking coffee.

But Reese's eyes suddenly widened. "Mors venit quia vos?"

Holy crap! I nodded like an anxious bobble head. "What does it mean?"

"Death is coming for you."

14
Make It Rain

eese's face had gone sallow, and even an hour later, the color hadn't returned to his cheeks. Apparently, "Blood for blood" was a Heavenly mantra the Angel of Death liked to use—when he claimed your life. Whatever Raelynd and Blaine were up to with their Blood Binding ritual, it had been enough to warrant Death's attention. And I was evidently the easiest target to reach. If Hell needed my blood for some demonic ceremony, then Heaven needed to ensure they wouldn't get their hands on it.

After breaking back into Blaine's Cutlass, Reese dropped off the book, but not before we took as many pictures of the inside pages as possible. Reese took my hand and brought it up to his lips, placing a soft kiss on my knuckles as he spun the truck into my aunt's driveway.

I froze at the sight awaiting me on the porch. It was the first time I'd seen Officer Hernandez after the night he was possessed, and the poor guy was looking rather worse for wear.

A large bandage covered his nose, and he was sporting a matching set of black eyes, bruised to a sickly mix of purple and blue. Jenna gave him a kiss before he made his way to the patrol car parked by the curb. I would've been proud of my handiwork, if not for the fact that an innocent man now had to pay the punishment for something he himself didn't willingly do.

Why haven't they used my blood yet? It was the question that had been eating away at me since we left the eatery, and even now, I couldn't bring myself to ask it aloud.

Blaine found me. Why didn't he just finish the ceremony?

"You can't run forever," he had said the night I fled Mystic Harbor. *"The time will come when we'll need to consummate our bond. And I* **will** *come to collect you."*

We... We needed to complete the mating ritual first.

At least I could take comfort in that. There was no way I would *ever* consummate that damn bond. Not while I was in my right mind.

And that very thought haunted me more. My right mind. How long would I still have that? How much time did I have until I turned into some besotted, love-struck halfwit? I sank down into the seat.

"You want me to come back later?" Reese whispered.

"No, you should head home." He tried to argue, but I wouldn't have it. "You've already missed your last shift at work, not to mention two days of school."

"You're not getting rid of me that easily," he sighed. "I'm gonna drive up to my place and take a look at my father's journals, see if I can find out anything more about the sigil. As soon as I'm done, I'll come back."

"Miss you."

He winked, giving me a playful shove as I climbed out.

"Jerk."

"Princess."

We both shared in a laugh, but my amusement died as I looked back to the house, seeing Jenna still waiting on the porch.

"What happened to Hernandez?" I asked innocently, nodding back to the patrol car as I came up to greet my aunt.

"Not sure," she huffed. "He had a few too many beers the other night. I found him passed out on the couch with blood all over his face when I came home. He thinks he may have slipped and just hit something." She eyed me for a long moment. "And yet, it was still the *second* most shocking thing I saw yesterday morning."

Crap.

"A strange young man in your bedroom, huh?"

"About that…"

Jenna held up her hand, and my heart sank. I knew what that gesture meant. My mom used to do it anytime she was at wit's end with me. "I was a teenager once, too. And you're almost eighteen. What you choose to do with your life is solely up to you."

Oh yeah? Tell that to the jackass living next door…

"But it would still be irresponsible of me not to worry," she added. "I know things haven't been easy with your folks, and no one could blame you for wanting to act out a little—"

"That is *not* at all what it was," I said, cringing at the very idea. "Trust me."

She sighed, noting my evident disgust. "Who's the boy?"

I followed her gaze down at the old beater truck rumbling down the street. "Ah..." Reese and I had never talked about what 'this' was between us, never put a label on it, so I called it the best I could. "He's my best friend."

Lazily stretching my arms above my head, I awoke from what I was sure to be a full night's rest. Instead, I found bright blue letters glaring back at me, saying "10:09 p.m." I'd only been asleep for a few hours. Rolling over, I nestled back into the pillows when lightning flashed through the edges of the window shades, followed up by a thunderous roar that rattled even my bed. No way was I going to be falling back asleep anytime soon with that racket outside. That figured. I'd been running on fumes the past few days. All I wanted was a decent night's rest, and I at last got to sleep in a bedroom where Blaine wasn't ten feet away. I knew that much, because that familiar heat in my chest was notably absent. He wasn't home, at least for now. So of course, this had to be the night that the weather wanted to rival the freaking thunderstorm from *Frankenstein*.

So long, sleep...

I fished around my nightstand for my phone and shot Reese a quick text. *"Where R U?"*

"Heading back now. Be at your place as soon as I check into a motel. About 1 hr. Your aunt home?" he messaged back a moment later.

"She's working a shift at the bar. House is empty."

"Good :)"

I didn't want to think about what that meant. After yesterday, I couldn't bring myself to try anything...physical, again. Not till I got a better hold on my so-called 'power.'

My eyelids sank shut, but a moment later, a voice suddenly cried out in the distance. I sprang awake, finding myself standing upright and...out in the freezing cold.

Broken branches cracked under my feet as I crept through a thicket of trees. Batting my way out into the open, I found myself standing at the edge of a forest with a massive field sprawling out in front of me underneath a dusk ridden sky. Iron posts were stationed across the border of the tree line with an electrical lantern hanging from the top of each pole. Strange cackling echoed behind me in the distance from what I prayed was only an animal, a very small, non-lethal animal.

"Hello?"

Dead leaves swirled about my ankles as I trudged further out into the grassy field. I could only faintly make out a few large, dark objects up ahead. A lump formed in my throat, encouraging me to turn back around. I hadn't the slightest idea where I even was, but standing out in the open seemed just as risky as returning to the unknown of the forest. I started to turn back around when an ear aching boom erupted from the boundary line. A sharp whistle rang through the air before a devastating bang hammered into the ground in front of me, the terrain vibrating from the impact.

A scream lodged in my throat as I whirled back around, running further out into the field. I felt like a rat trying to scurry away. I didn't know where I was going, what I was actually running from, or how the hell I even got here, but I continued to run until the dark objects up ahead came into plain sight. Cannons. Suddenly, blasts ignited in front of me as well, seemingly coming from the unmanned artillery.

Pattering triggers and a volley of gunfire accompanied the detonation, and I dropped to the ground as the shots whizzed right by my ears. I draped my hands over my head, as if that would actually help. The earth continued to shudder as thunderous roars hailed across the field. I managed to sneak a glance up from my trembling fingers, seeing nobody in sight. Bemusedly looking about, I saw the grass was completely undisturbed, despite hearing and feeling the impacts beside me. What the hell?

"Kat!" The voice barely managed to carry above the hysterics.

I stole a look over my shoulder, forcing me to stand. Long pale blonde hair whipped about in the aggressive wind, beating the woman's face. I outright stumbled back, tripping over my own feet until I fell flat on my ass. It... It was *me*. Or at least my mirrored image. This imposter made her way out from the forest, not seeming to take the gunfire into account as she walked unreservedly towards me in plain sight. Every last detail from her nose to the curve of her lips was an exact rendering of me. She wore a long purple gown, the ends of the skirts muddied and tattered as if she'd been running through the forest for hours on end. I remained frozen, unsure of where to go.

"I'm not here to hurt you," she called out.

Like Hell she wasn't! Scrambling back up to my feet, I tried to run further when flames manifested in front of me. Shrieking back, I fell to the ground as the heat from the inferno rushed out at me.

"Listen to me, you must listen," my creepy clone insisted, her voice frighteningly closer.

"Stay away from me!" I screamed, turning around to see her no more than ten feet away.

She stayed where she was, her opened palms extended up and out towards me, as if to signal good intentions. I cowered back on instinct, feeling the warmth of the flames breathing up my spine.

"I need to warn you," she pleaded over the gunfire. "You're in danger."

"No shit, Sherlock!"

She shook her head. "No, this isn't happening. This battle, it's from the past."

"What the hell are you talking about?"

"The past, it's linked with the present. What's happening to you now has happened before," she insisted over the riotous clamor of cannon fire.

I whirled around, looking at the field again. "The vision," I muttered. "This is where I die."

"Yes, and that's why I have to warn you!"

An explosion detonated not three feet away, the invisible force knocking both of us back from the other.

"He's going to kill you!" she bellowed.

"What?"

Artillery fired and blasted and rocked the earth, drowning out the woman's words. "...going to kill you! I've seen it."

"Who?" I demanded. *Blaine? Raelynd?*

The world abruptly fell silent. Still. As if someone had thrown a blanket over us, the sky darkened so suddenly to the point that my doppelganger became barely visible.

"You need to wake up, now!" She sprang forward, her hands slamming into my shoulders.

Rocketing backward, I expected to hit the grass, but instead, I fell into a mass of sheets and pillows as a searing pain hit my arm. My omen rune.

"Shit, grab her!" barked a gruff voice.

My eyes flung open as I sprang up from my mattress, seeing two brawny men standing over me at the end of my bed. Screaming, I rolled sideways and scuttled out from under my sheets, hitting the hardwood floor. My bare foot thrust into one of the men's shins as I grabbed the baseball bat out from under my bed, jamming the end cap up, right in his groin. He dropped to the floor with a howl, and the other attacker rounded the bed to my side.

I quickly climbed to my feet and gripped the bat, swinging all-out at him. He threw his left arm up, and it took the full impact. Barking out a painful cuss, he didn't relent as I failed to draw the bat back up in time for another swing. He rammed his full weight into me, slamming me into the wall. My whole body stung and my diaphragm contracted, forcing all the air out of my lungs. The man gripped both my arms and tossed me down onto the floor. I tried climbing back up to my feet, but I couldn't breathe and my legs buckled out from under me.

"Goddamn it!" The other assailant groaned, still holding his groin.

"Seems like this one's got some fight in her," laughed the man standing over me as he pulled out a syringe from his jacket.

I lamely swatted my arm at him as he approached with the needle primed and aimed at me.

"Okay, now you're just embarrassing yourself." The man snickered at my pitiful attempt and batted my hand away. He pushed me back onto the floor and laid over me, pinning down my legs and wrestling my arms away as my cell phone rang from the top of my nightstand.

"Stop!" I croaked, feeling the tip of the needle press into

the side of my neck. A riotous hum vibrated in my ears, and every nerve in my body sparked to life as a rune ignited. My hands flexed outward, and the man laying over me suddenly catapulted across the room before hitting the wall on the far side.

With lungs heaving angrily with restored air, I rose to my feet with a ferocious surge pumping through my veins.

"Shit!" The guy on the ground looked up at me, eyes as wide as saucers. His shoes squeaked against the hardwood as he hurried back towards the doorway.

The energy brewing inside me burned through my fingers as I gripped my fists closed, ready to watch him hurl out into the corridor, clean off his feet. Only, my legs gave out on me. Confused, I collapsed to the floor, finding my limbs unwilling to cooperate with me. I couldn't move! It was then that I acknowledged the soft pain in my neck. The syringe. It hadn't just pierced my skin. It had been administered. Darkness immediately began clouding my vision.

I had to keep fighting it.

"Awww, what's the matter, Blood Whore?" The man I'd tossed across the room limped over to me with a winded laugh. "You expecting your evil prince to come and rescue you?"

He leveled a swift kick to my stomach, sending stars to explode in my vision. All I could do was wheeze as the air was ripped from my body. I couldn't even scream.

The man leaned over me, only laughing harder. "Well, well, well. Seems the bitch can feel pain, after all. That'll only make this more fun."

My phone continued to sound off, the vibration eventually rolling it off the stand onto the floor. It lay just a couple feet away, close enough that I could see Blaine's name on the caller screen. I willed my body to move, thrashing my arms and legs any which way, but they weren't obeying, not budging an inch. The only thing I could muster was a pathetic whimper. A muffled whisper resonated deep in my mind, but for the life of me, I couldn't make out the words. Not with the heaviness clouding my mind, dragging my eyes shut.

"How long will that knock her out for?" asked the other attacker.

"About a half hour."

"Reynolds is still at least a few hours out. What do we do in the meantime? Dose her again?"

"Nah, we don't know how much her body can handle. Nathan wants her alive, at least until he can get some answers out of her."

"So what, then?"

The man above me snickered, his arms reaching down to grab a hold of me. "Oh, I have an idea..."

I never heard what that idea was exactly, but I didn't really need to. My conscious slowly slipped back into reality, my body sore and sluggish. What felt like cement lay beneath my fingers, a solid slab from what I could feel out in the darkness. And I quickly realized I didn't have a lot of room. Lying flat, my elbows could barely move a couple inches to the sides, and my feet found the same resistance as I tried to flex my toes down.

The space was too warm. Every breath I took seemed to ricochet back onto my face. I raised my hands, only for my palms to press flat against another cement slab not half a foot above me. Panic tore through me in an instant, my hands desperately pushing against every surface without give.

Pale blue light poured into the limited space, confirming my worst fears. I was in a…tomb. Not a coffin or a wooden box you hear of people being buried alive in. It was an *actual* tomb. All four walls encasing me were aged concrete!

I screamed as loud as I could, even after my vocal chords went raw. "PLEASE, SOMEONE! HELLO, CAN ANYBODY HEAR ME? PLEASE!"

Hot tears blurred my vision as I continued pounding my fists into the unforgiving slab above me. Whether it was mere minutes or an entire lifetime, I couldn't tell. My entire body felt like it was on fire as I began hyperventilating.

There was nothing.

Only silence met my pleas through my gasping breaths. I was losing oxygen…

I'd either suffocate to death, or manage to live just long enough for Mr. Reynolds to finish the job.

I was going to die…and so would Blaine. And it was all my fault.

You stupid, stupid girl.

"Please," I whimpered, feeling the suffocation coiling itself around me, pressing into my lungs.

"Kat!" The voice echoed in the corners of my mind.

Blaine.

I cried out his name, though it didn't do me any good. It wasn't like he could hear me from in here, and I had no idea how this mental communication worked.

"Where are you?"

I don't know. I don't know. I don't know.

Panic surged through me harder. I was trapped

between four old slabs of concrete. That's all I knew.

Blaine's voice seemed to mellow in my mind, taking on a more soothing tone, as if trying to calm me in turn. *"Breathe, Kat. Okay? Just breathe for me."*

I couldn't. The air was getting thicker, and I had no idea where I was. No idea how to help him find me.

"I'm coming," he assured, but all rationality was gone, only making me cry harder. My greatest fear since I was little was drowning, after my cousins threw me into their pool even though they knew I couldn't swim. The half minute I spent underwater felt like an eternity as the water choked me, robbing me of any chance for air until Jenna leapt in to save me.

And it felt like that all over again.

I was struggling to drag in a feeble breath, and my terror only made it worse. I knew I needed to calm down, but instinct wouldn't let me. Blind panic was real, and it was literally killing me faster.

The space only burned brighter from my runes, the heavy vibrations rattling my arm, all the way into the rest of my body.

"You have to calm down," Blaine demanded. *"If your runes ignite, and the power isn't enough to blast away the concrete, it'll rebound back at you. You'll die."*

Concrete?

He knew I was in concrete!

I clung to what little hope that brought. Despite my panic and the flood of thoughts that came with it, he'd still been able to reach into our bond and sort through the chaos of my mind to work out what was happening.

Couldn't he just shut down my runes, though? He'd already done it before—

"I have to be touching you for it to work."

I shrieked, clutching desperately at my arm as the barely contained energy continued pushing against the inside of my skin. It begged for release, and the power soon turned baleful, eventually thrashing so hard I screamed. The very action smothered me as I tried to refill my lungs. The pale blue space started to dim, but it wasn't from my rune dying. It was me. The details around me had distorted, and I couldn't fend off the gray haze invading my vision.

"Kat?"

"I'm sorry," I whimpered.

The invisible bond we shared tugged at me, trying to assure me I wasn't alone. *"Don't,"* Blaine whispered. *"Don't you dare say that to me."*

I'm sorry.

I'm sorry.

I'm so, so sorry.

"Stay with me." The words were nearly inaudible, pained. *"Don't you fucking leave me."*

He was too far away. I could feel it, hear it in his voice. He was still trying to figure out where I was, and my body was already shutting down.

"I'm sorry," I mouthed, unable to muster the breath.

"Don't…"

I couldn't even tell if my eyes were opened or closed. Everything faded to black, silence inviting me to enter into a freefall as the world collapsed around me.

Control

*A*n unspeakable calm washed over me as my body was suddenly suspended in a bitter abyss. The stinging cold encased itself all around me, the swirling vortex yanking me in every direction. I punched and kicked, and the thick atmosphere rippled as hollow gurgling filled my ears. It teased me, challenging my lungs to react on instinct. I tried to catch my breath, but to my horror, nothing but chlorinated water flooded my airways. I was drowning!

My chest heaved as pressure fell down on it. Not the same pressure that had stolen my breath.

Hands.

Hands pressed down into my chest in a repetitive pattern. It vanished, only for lips to cover my mouth as they invited air back inside my lungs. Again. And Again.

I gasped.

There was too much oxygen and yet not enough. My lungs heaved, desperate to take in as much as it could get, simultaneously making me choke on the abundance. My eyes fluttered open, the darkness slowly subsiding. For the first time in my entire life, I was all too happy at the prospect of finding those pale blue eyes resting above me.

Blaine.

But as I blinked and my vision cleared, I didn't see that bleached blonde hair or iridescent gaze peering down at me. No…

Dark blonde hair and unfamiliar hazel eyes came into view, and a new wave of panic settled in.

Not Blaine.

I thrashed my exhausted limbs, kicking and clawing at the stranger like a cornered animal. The young man just gripped me by the forearms and pried me off the stone floor I'd apparently been sprawled out on. I quickly realized why he wasn't putting up any ounce of a fight with me. The moment I was hauled up to my feet, my knees buckled, and I collapsed back onto the ground. Whatever drugs I'd been given were still kicking my ass as I pathetically swatted at the man to leave me alone.

My hand connected with his cheek, and he didn't so much as blink upon impact. With all my mustered strength, I'd barely manage to give him what amounted to a light pat. Someone snorted behind him. The blonde just scowled, taking better care this time as he pulled me up against his body and lifted me clear off the ground in his arms. I writhed and flailed like a dying fish in his hold, spotting the spectator lingering in the doorway. The same asshole who had stuck me with the syringe.

Blaine? I kept repeating his name in my head, waiting for a response. Where was he?

I couldn't ignore the metallic tang. It wasn't a scent though. It...it was in my mouth. I looked at my arm. All my runes were still intact, but not a single one was alit.

Something was wrong.

Whether I cared to admit it or not, there was a part of my mind these past couple of months that had been carved out and constructed to instate Blaine's presence inside. It was like an invisible bridge, a conduit linking him to me. As much as I dug through my mind though, I couldn't find so much as a scrap of it anywhere. That tug—the essence snaked around my bones—was unnervingly still.

"W-what did y-you do?" I croaked out, choking on my raw vocal chords.

The stranger didn't answer.

An upsurge of wintry air crashed into my sweat-drenched frame as he carried me outside, the impact stealing the breath right out of me. He just held me closer, letting the heat of his body melt into mine. It did little good. My body only grew colder with every passing second. Not just on the outside, but in my very core. I could feel the energy draining from my body.

Find me.

Find me.

I couldn't ignite my runes. I couldn't fight back. I couldn't even stand on my own two feet.

I *needed* him.

The tears in my eyes burned, freezing on my cheeks as they tumbled off my lashes. Blaine was going to find me. He had to.

My pleas to him merely echoed in the bottomless crevasse of my mind. I didn't dare make a sound, but tears continued pouring down my face as my entire body shuddered.

My head rolled to the side, revealing exactly what I had expected. I'd been trapped in a mausoleum — in the middle of a cemetery. The metallic taste coating my tongue only grew stronger, and as hard as I tried to keep my eyes open, they sank shut once more.

A blur of burgundy and gold stirred before my vision as I came to once more.

With the coldness that had seeped into my limbs, my body had instinctively pulled itself into the fetal position in an attempt to cling to any warmth it could gather. To my surprise, I found an old wool blanket draped over me. I continued to blink away the drug-induced haze, realizing the floral patterns in front of me were part of the backing to a sofa.

"Hey, stranger."

If I had an ounce of strength in me, I would've jumped at the sound. Instead, I pathetically groaned as I rolled over, seeing the same dirty blonde-haired guy from the tomb seated across from me in a matching seat. It was the only other piece of furniture in the expansive room that wasn't covered with a white sheet, and remnants of stirred dust coated the splintered hardwood floors. Even the windows were boarded up. We were evidently in an abandoned house, the smell of built-up soot choking the air from the burning fireplace.

I attempted to pull myself up, cursing at the pain tearing through my stomach.

The stranger grimaced, his nostrils flaring in disgust.

Only... the sentiment didn't seem to be directed to me. "You okay?"

There was a peculiar drawl to his words, evidence that he clearly wasn't from the area. It sounded like a western twang or maybe a faded Texas accent. If it weren't for my current predicament, I would have been inclined to find it cute.

Peeling up the hem of my shirt, I cringed at the large black and blue splotch staining my abdomen. Either I was healing incredibly slowly, or that kick to the stomach I'd taken back in my bedroom had done more damage than initially thought.

"Sorry about my colleagues," the young man huffed. "They have about as much tact as they do brains."

Even sitting down, it was clear that the stranger was tall. Lean muscles made up his body, poorly concealed beneath worn jeans and a fitted thermal. His jaw and cheekbones were cut at hard angles, and his mildly cultivated five o'clock shadow had me estimating him to probably be in his earlier twenties.

Despite my swirling emotions, not a single rune on my arm so much as tingled, and that bottomless pit in my stomach returned as I once again found myself unable to tap into the mental bond to Blaine.

Distant footsteps sounded from a backroom, and he could see the rising panic in my eyes, giving me a sympathetic half-smile. It could all very well have been an act...but there was consideration in his voice, in his eyes.

"I'm Nick," he said, extending his hand out to me. When I only cowered back at the gesture, he sighed softly. "I promise I don't bite."

"Yeah, well, last time a guy said that, things didn't go so well for me," I muttered, rubbing the scarred fang marks on my neck.

The stranger's expression softened all the more as he studied me, seemingly fixated by my eyes. "Do you know the name of your birthparents?"

I was about to shake my head when heavy boots galloped into the entryway.

"Don't waste your breath," scoffed one of my captives, donned in red flannel—the same guy I'd hit in the balls earlier. He came closer, but still kept a healthy distance, as if I would crush his manhood again. Oh, if only I could... "The bitch is as good as gone." He leaned in, casting me a mocking smile. "Isn't that right, Blood Whore?"

What the hell was with this whole 'Blood Whore' thing, anyway?

I only had two (albeit *horrifying*) close encounters, but to this day, I'd still never bitten anyone, let alone sucked their blood. I didn't bother masking my hatred as he drew nearer.

"Just wait till Reynolds gets here," he seethed in wicked delight. "You should've seen what he did to the last Underworlder he interrogated. Peeled the flesh right off the bastard's bones."

After witnessing the horrors Mr. Reynolds and his men implemented on Blaine, I didn't doubt it for a second.

"Maybe we could get an early start on proceedings," my attacker further prodded, stealing a glance at his watch. "Nathan's flight shouldn't be coming in for another few hours. Wouldn't hurt to take a little peak at what your insides look like."

The blonde—Nick—just shot him a warning look as his companion plucked out a massive dagger and admired the blade before me. "Neither of you is to touch her."

The third guy in the room, the one who'd stabbed me

with the syringe earlier continued lingering in the entranceway, merely rolling his eyes.

"I mean it," Nick growled.

"So what do you expect to do in the meantime? Keep making puppy dog eyes at her?" challenged Mr. Flannel.

The blonde didn't appear the least bit fazed by the remark. "No," he drawled, "the Sagax will be here within the hour."

Syringe and Flannel both blanched.

Ooookay, definitely not reassuring.

"Why the hell would you summon that... that *thing*?" Mr. Syringe demanded.

"Because you morons shot our guest here up with Syrifian before we even had a chance to speak with her, meaning we can't use it again for another twelve hours without killing her. And we can only dose her up with so much Devil's Pod at a time to neutralize her magic," declared Nick. "We can't afford to idly sit around till Reynolds shows up."

"Let *us* take care of it," insisted Mr. Flannel, gesturing all a bit too eagerly at himself and his friend. "Give us a half hour with her—"

"*No*," Nick snapped. "We wait for the Sagax."

It seemed like both an eternity and mere minutes passed when the raging embers of the fireplace suddenly petered down to almost nothing. Billowing black smoke formed in the far corner, urging Syringe and Flannel to the other side of the room. Nick, however, only rose up from his seat and headed toward me, kneeling down to wrap the worn wool blanket around me tighter.

"Just be honest," he whispered, nearly inaudible over the other Reapers' curses.

Nick stepped away, revealing what had caused such a commotion from his companions. Strolling out of the swirling black cloud appeared a woman, her long, bell-sleeved white gown dancing about the ground on a phantom wind. Her skin was ghostly pale, nearly indistinguishable from the pallid shade of her very dress, as bone-straight onyx hair draped over her shoulders, her back, all the way down past her waist. I couldn't see her feet beneath the flowing skirts of her gown, and the fabric never extended or pulled to suggest she was even walking. Her tall, slender frame seemed to glide across the floor, as if hovering above it without so much as a step.

I couldn't ignore the hair prickling up on my arm. I was already cold, but the goose bumps that formed were from something else entirely. This woman was fifty shades of wrong! Even her lips and eyes were leeched of color, the green swirling in her irises so faint that in the flickering firelight they too appeared nearly white.

"Relieve yourself of your weapons, or relieve yourself from the premises," she cooed, her voice a delicate, soothing caress.

I hadn't realized there were other men lingering in the hallway until several more pairs of footsteps hastened out what I suspected to be the front door. Syringe and Flannel seemed eager to follow suit, but decided against it, easing down to their knees to discard the blades and various weapons decorating their persons. Upon sliding the hidden arsenals to the other corner of the room, they slowly rose to their feet, receiving an agreeable nod from the fair maiden.

She came to stand before me, and every instinct told me

to run. If the heaviness in my legs didn't make me feel like I had cement laced in with my bones, I would have attempted it. Hell, everyone was now apparently unarmed. Maybe I could at least try...

The thought vanished the instant the woman's fingers stroked the underside of my chin. Cold shot through me, locking every last muscle into place. I could barely muster the power to drag in a breath as ice seeped into my limbs, my mind, my heart.

Amid her fluid gestures, the Sagax's head suddenly twitched at a crooked angle as she studied me. The movement was unnatural—animalistic, like a vulture inspecting its prey, though her face remained unnervingly neutral. With her flawless features and bland expression, she reminded me of a doll. A creepy-as-fuck doll, but a doll no less. "What a pretty little thing," she mused, peering down at me. "A truth for a truth, my dear. Which one of my brother's younglings marked you?"

Her brother's younglings? I didn't know how to answer, not the least bit sure what the hell she meant, opting to just shake my head in response.

"You don't know which young prince marked you?"

I attempted to swallow down the massive lump in my throat. "Blaine."

Her head shifted in the other direction as she continued to peer down at me, the gesture holy aberrant. It was the only hint she provided, prompting me to further elaborate.

"Sitri," I muttered.

"Ahhh." The sound was so cool, her vocals vibrating softly like that of a dove as she finally released her hold on me. Her hand fell away, allowing what little heat I had to replenish me. "Astaroth's son. How fetching."

The Sagax strolled around the back of the sofa, coming

up behind me. That same ice shot through me once more as she peeled the wool blanket away from my neck, gifting me with a fresh wave of nausea and revulsion in its wake at the contact.

Not there.

Not there.

Not there.

Anywhere else but there.

"The Prince bit you."

It wasn't a question, but I nevertheless managed to nod, praying the answer would suffice her curiosity enough that she'd get her hands off me. I silently thanked the Lord she did as she rounded back around the couch. If I bared my fangs here, I'd be dead before I hit the floor.

"Tell me, child, do you love him?"

"Blaine?" I actually barked out a breathy laugh at the absurdity. "No."

The woman craned her neck again, her brows furrowing ever so slightly, as if waiting for something — waiting for me to retract...I didn't know. I stole a look over towards the others. Syringe and Flannel were only eyeing me bitterly. Clearly, I wasn't convincing them, but Nick...

Nick was gawking at me as if I'd stripped naked and started dancing on the sofa cushions. "You ran away with him though, after you were bitten..."

"No, I ran away *from* him — as well as everyone of the Reaper variety," I gnashed, glaring at Syringe and Flannel. Nick just continued to gawk, as if unable to process what he was hearing. "Reynolds already tried killing me when I was just a Changeling. The moment he suspected I *may* have been bitten..."

"He didn't *know*?"

"No, he was only aware that Blaine wanted me. Not

that I'd been bitten. And even after the fact, I did everything I could to get away."

The blonde's eyes shifted between me and the Sagax in disbelief. The woman simply nodded.

"Bullshit," Flannel sneered. Nick opened his mouth in protest, but his companion beat him to it. "You can't seriously be buying this. Come on, Holloway. You of all people know better than anyone what their kind can do. Even if she *thinks* she's telling us the truth, it's probably only because that bastard brainwashed her. She's nothing more than a puppet by now—"

"Shut up!"

The fury in Nick's voice...it brought the room to a standstill.

Flannel grimaced.

Whatever he had just said, it clearly wasn't about *me* anymore. I could see it in Nick's eyes. I'd seen that look before—right after I nearly bit Reese, when he watched me drive away. The loss, the desperation.

The blonde ran his hands over his face, trying to collect any sense of composure. "Where is he?"

The Sagax looked to me, but I just shook my head.

"Your mate," Nick gritted. "Where is he?"

"I... I don't know." He said to be honest, and I guess in a way, it was the truth. I knew Blaine wasn't home, and I had no idea where he was before I lost communication with him.

"Who killed Russell Hurst?"

Tears pricked my eyes at the very thought. I wanted to forget everything about the night of my Great Rite, but that moment...it would never go away. I still woke up sometimes, feeling that silver chain lynched around my throat as Russell tried strangling me, feeling the warmth of his blood drenching my body as Blaine slit his throat. "He did," I choked.

"Do you know what happened to his blade?"

I shook my head again. "Blaine may have taken it, but I'm not sure."

I nearly screamed as that hoarfrost bristled up through my arm as the Sagax took claim of my hand. She wrenched it out from beneath the blanket, scoping the entirety of my runes.

"Quite curious," she cooed.

A scream tore through the distant air, making the Sagax's head snap up. Everyone went silent as Flannel inched his way to the front window, peering through a small gap between the nailed boards. More footsteps tiptoed through the foyer hall, and another group of armed men passed by the entranceway. Nick exchanged a series of tactical hand gestures with them before the faction headed outside.

Indistinguishable mumbles came through the walkie-talkie strapped to Syringe's belt. Somehow, he seemed to understand the mumble, because he cursed. "Sullivan's not picking up."

"Is it her mate?" asked Flannel, looking to the Sagax.

"That… I cannot say." The pale woman sniffed the air. "Though I should tell you, you're outnumbered, young man. Your visitor comes with friends."

An enraged howl bellowed, and by the booming echoes, it was close. I knew that sound, and so did everyone else in the room.

"A truth for a truth, my dear. I would very much like to meet your mate, when you have the time," the Sagax cooed, tapping the rune on my ring finger. "Praesidio tuus cor, regia puella."

Before I could ask what that meant, the Sagax's form was already melding into the inky black cloud stirring in the far corner.

"Protect your heart, royal girl," she cooed softly.

Just like that, she was gone.

"Real helpful," Syringe spat, reclaiming his discarded weaponry from the floor.

Nick ducked into the hall, returning with a double-gun shoulder holster he threw on over his thermal before concealing it beneath a beaten leather jacket. Loaded with fresh ammo and accompanied by several silver blades, there was no doubt about it; Nick was ready for a blood battle, as were his compatriots.

The walls shook as a deafening blow struck the front of the house just beside the bay windows. Snarls and furious roars accompanied the volley of gunfire as screams filled the air.

The front door ripped open and slammed shut just as swiftly. Three blood spattered men staggered into the entranceway, their arms and legs and torso slashed with vicious claw marks.

"We have to move! Now!" one of them demanded.

"What are we looking at out there?" asked Syringe.

"Hellhounds. At least half a dozen."

Something cold pressed into the side of my head, and I turned to find the barrel of a gun aimed between my eyes. "Get moving, Blood Whore," growled Flannel.

Nick protested, but Flannel wasn't hearing any of it. He slammed the butt of the revolver into my temple, and my heavy limbs sent me toppling onto the floor. I was instantly pried up to my feet and dragged through the house to the garage. There were two SUVs already parked inside, and I was immediately tossed into the backseat.

Nick was shoved in beside me, and another Reaper climbed in through the opposing door, effectively pinning me between the two. The bloodied Reaper snatched hold of my wrists, snapping cuffs into place. I gasped, feeling my flesh burning inside the manacles.

Silver.

Given that the house was abandoned and that the only illumination came from the vehicles' interior lights, I safely assumed there wasn't any electricity to draw the garage door up. All but one of the men loaded up into the SUVs as the engines turned over. The lone Reaper pulled the emergency cord and flung the door up, allowing the vehicles to tear out of the garage. We lurched forward, only to crash to a halt as a mammoth wolf cut into our path. Shots rang out from every direction, and the beast snarled as multiple rounds clipped into its black mass of fur.

With an effective distraction, I readied my position, unable to bring myself to exact my plot out on Nick. Instead, I turned to the unsuspecting Reaper on my right and slammed my elbow into his nose. I tried reaching for the handle as his eyes instinctively teared up, only for him to blindly nail a fist into my already beaten temple. My body was suddenly hauled up against Nick, and before I could react, I found one of his hands wrapped around my forearm and the other prying the handle free. In one swift motion, he pulled me over his lap and threw me out the door.

"Shit, get her!" barked one of the men.

Hitting the lawn, I looked back up just long enough to see Nick mouth, "Run."

With legs made of lead, I staggered upright and took off—or rather more *stumbled* off. Every five feet, I face-planted into the grass, still unable to get my unruly limbs to work with me. But I kept moving. The entire property was surrounded by trees and overgrown brush, not another house in sight.

Shit.

Snarls and howls and gunshots sounded off all around me, growing quieter as I pushed on through the thicket. My heart thundered as cold lights came into focus.

A streetlight!

Twenty more yards, and I'd reach the road.

Something whizzed past my ear, and I shrieked, stumbling down. A flurry of beams highlighted the line of trees, and I quickly realized they were flashlights. I only made it another five yards when something struck the tree right beside me.

Was that...a tranquilizer dart?

"I think I got her!" a voice behind me called out.

It was too close.

There was still forty-five feet set between me and the road, and I hadn't seen a single car even pass by yet.

And then I felt it.

Not a dart, but...

I didn't have time to waste. I quickly reached up and pried the dart loose from the tree bark. Not a moment later, footsteps and flashlights swarmed me from behind. I kept the fetching of the dart dangling loosely between my fingers as I let the heaviness in my body drag me down to my knees.

16
Kill For You

Hauling me out of the brush, the four Reapers continued taunting me while dragging me up to the roadside. Every last one of them cackled and snickered as they informed me that all my so-called "friends" had been put down like the miserable mutts they were.

Keep laughing.

The SUVs barreled towards us, only slowing down once the drivers caught sight of the men around me waving their flashlights. Hoots and hollers greeted us as the Reapers inside the vehicles saw what their comrades had in tow, everyone but Nick. He paled.

Thankfully, nobody else appeared to have noticed, both now and his help in my escape, because they just cheered as my limp body was dragged back toward the backseat where he sat. Nick got out and had to make a conscious effort *not* to help me as I stumbled to climb inside with my bound hands. The skin around my wrists was a sickly red, the flesh blistering over as every movement chafed it more and more.

My evident pain appeared to please the bloody-nosed Reaper seated on the other side of the backseat. His nose hadn't been perfect to start with, but now, it was bent at an ugly angle, all thanks to my trusty elbow.

"Better get use to those," he snickered, grabbing my cuffs and yanking me inside. The silver bit into my burning flesh with such pressure, I couldn't hide the pain as I cried out.

Nick climbed in after me, and I collapsed my exhausted, injured frame against him.

"Awww, I think she likes you," laughed someone from the front seat. I didn't bother seeing who, letting my eyes sink shut. "Considering the dose Bill hit her up with, she'll be as harmful as a declawed kitten."

"You drugged her?" Nick couldn't mask the anxiety in his voice.

"Relax, it wasn't Syrfian. Okay? It's just some Diazepam."

"A shit-ton of it, but yeah," laughed another voice.

The cars started on down the road, and I tried not to grimace at the cuffs biting deeper into my wrists. I just kept my eyes shut and my body slack like the good little drugged-up Blood Whore that I was...supposed to be. The engine revved as the cars picked up speed. We drove for a couple minutes with my fellow passengers exchanging in overly embellished retellings of the fight back at the abandoned house. The very same men who'd run inside screaming were now declaring themselves victors as they proclaimed to have taken out each of the Hounds. By their accounts, there would've needed to be an army of wolves to even come close to matching their imaginary body count. Still, Nick didn't say anything.

The subtle warmth lingering in my chest roared to life, and it took everything in me not to laugh.

"Think that's cute?" demanded Bloody Nose beside me, noting the evident smile I couldn't hold back. "Something tells me you won't find any of it to be amusing when Reynolds gets his hands on you." His fingers grazed down my arm as he leaned into me, his breath warming my ear. "And just wait till I get my turn."

The menace in his voice had provoked something deep within me, an equal cruelty. A low, vicious laugh eased from my throat. The pleasure in it sounded so foreign to my ears. Monstrous even. I finally opened my eyes and turned to him, biting my lip. My teasing smile only infuriated him more as he continued his taunts, but I didn't so much as say a word.

"Leave her be, Brett. The bitch is crazy," remarked the driver.

"Is that it?" Bloody Nose sneered. I merely snickered. "You got something to say?"

It was my turn to lean into him as I whispered softly, each word as smooth and lovely as silk. "I'm talking to a dead man."

The grip on his rifle tightened as his eyes snapped down to my hands, expecting to see me holding some kind of concealed weapon. Yet, I held nothing, and not a single rune was lit. He scoffed, the tension in his shoulders easing for just a split second before a thunderous roar pummeled in front of us. Everyone's attention shot forward, watching the speeding SUV ahead of us suddenly swerve sideways, tires squealing as rubber burned into the pavement. Between the momentum and the unnatural angle, the vehicle spun and all-out flipped. Rolling again and again into the oncoming lane, it finally crashed to a halt, landing upside down as it fell into the ditch.

Everyone in our car was suddenly thrown forward like crash test dummies as the vehicle squealed to a stop. With rifles and handguns at the ready, the men surveyed the abandoned rural road. The air rippled ever so slightly, making the hairs stand up on my arm. I knew that feeling all too well.

"Get us out of here!" demanded Bloody Nose.

The driver continued pushing the gas pedal to the floor, but the wheels just spun uselessly against the asphalt, not carrying the car an inch. Smoke poured across the front hood as the tires were clearly burning out from the full-throttle rev on the engine. And yet, we didn't move. "I can't!"

Metal shrieked as something carved alongside the passenger doors. Bloody Nose and the man up front both yelled before an annihilating mass slammed into the side of the SUV. The vehicle rocked, the impact shattering the windows. Guttural snarls emitted from the darkness, commanding everyone's attention. With their guns primed, the aim shifting aimlessly around the shadows, not a single Reaper paid mind to the dark figure up ahead that just so happened to be sauntering down the street right for us.

Those startling pale blue eyes gleamed in the headlights even before the platinum dyed hair was discernible. A single gunshot went off, presumably from someone trapped in the rolled over SUV. But Blaine didn't stop. At last, everyone's attention cut to him, but they couldn't seem to discern where to aim: the stranger or the hidden Hounds lingering in the darkness. Curses came from the overturned car, and several figures staggered up from the ditch, one hurling something right for the Dark Mage.

Blaine simply raised a hand and waved it towards the offender. The object froze midair, only to switch paths and catapult right back at the Reaper. The oval device dropped into the ditch beside the SUV.

"Grenade!" one of the men screamed.

The bloodied crew frantically leapt away as the device detonated. The blast sent the SUV's backend bucking up as the vehicle ignited with a blast wave that knocked the men to the pavement, their hands instinctively shielding over their heads for protection as flaming metal and scraps rained down on them. If they still had any gusto to attempt another strike against him, they weren't given the window. A black mass of fur emerged from the forest. The Hound circled around the fallen men steadily, like a Great White Shark preparing to make a surface charge at the first man who so much as moved.

Mr. Flannel upfront in our own SUV shot off a few rounds into the darkness beside us, praying to hit something before he reached out the shattered window and primed his aim towards Blaine. Before he could even center his shot, another black mass slammed into the passenger side door again. This time, the Hound's strike was intended for more than a scare. One second, Flannel was strapped in the front seat. The next, his body was snatched right out of the window, his feet kicking helplessly as the Hound dragged him into the darkness.

A hail of gunfire sounded all around me as large masses surrounded the vehicle. Nick grabbed hold of me and pulled me down to the floor, using his body to shield me from the chaos. The SUV jostled and thrashed and rocked. Screams cut through the air before everything suddenly went quiet. Nick and I both stole a look up around us, finding the inside of the cabin empty. Bloody Nose and the driver were gone.

"You okay?" he whispered, slowly easing himself back onto the seat.

I nodded. "Thank—" The unmistakable *click* turned my stomach as I looked up to find him deathly still, his hands raised in the air. I pulled myself off the floor to discover the barrel of a gun pressed into his temple from someone outside. The unrepressed intensity in Blaine's eyes set my blood cold. His entire arm was ablaze with runes, but he wasn't bothering to use them. This was personal. He wanted the damage—the kill—to come from his own hands. *"Don't."*

I wasn't sure if I said the word out loud or only thought it, but he flinched, his chest heaving furiously as he barely managed to rein in his wrath.

"Throw your weapons outside," he growled to the Reaper. "Slowly."

Nick did as commanded, reaching inside his jacket and lobbing the guns from his dual shoulder holster onto the pavement.

"The other one," Blaine snarled.

The Reaper grimaced, removing the concealed pistol strapped around his ankle as well.

Blaine stepped back, his own gun still fixed on Nick, as he reached inside the shattered window and unlatched the door. He motioned Nick out, and I followed in suit, but the heaviness in my legs sent my knees buckling under my weight. The two managed to catch me before I ate a mouthful of asphalt. Blaine's eyes went to the silver cuffs—and the scorched skin covering my wrists. He pried me away from Nick, the barrel of the gun centering between the Reaper's eyes.

"He helped save me," I said gently, resting my bound hands on his forearm.

To Nick's relief—and my own—the Mage lowered the gun under my hold.

Headlights blinded me as I turned to the rumbling and crackling that made its way towards us. A familiar black Escalade rolled up with a familiar ruffian positioned behind the wheel. Only, the vehicle wasn't looking so resplendent. The front bumper of Val's beaming new Cadillac was dragging along the pavement, the grill crinkled and cracked.

"You're a real bastard, you know that?" Val jeered to his brother, thumbing the cut on his forehead. "Romeo, here, insists on driving, only to pass out behind the wheel—going 90 miles an hour, mind you. Sent us flying off into a damn cornfield."

The air left my lungs as I peered up at Blaine. He hadn't just passed out. And by the knowing look he returned, he knew it, too.

Val took a better look at the current spectacle. The burning van, the bloodied men, the Hounds returning to the road with crimson tarnishing their startling white teeth; all of it. "And then you run off to have all the fun without me, while I'm stuck hauling my poor baby out of Farmer Ted's field? What a jip."

Ignoring the remark, Blaine turned his attention back to the Reaper. "Where are the keys?" It wasn't so much of a question as it was a command, lifting my burning wrists.

"I don't have 'em. Brett... the one who put 'em on... your Hounds ran off with him," Nick muttered.

"Can I at least take *him* out?" remarked Val mischievously, motioning to the Reaper.

"Only if I get to take *you* out next," I rebuked, cutting him a warning glare.

He only chuckled.

Blaine let out an ear-aching whistle, apparently summoning one of the nearby Hounds. He said something to it in Latin, and the massive wolf bounded into the woods.

"There's another outfit on its way," Nick said lowly, as if he were at risk of the other men still lying on the ground up ahead overhearing. "Twenty Reapers, strong. And they're just as eager to get their hands on the two of you. Wherever you're heading, I'd suggest staying off any of the main roads. They've hacked into the traffic cameras, so they have eyes on all highways, interstates, and major intersections."

Blaine just eyed him suspiciously.

"Thank you," I offered in turn.

Nick nodded, recoiling as the gigantic wolf returned to the roadside with metal dangling between its bloodied lips. The Hound dropped it, and I shared in the Reaper's sentiment, realizing what it was. Keys. Bloody keys.

Nick crouched down to retrieve them, but the Hound merely snarled at him. "Unless you want to burn yourselves as well, let me help."

Blaine nodded, and the Hound retracted in allowance.

The Reaper grabbed the set, sifting through the collection before he singled out a particular key. It was tiny, a simple metallic post with a circular butt. I cringed as he was forced to grab the cuffs bound around my wrists to find the lock. Relief was immediate as the silver unclasped.

The Hound on Blaine's other side snarled, its gaze homed in on something in the distance the rest of us couldn't see.

"Time to move, people," called out Val.

With an arm secured around me, Blaine turned to guide me over to the Cadillac when Nick's hand suddenly clasped around mine.

"Good luck," he whispered, releasing his hold slowly enough that I could feel the crinkled slip of paper now pressed into my palm. I nodded, balling it up just in time before he let go.

Blaine assisted me into the backseat of the Cadillac, his skin sickly pale as he struggled to haul himself up in after me. I watched Nick's frame illuminate in the red glow of the taillights as Val drove us away, giving him a parting wave before the Reaper disappeared into the night.

Take Me Down

W here are we going?" I asked Val, unable to make out any of the scenery of the pitch-black back roads.

"The Hideaway."

"Why?"

"Because, Lover Boy back there needs a doctor, and it's not exactly like we can take him to the E.R."

"What are you talking about?" I knew the two had been in a car accident. Hell, Val had literally torn the deployed airbag right out of the steering wheel. But he, at least, seemed to be fine...

"Not sure if you noticed, but he was shot," the ruffian acknowledged, so offhandedly you'd think it was a simple as stubbing your toe.

How could I not see that? The black material of Blaine's jacket made it a little less obvious, but upon closer inspection, the blood marring his entire bicep became evident. When…?

The Reaper from the overturned car.

I assume he had missed. Blaine hadn't so much as flinched —

"The bullet went through," my mate muttered. "I'm fine."

He looked anything *but*. His eyes kept fluttering dazedly, as if battling to hold them open, and his breathing was labored.

"I just need to rest…"

Val accommodated the Cadillac with the bend in the road, the shift in direction sending Blaine to topple into me.

With the remnants of the drugs still in my system and the fact that my wrists were killing me, I couldn't muster enough strength to prop him back upright, leaving me with no choice but to let him collapse into my lap.

"I'm sorry," he muttered, nearly breathless.

"For what?"

"For not being there…"

"Blaine?" I swept the hair from his ashen face, not getting a response, even as I shook him. "*Blaine?* Val, pull over!"

Rumbling into the gravelly shoulder of the road, Val threw the car into park and climbed out to join us in the backseat. He checked his vitals, not appearing to like what he found. "It's not from the gunshot," he huffed. "Though I doubt that's helping him any."

"Then what is it?"

"How much energy did he use back there?"

"Energy?"

"Magic. Even for how strong he is, he still has his limits, especially without the mating ritual consummated. Plus, he used up a bunch of energy earlier."

Energy? Magic? In all my stupidity, I'd just assumed his power was somehow infinite. "I... I don't know."

"Shit."

The Hideaway was still fifty-plus minutes from wherever it was we currently were. And since Blaine didn't require a doctor to remove the bullet, Val decided it wasn't apparently worth the drive. Instead, he pulled out his cell and started relaying our predicament to someone on the other end of his phone call, simply replying "yes," "no," and "not an option."

"Let me see what I can do," replied a soft feminine voice on the other end of the call. "I'll call you back if I find anything."

"Where're we going?" I demanded.

"My place, I guess," said Val, turning onto another abandoned back road.

"Can I borrow your phone?"

The Mage didn't really have room to argue, because despite Blaine still lying unconscious in my lap, I managed to reach forward and snatched the cell right out of Val's hand. "Help yourself," he muttered.

I ignored him, trying desperately to remember Reese's phone number. The damn thing was programmed into my cell, so it wasn't like I'd made the effort to memorize the digits, but I was pretty sure *this* was it.

Or not...

Apparently, I'd just woken up a rather perturbed old

man. It was, after all, past midnight, so I couldn't exactly blame the poor guy. I made a second attempt, and wound up calling a 24-hour donut shop. Seriously? Did enough people *really* need bear claws at three in the morning to warrant this? I hung up and prayed the third time was the charm. All it took was a questioning, "hello?" from me to get my answer.

"Jesus Christ! Kat?" Reese sighed. "Where the hell have you been? I've been calling your phone for hours! And you weren't answering your door either. I thought... Wait, whose number are you calling from?"

I collapsed into the backrest with relief.

"It's a long story, but I'm alright," I assured. "I need you to go back to wherever you checked in, if you're not already there, and just lay low. Can you do that?"

"Yeah, but...what happened? Are you hurt?"

I could hear the panic in his voice, even now, and tears swelled in my eyes. If this was what he sounded like *after* I assured him I was okay, what had he been like before? "Reynolds found me. Or more, his *men* did. But I got away."

Since Reapers now knew where I lived, it didn't seem like much of a stretch that Reynolds would have spies scoping out my aunt's house, especially now. And if Reese showed up... I shook my head, not willing to venture down that rabbit hole. Imagining him being tortured for information—all because of me—I wouldn't have been able to live with myself.

I told Reese as much, opting to leave out that last bit, and made him promise me to keep an eye out, to make sure nobody was following him, and to stay hidden for the time being.

He did.

And his assurance was the only good news I had as I hung up, because Blaine groaned ever so softly beneath my hand. I hadn't even realized I'd been absentmindedly stroking his hair. The guy looked like death warmed over. Val echoed the sentiment upon pulling into some dingy motel off the interstate, seeing his brother still unconscious and paler than ever. Parked right in front of Room 108, he turned off the engine and climbed out of the car. Just as he opened the back door to where I'd been seated, familiar chestnut brown hair came into view, washed out in the hideous long-tubed fluorescent lights overhead as the fixtures sputtered on and off.

The young man seemed to notice me at the exact same second, because the ice bucket in his hands almost slipped from his grasp.

Reese?

He didn't say anything at first, his eyes shifting up and down from my face to...

Blaine was in my lap.

Blaine Freaking Ryder was in my lap!

Val cast me a look that seemed to say, *"What the hell's with you?"* as he tried to calculate which way would be easiest to haul his brother out of the backseat... and off my freaking lap! He finally looked over his shoulder at Reese. "You two know each other?"

I wasn't sure if it was the look on my face or something else, but the Dark Mage did a double take.

"Ah-ha," he crooned. "The magician."

I shot him a warning look, not the least bit in the mood for any of his bullshit. Not right now.

He seemed to sense as much as he turned back to Reese and said, "Mind giving us a hand? Or is that bucket all you can handle?"

The fact that I was clearly annoyed — and *not* scared of Val — was the only assurance to Reese that it was okay to approach the Dark Mage. He set his recently filled ice bucket on the hood as Val instructed him to grab Blaine from the other side of the backseat as Val heaved him upright off of me.

Apparently, dragging an unconscious/seemingly-dead man out of your car and into your room was a perfectly normal occurrence in these parts, because a couple of guests walked past us and didn't pay any mind as the guys hauled Blaine into Room 108. With my legs unsteady beneath me, I took my time hobbling in behind them, arriving just in time to see them toss Blaine onto the mattress.

Since neither Val nor Reese seemed to be a particular fan of the Crown Prince, they didn't exactly treat him with care. They lobbed him like he was nothing more than a sack of potatoes, watching him hit the edge of the box spring only then to topple off onto the floor. Reese pinned a hand to his mouth, at least *attempting* not to laugh, as Val outright snickered.

I stepped between the chuckling pair and gave them both a swat in the chest, immediately regretting it. My wrists silently screamed at the action. The slightest movement pulled and stretched the scorched skin, bringing me to the brink of tears. It *should* have at least begun to heal, but the charcoaled flesh and burning blisters were just as savage as they had been the moment Nick removed the silver manacles.

Recovering from their amusement, Reese and Val returned Blaine to the bed, taking better care this time as they set him closer to the center of the mattress. A cell phone sounded off outside, and Val cursed, realizing it was his.

"Sooo, how's your night been?" asked Reese, attempting a half-smile upon the Mage's departure.

"Oh, the usual. Kidnapped, drugged, nearly killed. And let's not forget the gunfights, interrogation, and brutal mutilation by Hellhounds."

Reese's mouth dropped.

Yeeeeah, I kinda, sorta, *maybe* left out a few details on the phone, and his inability to find the right words hardly came as a shock. "So, you're staying here, too?"

He managed to nod.

Now that I thought about it, it wasn't that surprising both he and Val were here. The only nice place to check into around Evermore that wasn't a Bed & Breakfast was the Grey Wolf Resort. It wasn't overly expensive, but it would still take a hit to your wallet, leaving you with some less than stellar alternatives. I supposed the Moonlight Motel really wasn't as bad as it looked from the outside, and it was infinitely better than the fleabag down the block. I was pretty sure you required a rabies shot before you were allowed to check into that monstrosity.

Reese's gaze fell to my wrists and then to the unconscious Mage. "Kat, what the hell's going on?"

"Hey, what do you know about Transference?" asked Val, poking his head back inside the room.

"...That it's a three-syllable word?" I offered.

Reese chuckled. "I think he means Demonic Transference."

"Oh, right. *That.*" I fake-laughed, thumping myself upside the head. "How silly of me."

"It's when two demonic creatures exchange energy between each other, essentially trading their essence. It can be given or stolen, depending on the situation," clarified

Reese.

"You up for it?" Val asked, looking to me.

"Up for what?"

"Giving Romeo, there, some of your mojo," he said, gesturing to his brother.

"I...I can't."

"Now is not the time to be coy, Doll Face. If he dies, well...I'll let your imagination fill in the rest."

I rolled my eyes. "I say I can't, because I *literally* can't. My runes aren't working."

"Come again?"

"I was dosed with Devil's Pod. My magic is dormant."

"Shit." Val returned to his phone conversation, making mention of stuff I had never even heard of, so I eventually tuned him out.

"Why would you need to give him your energy? What happened?" Reese asked me.

I recapped as much as I could manage to wrap my own head around when he leaned in and kissed me. I froze. "What was that for?"

Reese took a hold of my left hand, careful not to touch the skin on my wrist. "Dr. Madsen called me on my drive back. He thinks he found someth—"

Val interrupted again, sticking his head back into the room. "Have you bitten him, by any chance?"

"*Excuse me?*"

"Blaine. Have you bitten him?" By the look on my face, he didn't really need an answer. "That would be a *no*," he said into his cell as he headed back outside. Low murmuring continued, and he sauntered back into the room not a moment later, hanging up the phone.

"You find something that'll help him?" I asked.

"Yep, you're gonna bite him."

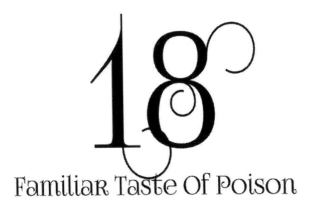

Familiar Taste Of Poison

A pparently, stubbornness was a familial trait.

"I think you may have to get your hearing checked, because I just told you. I. Have. No. Magic."

If anything, *I* should have been the one rolling my eyes, but instead Val took up the role, letting out an annoyed sigh. "You don't need magic to activate your fangs. Granted, you won't be able to trigger them by smell, but you *can* still do it."

"He's already infected with the demonic virus though. Why would biting him help?"

"It just will."

"How do you know?"

Val collapsed into the old worn chair in the corner, rubbing his temples. "I just do."

Well, wasn't he just a wealth of information. "Can *you*

trigger your fangs?"

With no more effort than opening his jaw, those elongated incisors jutted out.

"Great, then why don't *you* bite him?" I countered.

A devilish grin played at his lips as Val ran his tongue over the curve of his fangs. "I'm not his mate, Doll Face. *You* are."

I couldn't bite him.

I couldn't.

Even if I could trigger my fangs, I didn't know the first thing about how this whole "transference" thing worked. How hard would I need to bite him? Where would I have to bite him? For how long?

"It's really not complicated," Val assured. "I'll explain everything step by step."

I looked down at Blaine, praying I'd find a little more color in his cheeks. But his skin remained ashen, his breathing more labored. "Reese…"

He was at my side instantly, but I shook my head.

"I need you to leave the room."

Val's lips peeled back in a wicked grin, stealing a peak through the curtains, presumably to watch Reese pace outside. "I think you hurt Lover Boy's feelings."

I just shot him a dirty look as I yanked the drapes closed and shoved him towards the mattress.

"Wanna make this a threesome, eh?"

If I didn't require his assistance, I would have turned his face into a crater where his nose was supposed to be. "I can't risk having Reese in here when I trigger my fangs." Not only because I wasn't sure if I'd turn on him, but I also couldn't bring myself to relive the horror of having him look at me like that again.

"And how do you presume to do that exactly?"

"You have to touch my neck," I said, pulling the hair away from my exposed collar.

That wicked delight of his only heightened. "And…?"

"And *nothing*. Just be ready."

"For what?" He didn't give me a chance to answer, all too eager to run his fingers down the length of my neck as I sat down beside Blaine on the mattress.

The moment Val hit my scars, I doubled over and gasped. He seemed to understand, because he rested his entire hand over the markings as I writhed under his hold. Without any scent to assist the transformation, the fangs only teased at the roof of my mouth, not quite breaking through the gums. The revulsion hit in full force, and I began mindlessly thrashing at Val to let go of me.

But he held firm, his voice nothing more than a whisper. "Give into it."

I clung to the bed sheets as my fingers curled into fists. "I can't!"

My entire body convulsed, as if at war with itself. The pain in my jaw became unbearable. It felt like someone had just jammed a couple screwdrivers into my gums!

"Your body wants it. It's *you* who's holding back. Let go, Kat."

Val was right. All I could see was Reese's face, the fear, the aversion… Even without my magic, this was what I was, what I had become.

"He *will* die if you don't do it." Val grabbed my chin, forcing me to look at his brother.

I wasn't sure if it was the threat of me possibly dying, or perhaps just seeing Blaine so helpless, but instinct finally took effect. That ravenous impulse sent my fangs slicing through the roof of my mouth as red filled the corners of my vision.

"That a girl."

Val really should have heeded my warning. With his hand still on my neck, I involuntarily whirled on him, tackling the Mage so hard, his body slammed into the wall beside the mattress. My forearm pinned against his windpipe as I watched the pulse in his neck throb, practically begging me to tear into it—to tear the artery. I wanted to *kill* him for touching me there.

I wasn't sure if it was the red encasing my vision, but the lights pouring out of Val's remaining runes glowed like a Sith Lord's lightsaber. Without magic aiding my effort, he managed to use his own strength to ease me off of him.

"Down, girl," he beckoned.

Shaking, I finally regained composure, seeing the red peter out of my vision. At first, I panicked, grappling at my mouth, afraid my fangs may have retracted. They were still there.

I couldn't waste time. I climbed back onto the bed, unsure of the next step. I needed to bite Blaine, but where? His wrist, perhaps? I lifted it up, feeling the weakness in his pulse. I was running out of time!

"The neck."

"*What?*"

Val tapped the exact spot on his own neck where Blaine had bitten *me*. "It'll work faster there."

Struggling to pull Blaine into a sitting position, I stood on my knees behind him. This had to be precise. "What do I have to do after…?"

"After what?"

"You know... Do I have to drink...?" The very thought tested my gag reflex.

"Drink his blood?" Val laughed at me as if I was the cutest thing in the world. "No, Doll Face. Just let your instincts guide you."

Considering those very same instincts were telling me just a moment ago to tear into the ass-hat's neck like he was a human hamburger, the sentiment was hardly what I'd call comforting.

Lowering myself down to the back of Blaine's neck, I started estimating where the exact spot had to be when I suddenly found myself leaning into him, breathing in his scent. The fresh coastal fragrance lingering on his skin had me moaning as I intuitively traced a path down to the right side of his neck. All my calculations, all my questions, all my nerves; they melted away. I didn't need Val to tell me. I *knew* this was the spot.

My left hand cupped the underside of Blaine's jaw, tilting his head to the side, exposing the entire length of his neck to me. It invited me to slice my teeth into it. And I did just that. Not a thought, not a moment of hesitation. Intuition consumed me as my fangs sank into his flesh. The reaction was immediate. Blaine's wilted body went rigid, shuddering ever so slightly under my touch.

Giving someone your energy should have left you tired, drained, weak... Wasn't it?

I had expected to feel faint, or at least lightheaded. But the euphoric potency wrapping itself around my bones had my toes curling under. The high I'd gotten from kissing him at the Hideaway paled in comparison to the delirious warmth enveloping me, consuming every inch of my body. I didn't want it to stop.

I never wanted it to stop.

None of my runes had ignited, and yet I could feel the energy pouring into me, bringing me to the very brink of unadulterated ecstasy. Blaine fell slackened again, his weight leaning back into me, and I looked up at Val, my fangs still buried in his brother's neck.

The cruel smile painted across the Dark Mage's lips was pure menace, and ice instantly filled my veins as realization dawned on me.

"Well done, Doll Face."

This wasn't right. I wasn't supposed to be feeling this way. All I could think was *What had I done? What had I done? What had I done?*

I'd been sucking out what little energy Blaine had left in him! It was the only logical explanation for what I felt. I was supposed to be *giving* him a part of myself, but all I had done was devour whatever linked us. And I couldn't bring myself to stop! Had this been Val's plan all along? Eliminate his brother from the picture all together? If he was dead, what other option was there but to name *Val* Crown Prince? The wickedness seeping off him told me everything I needed to know. I'd fallen for it. I'd fallen right into whatever sadistic trap he'd constructed, all without *him* getting his hands the least bit dirty. I'd done everything for him.

The sweet electrical pulsation coursing through me at last subsided just enough that I managed to regain control of myself. I pried my fangs free from Blaine's neck, collapsing back into the headboard, taking him with me. I began shouting his name, *screaming* it, begging him to open his eyes as I shook his unresponsive form.

I hadn't even heard the door open over my hysterics, finding Reese suddenly at my side.

"What happened? *Kat?*" He kept trying to get me to

answer him, but I just sat there, sobbing.

I'd killed him. Maybe not entirely, but he was going to die, and it was all my fault!

I was going to die.

Val just chuckled, scooping up a bottle of vodka he had stored inside the top shelf of his mini-fridge, and casually strolled over to the chair in the corner.

Whether it was from the drugs or my hysteria, I didn't know, but I couldn't even feel my legs beneath me as I launched myself at him. I got as far as falling into him, feeling my nails tearing into his cheek when everything suddenly started to dim.

No, no, no, no!

Arms secured around me, and I wanted to scream, knowing exactly who they belonged to.

I was going to die in the arms of the very man who had just tricked me into killing myself!

I couldn't figure out how light was pouring back into my vision. Pinching my eyes shut, I demanded my eyes to focus. Upon reopening, the bright neon blue lights converged and sharpened into two legible words. "Motel" and "Vacancy." I was looking out of a half drawn window, noting it was nighttime. Disjointed fragments of half-thoughts floated about my mind, but in my lethargy, I couldn't seem to piece any of them together. I didn't feel exhausted. I felt...drunk. How long had I been asleep? How did I get here? What happened?

Everything hit me all at once; Blaine's body, Val smirking, me passing out. *What happened?* That rat bastard tricked me! But how was I still here? How was I still alive?

Something was digging into my side beneath me, and I rolled over, trying to find relief. I quickly realized I was lying on the bed, because platinum blonde hair gleamed directly in front of me, the hint of black roots visible up close. If I wasn't feeling so woozy, I would have sprung up from the mattress. Not because I was scared, but because I was so utterly taken aback.

Blaine was alive!

And not only that, but there was a healthy glow blossoming on his resting face.

How?

"Vestri 'pono super brachium meum."

I yelped. Literally *yelped* at the sound of his voice.

He peeled a groggy eye open and cast me a lazy, lopsided smile.

"What—what does that mean?" I managed to ask.

"You're laying on my arm."

"What?" I looked down at my other side now, realizing that my discomfort was indeed thanks to the muscled appendage wedged beneath my ribcage. He only chuckled as I scrambled up. "Oh! Sorry!"

And I only wanted to *keep* apologizing when I realized it was the very same arm he'd been shot in, seeing dried blood staining his bicep. But wait… Dried? He…he was healing, too? And so was I! My wrists still ached, but the pain was nothing to how it had been, and the skin had lightened up to a pinkish-red, the blisters and charcoaled flesh almost completely gone.

Blaine's fingers idly teased through the ends of my hair, and that familiar tug in my chest urged me to lie back down. I made sure *not* to crush his arm this time as I settled back onto the mattress and faced him. Warmth still coiled through my body, and I found my eyes sinking shut again when a soft kiss pressed to my forehead.

"Awww, how adorably nauseating."

My eyes flew back open.

Leaning against the open doorway stood Blaine's insufferable bastard of a brother. I tried willing my runes into action, but only a low buzz tickled the surface of my skin. At least it was something. But I really, really wanted to smash that bottle of vodka in his face. Before I could make a move for him though, Blaine was already charging at the door.

Damn, for a guy who was just knocking on Death's door, he sure could move. But he plowed past Val, and...

Something crashed outside. Thankfully, my legs had regained enough of their strength that I didn't collapse face-first on the carpet as I darted for the door.

Crap.

Reese's body was nailed to the front hood of the Escalade with Blaine's hand wrapped around his throat. I tried lunging for the two, but arms snatched me from behind, pulling me back. The runes on Reese's arm flickered, struggling to ignite.

"Not so easy to control them when you can't breathe, is it?" Blaine seethed, squeezing his grip even tighter.

"Blaine, stop!" I thrashed in Val's hold, but he refused to let go of me.

"How did they find her?" Blaine demanded, letting up his grip just enough to let Reese speak.

He just shook his head, unable to muster the words.

"How the fuck did they find her?" Blaine roared. His fist hammered down at Reese, and I gasped, seeing his Wrath rune ignited.

"Blaine, don't—"

His knuckles slammed into the hood of the car right

beside the Light Mage's head. Reese flinched, his eyes wide in unadulterated fear as he heard the metal crumple beneath Blaine's fist like it was tinfoil.

Blaine tightened his grip ever so slightly, as if it would force the words out of him. "How did Reynolds's men find her?"

"I don't know," Reese choked.

"Bullshit!" Blaine yanked him off the truck and whirled him around, throwing him into the side of the building.

Between the ongoing commotion and the ruckus from earlier, I had to wonder why none of the other guests had at least made a noise complaint to the front desk. My gaze shifted away from the guys, noticing a nearly indistinguishable ripple in the air. Wards. Val had set up magical wards around this place. It made sense now why no one else seemed to hear us, or why nobody reacted to Blaine being carried inside earlier.

Reese narrowly dodged the fist aimed at his head, sidestepping back to the open motel door. Val hauled me back inside, and with nowhere left to run as Blaine lunged for him again, Reese ducked in as well. The runes on his arm sparked back to life, but the bedside lamp suddenly hurled right at him. The energy he'd summoned managed to offset the strike, only to leave him vulnerable again as his runes died down once more. Reese didn't even have the chance to breathe as the air pulsated, the invisible force catapulting him against the tiny vanity counter just outside the bathroom.

Blaine was on him in a second, and Reese didn't dare move, feeling the barrel of the Dark Mage's revolver press beneath his jaw.

"What happened, Blackburn? You finally catch a glimpse of what she really is, and you couldn't take it?"

Reese closed his eyes, trying to regain his composure. His runes wouldn't work like this. He needed to fully concentrate.

Blaine smacked him, the power behind it jolting Reese's head to the side. The Dark Mage gripped the magician's jaw, forcing him to face him again. "Look at me, you fucking coward."

I could barely make out his eyes in the reflection of the mirror, but the murderous rage in them was unmistakable. Squirming in Val's hold, I finally managed to snake my arm out just enough to throw my elbow into his ribs. The asshole merely chuckled at my attempt, not the least bit affected, but he loosened his grip, allowing me to break free.

Stop,
Stop,
Stop!

I kept pleading the same word to Blaine as I raced to his side, but he wouldn't listen.

"You were the only other person who knew where she was," he seethed, those steely eyes cracking under his own anguish.

"Why don't you look at your friend over there?" Reese choked out.

Blaine laughed, but it was a cruel, vicious snarl. "My brother may be a lot of things, but stupid isn't one of them."

Val's brows furrowed. "Uh, thank you… I think."

"See, as much as he may hate me, he's far more concerned with keeping Kat alive," Blaine further elaborated, ignoring the remark.

"That's funny, especially since he was trying to kill you earlier," Reese rasped, his eyes shifting to the side of

Blaine's neck.

As if only now acknowledging the sting of pain, Blaine lowered the gun from Reese's jaw, using his free hand to reach up and finger the abrasion just above his right shoulder. His jaw fell slackened, apparently appalled by his discovery as his head snapped over to his brother. *"Did you bite me?"*

Val burst out laughing. Even as Blaine shifted the aim of his gun at him, he couldn't rein in his amusement.

Blaine cocked the trigger, but his brother just rolled his eyes, still chuckling.

I wasn't sure why I was coming to Val's defense, but I suddenly blurted, "He didn't bite you... I did."

Blaine faltered at the words, the air heaving from his lungs as if I'd hit him. He whirled around, his eyes immediately locking on mine. The feral edge in them had me stumbling backwards, and I barely managed to catch myself on the edge of the vanity sink.

"I'm... I'm sorry. You were dying, and Val said it would help..." I didn't know what I was saying. I just kept spewing out random nonsense, hoping he'd just stop looking at me like that.

"Oh, come on, brother. Lighten up." Val dared to approach, slinging an arm around Blaine's shoulder. Looking like the cat who ate the canary, he brushed the puncture marks with a feather light touch.

Sure enough, Blaine recoiled, his hand slamming defensively against the wound. He looked more feral than ever. "No..."

"No?" His brother parroted back, mockingly. "Oh, I see. You wanted it to be a special occasion, did you? Maybe have a bearskin rug and some grape soda on ice ready."

Blaine just kept shaking his head. "It couldn't have

worked, not if she didn't mean it..."

"Trust me, it worked just fine."

That ire in Blaine's eyes resurfaced as he turned to face Val, but the rest of his body had gone eerily calm. His brother seemed to relax, only making the impact more satisfying. The motion was nothing but one swift blur as Blaine nailed Val square in the jaw with a devastating left hook. The impact sent the towering male falling to the floor with a sharp *crack!* It sounded like he'd literally broken his brother's face.

Val still didn't look the least bit concerned, merely vexed as he tweaked his beaten jaw from the ground. "Hey, I did you a favor. If I hadn't, you'd both be dead."

"What did you do?" I demanded.

Val's grin only broadened as he climbed back up to his feet and slowly sauntered over. "*Me?* I didn't do a thing. You, on the other hand, Doll Face... You were spectacular. And it's all quite fantastic, when you think about it. He bites you to save your life, only for you to return the favor. How very kismet."

I was nearly breathless, feeling a wave of nausea wash over me. "What did I do?"

"You, Doll Face, finally completed your half of the mating ritual."

19
Shameless

I was going to be sick.

Like projectile-vomit sick.

Why was the floor spinning? I was standing still, yet the ground seemed to waver beneath my feet.

Reese seemed to have regained a morsel of his composure, enough to ignite a single rune, because he charged at Val. My body lurched, instinctively wanting to intervene, but the slightest movement sent my stomach reeling. I was going to be sick... I staggered, only tripping over my own feet in the process. Blaine seemed to have notice my current state amid the commotion, because he managed to catch me. I rewarded the deed with the most forceful shove I could muster, choosing to collapse sideways into the wall instead. The thought of his hands on me... And a metallic tang still coated my tongue. Was it his blood? Was it in my mouth?

I seemed to have recovered some strength back into my legs, because I darted into the bathroom. For the first time in my life, I *wanted* to throw up. I wanted whatever was in me to get the hell out. I wanted it all out, now!

But no matter how hard I tried, nothing came.

That's what the intoxicating rush of magic had been. I hadn't been stealing Blaine's energy. No, I had broken the final seal that had been keeping the Crown Prince's power captive in Hell. And I'd unleashed it...into *me* as well.

"You can't get sick with Devil's Pod in your system," remarked a voice from the doorway a moment later. It was only then that I realized the commotion outside had finally calmed down. I looked up to find Val standing there, his lip busted, the entire right side of his face bruised, and his perfectly groomed hair now a complete mess. "Its sole purpose is to contain dark magic, so it does everything it can to suppress your body's natural ability to expel it. The effects will probably last for a few more hours."

Reese came into my line of vision, shoving past Val to get to me. He, too, looked a bit beaten up from the tussle, sporting the beginnings to what was inevitably going to be a pretty ugly shiner beneath his left eye. Wiping the tears from my face, he gently coaxed me up to my feet and led me out of the bathroom. Val made a remark of some sort, but Reese just growled. "She's staying in my room."

"The hell she is." Blaine, still clearly not trusting Reese, moved in toward me, but stopped as I recoiled at the very sight of him. "Kat—"

"Stay away from me." I looked between the two brothers, sickened at the sight of them both. Blaine had rescued me, but at what cost? I was now claimed to him, and I had no idea what that even entailed. As for Val... I wanted nothing more than to bathe him in holy water. Even then, it still wouldn't be enough. What little information there was on mating bonds, one thing was adamant. Their consummating rituals were meant to be sacred—*intimate*. That's why Madsen and I had believed it to be sexual in nature. Seeing the sickening amusement Val found in tormenting his brother like this, robbing him of a tradition that was clearly meant to be respected, it had my fangs threatening to tear through my gums. And the very fact that it bothered me so much only had me wishing all the more that I could vomit.

I didn't know how long I'd been in the shower. Well after the shampoo and suds were gone, I just stood there, letting the hot water cascade down my face, as if I could somehow wash away the events of the night. Once again, my ignorance had put me one step closer to eternal damnation. I'd completed the mating ritual.

How could I be so stupid?

Did I honestly think that *biting* him wouldn't have had repercussions?

How would this affect the hex?

My dizzying array of questions and self-loathing was cut short as I closed my eyes. In the darkness, the steam of the shower suddenly seemed to be smothering me. I couldn't breathe! All I could see was the tomb, feeling the concrete pressed against my back. My eyes flew back open and panic arrested all my senses. The limited space of the tub closed in all around me as every last loose fixture in the limited space started to rattle. I would have thought it to be an earthquake, if not for the sudden pressure that slammed down into my arm. Most of my runes were lit, and the fury brewing beneath them only grew. The pain nearly sent me crumpling to the ground as I tore the shower curtain open and stumbled out. I barely managed to fasten a towel around myself before I cried.

Reese pounded on the bathroom door, begging to know what was wrong, asking me to unlock the door, but I couldn't speak. I couldn't move. I curled over and began sinking to the floor when I heard something pop. The lock on the door. My low line of vision had me seeing a pair of knees and feet, but I recognized the decorative Gothic boots.

Reese pushed the shower curtain out of my way and helped me up so that I could sit on the edge of the tub. "What happened?"

The air was still too suffocating in here. I tried to say as much, but found myself instead stumbling out of the bathroom. The immediate drop in temperature between the bathroom and the bedroom was a blessing, but it still wasn't enough. I staggered over to the door and pried it open.

"Kat, what the hell are you doing?" Reese grabbed my damp arms, hauling me back. "It's twenty degrees out there!"

I didn't care. I wrestled out of his hold and bolted out the door, clutching to the railing running along the entire exposed second story. The bitter cold stole my breath as the howling winds crashed into me, but I needed to feel the open air. Every time I so much as blinked, all I could see was concrete. And the painful toll of my runes still ablaze on my arm only made the nightmare all the more real.

Reese reached out to me, but he suddenly cowered

back, cursing under his breath as an unruly tendril of my power slammed down on his hand. I sobbed, dignity be damned, letting my body slowly sink to the floor. Everything around me rattled and vibrated, no doubt from my runes that only burned brighter. The lights overhead surged with electricity before the bulbs blew out. I couldn't contain the energy—

A warm embrace suddenly cradled around me despite my sopping wet frame. "You're okay."

And he was right. The moment his arms held me, the pain vanished, along with the pale blue lights burning up my arm. But I couldn't stop shaking my head. I couldn't stop sobbing.

"You're okay."

I could feel the energy resurging in me, the lights on my arm humming back to life, and blind panic seized me once more.

"Look at it." Blaine's fingers gently stroked over my omen rune. "It's not lit."

Again, he was right.

All the runes around it glowed so brightly, they illuminated the entire corridor, but the one in question remained as nothing more than metallic black ink.

"You're safe," he whispered.

The effects of the Devil's Pod had apparently worn off a lot faster than Val had predicted, because a half hour later my runes were raging worse than ever, still threatening to fry every electronic in the building the moment Blaine let go of me. He had to stand right outside the bathroom when I finally regained enough composure to wipe myself off and change into my clothes. We kept the door cracked open, allowing his hand to poke through just in case I needed to grab it.

Which I sadly did—a lot.

I couldn't make it more than ten seconds away from his touch without my runes reigniting, begging for sweet release. At least I didn't have to use the bathroom. Things were awkward enough as they were, especially with me fumbling about in the compact space, attempting to keep my newly found claustrophobia in check as I threw my clothes on behind the door. Last thing I needed was another freak-out, especially when I wasn't wearing *anything.*

Oh God.

Blaine had been holding me—and I'd been in nothing more than a towel! He'd even carried me back into Reese's room, his one hand clasped under my exposed thighs. The very same hand now sticking through the door. Could somebody die from humiliation?

Evidently not, since I reemerged from the bathroom a moment later, still alive. The vintage rock t-shirt Reese had lent me barely covered my butt, making my face redden all the more as I went to the vanity mirror to blow dry my hair. Blaine lingered behind me a couple feet, his gaze drifting down my completely exposed legs. That devil-may-care grin tugged at his lips the moment his eyes caught mine in the reflection.

He leaned in again to tap my shoulder, forcing my runes to settle down once more. I tilted the blow-dryer away from my head, purposely batting him in the face with a gust of hot air, properly tossing his already untamed hair. He only chuckled, and the playful tenor warmed my insides. *What the hell was wrong with me?* I felt…flushed.

The underside of my hair was still a bit damp, but I turned off the dryer anyway, unwilling to give Blaine anymore of a show by having to flip my head upside-down, essentially exposing more of my backside as I would have to lean forward. I caught Reese's reflection in the mirror. He remained seated in the far corner, the particular location allowing him a full view of the room — including us. Admittedly, he looked pissed off, and I couldn't blame him. Not when Blaine was allowed to watch me and touch me and hold me as he pleased. But was Reese mad…at me? I mean, I'd brought all this to him. How could he not be? Despite how sweet and amazing and supportive he was, he still couldn't help me. And all I was doing now was hurting him.

"Ready to go?" Blaine asked behind me as I pushed past him into the bedroom area.

Both Reese and I looked at him as if he'd spontaneously grown a second head, but Reese was a little faster on the uptake. "Ready to go *where?*"

"Val rented another room for the two of us just down the hall," the Prince clarified.

"Not a chance," Reese said vehemently. "You're not taking her anywhere, least of all to a private room."

Blaine pinned a hand to his chest in mock offense. "Awww, and to think I was doing it to save you the discomfort. Let's face it, Houdini. As long as Kat's runes are revved up like a deuce, I'm not leaving her side. If she unleashes that energy in the state she's in, it'll be a beacon to every supernatural entity in the area, especially Reapers. And that leaves *you* with only three options if we stay in this room, none of which you're going to like."

"Anything's better than leaving her alone with you."

"Okay." Blaine happily took a seat on the mattress, forcing me down with him. "First option, we all sleep in bed *together*, which I can safely assume none of us wants."

As expected, nobody argued.

"Second, you keep to your chair in the corner while *we* take the bed," he further offered, pulling me closer. "Or we can switch positions, where you'll spend the entire night in bed watching Kat curled up in my lap."

Definitely not that last one!

Or the second...or the first.

Crap.

They were all awful.

"Don't tell me the prospect of the last two doesn't excite you, love," Blaine's voice purred in my head.

I scoffed at the thought, trying to ignore the warm rush of heat perpetrating its way back in me as I recalled one too many of the dreams I'd had of him. Reese just worked his jaw, clearly coming up empty on a fourth option.

Blaine leaned back on the comforter, his fingertips drawing soft, idle lines up and down my arm until goose bumps kindled across my skin. I slapped his hand away, grinding my teeth as the runes started vibrating back to life again. Blaine crooked a mischievous brow at me in challenge, knowing I had no other choice. I gave him a good shove, but surrendered my arm back to him.

"Amor me vel odi me; ambo sunt in mea favor," he whispered in my mind.

I out-and-out glowered at him. "If you insist on doing that, at least do it in English."

"You're adorable when you're angry." Blaine winked, and I seriously doubted that's what he had previously said...or thought. Whatever.

Reese just stared at the pair of us, confused and

blatantly pissed off.

"I don't see what the big deal is that we share our own room," Blaine lazily sighed, stretching out across the mattress. "It's not like this is the first time we've slept together."

There had already been rumors back in Mystic Harbor that Blaine and I had been hooking up before his supposed "death." And seeing as how I hadn't told Reese about the morning I woke up in my room only to find Blaine in bed with me, I could clearly see he was questioning the fallacious gossip as well.

"We'll go to the other room," I muttered.

That look of anger Reese was sporting quickly shifted to downright shock. "You can't be serious!"

"We don't know who might be out there trying to track us. If Reynolds catches up, I'm not going to risk you getting pulled into the middle of this. I've hurt you enough as it is." I ran an exhausted hand down my face before casting Blaine another scowl. "And all this douche canoe's gonna do tonight is try pushing your buttons."

"Douche canoe?" I could actually hear him chuckle inside my head.

Before Reese could object, I grabbed Blaine and attempted to haul him up off the mattress. All I really did was just strain my arms. He didn't budge, at least not until he shot Blackburn a victorious, shit-eating grin, batting eyelashes and all.

"You're a jackass!" I plowed past Blaine into our new room, practically dragging him behind me until I reached the bedside. I furiously yanked away the sheets and prepared to crawl underneath, all too aware of his close proximity. I could even feel the heat from his body radiating onto mine as he stood behind me. Every muscle in my body locked, hearing a zipper draw down. I whirled around.

Blaine had already discarded his shirt, and he apparently was preparing to do the same with his pants.

"What the hell are you doing?"

That roguish grin of his only grew. "Joining you."

"Not like that you aren't."

"Well, some studies suggest that it's bad for a man's health to sleep in jeans." His smile was all fox as he nodded down at the faded black denim. "Some even say it could even cause infertility. And we wouldn't want that now, would we?"

"A hundred-percent of studies would prove that you'd be doing society a favor keeping them on," I shot back, snatching up a pillow and moving to the far side of the mattress.

Blaine tossed his jeans aside, thankfully leaving on his black boxer briefs, and climbed in beside me.

I immediately took a pillow and wedged it between us.

"What is this for?"

"What does it look like? It's a safety barrier, to prevent any unnecessary physical contact." I adjusted the remaining pillow behind my head and offered him nothing more than my hand.

"Ah, yes, how truly innovative. It's an impenetrable fortress, except... uh-oh." Blaine stuck his entire arm out above the pillow and waved his hand in front of my face. "Just as I feared. A security breach is possible, if not highly probable."

"Don't even think about it."

"Excuse me, Miss High-And-Mighty, but I wasn't talking about me," Blaine laughed. "No, my fears rest solely with you."

"Me?"

"Yes, I don't think you're gonna be able to keep your hands to yourself."

"Is that right?"

"Well, I don't mean to be arrogant here, but come on. Have you seen this?" He motioned to himself grinningly. "Let's not kid ourselves, love."

"What? You think I'm gonna manhandle you in your sleep?"

"I don't see how you could resist."

"In your dreams." Flipping him off, I jammed my head into the pillow and forced my eyes shut, trying to ignore the idle strokes Blaine traced along my offered hand.

"And in yours, love."

Exhaustion overpowered my anger, and sleep took me in a matter of minutes.

20
Demons

un shots reverberated in my ears as I startled awake from the same horrific dream I'd been playing on repeat. I looked around, and at first, I couldn't understand why I wasn't in my bedroom. Where were my posters? My Christmas lights? My Chinese lantern? It took a moment to remember what had happened, where I was.

The motel.

I looked over my shoulder, finding Blaine still lying beside me. A low groan emanated from the bottom of his throat, but he didn't open his eyes. His body twitched for a moment, and I noticed his breathing quickened. Another groan followed, and he suddenly jerked. It had been powerful enough that it should have woken him up, but he only murmured something I couldn't quite understand.

"Blaine?" I whispered.

Nothing. He was out cold.

But then he made a strange choking sound, as if gasping for air.

"Blaine!" I shook him, hoping to rouse him awake when my breath suddenly caught as well.

The motel room vanished as darkness overtook my vision. It took a moment, but warm glowing lights eventually came into view. The shadows peeled away as muffled music filled the air.

"What'd you say?" a gleeful voice yowled behind me.

I whirled around, suddenly finding myself standing in the middle of a crowd. Everyone's breath vaporized as they jumped about, rubbing their arms and hands furiously through chattering teeth as they all laughed and talked over the booming bass of the song.

A short sandy blonde haired boy stood staring at me expectantly. Something about him looked familiar, but I couldn't place his face.

"*What?*" The voice behind me caught me off guard. It was rich and lilted with a distinctive silvery quality.

Blaine?

I looked over my shoulder, and sure enough, there he stood.

"I said I'm gonna grab a beer. You want one?" the boy reiterated.

Blaine shook his head. "I'm good, man. Thanks."

What the hell? Where were we?

Blaine shoved his hands into the lined pockets of his jacket, shivering as another guttural wind coursed through the nightly air. I had to do a double take. Holy hell! I realized the real question was *When were we?* Blaine's hair…it was black, and it was also shorter than I'd ever seen it. A lot shorter. And his clothes… Since his reveal on the night of my Great Rite, Blaine looked like he'd been raiding Colin Farrell's wardrobe. Dark, rugged, and casual. But this? With a tailored peacoat, matching slacks, and Armani dress shoes, he looked every bit worthy of his old nickname "Gatsby."

"Blaine?" I bellowed at him, but he simply turned and headed over to a rickety set of wooden stairs. "Blaine? Blaine!"

I raced after him down to a path overlooking a reservoir where smoke stacks and numerous industrial buildings rested on the other side. None of this looked familiar, until a flash of light caught my eye. In the distance, I could faintly see what I realized was a lighthouse. Harper's Cove. We were in Mystic Harbor!

"Blaine!" I caught up to him, snatching his arm to turn him around. Only…my hand slid right through his bicep.

What the hell?

I reached out, trying to grab his shoulder. And yet again, my hand fell right through him.

Was I a…ghost?

Had I died?!

Blaine plucked his familiar Kevlar encased phone out of his pocket as it vibrated. I tried catching a glimpse of the text message that came up on the screen, but he put the cell away just as quickly.

"Shit," he muttered.

"Hey, sexy!" laughed a drunken girl to him from up above on the raised dock. "You gonna dance with me, or what?"

He attempted a polite smile, but it didn't reach his eyes. "Rain check. I have to take care of something."

She whimpered as Blaine began jogging away. I raced after him down the path running alongside the waterfront. We went all the way around the reservoir, going into the heart of the industrial complexes. Blaine navigated through the maze of factories before coming out onto the massive loading dock. By now, I'd given up on trying to get his attention. He couldn't *see* or *feel* or *hear me*.

Then I remembered this wasn't the first time this had happened to me. Once, I had fallen asleep in class, and I'd witnessed a murder that hadn't taken place yet. The other was the night I'd been bitten. I was locked in the back of Russell's truck and had passed out from my fever. When I thought I had awoken, I had somehow teleported myself back to the Reaper compound, in the prison cell with Blaine as Mr. Reynolds proceeded to torture him. Astral projection. Only this time, I was seeing the past.

"Pop?" he called out, peeking his head inside the vacant storage bays. "Oi, Dad? You in here?"

A distant clang echoed throughout the expansive, vacant space. Blaine followed the sound, coming to a large sliding metal door. He gripped the handle, struggling to heave it open. An empty beer bottle rested at his feet as he stepped inside the warehouse. Blaine took one look at the label and rolled his eyes. "Perfect."

Carefully maneuvering between loose pieces of rebar and pipes that lay strewn about the floor, he made it halfway into the room when a lone light flickered on overhead. We both gasped, seeing the figure in the back corner—only I didn't share in Blaine's relief as he got a better look at the stranger. Matted brown hair clung to the man's face as he staggered up from an old folding chair, ambling forward with uneasy steps. He would have been intimidating, given his broad build and lengthy stature, but he was a down-and-out mess.

"Pop, what are you doing out here...besides the obvious?" asked Blaine, motioning to the newly opened beer bottle dangling between the man's fingers.

"What I should've done a long time ago." The man stopped, letting the bottle clang to the floor. Blaine took one step toward him, but froze at the sound of an unmistakable click. He lifted his hands as slowly as he could, now staring down the barrel of a Smith & Wesson Governor revolver.

"D-Dad, put the gun down. Okay? You're drunk—"

Dad?

The man standing before us wasn't Blaine's adopted father, leaving only one other option.

It was his birth father.

The man's entire demeanor fell away as he straightened, his shaky hold on the revolver immediately steadying. "I should have done this years ago."

Blaine swallowed hard, his breath catching in his throat.

His father laughed, but it was a grievous sound.

"Pop-"

"I saw you...in the parking lot. I saw what you did to all those windows."

Blaine's already pale face somehow managed to go even whiter. "I didn't—"

"Yes, you did!" the man barked, clutching the side of his head with his available hand. "You know what's happening to you. Don't deny it."

Blaine cowered back a step, only to have his father center his aim right between his eyes.

"This has to be done, for the good of everyone. You're

only going to grow stronger, and you'll spread your plague to others."

"What the fuck is wrong with you?" Blaine gasped. "You'd kill your own son?"

"I'm not your father," he spat. "Your mother lied to me! All I ever tried to do was protect her, and how does she repay me? By fucking that filthy Underworlder!"

By the look on his face, I knew Blaine had no idea what the hell he was talking about. The young man just kept shaking his head. "You hear yourself right now? You're drunk! Just put the gun down…please."

"I've put this off for too long. It's time I set things right."

A deafening blast exploded into the air as smoke billowed from the revolver. My hands flew to my mouth, seeing Blaine stagger back. He stood shell-shocked in place for so long, he looked like a statue. I ran over to him, surveying him for a gunshot wound. Did the bullet somehow manage to miss him? Turning around, I followed Blaine's petrified stare. Not ten feet from us was a single bullet, hovering in midair. The air around it rippled as it continued to stir, but it wouldn't move forward.

Blaine's father—or whoever he was—cursed as he raised the gun again, relinquishing every round from the chamber. This time, I watched as each bullet froze in place alongside its companions. "Devil!"

Blaine's eyes were the size of saucers, and they only grew wider as he looked down. He lifted his left hand, staring horrified at the alien light that emitted from his palm. That's when I noticed, he didn't have any runes… Just as Blaine turned his palm outward, the bullets suddenly veered in the exact direction it faced, piercing into a crumbling plaster wall across the way.

I cried out his name, hoping to get his attention, but it was too late.

Dismay had overtaken Blaine, leaving him blind to his father. The man charged at him so swiftly, he nearly blurred. A sharp crack resonated as the corroded tire iron in his hand struck Blaine in the side of the skull. I screamed, but the sound fell upon deaf ears as I watched Blaine's body limply fall onto the concrete floor. His eyes fluttered wearily. He was still conscious!

Blood began to pool from the side of Blaine's head as he tried lifting his hand. It fell though once his father brought the iron down again for another swing. The jagged hook caught the side of Blaine's face, tearing right through his cheek. A strangled cry escaped the beaten boy as his entire backset of teeth was ripped clean from his jaw, splattering across the floor. His cry only split the skin further, exposing gory muscle and broken bone, the sight so heinous it even made his assailant retch. Blaine's frame convulsed as he gagged, trying to draw in a breath that wouldn't come. He barely managed to roll to his side before coughing.

He'd been choking on his own blood. A mass of crimson painted the concrete as Blaine blearily spit out the contents lodged in his throat. He could barely keep his eyes open. The man knelt down and pried Blaine's cell out of his jacket. The screen cracked as he slammed it down on the pavement, the final blow coming as his iron-toed boot hammered down on it for good measure.

Blaine's weak fingers grappled for the pipe beside him, but it was just out of arm's reach. Desperately clawing outward, his fingertips barely managed to grasp the end. He tried heaving it up at the man, but the metal cylinder clattered to the ground, proving to be too heavy. The man murmured an apology, the words barely audible as he raised the tire iron for the last time. He turned the device the other way around, having the pointed end faced down at Blaine. His hands shook ever so slightly. He couldn't go through with it… How could he? How could anybody do that—do *this*—to someone?

The man pinched his eyes shut as his grip tightened on the tool. And with that, he drove the iron down. I couldn't bear to look, but I wept at the unmistakable crunch that followed as metal sliced into flesh and bone. Nothing more than a guttural rasp escaped Blaine's lips. Another heavy blow followed, forcing me to open my eyes. The man staggered back dazedly, the tire iron slipping from his grip as a piece of rebar clattered to the floor from behind him. He tottered sideways, patting the back of his head. Blood soaked his fingertips. Had Blaine hit him? Had he made the rebar fly at him somehow?

The man's eyes rolled back into his head as his body collapsed. I yelped, knowing even before he hit the ground that he wouldn't quite clear the load-bearing column behind him. With the full weight of his body driving him down, the base of his skull clocked the pole, leaving a pitched ring to resonate across the desolate space from the blunt impact. Though knelt on the ground, I could nonetheless see blood blossoming out from his head, fanning the floor around his fallen frame.

"Blaine?" I turned back to him, still hearing shallow breaths scrape from his lungs. Trembling hands clung to his torso as he grappled at the skin surrounding the wound. He'd been stabbed nearly in the center of his chest, right by the heart. His father had missed…

Someone had to save him. He'd been brought back. He

had a Maker, right? Where were they?

Moments ticked away, and yet no one was here. No one was coming.

I couldn't even touch him. My hands repeatedly slid through his body as I tried desperately to hold him, to assure him he'd be okay. I couldn't help him. I was completely useless. All I could do was watch him as his body convulsed, watch him as tears streamed down his face, barely able to draw in a breath.

I cried out at the top of my lungs, begging for someone. Anyone!

Blaine startled.

Did...Did he hear me?

"Blaine?"

A distant light abruptly gleamed in from the entranceway. He angled his head up, taking notice to the source as well. It appeared to be headlights, but they were far-off. Blaine croaked as he attempted to call out, but the words were breathless, clogging in his throat. Against all odds, he rolled over onto his stomach. With one hand pressed against his chest and the other arm outstretched in front of him, he began to crawl. Reaching the slanted walkway at the front of the warehouse, Blaine clawed onto a latch nearing the bottom of the door. He heaved himself through, clumsily dropping to the pavement outside. His knees buckled under his weight, but bloody palms pushed off the asphalt, forcing him back upright. Short, visible gasps expelled from his lips, the blustery wind taking away my own breath as I frantically followed him.

The headlights came rolling up, eventually making the car behind them visible. Blaine made it not six more steps before finally collapsing to the ground.

He'd stopped breathing.

"Is this our boy?" The Englishman mused, climbing out from behind the passenger seat. He laughed as he approached the broken boy on the ground. "Gotta say, I was expecting him to be in better shape."

"Oh, he'll be tip-top when we're through with him," crooned a familiar voice behind the wheel. A black leather racing jacket came into view as the driver joined his cohort outside, observing Blaine with evident amusement.

Black inked over the Englishman's eyes as he knelt down. "What say you, Val? Should we get to work?"

The calm of the bedroom came back into focus as I jolted away, breaking my hold on Blaine as I gasped. I fell back, shaking. He shot awake, wheezing painfully for air. The blind panic in Blaine's eyes vanished as he too acclimatized to his surroundings, realizing where he was. His whole body still convulsed, his hands shaking as he wiped them over his eyes. A damp, cold sweat had perforated all the way through his shirt, and there was an unnatural clamminess to his skin. Worst of all, he still looked petrified.

"Blaine?"

My voice only startled him more as he jerked at the sound, his eyes snapping up to mine. I slowly drew back, noting the serrated blade wielded in his grasp. Where had he been keeping a knife? Under his pillow? Shame filled his eyes as he dropped his gaze to the weapon.

He hadn't even realized he'd grabbed it, fetching the blade on instinct alone.

The sight only made me want to cry.

Cry more.

Because I was already crying, feeling the warm streaks running down my cheeks.

His eyes slowly drew back up to meet mine. He looked downright horrified, letting the blade drop to the floor. "I'm sorry." The words were barely audible as he flung back the covers and darted into the bathroom, the door slamming shut behind him.

I remained there, sitting on the bed, shaking, knowing the feeling all too well. After the accident, after what Russell did, I still woke up nights in blind panic. But seeing Blaine like this... I couldn't rationalize it. He suddenly seemed...all too human. What other kind of horrors had he endured?

I'd been sitting back in bed for about fifteen minutes or so, hearing the water running on and off from inside the bathroom. The faucet squeaked off once again. Silence hung in the air for a good half a minute when a walloping crash sent me hurtling out of bed. Blaine cursed as I could hear bits of debris shower down onto the countertop and floor of the bathroom. Without thinking, I grabbed the knob and forced the door open, seeing the small mirror over the single sink smashed with a circular point of impact. Blaine's back faced me.

"What the hell happened?"

He slowly turned around, revealing a bloodied set of knuckles he was coddling with his other hand.

"Oh my God…"

"Don't!" he warned as I stepped inside.

I looked down at the broken fragments of glass around my feet and retracted back to the doorway.

"Go back to bed," he said lowly, extracting a sizable shard from the joint of his pointer finger. The skin sizzled.

I didn't move, watching blood slowly drip off between his fingers. "You need help with that. It's silver-coated glass. If you don't get all of it out, your body will heal with it still in there…"

"Please, just go." His breathing was jagged and his nostrils flared as he curled his injured fist. "Go!"

Blaine had never yelled at me before. Not like this. I actually jumped at the order. He looked like a feral dog. Unable to argue, I slowly retracted from the doorway and turned the corner back into the bedroom area. The door remained open, and I could still see Blaine's reflection in the remaining glass of the fractured mirror as I peeked around the corner, unable to muzzle my worry.

He gripped the edge of the counter, his shoulders shaking with every aching breath as he leaned forward, his eyes locked on the tiles. After a moment, his hands finally slid from the counter, only to take residency in the front strands of his hair. He staggered away, his back slamming into the opposing wall as he crumpled over onto the floor with a shudder.

I couldn't breathe…

An ache had settled in my chest, robbing me of air, along with my sanity.

He'd been killed, same as me, but by someone who claimed to love him.

I stayed curled up on the mattress, unable to shut my eyes. When Blaine eventually returned to the bedroom, he stood cowering back by the bathroom, his eyes focused on his clumsily bandaged hand.

"I'm sorry," he finally muttered, his throat raw. "I didn't mean to scare you."

The very sight of him threatened the tears burning behind my eyes to pour out. To see him so vulnerable and...embarrassed.

"May I?" I pointed to his hand, and he slowly extended it out as I climbed out of bed to meet him. Delicately undoing the dressings, I looked at the beaten skin and scathed knuckles. It was still too inflamed.

"I couldn't get a couple of the splinters out," he muttered, flexing his fingers. The skin stretched, revealing a few tiny glints of glass.

I didn't have tweezers or anything to help remove them, so I did my best, using the tips of my fingernails. Blaine kept steady, only letting out a low hiss as I removed the final particles. Before I even had time to clean the wound, the skin was already looking better.

Properly rewrapping the injury, I fastened it and returned his hand to him. "Is it bound too tight?"

Blaine flexed his fingers again and shook his head. "No, it's good. Thank you."

His eyes finally met mine, but his gaze fell away just as quickly as he moved around me.

"Are you okay?"

He nodded, still unwilling to meet my eyes.

It was a little chilly in the room, yet he still looked like he had fallen asleep in a sauna, his hair moistened across his forehead, his skin glinting in the low light.

"Hey, I'm serious."

His chest rose and fell, still too fast, still too panicked, when he finally met my eyes. "What did you see?"

One look at him, and I knew what he meant. He *knew*...

"Everything."

He sank down onto the mattress, his back resting against the headboard. His eyes suddenly seemed to find everything else in the room to be infinitely more fascinating, because he looked everywhere but back at me.

"Who was he?" My voice was so quiet, so weak, yet I could feel vibrations raking up my arm. I couldn't explain why, but all I knew was that I wanted to slam my fist through something. "Your...your father?"

Blaine grimaced at the word. "He wasn't my father."

I know, I wanted to say.

"I thought he was. Hell, *he* thought he was." Blaine laughed, but his breathing was still uneven, making it all the more aggrieved. "Since full-blooded female Reapers are so rare, it's customary for the women in their respective packs to be set up in arranged marriages with the Alphas, as to ensure they have the strongest offspring. The same thing happened to my mom. When she learned she was pregnant, she ran away. Donovan assumed it was because she didn't want their child growing up in their world. He finally managed to track her down, but she'd already given the child up for adoption.

"Donovan reached out to me when I was fourteen, explaining what had happened. He explained why I was the way I was, being able to heal so quickly and whatnot. He told me all about Reapers, and how he wanted me to join his pack. He told me that he was my birth father. I spent two years getting to know him, growing closer with him. We even started training together... And then I turned sixteen." His eyes fell into his lap, at his injured hand. "I didn't know what was happening to me. I started getting visions, seeing people's auras, and then one day I got into an argument with Trace in the school parking lot.

As soon as I yelled at him, all the windows around us blew out. The cars, the busses, the side of the building, all of it."

"*I saw what you did,*" his father had said.

"Reapers weren't supposed to be capable of doing that, and apparently, my old man witnessed it. It was only then that he started to put the pieces together." Blaine's injured fist curled, testing the bandages. "My mother never loved Donovan. She found out she was pregnant just before she was forced to marry him. It took her a couple months to plan her escape, and because she was only a month along when she found out, Donovan safely assumed I was his kid. But when he learned the truth...well, you saw how that went."

"But... Val. I thought he—?"

"He's my half-brother. Astaroth's other heir. Same father, different mothers."

Blaine's breathing finally seemed to calm, even if just a little bit, as I sat down on my side of the mattress. "If he's older, then why isn't he the Crown Prince?"

"He was, for a short while. Val actually knew I was his brother when we met a few years back, but he didn't want to tell me about it until I 'came of age.' As soon as he turned seventeen, Raelynd set his sights on him, and in consequence, it caused a chain reaction. Demons began talking, and then word spread to Hellhounds, and Mages, and eventually it got back to Reapers what he was planning. Val became public enemy number one." Blaine rested his head back against the headboard, his gaze drifting up to the ceiling. "If you met him a couple years ago, you wouldn't have recognized him as the man you see today. He decided to take the demonic approach, and turned off all his emotions. He doesn't feel pain, even physical. And I can't necessarily say I blame him. After what they did to him…no one comes out of that the same."

"What happened?"

"Let's just say he's had it rough." Blaine seemed rather disinclined to elaborate, so I took the hint. Conversation: terminated.

But I couldn't help recalling Raelynd saying something similar about Blaine as well. *"The world has not been kind to him…"*

The only thing I knew now with any certainty was that I didn't know the first thing about Blaine Ryder.

21

Way Down We Go

"Time to greet the day, lovebirds!"

The low hanging sun flooded the room through the opened doorway, and I blinked groggily, still too exhausted to lift my head. Val chuckled, his body shading the early morning light as he stepped into the room. As pissed off as I was with him, I couldn't bring myself to care enough to get out of bed. Maybe in a few hours. Or a few days. I nestled back into the warmth engulfing me and shut my eyes again.

"Uh, Doll Face..."

I groaned, blindly fishing around for the pillow that should have been next to me. The moment I got a hold of it, Val would be eating a cushion full of feathers...if only I could find it. My hand continued patting around the mattress, coming up short. I stretched my fingers out a little bit further, only to feel the edge of the...bedside. Wait, that *couldn't* be right.

"Ahem."

I peeled my eyes back open, looking up at the opened doorway. Val stood there smiling like the Cheshire Cat, while Reese—

If looks could kill...

I followed both of the guys' gazes, realizing I was on the whole other side of the bed. I lifted my head to find a naked, muscular torso resting beneath me. Blaine just sighed and stretched indolently, his eyes still closed as I noticed his rune-covered arm draped around my shoulders. Feeling the rush of heat reach my cheeks, I tried to toss off the appendage so I could sit upright. The moment I attempted to, Blaine's hold only pulled me closer, forcing my head back onto his toned stomach. He murmured something inaudible under his breath that I was pretty sure *wasn't* English.

The door slammed so hard, the old hinges rattled. Blaine finally opened his eyes at the thunderous disturbance, and I turned to see that Reese was gone.

"Would you mind?" Blaine waved lazily at his brother, shooing him outside. "Some of us need our beauty sleep."

"You're pretty enough, Sleeping Beauty," Val said, lobbing Blaine's discarded shirt at him. "We've got places to go, people to torture. All the fun stuff."

"What *places*?"

"It's not exactly safe here, so you two are going to be relocated. Probably to The Hideaway, at least for now. Raelynd's sent a ride to pick us up. It'll be out front in fifteen."

Relocated? I hadn't allowed myself to think too much

about the repercussions of last night, but hearing him say it out loud… It felt like a mallet had been thrown down into my chest. I had to leave. Just when I had been able to settle down and find some semblance of a home, I was going to have to leave it all behind again. Jenna, Hannah, Sam, school. Everything I'd rebuilt, gone.

I finally managed to heave Blaine's arm off me, and I hauled myself out of bed, realizing I didn't have any clothes. My dirty pajamas were probably still on the ground in Reese's room, and I didn't even have shoes.

Val must have noticed me uncomfortably fidgeting with the hem of my shirt as I kept pulling down on the fabric, desperate to make it cover more than the measly top inch of my thighs. He motioned to the little red luggage case parked beside the mini fridge.

The little Epi Leather carry-on case was unmistakable. It was part of the Louis Vuitton luggage collection my mom had bought me before our last family vacation. I cautiously approached it, pulling the bag up onto the couch so I could unzip it. Inside were a handful of my clothes, my picture frames, a couple pairs of shoes, and even my curling iron. If Val had gotten all this stuff...he would've had to have been in my aunt's house!

Before I could make the accusation, the Dark Mage snorted. "Relax, Doll Face. Your precious little magician was the one kind enough to pack your belongings. I never even got an invitation inside. Though, I did speak with your aunt. Told her you were going away with friends on a trip for Winter Break, and suggested that she perhaps go away for a bit as well. You know, until things settle down. Wouldn't want any demons or Reapers swinging by again looking for you while she's home."

I appreciated the thought, but there was only one

person on my mind.

Reese...

Without bothering to grab some fresh clothes, I pushed Val aside and ran out the door. I could feel eyes burning on me from down the hall as I pounded my fists on Reese's door. Val stood leaning against the worn brick wall outside Blaine's room, his head cocked in amusement as my fist suddenly struck...

Crap! I'd been so consumed in my need to give Val my most vicious glare that I hadn't realized the door opened, making me pound my fist into Reese's chest.

"Oh my God! I'm so sorry!"

He just scowled, also stealing a glance at the leather-clad asshole down the way. Reese merely nodded over his shoulder and pulled the door open enough to indicate my invitation. I immediately noticed the packed duffle bag resting on the corner chair. He was leaving, but where?

"That's not at all what it looked like back there, I swear. I don't know what happened. I'm so, so, so sorry, about everything!" The words were clumsy at best, but they were the only things I could think to say as Reese locked the door behind me. "I never should have bitten Blaine. I should've listened to you from the very beginning! I should've just run away the moment Blaine tracked me down here! I should've listened!"

Reese was shaking his head, and it felt like a vise grip had seized my heart, slowly applying pressure to it until the muscle would explode in my chest.

"It doesn't matter," he whispered.

"Don't say that—"

"Kat, listen to me."

"No!" I reached behind me for the doorknob. A stupid, childish part of me was convinced that if I ran away from him, if I could get out before he could speak, I'd be able to stop him from doing what I knew was inevitable.

But his palms came to rest on both sides of the door right behind my head. "Listen."

Not him too...

I couldn't lose him. Everybody else had already abandoned me.

"Dr. Madsen's found a cure."

My pounding heart seemed to skip a beat, maybe even two or three. *"What?"*

"You said the mating bond didn't work when the Angel of Death attacked you at school, right?"

I nodded. "My omen rune went off, but Blaine had no idea. The connection was somehow interrupted."

This little tidbit of information brought a sly smile to decorate his lips as he crooked his finger and gestured for me to follow him over to the bed. Pulling out printed copies of the ledger we had borrowed from Blaine, he found the page in question and handed the sheet over to me.

"'Sanctus Perimo...directly derived from the Latin words meaning 'holy abolishment,'" I read aloud. "'Seven holy swords were forged from Angelorum steel and given to Samael, also known in some scripts as the Angel of Death. The fuller of these blades is said to be brandished with angelic sigils that work to deactivate the effects of Black Magic. Any demon or Dark Mage will find their powers useless when in its presence, and when killed at the hand of these swords, any soul will be banished to eternal Purgatory. The angel Samael gifted one of these blades to a special offspring of men, who shared his angelic bloodline...'"

In other words, Reapers.

But... Purgatory? As in eternal suffering? More of Raelynd's words came to mind, what he had said about Blaine intervening when Russell tried killing me. *"The fact he would risk getting his very soul claimed is a true testament to his character."*

All the blood drained from my face as I stumbled back.

"It's well documented that runes can't be tampered with," said Reese, too consumed by the papers in his hands to notice I could be knocked over with a feather. "Even if you were to burn your entire hand and arm to destroy Blaine's mark and mating bond, the moment your skin healed back to normal, the runes would regain their power."

"...Yeah. So?"

"What if there was a way to maim the skin so that it *couldn't* heal?"

"By somehow swiping a blade from an avenging angel who wants me *dead*? That sounds like a suicide mission."

Reese just smiled. "You won't need to get it from *him*."

Nick's questions from last night hit me like a railroad spike.

"Who killed Russell Hurst?"

"What happened to his blade?"

The breath caught in my lungs. "Blaine."

"During the 18th century, when there was an upsurge in the art of dark magic, there was a blade reportedly used to permanently disable a Mage's runes. If it cut through the brand, the magic would cease to run through the rune, making it ineffective," Reese further explained to me.

Just like Val's runes.

"Why did Reapers kill all of them if they could be neutralized?" I asked. "You know, asides from the fact that they're assholes?"

"Because severing the power didn't cure them from the demonic virus. Their offspring would still carry the same dark magic. Reapers wouldn't risk that kind of energy being passed on to another generation." He sighed. "Are you absolutely certain the Angel's blade you saw was exactly marked like Russell's?"

All the puzzle pieces seemed to fall into place as the gears began working in my mind. "You should've seen Blaine's face when I mentioned that Death's blade shared the same symbols as the one Russell tried to kill me with. Blaine couldn't get me away from the school fast enough. And he himself has a sizeable scar on his unmarked arm, suspiciously right where Russell had cut him with that very same blade."

Reese beamed at me. "If this *does* work, if we can get our hands on one of these swords, then we can break both the mating bond and the hex placed on you. After that, finding a cure for the virus will be the only hurtle we have left."

"Yeah, but we don't even know where to start looking for the blade," I pointed out. "I haven't seen it in over eight weeks, and the last time I did, I was half delirious with the virus. I fell unconscious after Blaine used it to kill Russell." A knot formed in my stomach at the very thought of that night. But then something else ate away at me. "I still managed to use my runes to get the blade away from Russell when he came at me. If it's supposed to turn off all dark magic, then how did I have use of it?"

"That...I'm not entirely sure of."

"The sword could still be anywhere by now," I said,

admittedly deflating a bit. "And it's not at his house. I already checked that place from the basement floor to the roof shingles.

Three solid knocks thudded against the other side of the door. "Wrap it up, Doll Face. We've gotta get a move on," called out Val.

That pit returned to the bottom of my stomach, but Reese just took my hand, trailing his thumb over my runes. Tiny electrical pulses crackled along the surface, and I found myself leaning into him.

"I don't know when I'll get to see you again," I muttered.

"Oh, I wager it'll be much sooner than you think."

Before I could say anything, he pulled me in against his chest, seizing my lips. That very same electrical current worked its way across my mouth, into my face, tingling down my back, leaving me delirious and lightheaded in the best possible way.

"I love you," he whispered.

The door swung open on some kind of phantom wind. Magic no doubt. I turned back to where Reese had just been standing in front of me, but he was suddenly across the room. And that pissed off expression he'd been sporting earlier had evidently returned in full-force. Reese proceeded to glower at me—glower—as he pushed past me like I was some insufferable pest he wanted nothing to do with.

"Get the hell out," he growled.

I just gawked at him.

Paging Dr. Jekyll!

Where the hell did this come from?

"Ouch." Val smirked as he strolled into the room, interlocking his arm around mine. "You heard the man,

Doll Face. Let's go."

He turned us around and guided me out the door. I barely had time to pluck up my dirtied pajamas from last night as I stole a glance back at Reese, who *winked* at me. The message was clear. I was now the fox in the brothers' henhouse. Only problem, their henhouse was no henhouse at all. It was a shark tank. And there was blood in the water.

22

Build God, Then We'll Talk

Were we actually onto something? Could this hex really be broken? Could the mating bond be severed? Butterflies swirled in my stomach at the mere possibility. I had to keep telling myself not to get too excited, but I couldn't help it. The possibility of a normal life…it was too much for my heart to contain. There was a chance that Reese and I could actually have something between us, something that didn't include Blaine, or Hell, or fangs, or the risk of death, all standing in the way.

Val tossed me a plastic bag to throw my dirty clothes into, ordering me to change. Apparently, I was expected to look my best—or at least as presentable as I could be, all things considered—for when we arrived at the Hideaway.

I did as he requested, palming Nick's note as discretely as I could. There would be no knowing who might rummage through my belongings, and I didn't want to risk having the paper fall into someone else's hands. Tossing the stuffed plastic bag into my luggage, Val lobbed a pair of thigh-high boots on the bed, along with a satin top...and no pants, or coat. I picked up the blouse, realizing it wasn't a shirt at all—but an Italian lace-trimmed chemise dress.

"This is lingerie," I growled.

"Sorry, sis, but you're about to become the Crown Princess of Lust. You need to dress in something more... well, *lustful*. This is gonna be the first time you're presented to Raelynd's crew with your new title, and no offense, but..." the Mage drawled, plucking out a few assorted items from my bag. "A pair of old jeans and a *Walking Dead* t-shirt ain't gonna cover it."

"Yeah, well, *this* isn't gonna cover anything either," I snapped, waving the garment at him.

Val pretended not to hear my objections as he slung my carry-on bag over his shoulder and exited the room, calling out, "Ride's here."

I barked at him to return with my clothes, but he merely whistled, trotting down the railed steps to the parking lot. I grabbed the chemise off the bed and held it up against myself. The damn thing would've been lucky to reach my mid-thighs. On top of that, I looked out the window just as a stretch limousine rolled up in front of the building.

Just perfect.

I'd already spent the night outside in nothing but a towel, then a t-shirt, and now I had the humiliating pleasure of having to walk past all the rooms on both the second and first floor dressed like a high-end hooker.

I snatched up the boots and forced my feet into them,

not even bothering to unzip the long stretches of leather that came up to the lower halves of my thighs. The room remained suspiciously quiet, and I found myself slinking over to the bathroom, straining to hear any signs of Blaine. It wasn't till I rounded the corner that I realized the door was cracked open and the light was off. He wasn't here. But the mirror was…miraculously fixed.

Hurrying back to the window, I checked to see if the coast was clear and quickly changed out of Reese's shirt and into my so-called 'outfit'. It thankfully wasn't as revealing as I had feared. My chest was a bit too out on display for my liking, but it didn't appear to leave anything blatantly exposed. The design still would've been conservative by Vegas dress standards, though that didn't say much. Darting over to the phone, I unfurrowed my fingers, palming the note Nick had slipped me. It was a wrinkled up business card with a phone number scribbled on the back. I'd wanted to call it before I got into the shower last night, but I also didn't want to risk someone possibly tracing the number back here. Since everyone was evidently leaving, I didn't see the harm now.

The phone rang, and on the third ring, a familiar voice welcomed me on the other end—but not the voice I'd been prepared for.

"A truth for a truth, my dear."

I slammed the phone back onto the hook.

Why the hell would Nick give me her number? Why the hell did someone—or rather *something*—like the Sagax even have a phone?

A light knock sounded at the door, and I jumped upright. Panicked, I shoved the business card into the leggings of my right boot just as the door opened. Blaine stood on the threshold, about ready to say something, when he took in the sight of me. His lips tipped up in evident amusement. "Not that I don't appreciate the view, but dare I ask?"

I gave him a pointed look, and he sighed, knowing full-well who the culprit was for my new apparel.

"Here." He slipped off his jacket, but I just scowled, trying to move past him. He cut me off though, draping the leather around my shoulders. I couldn't help but discern the bullet hole accessorizing the right sleeve. Despite my quiet fury, I still reveled at the heat lingering in the jacket's lining as he shut the door behind us.

Val greeted me with a slow, mocking clap as I stomped my way down the stairs.

"Open the trunk," Blaine ordered from behind me.

"Whatever for?" his brother crooned. Receiving no answer, he still laughed from what I could safely assume was Blaine casting him a brutal glare. "Sorry, but the Boss insisted. Her outfit stays right where it is."

He enunciated those last four words with particular delight as he opened the back door of the limo to usher me inside. Val's gaze lingered over my body, simpering with approval as he strolled over to the front passenger door. "And he also encourages *you*," he added to his brother, "to put your unique skill set to use, Prince. We're gonna be on the road for a while."

His low laugh was cut short as he shut the front door behind himself, leaving Blaine and me wholly alone. I wasn't about to ask what that last remark meant, opting to climb in back. As soon as I slid onto the seat, I froze.

Red rose petals littered the plush extended seats as chilled champagne sat on display by the mini-bar alongside a couple boxes of chocolate covered strawberries. Seeing no sign of me scooting over to accommodate him, Blaine knelt down and stole a look inside, clearly wanting to know what had robbed my attention.

The privacy divider between the front seat and the back compartment rolled down just long enough for Val to peek inside and purr at our matching scowls, "Enjoy yourselves."

The door shut beside me, making me jump. A part of me expected to hear raised voices, expected Blaine to start arguing with his brother. But the other back door opened, and Blaine joined me, settling into the elongated, plush side bench. Seeing as how he was in front of me now, I immediately crossed my legs as he turned to face me, acutely aware that his eyes lingered on the portion of skin displayed between the end of my chemise and the top of my boots. It wasn't flirtatious. If anything, he looked perplexed.

"*What?*" I finally demanded.

Blaine merely shook his head. "Nothing. It's just...I'm trying to determine whether or not I want to know if that belongs to you," he said, gesturing at the scrap of fabric covering my body. "On one hand, if my brother found that someplace else and gave it to you to wear..."

I hugged his jacket tighter around myself. "It's mine."

"Which brings me to my next dilemma: determining who you bought it for."

My cheeks flushed. "Excuse me?"

"Well, I've already seen what kind of clothes you prefer to sleep in, and lacey lingerie isn't it. So, based on the evidence, I can only infer that you purchased this for someone else's viewing pleasure." He didn't seem particularly pleased at the thought. "I mean, seeing as how I'd know," he said, tapping the rune on top of his hand, "you haven't been with Blackburn yet, but that doesn't rule out intent."

"It was for Adam." The very thought of my ex churned my stomach, even more than Blaine did.

At least *he* had a reason. Blaine was damaged. But Adam... He was a good person. A kind person. His father was so consumed by grief and hatred that he would kill the girl who he considered to be his own daughter, and even knowing this, Adam had still handed me over to him. He had let Russell take me to what he knew would be my death, because despite all his kindness, he had given up on me. I had known him my whole life, had loved him for most of it, and yet, as soon as Blaine told him there was no cure, no hope of ridding me of the demonic virus, Adam had made the decision that I was beyond saving.

Blaine seemed to share in my sour sentiment, his chest heaving as if trying to control a sudden surge of anger.

"I bought it at the beginning of the summer while I was on vacation. I was saving it for what was supposed to be our one-year anniversary."

A little bit of the light returned to Blaine's eyes as he worked out the details. He knew. I'd never gotten around to wearing it for Adam, seeing as how I broke up with him the week before said anniversary. After I met *him*.

"I should've burned this stupid thing the moment I unpacked it at my aunt's house," I murmured.

"Why did you bother packing it if you seem to hate it so much?"

"I didn't realize I had. I kind of left Mystic Harbor in a bit of a rush," I said, cutting him a glare. "I'd literally just thrown whatever fit into my luggage."

We were on the road for a good ten minutes or so before Blaine finally spoke up again, motioning to the vintage t-shirt bundled up in my hands. "You work things out with Blackburn?"

"Why don't you ask your brother?" I grumbled, turning my attention outside. The early morning sunlight had been long devoured by a grisly collection of storm clouds rolling in from off the coast. It only appeared more abysmal through the vehicle's tinted windows as the scenery passed by.

When I finally looked over at him, Blaine appeared both surprised and pleased. The latter had my fingers curling into fists at my side. There was no way Val didn't already tell him all about what he witnessed between Reese and me at the motel, but Blaine clearly hadn't believed it…until now.

He nodded, more to himself. "It's for the best."

"Of course *you* would say that."

"Indeed I would," he affirmed. "I don't trust him."

"Yes, and I'm sure that judgment comes from a wholly impartial standpoint."

"He's trying to *fix* you."

"So?"

"That implies there's something wrong."

"There is," I growled.

Blaine's shoulder shook as he tried to repress a laugh, but it didn't stop his smile from broadening. "'You may choose to look the other way, but you can never say again that you did not know.'"

"Excuse me?"

"William Wilberforce."

"I know the quote," I said, rolling my eyes. "It was pinned up in Mr. Hopkins's classroom."

"Then you may want to pay better heed to it." The Prince stretched his arms out across the backrest of the plush bench, laxly perching his feet up on the end of the bar. "Never in a million years would I have guessed that Blackburn would be the one to sweep you off your feet. Quite clever, that one. When Daniel told me that Harry Houdini back there had weaseled his way into the picture, I couldn't believe it—not till I saw it with my own eyes. Tell me, love, what sweet nonsense has he filled your head with to make you turn such a blind eye to him?"

I yanked his jacket off my shoulders and flung it at his face. The fabric was heavier than I had anticipated though, making it plop in his lap instead. "I can't turn a blind eye to a scheme that *doesn't* exist."

"Is that so?" His amusement didn't wane as he beheld me, admiring me like I was the sweetest, silliest thing he had ever seen. "So a guy who has treated you like shit for well over a year miraculously wakes up one day to become your White Knight, and you find nothing odd about that?" He only further chuckled. "And you say *I'm* crazy."

"It didn't happen like that," I snapped.

"Well, I'm all ears, because if I recall correctly, you yourself referred to him as an 'Abominable Ass-hat' on more than one occasion. Hell, I saw it with my own eyes. Blackburn acted like you were the Second Coming of the Seven Plagues." Reaching forward, he plucked up the chilled champagne bottle and untwisted the wired cage surrounding the cork. Considering the number of dinner parties and fundraisers our parents had hosted and dragged us to, the act was nearly perfunctory as he draped the offered towel over the cork and rotated the bottle down until hearing a soft *pop*. He filled one of the empty flutes and offered it to me, but I merely scowled at him. Blaine just shrugged, taking a sip. "Why the sudden turnaround?"

"Unlike you, Reese actually has a conscience. He saw what was happening to me, and unlike you," I added again, "he was actually there for me when I needed help the most."

A flicker of satisfaction rang through me, seeing that smug amusement finally fade.

The muscles in his jaw tightened, highlighting the sharp cut of his cheekbones all the more. "If I could have been there for you, I would have. And you know that."

I couldn't deny it. Not really.

Blaine had explained it to me the night I discovered he wasn't dead. In order for him to even claim me as his hellish bride, I had to perform each of the seven deadly sins. And to ensure I wouldn't have any assistance, he was forbidden from revealing himself to me until I completed all but the last one.

"Why do you hate me?"

I wasn't sure what startled me more: the question, or the earnestness in which he wanted to know. "If you even have to ask that, then you're not in a position to understand."

"I'm *trying* to understand."

"No, you're not." I tried muzzling my rage, but I could already feel the vibrations coursing up my arm. "If you ever cared about me, you wouldn't have done any of this."

"Save your life?"

"Put me in danger!"

The interior lights around the bar suddenly flickered. His gaze dropped to my arm, seeing the Wrath rune ignited. My fist wrapped tighter about the handle of the armrest, and I could feel the electrical pulsations emitting from my fingertips. The vehicle sputtered shakily in response. I couldn't have controlled it even if I had wanted to, but at that moment I didn't care.

A warm caress seemed to coax through my mind, as tangible as a hand running over my skin. He was in my head… *"I'm trying to help."*

"Stop." The word came out as nothing more than a pitiful whimper. I forced my eyes shut, as if it could help force him out, but fingers suddenly brushed beneath my chin.

He was right in front of me. I still hadn't opened my eyes, but I could feel his breath stir against my lips as he whispered, "Don't do that, love. Don't shut me out."

"Stop calling me that!" I brought my hand up, blindly slapping him in the face, but the moment my palm connected with his cheek, his own hand wrapped around mine, pinning it there in place. I finally opened my eyes, finding him knelt before me, his right knee resting between my thighs. When had I uncrossed my legs?

And oh God, his lips…

Why was he so close?

Why was his hair black again?

Why was he kissing me...there?

I shook my head, waiting for the images to disappear, but all I could see was that wood paneled wall from my dreams, feel Blaine touching me, hearing him whisper in my ear.

Then…blood. There was blood everywhere. All over my hands. And Blaine…

A gun blast erupted behind me. My throat was raw, the windpipe aching as if I'd just screamed when I shot back into reality. I must have, because Blaine was gripping my shoulder, his eyes wide in alarm. The runes lighting my arm made everything from the muscles to the very skin atop it burn with exhaustion.

"Hey." Blaine's fingers gently wrapped around my wrist, and the ache in my arm vanished the moment the runes subsided. He opened his mouth to say something, but he suddenly froze before jerking back. Like a single image spliced into a film reel, the bloodied field from my nightmare flashed into my vision again. Fear and anger flooded Blaine's eyes in an instant as his gaze fell to my chest, where my hand remained pinned over my heart. "What the hell was that?"

Did he just…?

I shied away, feeling an all-new surge of panic, but as I tried recoiling from him, that invisible pull in my chest hauled me back to him. His hands suddenly cupped my face, and despite my best efforts, tears escaped off my lashes as I forced my eyes shut.

"Look at me, Kat."

Against all will and better judgment, I did.

"What the hell was that?" he asked again.

"What're you talking about?"

Blaine gave me a pointed stare, clearly not in the mood for my feigned stupidity.

"It's… It's how I die."

For the life of me, I couldn't stop talking. Not with him looking at me like that. Not with him whispering words into my head. I didn't know what came over me. The next five minutes was a blur of contradictions. I kept telling myself not to speak, kept demanding that I keep my mouth shut. But that strange tug, that *influence* rooted inside my chest…it wouldn't let up. It wasn't until I relayed every last detail about what had happened with the fortuneteller that I finally found the will to stop. *"His influence is nearly impossible to resist, thus turning anyone he captivates into his unwitting servant."* The words from that journal Reese's father had left behind rang through my mind, stealing my breath in the process.

Oh God…

It really was happening.

That pull I felt when he was near… The dreams… *This…*

The hex was going into effect.

Just as I regained enough of my senses to react, Blaine withdrew from me on his accord, reclaiming his seat on the elongated side bench in front of me. He ran a hand over his face, his own breathing now jagged. "And you saw this only after she touched the mating rune?"

I nodded, relieved by my momentary hesitation. At least I could still control my body…for now.

Blaine's face had gone sickly pale. *"Blood for blood."*

"H-how do you know that? Did you see what happened? I mean, *all* of it?" I'd never had such a luxury. In my vision, I always felt the pain, but only ever caught glimpses of images and muffled voices. Nothing perfectly clear.

He shook his head, more to himself. "Have you ever seen a sigil, in this dream?"

"A snake." I could see it in his eyes. He knew what I was talking about. "But how do you…?"

"That's also how I die."

"What?"

He turned his attention outside, as if the answer could be found on a mile marker. We appeared to notice the same thing, because our eyes locked on one another's at the exact same moment. Blaine immediately hit the button to roll down the privacy divider, but it didn't budge. He cursed under his breath, fiddling with the gadgets to no avail.

I noted the button on the panel beside me and turned on the microphone function. *"Val?"*

"Yes'm?" he answered in the most sugary tone.

"Where are we going? We just passed the off ramp for the Hideaway."

"Change of plans," Val purred. "We're heading up north."

Blaine and I both paled. "North where?" we asked in unison.

The Dark Mage up front chuckled. "Good ole Mystic Harbor, Maine."

"What?"

Mad World

Surely, this had to be some kind of joke.

Blaine said as much, but his brother only laughed harder.

"There's been some suspicious activity at the Hideaway, so Raelynd wants to play it safe—take you somewhere protected. You two lovebirds will be staying at your family's estate," Val cooed.

"My 'family' thinks I'm dead," gnashed Blaine. "What do you expect me to do? Waltz into their house, throw a white sheet over my head, and go, 'Boo!'?"

"Always with the dramatics," Val drawled, the amusement in his voice barely contained. "No, I meant the *other* estate."

This didn't seem to assure him any. Blaine settled back into his seat, looking like someone just handed him *another* death sentence. And the mood didn't lighten any over the course of the next hour. If anything, his misery found company in me as familiar landmarks and shops came into view as we drove over a river I knew all too well, accompanied by a sign that announced, *"Welcome to Mystic Harbor."* Not a moment later did we pass The Office, Mr. Reynolds's waterfront bar on the south side of town. Adam's Jeep Wrangler was even parked out front. This place used to be my home away from home. I spent hours upon hours after school curled up in the back booth with Adam, doing my homework. I'd even memorized the entire catalog of the jukebox machine. Now, the sight only had bile rising up my throat, had me cowering away to the other side of the car. It didn't matter if the windows were tinted or not. Being this close made me feel like an escaped convict driving past FBI headquarters, as if anyone and everyone was out looking for me and I was on enemy territory.

The feeling didn't lessen as we drove past the mall and into Old Port, the 19th-century shopping district made up of cobblestone streets and historic buildings. I'd always loved taking early morning jogs through here during the summer, seeing the dew settle into the moss covered roofs. When the natural mist met with the break of dawn, the entire district glowed in gorgeous golden hues. But today, it only reflected the gloom resonating from within the car. It seemed as if the storm was chasing us up the coast, because the sky only grew darker, making the earth tremble in its quake as roar after roar bellowed overhead. Everyone scurried about the sidewalks, umbrellas in hand, as they raced for their cars. The rain coming down was only a light drizzle, but the lightning flashed above us like a siren, warning the town of the impending storm, perhaps warning them of *us*.

I couldn't have thanked the driver enough that he decided on taking the back roads along the coast. If we'd headed up north on Main Street, we would have inevitably taken DuPont Lane, which went past my folks' place. My stomach dropped, however, as the pier came into sight, along with the advertisement for Slippery Pete's restaurant. The last time I'd been here was when I'd leapt out of a moving car to get away from Blaine, where I'd accidentally hit him with enough energy that it had stopped his heart—and *mine*. To my surprise, the limousine turned onto an unfamiliar side street, leading us southbound into a forested collection of reclusive estates. This must have been where Blaine had been planning on taking me—if I hadn't escaped.

I'd been to the Ryder's estate in town on several occasions, mostly for dinner parties and fundraisers my mother had co-organized with Blaine's mom. The place was pretty much a castle, even by Mystic Harbor's haughty standards. I expected as much from this estate when we continued along down the coast, eventually coming to the end of the road. Large wrought iron gates greeted us as the limousine turned onto a long private driveway. As if on silent command, the gates drew open, despite no one manning the entrance. There wasn't even a call button.

I looked to Blaine, hoping for some clarity, but he still refused to meet my eyes. It was unnerving. Somehow, Blaine *not* talking made him all the more intimidating. Seeing him in quiet contemplation, seeing his eyes shift every which way as the gears in his head turned over, it promised an unspoken wrath.

The narrow road continued down another winding

bend, encased by trees that domed over the path. At last, in the center of the thicket made of elder maples and evergreens rested an English Tudor estate. It could easily be classified as a manor, but it wasn't nearly as gaudy as Blaine's family home. There weren't any other houses in sight, made all the better by the lush greenery obscuring distant eyes. It was surprisingly quaint, if not for the sudden procession of cars pulling up in back of us as our driver took us to the small courtyard out front.

"Welcome to Haven Crest," announced Val not a moment later, ushering me out of the back of the car. "This is where all the magic happens."

"Magic?" I asked, unable to control the nervous crack in my voice.

"Indeed." He slung an arm around my shoulder, drawing me up alongside him. "Here, nobody can hear you...scream," he whispered balefully.

The double meaning wasn't lost on me. It didn't matter what kind of 'screaming' he was insinuating. All I knew was that I didn't want any part in it. The series of unfamiliar black vehicles pulled up, and armed men stepped out to greet us. Panic ran rampant in me until I spotted the man sitting on the hood of the Land Cruiser that had already been parked out front when we arrived. It was a different face than the one I'd last seen him sporting, but the mannerisms were uncanny.

"Well, if it isn't my favorite couple?" Raelynd flicked his cigarette to the ground, crushing it beneath his boot heel upon leaping off the hood. The joyous way the demon greeted us, rubbing his hands together in anticipation, you'd think we were bricks of cocaine being presented to an addict. "Valor has told me the exciting news."

He grabbed Blaine's shoulders as if to pull him into a

hug. Instead, the demon grabbed the collar of the Mage's shirt, yanking both sides away from his neck, exposing the fang marks I'd left behind. Raelynd outright purred at the sight, unable to rein in his curiosity. He ran his fingers across the scars, and Blaine immediately tried pulling away, obviously feeling the same revulsion that always accompanied the deed anytime somebody touched my own.

The reaction pleased the demon all the more as he laughed, turning his attention to me. "You, my darling Princess…" His eyes scoped me from head to toe, clearly appreciating Val's *delicate* choice for my outfit. "Well done. I knew you wouldn't disappoint." The man made no effort to contain his enthusiasm, howling out into the tempestuous air.

Maybe he *was* high… He surely acted like it.

And I didn't dare glance at the other people in attendance, feeling their eyes burning on me as they, too, took in my so-called dress. I instinctively tugged down on the chemise, trying to pull the fabric further over my exposed thighs, but Val's hand clasped discreetly around mine. He shook his head, ever so slightly. A silent plea.

"Do you have any idea what this means?" Raelynd's voice startled us both, and Val let go of me, but not so fast as to look suspicious. He knew better than to upset the Boss. But the demon didn't seem to notice in the least, still consumed by his own enthusiasm. Raelynd's hands fell from Blaine, only to wind up cupping my face.

The fire in his eyes was equally crazed as it was delighted, like I was the oasis in a barren desert. Before I could even think to push him away, the demon smacked his lips against my cheek. It only lasted for a second, and he pulled away, his laughter so manic it could give the

Joker a freaking run for his money.

One look back over at the Crown Prince's dour expression, and he finally gave an exasperated sigh. "For pity's sake, mate, you look as if somebody's just walked over your grave. You've got your girl, a lovely place to lay low, and a house entirely to yourselves. What could you possibly be sulking over?"

"What was wrong with the Hideaway?" Blaine demanded. "Why the hell would you bring us *here* of all places?"

"As far as the Hideaway is concerned, those matters are still being investigated. As for the second inquiry," the demon crooned, "when you escape from prison, where do you run?"

A shiver prickled up my spine at the mention. It appeared I wasn't the only one who viewed us as fugitives.

Raelynd pulled Blaine in closer, as if to tell him a secret. "You go as far away as you can, as any smart man would. Those Reapers will be looking at every airport, train station, and border crossing they can get footage of. And that is precisely why *this* is so perfect. The absolute last place that any of those bastards will be focusing on is right under their noses."

"Forgive me, but I can't say I feel particularly comforted, given that demons already tried kidnapping my mate," Blaine snarled. "And last I checked, I'm not the only one around here with permission to get inside."

"No need to worry about your previous security detail, I assure you. I had your brother dispose of that demonic lot after your little run-in with that Angelorum blade," Raelynd drawled, uninterested. "Good help really is hard to find, isn't it?"

I stole a questioning glance at Val, who in turn merely smirked and pointed to the ground. I gulped.

Hell... He had sent them to *Hell*.

Raelynd waved a hand, as if to clear his thoughts. "But no bother. Not a single soul will be allowed now inside the manor unless expressed specifically by *you*, or your darling Katrina."

Blaine still didn't appear satisfied, but nevertheless nodded.

"Fantastic!" Raelynd clapped, and there were hands all around us, grabbing sets of luggage and bags from the trunk—all of which belonged to me. Did Blaine not pack anything?

Raelynd's cronies carried everything up the steps, neatly filing it beside the front door. Blaine grumbled, "Thanks," but the tone sounded an awful lot more like "Piss off" as he hooked his arm around mine and escorted me up the front steps. Without so much as a key, the door opened on silent command the moment we reached the porch.

Every muscle in me locked up as I stared inside the darkened foyer, and I didn't budge, even as Blaine tried to coax me over the threshold. The only thing I wanted to do was run in the opposite direction. Run down the driveway, the street, the coast. Run as far as I could until my feet bled and my lungs gave out. I could even feel myself slowly easing a step back.

Go now! that little voice in my head demanded. *Run!*

But Blaine's thumb traced over my left ring finger, and something in me settled. "*It's okay*," his voice assured to my mind. Those two simple words, and suddenly my feet were moving forward.

No.

No!

Go back!

But neither my feet nor my legs was listening to me, carrying me inside. I rubbed my arms, for the temperature of the interior wasn't fairing much better than outside. With a wave of Blaine's hand, embers roared to life in the fireplace to my right. Okay…that was both really cool, and really unsettling. And it was the only real light in the vast space, considering that all the windows were closed and covered.

The golden glow highlighted what I assumed was the sitting room. Rich oak furnishings, plush leather couches, and matching sofas filled the living space, accessorized by hanging pendant lanterns, candle chandelier wall sconces, and wrought iron fixtures. There was even a full-sized medieval suit of armor, along with mounted filigree blades, and red tapestry curtains on display by the fireplace, assisting the manor's wood and brick elegance. It was like being in a modernized renaissance manor, seeing as how there was still a flat screen television and sound system residing on the back wall.

"You can choose whichever bedroom you like," Blaine said, pulling my attention back to him. "Just let me know. I'll take everything up when I get back."

I looked behind him, noting he'd already carried all the luggage into the main foyer. "You're leaving?"

A small smile. "Why? Are you gonna miss me?"

"What? No!" I realized I sounded weirdly defensive, and all I wanted to do was kick myself. The outburst earned Blaine a chuckle, bringing heat to my cheeks. *God, what was wrong with me?*

"I'll be back in a couple hours. Don't invite anyone in,

alright?"

The moment he exited the front door, I immediately threw all the locks into place and fished around for any light switches. Ebony wood decorated everything from the vaulted ceiling rafters to the intricately hand-crafted panels and railings of the main staircase. The same gorgeous woodwork domed the entire entrance hall and appeared to carry on up to the second floor.

Two hours. That's all I had. And this place was enormous. It hadn't looked like much on the outside, but I discovered as I walked the main hall that the property extended so much further back than I had anticipated. I had to be fast.

The more rooms I investigated, the more Victorian décor I uncovered. Reese would've loved this place, if not for the Dark Prince currently residing in it. Not one inch of the manor went underappreciated. Beautiful wood parquet floors, rich red carpets, stunning crown molding... There was a freaking library! Not just a room with some bookshelves. An *actual* library. It was even equipped with one of those rolling ladders to reach the higher ledges, along with a spiral staircase that led to an upper level.

Spectacle after spectacle, and yet... no sword.

The only blades in the house belong to the coat of arms above the fireplace, but there was nothing special about them. Although, they were a hell of a lot heavier than I'd expected, especially when I pried them off the wall, shield and all. I'd wasted ten minutes alone just trying to get it back up.

And my frustration wasn't doing me any favors. It had sparked a couple runes, resulting in three ruined door knobs, a shattered drinking glass, and me *nearly* tearing down a shelf full of antique porcelain plates. Unless I wanted it to look like King Kong threw a hissy fit in here, I had to give my investigation a rest, even with an hour still left before Blaine came back.

I collapsed on the couch in the sitting room, practically sinking into the plush cushions. If I got to take anything with me from this experience, I called dibs on this baby. It was like falling onto a cloud. Just as my eyes began to sink closed, a sharp *ring* sent me startling upright. I scrambled off the sofa, scouring the room for a telephone, but the only one was an antique handset, which wasn't connected to anything. Following the sound, I made my way back into the foyer, discovering that it came from inside one of my bags.

I pulled out a phone from a side pocket of a carry-on, but it wasn't my own. Neither Val nor Blaine had been kind enough to give that back to me. The cell in my hand was a cheap plastic thing that I quickly realized was a burner phone. "Hello?"

"Hey, Princess."

I outright squealed. "Reese?"

He laughed. *"Miss me?"*

"I could kiss you right about now!" Without my phone, I had no idea how I would have been able to get in touch with him. "You'll never guess where I am."

"Mystic Harbor?" It really wasn't a question.

"Dare I ask how you know that?"

"I may have overheard a certain phone call from a certain leather-clad asshole whose name rhymes with Pal."

Now it was my turn to laugh, recalling what he had told me before I left this morning. I told him I wouldn't know when I'd see him again. His response: "Oh, I wager it'll be much sooner than you think."

"Do you think you'll be able to sneak away for a little bit?"

"I've only got about an hour before Blaine returns," I grumbled. "Where are you?"

"Heading over to Carly's beach house."

"Carly?" I nearly choked at the name drop. Reese and she had always gotten along about as well as lead and gunpowder.

"Save the sarcasm," he said. *"Nobody really knows about her parents' place off the coast, so she's letting us use it when we all need to meet up."*

"All?" I questioned.

"Dr. Madsen's making a special trip down here, says he has something you may want to see."

I had stayed at the beach house with Carly for a girls' night-in after she and Daniel got into a fight. If my calculations were correct, it was only a few miles away. "I'll be there."

Darting over to my luggage, I changed into a set of workout clothes and sneakers before gathering my hair back into a ponytail. With an oversized hoodie pulled on over my head, all my runes were concealed, along with my face. I didn't see any cars left out front, but I didn't want to take my chances getting caught, so I slinked out back through the family room.

Holy Moses!

Stepping right out on the wraparound porch, I realized there wasn't any land backing the property. Overlooking the ocean, the stormy Atlantic tides crashed against the rocks beneath me, sending chilling droplets to splash up within arm's reach. The scenery was downright breathtaking.

It took considerable effort to tear my attention away from the view, but I snuck a peek around the bend, checking to see if the coast was clear. No one appeared to be on the property, so I took off running. The trip was a bit longer than I'd anticipated, by another couple miles, but one benefit to being Supernaturally-inclined: endurance. Between my speed and prolonged energy, I reached the property in under twenty-five minutes, leaving me about ten minutes to visit.

Trotting up the driveway, I immediately spotted an unfamiliar black Benz pulling in behind me. Madsen, probably. Only…

"Hey there, Doll Face."

Shit!

I Write Sins, Not Tragedies

I pitifully turned on my heels, finding Val stepping out of the vehicle.

"Whatcha doing?" he teased.

"Visiting a friend," I snapped. "You?"

"I may not be allowed in the house, but that doesn't stop me from keeping an eye on you. And my brother thought you may require some looking after, so I obliged."

"Kat!" Footsteps trampled down the porch, and I barely had enough time to turn before being tackled into a hug.

"Hey, Car," I choked out. With my irritation still flaring from Val's little drop-in, I didn't dare hug her back, afraid that my unruly magic might accidentally make me snap her spine. Instead, I just patted her as gently as I could.

"Who's your friend?" she asked, biting her bottom lip as she pulled away from me. Add in her batting lashes, and it was evident she liked what she was seeing.

And Val didn't seem the least bit opposed to her

flirtations either.

I rolled my eyes. "Carly, Val. Val, this is my friend, Carly."

The ruffian took in my beautiful blonde friend, admiring her from head to toe. Car had an odd way of appearing both posh…and a bit risqué. Her butterscotch hair and lash-grazing bangs were bone straight with such gloss that every silky strand shone in the simplest movement. She wore a simple black top adorned with lace sleeves, not an inch of cleavage on display. It was the red plaid mini skirt, whose length just barely met with the school's dress code, that had Val ogling. With the black thigh-high nylon stockings, matching lace garter, and towering stilettos, she looked like a sophisticated, yet naughty schoolgirl.

The Mage bowed—literally *bowed*, before taking her hand into his and planting a kiss atop it. "Pleasure."

Her smile only broadened.

"This is Blaine's brother," I interjected, watching Carly instantly blanch. The girl outright scowled as she ripped her hand free from his.

"*He's* not here, too, is he?" she growled.

"No," I assured.

"I'll be inside." Car spun around and stomped back up the steps, slamming the front door behind her.

Val knew precisely why I'd thrown in that little fact and he shot me a dirty look in response. I only smiled back at him sweetly.

"Was that really necessary? I can play nice," he said, looking over my head into the front windows, as if he could see through the drawn curtains.

"Considering your brother's responsible for turning her boyfriend into a murderous monster who tried to kill her, yes, it's entirely necessary."

"So she's single, then?"

I didn't care if my runes were lit or not. I all-out punched him in the arm.

He didn't so much as grimace. "What? It's a legitimate question."

"Did you miss the part about Daniel being a *Hellhound*?"

"Who?"

"Remember the guy who started harassing me at the Hideaway?"

"That halfwit?" Val snickered. "Blaine didn't do that. That was m…" He glanced down at my arm, seeing more runes glowing beneath the sleeve of my hoodie. He couldn't even keep a straight face. "I mean… That was m-my friend."

"Your 'friend'?" I derided.

"Uh-huh."

"And pray tell, what's your *friend's* name?"

"…Bob."

"Bob? Bob the Mage?"

His shoulders shook in silent laughter. "Yep."

"Sounds fearsome."

"He is."

I punched him again, this time nailing him in the face.

Val, being the cold hearted bastard he was, may not have felt pain, but his ego could still certainly be bruised. Along with his vanity. And by the blood pooling down his upper lip, he knew the damage had been done. "Son of a motherf…"

"Now, be a good little lapdog for your brother, and stay put," I scoffed, retreating up the steps. My victory was short-lived, however, as I pulled the front door open—and slammed into an impenetrable wall of air.

"Missing something?" Val drawled behind me.

I didn't even bother turning to him as I hit the doorbell, simultaneously flipping him off.

Carly appeared in the front entrance a few seconds later, still scowling at the jackass in the driveway. She did seem appeased though, noting the blood he tried and failed to clean up. "What's up?"

"Can you invite me in?" I murmured.

Her nose scrunched up in confusion before realization hit. "Oooh, sorry! I totally forgot!" She pushed the door all the way open. "Please, come in."

"Thanks."

"Does that invitation extend to me as well?" Val drawled.

Carly tilted her head, as if contemplating the inquiry. He wasn't using his creepy powers of persuasion, was he? Crap! I reached to yank her inside, but she brushed me off.

Car gestured down the stretch to where a small boating dock rested over the water, and said all so sweetly, "I invite you to take a long walk off a short pier." She even imitated his sugary smile before pulling me inside and slamming the door shut.

Either Val liked a challenge, or he may have just met the first human immune to his 'charm'.

Hands grabbed a hold of me from behind, and I gasped, feeling heat flood my chest. The scent of honey and musk tickled my nose, and I sighed, letting myself melt into the embrace.

"Hey, Princess."

I'd gotten so used to that feeling being associated with Blaine, the surprise was beyond welcoming.

"Your doctor friend is in the living room with Mark,"

said Carly, pointing to the left.

"We'll be with you guys in a minute. I just want a quick word with Reese." I prepared to steer him away when a hand fell on my shoulder.

"I'm afraid I have to request that 'minute' first," declared Doctor Madsen in that distinct Danish lilt. "Please."

He looked just as I remembered, down to the tweed blazer and oxford button-down. Even the same earnestness remained in his russet eyes as he guided me toward the back of the house and into the kitchen, easing the swinging door shut to make sure we didn't have an audience.

"I know this is a delicate subject, and I can only suspect you'd prefer not to have Mr. Blackburn privy to the exact details, but I have to ask," he said softly. "Have you experienced any...warning signs, that perhaps the hex is taking effect?"

I didn't even realize I'd been gripping the counter until I felt the quartz surface splintering beneath my pressing palms. He seemed to notice the same moment I did, because he rubbed his eyebrows jadedly as I yanked my hands away.

"How bad is it?"

"I keep having dreams..."

This seemed to pique his interest. "What kind of dreams?"

"The kind where I keep getting killed," I murmur, "along with some other...intimate ones." I was probably blushing from head to toe, and for the life of me, I couldn't bring myself to look him in the eyes, settling my gaze instead on his shoes. I felt too ashamed.

"You know this isn't your fault."

"I know." But it didn't change anything. It didn't help ease my trembling hands. It didn't help erase the tears building behind my eyes. It didn't help me forget the things I'd seen last night, the details no one else knew about Blaine. Before I could react, Madsen's arms were wrapped around me, pulling me into a hug. His jacket smelled of coffee and cigars. *He smelled like my dad.* The thought made my knees buckle. I tried to find something else to say, something constructive. But I couldn't, not as my mouth trembled. "I'm scared."

It was barely a whisper, and the Light Mage only held me closer, so wholly unafraid that I'd hurt him.

"We're not giving up on you." A floorboard creaked somewhere behind Madsen, and he finally pulled away, looking less than pleased. "It's not polite to eavesdrop, Mr. Blackburn."

The swinging door leading to the main hall eased open, only to reveal Carly, along with my other old friend Mark McDowell, standing on the threshold.

"Sorry," Carly lamented. "It's just us."

Madsen only deflated all the more. "If only." He strode across the kitchen to the other door that headed into the dining room and pushed it open. Sure enough, Reese was on the other side, looking just as guilty as Mark and Carly. "What did you hear?"

Reese just kept his eyes fixed on me, sorrowful in a way I'd never seen before. Madsen turned to the others when it was clear he wouldn't answer.

"Nothing," Car blurted, "I mean…not much, anyway."

"Yeah, apart from Kat having the hots for Blackburn whilst fantasizing about a psychotic nutcase," Mark added impassively. *"Nothing."*

"Since it appears nobody here can respect boundaries, I suppose we shouldn't waste anymore of what little time Katrina has left before she has to go." Madsen gestured for us all to take seats as we congregated in the living room before handing me a manila envelope. It didn't have a return address, but it was addressed to:

Dr. Jonathan Madsen - Whitmore University, 418 Winsor Rd. Creighton, Maine.

I looked up at him, but he merely gestured for me to open it. Adjusting the prongs, I tilted it until an old piece of parchment slid into my hand. There were words dictated all across the aged paper, but it wasn't written in English...or even Latin for that matter. "What is it?" I asked.

"Something I suspect only a well-connected sibyl would be able to find."

"Lucinda?" Well, hot damn.

"It's an ancient ritual, inscribed by pagan high-priestesses." The doctor reached into his pocket, thumbing what appeared to be a necklace. On closer inspection, I could see the pendant was in fact a stone of some sort, made up of green jasper and flecks of earth red. "And this is what they call a Bloodstone amulet. When performed with this, the ritual is said to be one of the most powerful casts known in natural magic."

"What does it do?"

"With a blood offering, it can allegedly remove even the deepest rooted hexes."

Everyone perked up at the sound of that.

"But...blood offering?" Carly questioned, looking a bit queasy.

"It only requires a few drops of blood," assured Madsen.

"Hell, what're we waiting for?" said Mark, nodding to me. "Let's get this show on the road, before she has to hit the road."

"Blood magic is not something to be trifled with," said Madsen. "With a pagan ritual as powerful as this, it presents a threat to the host. When cast, the stone's energy would literally rip the hex's blight out of Katrina's body, no matter how deep it may be rooted. It could very well kill her. Only until it's absolutely necessary should we ever consider using this."

Reese was already shaking his head.

"Do it."

Everybody froze, all four pairs of eyes slowly sliding over to me.

"What the hell are you talking about?" Reese demanded. "You heard what Madsen just said—"

"Blaine can already get inside my head," I murmured, slumping back into my chair. "When we were driving up here, he touched me, and he saw my vision. He saw how I'm supposed to die. And when he demanded to know about it, I told him about what happened with Lucinda. I didn't want to, but I couldn't help it... It's only a matter of time before this gets worse."

"No." Those amber eyes flared like raging flames as Reese took my hand. "We'll find out where he's keeping the Sanctus blade, one way or another."

"I know we can't kill him, for obvious reasons, but why don't we just kidnap him?" asked Mark. "You know, go all *Casino Royale* on his ass, and beat the answers out of him till he tells us where the sword is."

"If I recall, that didn't turn out so well for the interrogator," I grumbled. "Besides, we're talking about the same guy who escaped silver shackles and a literal prison cell after being shot and repeatedly tortured. If Mr. Reynolds couldn't hold him, we wouldn't stand a prayer."

"We can always offer him an incentive," Mark offered.

"Like what? Cold beer? This isn't Shawshank."

He seemed to ponder this, stroking his chin for added effect. "I got it!"

The whole room shared in a collective eye roll, waiting for the moronic punch line. Sure enough, Mark delivered.

"Lap dances."

Carly immediately slapped him in the arm.

"Owww!" he howled. "What? The guy's still human, right? If someone like Kat offered me that in exchange for imprisonment, I'd save her the time and handcuff myself."

"Could you *try* to be serious?" Reese growled.

"Oddly enough, Mr. McDowell has a point," said Madsen.

Everyone's heads, including Mark's, snapped to the doctor, openmouthed.

"Not about the method," Madsen amended. "But the underlining concept has promise."

"What are you talking about?" I begged, praying the outcome didn't end the same way Mark's had.

"You need to get closer to him."

"Closer? He went from sleeping next-door to literally being in the same house," I said. "You don't get much closer than that."

His jaw tightened. "That's not what I'm suggesting."

Everybody gawked at him in horror.

"You don't seriously mean—" Reese couldn't even

finish the thought, springing up from his seat. "No."

"If you have a better alternative, I'm all ears," said Madsen, watching the Mage pace the length of the room.

Reese cut him a lethal glare. "Anything would be better than that!"

"The Angel of Death is never going to lend his blade to us, no matter how noble the cause may be. And the Crown Prince of Hell isn't going to disclose where he's hidden the one in his possession. Not to Kat, not without trust," he said, gesturing at me. "She needs to give him incentive. She needs to convince him."

"Of what?" Reese seethed. "That she...*wants* him? Kat can barely stand the thought of being in the same room with that psycho, let alone..." His words fell away as everyone's gaze redirected to me.

I remained silent, feeling the immobile floor somehow spinning beneath my feet. "I can't."

"I'm not sure there's another option," Madsen muttered. "We don't know how much time we have left before the hex takes over. It's at least worth a shot."

I couldn't stop shaking my head. "Blaine may be crazy, but he's not an idiot. There's no way in hell he'd buy into that. I can't go from telling him I hate him to suddenly asking to become best friends. If anything, he'll find a way to take advantage of the situation. We don't know anything about how this hex even works. For all we know, being around him that much could accelerate the process!"

"Alright, what's the alternative?"

I searched every dark corner of my mind, hoping for a light bulb, a lifeline, anything at all. But there was nothing. No saving grace. I had but two choices: Admit defeat, or venture to the last place any sane person wished to travel—behind enemy lines.

World Outside

I needed to convince Blaine that he could trust me. Should've been easy enough.

A.) He fancied me.

B.) He was nuttier than a bag of raccoons.

All I had to do was throw in a few smiles, an occasional compliment, maybe some eyelash batting. Easy-peasy, right?

Wrong.

So utterly, horribly wrong.

If he'd been your average, run-of-the-mill lunatic, it may have worked. But Blaine could sense and even smell my emotions, which made things infinitely trickier, especially when my anger had me destroying small portions of the manor, one bit at a time. As it turned out, that little bite I'd given Blaine came with a lot more punch than I had bargained for. It seemed whatever drugs I'd been given had still been lingering in my system to some

310

degree, because as the day progressed, the more aggressive my runes became. I was growing stronger.

Assuming Blaine slept in the master bedroom at the far end of the hall, I chose my living quarters to be as far away from his as possible. He suggested a closer room, but I assured him I'd be fine, finding a lovely handcrafted canopy bed awaiting me. The mattress was relatively soft, although the comforter smelled a little musty, making me wonder when the last time someone had even slept in here, if ever.

It was only eight o'clock when I turned in, ready for sleep to grant me a temporary reprieve from all this. I'd made it through the night just fine...until a certain dream had me up in a frenzy. I awoke in blind hysteria, my runes already lit. The moment I shot upright, the energy pulsated from my hands, shooting out on all sides. The force struck every one of the canopy posts, splitting them in half.

I shrieked as the wooden beams crashed all around me, and the fastened canopy sheet followed in suit, blanketing down on me like one of those animal capture nets, ensnaring me beneath its material. With the heavy posts collapsed on the floor, I struggled to wrestle my way out from under the fabric, finding Blaine standing in the entranceway already shaking his head.

"Don't even start." I slumped back under the canopy, wishing I could die.

My morning didn't fare much better. The tiniest fleck of frustration had me ripping off another few doorknobs, a sink faucet handle, and even the showerhead. By the time I entered the kitchen, I realized something. If I played my cards right, I could use this to my advantage. Kill two birds with one stone.

Blaine wanted me to play along. Fine by me.

"I want to take you up on your offer," I announced, taking a seat at the island across from him.

Blaine's focus had been concentrated on whatever book he was reading, but the declaration definitely earned his attention. "Offer?"

"The night of my Rite. You said that you'd help train me, to help me control my powers. I want to take you up on the offer."

He leaned against the counter, taking a long moment to look me over. I waited with baited breath and prayed I didn't appear too suspicious. Could he smell the lie? His eyes studied my face, and it felt as if the guilt was painted across my forehead.

He finally set down his coffee mug. "Is this really what you want?"

"No."

A small smile tugged at the corner of his lips. "I appreciate the honesty."

He *could* tell.

Crap.

"I don't want *you* to train me," I clarified, "but you're the only one who can. Being that Reese is a Light Mage, his runes don't work the same way as ours do."

"So you're asking me as a last resort?"

"Pretty much."

He nodded, seeming to consider. "When do you want to start?"

"Do your worst."

There we stood, in a training room. I'd combed every

inch of the manor, and had never spotted it. Though, I couldn't blame it on being dimwitted. The entrance to the basement stairwell was made of the exact same wooden paneling as the length of the walls, making the doorway undetectable to the naked eye. It wasn't until you pushed on the specific plate that it opened. Tucked away in the far end of the basement, the training room was about the size of a basketball court, lined with exercise equipment along with an entire wall decked out in various weapons.

I gawped at the dagger Blaine set in my hands. "You want me to stab you?"

He smirked. "I'd like to see you try."

This wasn't common cutlery. The hilt of the dagger was adorned with filigree, and the blade had to be at least ten inches long. By the looks of it, I guessed it was an antique.

"Are you crazy?" I looked up at him, immediately realizing who I was talking to. "I mean, obviously you are, but I didn't think you were suicidal."

Blaine laughed. "It's not silver." Seeing my unwillingness to even test it out, he came up and took the weapon back from me by the tip of the blade. He held it between his fingers, letting me take note that it wasn't burning his skin. "Unless by some miracle you can manage to decapitate me, I'll be fine," he assured. "Just try to avoid the eyes. From what I hear, that is *not* a pretty healing process."

He extended the dagger back to me, allowing me to wrap my hand around the hilt. "I thought you were going to help me control my runes," I said.

"We'll get to that, but you also need to learn how to fight without relying on them. If the Angel of Death really does have it out for you, then you won't have the luxury of using any magic to defend against him." He took a healthy step back and beckoned me to follow. "Let's see what you've got."

I positioned myself, readying the blade, and he immediately shook his head. "What?"

"Your body's all wrong."

"I've never heard you complain about it before," I ribbed.

"Your stance is wrong," Blaine clarified, unable to fight the grin pulling at his lips. "You have your fighting arm angled behind you. Here." He came over, turning my whole body to the left. "When you're facing your opponent, you want your dominant side—which for you is your right—to be coming forward. When you're turned the other way, you're leaving the entire unarmed side of your body exposed. Plus, when your fighting arm is further back, you're losing most of your reach, making it that much more difficult to strike your attacker."

Made sense.

"This way," he said, repositioning my feet, "your attacker has to find a way past the knife in your hands to get to you. And always try to leave your free hand up guarding your throat. It's the most effective area to strike, even with our kind."

With my newly acquired position, Blaine urged me once again to come at him. I wasn't going to lie. The idea of being allowed to stab Blaine sounded pretty good. In fact, it was a fantasy of mine. Only, it was much harder than it looked. Even without any weapons to defend himself with, he averted every swipe, strike, and slash I threw at him. Every move was so effortless, it only fueled my fury, making me all the more imprudent.

At last, he caught my arm, the knife still a healthy distance from his neck. "You're exhausting yourself."

"Am not," I panted.

Yeah, real convincing, Kat.

"I can smell your anger, as well as see it," he remarked, pointing at the glowing rune on my arm. "The more energy you waste on ineffective strikes, you're only giving your opponent the upper hand by wearing yourself out."

I pulled away, tossing the blade aside, unable to bottle my annoyance.

"You already have the necessary skill set," he sighed. "I've seen it for myself. Our bond gifted you my fighting abilities. You just need to learn how to tap into it, and maybe brush up on a few techniques. It won't be that hard, I promise."

Still peeved, I bent down to reclaim the dagger when it suddenly slid away just out of reach. I took another step forward, and yet again, it skittered across the floor. I shot a dirty look up at Blaine, seeing his finger crooked toward the dagger. No doubt magic. "Will you stop it?"

He shook his head. "Leave it. I want to see what you can do with hand-to-hand combat."

"I'm not going to learn anything if you keep jumping from subject to subject," I scoffed.

"We'll come back to it later," he assured. "Anger and sharp objects don't generally mix well. If you pick up the blade again, the only person you're most likely to hurt is yourself. Let's stick to fists till you dial it down a few notches."

I took a moment, pretending to collect myself, when in fact I really needed it to catch my breath. God, didn't he get sick of always being right?

And the prospect of fighting him only became less and less appealing as I looked back at him. Having tossed aside the hoodie he'd been wearing, Blaine showcased his lean, inverted triangular frame in all its glory, hidden beneath nothing but a fitted black wife beater tank top and a pair of workout sweats. I could even see the ripples in the shirt's fabric where his six-pack rested. Match that with toned biceps, broad shoulders, and defined pecs, I felt about as threatening as a basket of kittens.

"Okay, show me what you've got." Blaine motioned me forward, still not bothering to take any stance. He stood not five feet ahead in front of me, his arms laxly at his sides as if he didn't have a care in the world.

Without anything to go off of, and admittedly self-conscious of any further criticism, I held up my hands. I'd taken self-defense courses before, so I at least knew to bend my knees and keep my elbows tucked in. Except…which side was I supposed to turn my body toward again?

Crap.

Was the technique for punching the same as knife-fighting? For the life of me, I couldn't remember. With Blaine's eyes homed in on me, on my *body*, anxiety hit in full-force. Desperately grasping at any scrap of memory for help, I still drew a blank.

How the hell was I ever going to pull this off? Every time Blaine touched me, it took everything I had not to run away screaming. And now? I literally couldn't stand in front of him without becoming flustered.

One look at him, and I already knew whatever I was doing had to be wrong. I immediately dropped my hands.

Blaine sighed. "If you're that uncomfortable, we don't have to do this."

"No." I shook my head. "I need to learn."

He nodded. "You had it right the first time." Blaine adjusted my stance so that my dominant leg and punching hand were positioned further back, like how I'd been when first holding the knife. "Make sure to stand square. The power of your punch starts in your legs. Keep them bent, and use your hips to guide your body." He demonstrated beside me, illustrating the perfect technique. Just as he said, the energy travelled up his torso and into his arm, allowing him to throw a forceful jab. Blaine repeated the action, purposely slower to further illustrate each step.

After showing me various punching methods, my 'teacher' wanted to see if I could put his lesson to use. To say it bruised my ego all over again would've been an understatement. That challenging brow, that smirk teasing at the corner of his lips, that condescending nonchalance; it all made my blood boil. Time and time again, I managed to punch into nothing but air as he casually sidestepped and parried each attempted strike like he was facing off against a toddler. At one point, he even yawned!

That was the last straw. The moment I pulled away from him, my runes reignited as I clenched my fist. Without my permission, the power brewing inside me exploded, clearly deciding to show Blaine who was boss. Something shot off the small bench in the corner and hurled right at the back of Blaine's head, smacking him in the base of his skull.

I nearly yelped, uncertain of what I'd inadvertently thrown. The entire section of the room was covered with weights and weapons, all of which could do some serious damage.

I expected him to scream or curse, or do...something. Instead, he just looked baffled. Something thudded behind him on the floor, and he turned around to see what I now realized was a water bottle.

"Cute," he smirked, kicking it back over to the sidelines.

A freaking water bottle? *Seriously?*

Not only had I involuntarily Hulked out, I couldn't even do *that* right, picking the least effective weapon known to mankind. In all of human history, no one's autopsy report was ever going to read 'death by water bottle.' Along with the damn thing being only half-full, it didn't even have the decency to be well-made. It was one of those stupid environmentally friendly bottles where the plastic was so thin, you could crinkle it up in your hand. I might as well have hit him with a party balloon.

"May we proceed? Or do you wish to continue your tantrum?" he asked, getting an eye roll for an answer.

I wasn't sure if he had started taking it a little easier on me, but my self-esteem got a much needed boost for the next half-hour after I managed to land a couple decent punches. Sure, they only connected with his arms and chest, and he didn't seem the least bit fazed by them, but at least I wasn't swinging uselessly at the air.

"Turn around."

"What?"

"We need to test your reflexes," said Blaine, apparently switching gears into our next subject. "In a perfect world, you'd always face-off with your opponent, but unfortunately, that's rarely the case in reality. You'll need to learn how to defend yourself against ambushes."

Turning my back to him was the last thing I wanted to do. It hadn't done me any favors in the past. Hell, the fang marks scarring my neck were proof enough. But none of this was about trying to make me feel warm-and-fuzzy. I needed to learn things like this, and I needed to convince Blaine that I could at least tolerate being around him. It was the first step in the right direction, and if I had any hope of gaining his fullest trust, I had to work fast, comfort be damned.

I did as instructed, trying to ignore the quiver working its way up my arms. It wasn't from my runes. It was pure, unadulterated anxiety. I gripped my hands together, as if I could squeeze out the unease. My heart only pounded faster as haunting music suddenly blared across the training space from speakers I hadn't realized before were mounted into the corners of the walls. I whirled on my heels.

Blaine merely twirled his finger at me, indicating that I needed to turn back around. He didn't want me to hear him coming—whenever he decided to. I stood stupidly for a good minute, straining to hear over the gorgeous, dark melody. Without a sound, his only hint came from the breath of air hitting my neck before his arms wrapped around me. I'd expected him to rush me, ensnaring my hands to my sides as he pulled me up off my feet. I'd expected him to attack me. But his hold wasn't so much of a hold as it was…an embrace, feeling his body pressing up against my back. Even with his taut muscles and sculpted arms, the embrace was so startlingly gentle.

His lips were so close to my ear that his breath warmed it, and all I could suddenly see was that wood paneled wall from my dreams. All I could feel was his mouth on my shoulder, his hands roaming my body, our lips crashing into one another. Every inch of me went flush at the recollection.

"What do you do?" he whispered.

"Huh?" I muttered, snapping myself back into reality.

"When your attacker grabs you like this, what do you do?"

I seriously doubted my attacker would be holding me 'like this.' "I...I don't know. Stomp their foot?" It had worked with the demon possessing Officer Hernandez.

"Nice sentiment, but it only works if they're standing still. Most of the time, your attacker will try lifting you off the ground, dragging you backward. Chances are you won't get the opportunity."

"Head butt?" I attempted again.

"If they're not too tall, it's a possibility. But you need to think in guarantees." He gently kneed the back of my leg. "I want you to take your right foot and pivot it to the outside of my left foot, as far back as you can."

I wasn't sure where he was going with this, but I nevertheless did as he said.

"When you do this, grab the fabric of my pants just above my knee. This'll help steady your weight when your center of gravity lowers," he further instructed. "Once you have your footing, extend your right arm out."

To my amazement, the maneuver forced his arms to pull apart, effectively breaking his hold on me.

"Now, take your right leg, position it behind my left foot, and bring your knee into the back of my leg. Then, fall back."

"Seriously?"

All I got was a soft chuckle.

I did just that. With my arm still extended and his knee buckling under, I actually managed to take Blaine down with me. In fact, my stance had allowed him to fall beneath me, letting me avoid the impact of his weight.

"See where your right arm is?" he asked, lying down beneath me, our limbs still tangled together. Thank God my back was still to him and not my face.

I flushed nevertheless, noting that my elbow was just

above his…unmentionables.

"That's your target. You hit him there, and I promise you, he won't be getting back up anytime soon."

"Oh…okay," I muttered stupidly, involuntarily shifting.

Blaine suddenly let out a breathy laugh after a moment, and I startled at the sound. "Not that I mind you laying on top of me, but would you mind letting up your elbow?"

"Oh…God! Sorry." I scrambled away, realizing only just then that my shifted position had my elbow digging into his solar plexus, which probably wasn't helping his breathing any.

He only laughed again, climbing back up to his feet to meet me. "For the record, that's another effective area," Blaine said, tapping the same spot below his sternum. "If you hit that hard enough, the impact will cause the diaphragm to spasm, cutting off your assailant's air supply."

"Did you learn all of this from…?" I couldn't bring myself to say his name, not wanting to upset him.

"My brother taught me most of this." To my surprise, he actually smiled. "Let's just say the pupil surpassed the master."

Blaine proceeded to show me how to break free from an underarm "bear hug" hold, which even I had to admit was kind of fun. Hooking my hand around Blaine's arm, I turned to the side and hooked my foot under his leg, throwing him to the ground in a backwards roll. Move over, Black Widow. There was a new badass in town.

Okay, maybe I wasn't *that* awesome, but knowing I could at least defend myself now still felt pretty good.

Five maneuvers later, and I needed to ask. "My attacker isn't going to be coddling me, so…why are you?"

Blaine's throat bobbed.

"I mean, I can take a few bumps and bruises. You don't have to handle me with kid gloves," I amended.

"I don't doubt your resilience. I just didn't want to scare you."

"What do you mean?"

He gave me a knowing look. "It doesn't take clairsentience to know you're afraid to be around me."

I could feel blood rushing to my cheeks, only further proving his point.

"It's hard enough learning things like chokeholds when you do trust your instructor. I highly doubt you'd feel comfortable with me, of all people, wrapping my hands around your throat, especially with any kind of force." Before I could attempt to deny or even admit it, he only stepped further away. "I get it, really."

Blaine headed over to the other side of the room and grabbed a pair of focus mitts, but even I could see the tension wrought in his shoulders. He began explaining some kicking techniques, but my mental filter seemed to break as I cut him off, blurting, "How *do* you get out of chokeholds?"

I couldn't help it. After being attacked by Brittany, the cheerleader-turned-Hellhound, and then nearly strangled to death by Russell, choking was an all-too familiar reoccurrence for me. Having a little know-how couldn't hurt.

Blaine's entire frame stiffened. "Kat—"

"I wouldn't be asking if I didn't think I needed to learn it. I'm tired of being a victim, and I'm tired of always running away. I want to fight." Because that's exactly what I was doing at this very moment. I was fighting for my life. I was fighting for my freedom.

He reluctantly tossed the mitts aside and met me at the center of the room. "You sure you're up for this?"

I nodded, adamant in my decision. That confidence wavered, however, the moment he came up behind me, securing the inside of his elbow against my windpipe as he wrapped his arm around me. Again, he made sure the hold was gentle, allowing me to break away at any moment if I wished. And I silently thanked him for it.

"Okay, first thing you need to do is protect your airways," he said. "I want you to take both your hands and grab my arm on each side of my elbow. Bring your shoulders up, tuck your chin down, and drop your knees. It'll relieve some of the pressure." He nudged my right foot. "Now, take your foot and pivot it behind mine."

"Like what I did with the bear hug?"

"Yes, only this time, it'll be the foot on the same side as the arm I'm using to choke you with. Your right foot goes behind my right foot. It has to lock up my leg, so make sure it's directly in back of it—calf to calf. Then, turn your body all the way around and pull my arm down diagonally."

With his right leg pinned against mine, I did a 180-turn and wrenched him across my body, letting him trip back and fall to the ground.

Holy crap.

I actually sighed, begetting a roguish grin from Blaine.

"Enjoying beating me up?" he drawled, propping himself up on his elbows as he remained lying on the floor. One deep breath, and he seemed to get his answer, catching whatever scent I was giving off. I wasn't even sure what I was feeling. Anxiety? Relief? Liberation? It was all one big blur. All I knew was that my uncertainty left me yet again at a disadvantage, which only appeared to please

Blaine all the more.

"Join me."

"What?"

He patted the floor beside him. "For our next position."

His inflection on that last word made my heart rate tick up a notch. The hesitation he'd exhibited a moment before was nowhere to be found, replaced by a bravado that exuded the pure sexuality his title of Crown Prince promised. It was a dare. A challenge. And the very moment I'd been dreading. But I lowered myself to the floor, lying beside him on the mat. With the hope that I could steady my thrumming pulse, I closed my eyes.

Even behind my eyelids, I could see the shadow cast above me, obscuring the overhead lights. My breathing hitched, feeling the pressure settle on my hips. I at last opened my eyes to find Blaine straddling me, his hands positioned on either side of my head, his face lingering just above my own.

That godforsaken pull in my core had my back threatening to arch off the floor, pleading with me to eliminate the sliver of space resting between us. To my relief, he sat up, just enough that he didn't have to rely on his arms for support, because his hands settled on my neck. But they weren't holding me. His thumbs traced the lines of my jaw while his fingers caressed the nape of my neck.

Without a word and without instructions, my right leg suddenly bent up, locking my foot behind his. As if he were the puppeteer to my very own limbs, my hands automatically drew up next and gripped his left forearm. How was he doing this? A faint magnetic pulse radiated from his skin, rippling into me. It was only then that I realized I was touching his runes. I'd never done that before. I could feel the energy pulsating from the metallic black ink, an invisible bond that silently summoned me. I pulled down on his secured arm just as the left side of my hips bucked up. With my foot pinned against his, Blaine's weight toppled to the side, and I suddenly found myself straddling *him* instead.

I'd done it.

I didn't know how, but I had escaped his hold…only to find myself in a new position that had my cheeks probably reddening to the color of strawberries.

His eyes gleamed up at me with silent approval.

What a shame, I thought, peering down at the striking young man beneath me, *to be so beautiful on the outside, only to possess such a blackened heart.*

"It may be black, love," his voice purred inside my head. *"But that doesn't mean it still can't be made of gold."*

I stiffened.

He *could* read my thoughts.

"Not always," he assured, still not speaking a word aloud. *"Only when you let me in."*

When had I done that?

His palms settled on my waist, exploring the curves of my body as his fingertips gently raked up the small of my back. The sensation somehow left both warmth and goose bumps perforating in its wake, leaving my skin to ache as he pulled his hands away.

"Ahem," coughed a voice over the thrumming melody.

As if I'd been slapped, my head snapped to the side, seeing six feet of racing leather and hair product standing haughtily in the entranceway.

Val.

26

Gods and Monster

H ope I'm interrupting," drawled the Dark Mage.

I scrambled up to my feet, brushing invisible lint of myself as to not look too flustered.

Yeah, that ship had long sailed.

I thought Blaine and I were the only people allowed in the house. *How was he even here?*

I wasn't sure if Blaine could still read my thoughts or if my look of unbridled confusion and horror spoke for itself.

"I invited him inside back when we were still on good terms," Blaine muttered. "A decision I deeply regret."

His brother pinned a hand against his chest and staggered back in mock offense. "Oh, how cruel you can be."

"I thought we agreed that you wouldn't come in here," Blaine snarled, rising to his feet.

Val merely rolled his eyes. "Cool your jets, okay. I got

tired of ringing the bell, so yes, I let myself in. It's not my fault you wouldn't answer the door. And it's no wonder. You probably couldn't even hear me over...whatever the hell this is," he said, waving a dismissive hand in the air to indicate the music. Despite the slick product keeping his hair intact, the rest of Val glistened in the warm glow. It seemed those storms headed north after all.

The strum of violins settled, silencing the room enough to hear the low rumble of thunder.

"What do you want?" demanded Blaine.

"I'd try to show a little more appreciation if I were you," said Val, "considering I come bearing important news."

His brother still didn't appear impressed. "You've got twenty seconds to become interesting."

Val laughed. "Well, it appears you and your sweetie here are the Underworld's new Bonnie & Clyde. The good ol' Angel of Death has just issued a bounty on your heads, and Mr. Holier-Than-Thou himself appears to be pretty desperate. Despite the fact Death despises all things Hellbound, he's resorted to commissioning demons to do his bidding. By the sounds of it, there's one hell of a reward for whoever brings the pair of you in."

The creature at the shopping district. The demon at my aunt's house. They weren't sent by a rival noble. They'd been sent by the very man destined to kill me. Blaine and I both paled, only making Val's grin grow.

"Have I earned your attention yet?" he crooned.

"What's the reward?" I asked.

Val shrugged. "Not sure. Anyone who actually knows isn't saying anything, which only means the payday has to be something pretty special if they don't want to risk tipping off any of their colleagues, even under means of torture."

Blaine's eyes narrowed. "The 'incident' at the Hideaway?"

"After the whole Reaper attack, Raelynd had planned for you to stay there, but the reported timetable had been skewed. A group of demons ambushed the joint, believing you two would be there. Hence, the hush-hush plans to ship you off here, instead. Gotta give it to your old man though," Val said, gesturing to me.

Blaine's eyes were suddenly the size of saucers as he shook his head as discreetly as he could, commanding a silent, "SHUT UP!" to his brother. But it was too late.

"It is a clever idea," Val went on. "What better demographic to target to do your dirty work than a bunch of immoral pests who are only out to save their own skins?"

"*My old man?*" I blurted. What the hell was he talking about?

My shock apparently registered to Val, because he winced. Though, he didn't seem the least bit sorry as he smiled back at his brother. "Whoops, guess you hadn't told her yet, had ya'?"

"You mean…?" The Angel of Death was my… I whirled on Blaine. "You *knew*?"

The bastard couldn't even look me in the eyes.

I'd asked him before who my parents were.

"*You're better off not knowing,*" he had said.

I pushed Val out of the way and raced upstairs.

Blaine tapped on the bedroom door, slowly easing it open when he didn't get a response. I'd left him in the training room about an hour ago, and hadn't heard a peep from him till now. His eyebrows shot up in surprise at the sight of me. He'd probably been anticipating that he'd walk in on me crying or tearing the room apart in a fit of fury, but certainly not *this*. Fresh out of the shower and in a new set of clothes, I pulled on my jacket and calmly shoved my feet into my shoes.

"Going somewhere?" He apparently wasn't a fan of being ignored, because when I failed to answer him yet again, he appeared at my side, plucking Reese's burner phone right out of my hands. "I know you're upset," he said, taking note of my inexplicably unruffled expression. "Or…at least, I *suspect* you are, but running out of here isn't the answer."

"I'm not running," I simply said, snatching the cell back. "I have somewhere I need to be."

He sighed, clearly trying his best not to lose patience with me. "It's not safe for you to go out, not by yourself."

"Fine," I shrugged. "Then come with."

We were on the road for about twenty minutes when I directed Blaine to pull off a stretch of back roads into the parking lot of an old dive bar. A tacky neon sign greeted us as we headed inside, where we were then ambushed by a buoyant redhead in a tight white t-shirt and short-shorts. The mass of people made the small space a bit stuffy, but it certainly wasn't warm enough to warrant that kind of outfit. Though, I didn't think she had much say in it. I noticed her nametag and gave the room another onceover, spotting several other girls in the exact same uniform.

"Hey, handsome," declared the waitress, practically

skipping over to us, her attention totally focused on Blaine. The name ROXY was printed in big bold letters on the left side of her chest. "Can I interest you in a booth? Perhaps start you off with a pitcher of our finest?"

"That won't be necessary. They won't be here long." Two simple sentences, and yet that Texas drawl was unmistakable.

Blaine and I both turned around, finding Nick seated at an otherwise empty table.

"What the hell are we doing here?" Blaine demanded to my thoughts.

It wasn't until yesterday afternoon, when I had changed out of my ~~lingerie~~ outfit after coming to the manor, that I paid closer mind to the business card I had shoved into my thigh-high boots. The number scribbled on the back may have been for the Sagax, but Nick had also circled the bottom of the front, writing "me" beside the business's listed phone number.

I gave Blaine the sweetest smile I could find. "Well, since you've proven to be stingy in the information department, I've decided to take matters into my own hands." I sauntered past him and joined the Texan at his table.

Blaine seemed less inclined to follow suit, but after surveying the room, he finally planted himself beside me.

"You two know how to piss off some serious bigwigs, I'll give you that much," Nick sighed, downing the last of his beer. Roxy came back to the table, all too eager and sweet, insisting we order something. Given Nick's rather ruffled state, it came as no surprise that he ordered another beer, while Blaine just shook his head.

Knowing she wouldn't leave until at least one of us relented, I asked for a coke, happy to see her skip away to the bar. "What have you heard?"

"Reynolds has rallied at least five large Reaper packs to join him in your manhunt," Nick said lowly. "And if word-of-mouth is correct, then he's also teamed up with someone rather influential Upstairs."

"Let me guess, the Angel of Death?" I remarked flatly, more annoyed than anything.

Nick tried not to chuckle. "That name puts the fear of God in most people, but…ooookay. Yeah, Samael."

I looked to Blaine for clarification.

"Samael is Death's real name. It means 'Venom of God'."

"Oh, that sounds…lovely." I wasn't aware of how odd it must have seemed as an outsider, witnessing the silent exchanges between Blaine and me, until I realized I'd said that last bit out loud, seeing Nick's eyebrows crooked in confusion. "Sorry."

This at least earned Blaine a small smile.

Nick just shook his head. "Anyway, the guy's pretty pissed that you're trying to break the Anastasis Seal."

"Anastasis?" I turned to Blaine again, but he looked equally confused.

The Texan leaned back in his seat, half-laughing. "You two have no idea what's going on here, do you?"

"Apparently not," I muttered.

"You know how God flooded the Earth way back when to wipe out all the Mages and fallen angels?"

We both nodded.

"Well, the only reason people like you even exist anymore is because a 17th century coven of witches managed to resurrect the demon Azazeal back to Earth in bodily form, allowing him to repopulate the world with Mages. Heaven counteracted the movement with a group of angels who willingly fell from Paradise so they could create Reapers, hoping to wipe out all you guys again, along with the coven. Only problem, the seal that was used to bring the demon back was still open for anyone powerful enough to perform the ritual. To prevent more demons from being resurrected, Samael had to build another seal around it to block its power. The ward was bound by the blood of those angels who fell to protect us. Each one of them made an offering at seven different locations around the perimeter of the area in question to form an invisible wall that no demon can cross." Nick pulled out an old leather-bound journal from the manila envelope beside him, unfolding an equally old map from within the pages. He laid it flat on the table, showing seven distinct markers placed around the outside of the drawing.

Nothing about the map looked familiar, except the name inscribed along the river at the top of the page. "West Fork?" Holy crap! "This is Mystic Harbor."

"South of it, actually. But yeah. Jameson Battlefield, where Azazeal was originally summoned, has more supernatural energy there than anywhere else you're gonna find in this hemisphere," said Nick. "The only problem: demons can't get to it so long as the protection ward is up. Whatever your bosses wish to do there is going to require summoning some serious amount of energy. That's where you and the others come in." Nick flipped through the journal, cutting to a specific page, and slid it over to us. "To terminate a spell such as this, you have to offer the equivalent of the same magical properties used to enact it. The blood sacrificed was entirely angelic. Considering there's been three-hundred years of humans mudding the angelic gene pool, far more blood would have to be sacrificed from a descendant to match the properties the original angels provided."

A pit formed at the bottom of my stomach. "How much?"

"Based on the number of girls your kind has killed and drained over the past two months, all of it."

My stomach hollowed out. All I could think about was my vision eight weeks ago of that poor girl whose throat had been slit by Hellhounds.

Nick proceeded to lay out a modern map of Mystic Harbor and placed it beside the old one. He circled a number of positions on the bottom of the current map with a red marker. "These are where each of the bodies were found." He overlaid the two maps, and sure enough, the location of where that girl had been killed coincided with one of the seven blood offering sites. She'd been killed to help break the ward. And there had been a murder at each of the marked locations, except one. "If you think your bosses are pains in the ass now, imagine every last one of them in their true bodily forms. Each of them used to be a powerful Mage or a fallen angel, either killed in the flood or taken out by Reapers following the coven's uprising. As soon as your bosses find that last candidate, all Hell's gonna break loose. They've been holding onto centuries, if not millenniums, of aggression. War would be inevitable. Hence, Samael's desperation to take you two out."

Amid my internal panic at the thought of a holy war, Blaine didn't look the least bit impressed. "Can you really blame them? Some of those demons you're talking about were 'Light' Mages when they were alive. Angelic. Your kind still hunted them down without cause, apart from your own fear, and damned them to eternal suffering, forcing them to live as parasites on unsuspecting victims just so they can feel something. If every time I looked in the mirror, I saw a new face staring back at me, I'd be pretty pissed too."

I had never thought of possession that way.

"I'm not saying our ancestors never made mistakes—"

"Yet you guys are fast to pass judgment on us," Blaine countered. "The whole 'Light' and 'Dark' thing is pretty hilarious. Mages inherit either Nephilim runes or Enochian runes, and you are all too eager to throw the 'evil' label on the one that gives the slightest bit of trouble. Multiple Reapers have tried to kill my mate, one of your kind *did* in fact kill me, and a group performed such unspeakable atrocities on my brother that you made him into the monster you claimed him to already be. We never did anything to provoke these attacks, and yet you've affectionately labeled yourselves as the 'good' guys."

"So what? You think you're the hero in all this?" Nick scoffed.

"Me?" Blaine laughed. "Hardly."

"Because *your* kind killed my family, kidnapped the person I love, and brutally butchered a number of my friends and colleagues. I've never done anything to ever hurt you, just as you haven't to me, but that doesn't change hundreds of years worth of bad blood. One side kills someone, the other hunts them down, the original side retaliates, and the cycle just goes on and on. Your kind will continue to hunt me till the day I die, and nothing I do is going to change that."

"If we're your mortal enemies, then why are you talking with us?" Blaine asked.

"Your mate is the only hope I have right now." Nick slipped the information back into the journal. "If your session with the Sagax has taught me anything, it's that you're not like the rest of them. And I'm putting faith in you that you'll do the right thing, when the moment comes."

"What do you mean? Where do we fit into this?" I asked. "I mean, specifically?"

"Royal blood goes a long way, and the fact that you two are mates only makes your potential energy that much stronger. A few drops of blood from you guys are all your bosses will need. I'm asking you to not let that happen." The Reaper placed everything back into the manila envelope and sealed it. "Samael has informants on Earth that he sends word to, but it's not like he can just pop down here whenever he feels like it. So it's a pretty big deal that he's scheduled to arrive in the next day or so, and Reynolds is planning a full-frontal assault to take place when that happens. Both of them are desperate enough that they will do just about anything to draw you out. My advice: get as far away from here as you can, and hide anyone who could be used as leverage against you."

"And you're telling us this out of the goodness of your heart?"

"Not entirely, no." Nick slid the envelope to us. "Someone I love was taken by your kind. I need someone with an ear close to the ground, someone who can ask questions about her and not raise suspicion. I suspect, being who you are, it wouldn't be that much trouble to at least ask around."

"We'll do everything we can," I assured, taking the packet.

The Reaper nodded, but it couldn't mask the grim expression, and it broke my heart. I'd seen that look before. In the mirror. In my hands rested the only glimmer of hope he had of finding whoever it was that he cared so much about. I tried to think of something else to say, but

Blaine hauled me up, clearly wanting to get the hell out of here.

"What happened to Val?" I asked the moment he pulled me into the parking lot.

"What happened to me *when?*"

Blaine and I both stopped, finding his brother leaning against the Benz we had ~~stolen~~ borrowed for our little excursion.

"Mind telling me what you're both doing out and about, in *my* car no less?" Val inquired flatly.

"Well, you guys didn't let me drive my Cutlass up here, so I have limited means of transport," said Blaine, rounding the vehicle to the driver's door.

Val pinned a hand to his chest and forced him away. "Yeah, and you crashed my brand new Cadi, so there's no way in hell I'm letting you get behind the wheel again. Besides, Maddox should have your precious Cutlass up at the manor in a few hours. Back seat, now."

We were on the road for only a few minutes when we came to a red light.

"Shit!" I grabbed Blaine by the collar and hurled him down across the seat into my lap as I threw my hood over my head.

Val angled the rearview mirror at us. "Should I even ask?"

Blaine tried lifting his head, but I immediately pushed him back down. "It's Syringe," I sneered, motioning to the SUV pulled up beside us.

"What?" Both brothers tried to steal a look over at the vehicle, but only Val managed as I struggled to keep Blaine down.

"That's the bastard that drugged me in my room," I clarified, nodding to the familiar face across the way. I'd thought for sure those Hellhounds had ripped him to pieces on the road. Pity.

"You want me to take care of him?" asked Val, opening his glove box where a revolver rested amid some paperwork.

The idea sounded fantastic, but alas I shook my head. "No, we can't afford to draw any unwanted attention. And with Angel Face over here," I said, gesturing to Blaine, "his hair hardly makes him inconspicuous."

That mischievous grin greeted me as the Prince peered up from my lap. "Did you just call me Angel Face?"

"It's from *Fight Club*," I clarified, giving him a light swat on the head.

"I know. I just like hearing you say that."

Syringe got a green arrow. As soon as the SUV began rolling through the intersection, that inexplicable tug in my chest beckoned me. Blaine must have felt it too, because he shot up and looked out the window. "Follow him," we both ordered.

Another Way to Die

We'd been tailing the Reaper for about five minutes when the burner phone in my pocket rang.

Reese.

"Hey, what's up?" I answered.

"Montgomery?"

"Mark? What are you doing with Reese's phone?"

"They took her," he panted.

"Who took who?"

Blaine snatched the phone, hitting the speaker button.

"School just got out, and the three of us were heading into the parking lot when a group of armed men in ski masks came up behind Reese and stabbed him with some sort of syringe. They were about to grab him as he passed out, but another guy showed up and said something about Blackburn being off-limits. So the bastards grabbed Carly instead!"

"And you let them take her?" Val barked.

"Did you not hear the part where I said 'armed' men?" Mark

snapped back.

"Pussy."

"Who the hell is this?" demanded McDowell.

I swatted Val in the arm. "Forget him. Did they say anything else when they took her?"

"No."

"Did you see any of their faces?"

"No."

"Did you see what direction they headed in after they took her?"

"Uh...No."

"Gee, isn't he just a wealth of knowledge," Val scolded. "Can you at least tell me what color the sky is?" he further mocked.

I smacked him again.

"What? It's not my fault this kid's about as useless as a chocolate teapot."

Mark had more than his fair share of colorful names for the Dark Mage, but we didn't have time for this.

"You two can get back to your dick-measuring contest later. Focus," I demanded. "Where's Reese right now?"

"He's still unconscious," Mark confirmed. *"The police should be here any moment."*

Blaine shook his head. "Are you still in the parking lot?"

"Ah...yeah." Mark clearly hadn't anticipated hearing from his old friend. *"Ryder, is that you?"*

"Get Blackburn out of there. Now," Blaine demanded. "Don't wait for the police. Just load him up into your car and go somewhere safe, okay? Lay low."

The skies only turned darker as another batch of storms moved up from the south. It seemed like a safe assumption that Syringe would lead us where we needed to go, so Val kept a healthy distance behind him as we headed deeper into the forestlands. The Reaper's SUV eventually turned off into a gravel parking lot on an empty back road where a large cabin rested in the hillside. A sign out front read, *"Wayland State Park – Main Center."* Beneath it, someone had added, *"Due to Extreme Wet Conditions, The Park Is Closed. We hope to reopen on Jan. 1st."*

For a place that claimed to be shut down, there were still an awful lot of lights on inside the Park Center. And even though I had never been here before, the three men standing out front with guns holstered at their hips seemed the *teeniest* bit odd as well. Val headed further down the road and parked off on the shoulder. We got out and walked the perimeter of the forest preserve. Razor wire lined the tops of the tall chain linked fences guarding the property, making it impossible to slip through. It took about a half mile's walk more before we came across a small dirt path. It headed downhill, and fence continued, but I'd spotted a small gap in the curve.

Struggling to keep our traction in the wet grass, we slid our way down to the separation. I banged sharply against the fence as I lost my footing, trying to dodge a dead log as I snaked between the frameworks. The guys followed in suit, and we found the closest marked path that led back to the service center. No one was guarding the back of the extensive cabin, so we were able to steal a look through the window. Spears, terrariums, and old native artifacts filled several glass containers, while an arrowhead collection and various stuffed animal heads were mounted on the wooden walls. There was a security camera in the far corner of the main room, but it just so happened to be turned off.

Of course it was.

Something smashed out front. Skulking to the side of the center, we peered around the bend, getting a perfect view of the parking lot out front. A stiletto-clad foot was sticking out of the shattered back window of a dark SUV. I knew those heels anywhere, and Val knew those stems all too well.

Carly.

Even with a blindfold over her eyes and ropes binding her hands together, the girl was like a cornered wolverine. She thrashed and slashed out at anyone and everyone who touched her.

"Why didn't you shoot her up with one of the doses we gave you?" asked Syringe from the porch.

Three guys unloaded from the SUV, all struggling to yank the blonde out from the backseat.

"We already used the first on the boy," said the driver. "And Shamus tried subduing this little spitfire on the way over here, but she wound up sticking the idiot with the needle instead."

Sure enough, they opened the other car door, and an unconscious man with nail marks down his face slumped sideways, toppling out of the backseat.

"A girl after my own heart," Val purred lowly.

Syringe climbed down and met with Carly as she was dragged out of the vehicle. He whispered something to her and she finally stilled, feeling the barrel of his gun press beneath her chin. Val drew out his own gun, preparing to launch forward when Blaine gripped his jacket and yanked him back.

"*What?*" Val mouthed angrily.

His brother nodded back to the parking lot where two more vehicles were pulling up. Carly was immediately dragged up the porch and taken inside. Checking to see if the coast was clear, we hurried over to the back door, and Blaine manipulated the three sets of locks with a simple twist of his hand. Each unlatched themselves, letting him pull the door open. Voices carried from the front rooms, but no one appeared to be back by us.

The hallways wrapped around the many different display areas, giving us some much needed coverage as we made our way towards the lobby. Taking refuge behind a display showcasing an enormous stuffed elk, we could see the main foyer. Seventy-seven inches of pure muscles adorned with copper brown hair stormed through the entryway.

Mr. Reynolds.

His towering stature was once a great comfort to me…back when he didn't want to use it to snap me in half. So long as he was near, I always felt protected. The very sight of him, of the man I used to call 'Papa Bear,' now only made me nauseous.

"What the hell is this?" he demanded, slamming the door behind him so hard the glass inside it rattled. "Humans can't know about what we are. We are not allowed to take them!"

"No, *you're* not," remarked one of the men holding Carly. "You Reapers may have your own set of rules, but we, on the other hand, don't. Hence, why Samael hired us. We do the dirty work you precious little kiss-asses refuse to. Besides, if you didn't want us involving the human, why didn't you let us take the boy?"

I caught a glimpse of the group in the mirror, and realized they had black covering their eyes. Demons.

"Because I said so." An unfamiliar voice came from the entrance, but my breath caught at the all-too familiar figure that entered the room.

Reese.

I was ready to lunge forward when my brain finally processed the image more clearly.

No, not Reese.

If not for this man's matured facial features, French cut goatee, and additional twenty pounds of pure muscle to his physique, the resemblance between Reese and him was eerily remarkable. It was more than familial. It was damn near identical, down to the same almond-shaped amber eyes, cleft chin, and warm coffee-brown hair.

"What the hell?" Blaine's voice whispered to my thoughts.

I shook my head, as if it would make the image go away. It didn't.

"I've already made a deal with Gabriel. So long as he holds up his end of the bargain, the angel's son remains off-limits," declared Mr. Reynolds. "Is that clear?"

The demons rolled their eyes, but nevertheless muttered their compliance.

"What do we do with her?" Syringe asked, gesturing to Carly.

"Did you at least grab Blackburn's phone?" asked Reynolds. One of the demons nodded. "Then the plan goes as scheduled. Call her. We'll give Kat enough time to come back to town. Let her crawl out from whatever rock she's hiding under with that bastard. Tell her you'll text the address of where we'll meet up later in the evening. At nine o'clock, we'll make the exchange. The coven should be here by then. If Kat wants her friend to survive the night, she'll turn herself over to us."

Coven? An all new dread seeped its way into my bones. Why would Reynolds of all people need witches?

"And in the meantime?" One of the demons stroked a hand down Carly's arm, and she blindly threw her elbow into him. He returned the favor with a strike against her cheek. Unable to maintain her balance in her towering heels, the force of his backhand sent her to the ground.

"Put her in storage."

They obliged, not even bothering to pull her back up to her feet as they dragged her away down another hall. Another one of the demons pulled out a cell from his pocket, and I immediately recognized the red case. It was Reese's. He scrolled through the contacts, reading off the names, none of which were mine. But one stood out amongst the rest.

"Who has he talked with the most?" asked Reynolds.

"Some girl named Leia."

Of all things, I bit back a smile, and Blaine just rolled his eyes.

"Seriously? That's why he calls you Princess?"

I would have shoved him, but I wasn't about to risk giving away our position. I settled for a smirk. Blaine's eyes widen in horror as he seemed to realize something I hadn't. He frantically dug through his pockets, pulling out what I realized was *my* cell. The jackass had it this whole time?

He hit the volume key, making sure it was turned down, but that didn't stop the automatic setting from still letting out a low *moo* as it switched into vibration mode as it began ringing. The three of us may have been out of sight, but that didn't stop the lobby from sharing in a collective set of *clicks*. Everyone had just checked the magazines in their guns.

Crap.

"Time to go."

I prepared to bolt when Blaine grabbed my arm.

"Keep low."

The three of us took off through the display areas. The building wrapped around, ensuring that we never had our backs openly exposed. I did as Blaine ordered, hearing the volley of gunfire ringing out behind us. Val didn't miss the opportunity to return the favor, relinquishing as many rounds as he could amid our escape route. Glass exploded all around us as display cases and windows were shot out, and stuffing filled the space as bullets tore through all the various taxidermied animals.

The back door came in sight when the percussive torrent of a machine pistol annihilated the wall ahead. I barely managed to twist the knob of the door beside me, ushering everyone in before the shooter's aim locked on us. Blaine and I took one look at each other and swept our hands backward. The exhibit cabinet on the other side of the room hurtled across the open space and slammed against the door, barricading it shut.

"Go!" Val ordered, motioning to the window. He drew out another pistol, ready for battle as he reloaded.

"Don't be stupid!" Blaine grabbed him, trying to haul him away from the door, but his brother shoved him off.

"I'm staying."

"What the hell are you doing?"

Val muttered something I couldn't hear over the commotion outside the door. I'd never seen true anger from the Dark Mage, but the wrath stirring in his eyes was enough to turn my blood cold.

"What?"

"The one in charge," Val roared. "He killed Danika!"

Blaine froze.

"He killed Dani."

Blaine shook his head. "This is suicide! There's a dozen men out there, armed to the teeth. What chance do you honestly think you'll have of getting to Reynolds before they gun you down?"

Bullets tore through the cabinet before weight slammed against the door from the other side. Blaine finally managed to yank Val away as they met me at the window. I finally looked outside, finding that we were on the hillside of the cabin with nothing but a fifteen-foot drop awaiting us below. The only promise was the thick pile of leaves at the bottom. Blaine yanked the window open and helped me as I pulled my legs through first, feeding myself out of the window. I let go and fell into the earth, but I did not stop.

My body landed on the leaves, only to feel the ground give out as warped boards shattered beneath me. Splintered bits of wood and dead foliage rained down on me as I slammed into a cement floor.

"Kat!"

I tried to call out to say I was okay, but my lungs disagreed. I'd knocked the wind right out of me.

Muffled moans sounded somewhere beside me, and I rolled over in panic, seeing that I had fallen through the opening of some kind of storage cellar. A figured sat curled on the cool basement floor beside me, and I could faintly make out her long blonde hair in the dim light. Carly. Rasping for breath, I crawled over to her, prying the tape and gag from her mouth. Garden shears lay in the corner, and I snatched them up, slicing through her other binds. She yanked the heels off her feet, preparing to run. Carly froze though as she removed her blindfold, looking up at the hole I'd made in my fall.

A dark figure lurked over the hole, peering down at us.

"Awww, lookie who I found," Syringe chuckled, prying open the storm shelter door despite its stiff hinges. Light poured in from above, revealing a short set of stairs going into the cellar below the hole I'd created. The Reaper whistled out, clearly signaling his buddies, as he fixed his gun on us. "Ready to meet your maker?"

"Are you?" I threw my hands up, and the revolver was ripped out of his hold. I thrust my palms forward, watching the Reaper launch backward out of the entryway, airborne. I grabbed Carly, and despite the pain tearing through my lungs, I guided her up the stairs. Syringe was lying in a heap at the bottom of the hillside, amid a collection of tree trunks, and he wasn't moving.

"Don't shoot the Prince!" barked Reynolds somewhere above us. "We still need him alive!"

Glass shattered, and two bodies crashed into the grass ahead of Carly and me.

"Ladies," Val greeted as Blaine and he pulled themselves up to their feet. Blaine hobbled on what I could only assume was a sprained ankle, and I secured an arm around him as we took off towards the closest hiking path. It didn't take long for Reynolds's men to catch up.

A Reaper charged at Blaine, ripping him clean out of my hold. The young Mage drove his elbow into the man's ribcage before throwing a brutal knuckle into his jaw. The Reaper hit the ground, but swept his legs at Blaine's ankles, forcing him down as well. The Mage's reaction was instantaneous. Blaine threw a sharp elbow into the Reaper's nose, knocking him out cold. His friend arrived a moment later and rushed at us before the Prince could recover to his feet. Val gladly engaged him, but I wound up having to tackle the next Reaper that arrived. Considering I only weighed about one-ten on a good day, I didn't offer much of a fight as I locked my arms around his neck. It wasn't like I had much of a choice, seeing as how the Reaper seemed hell-bent on shooting Val. Unlike Blaine and me, he apparently was open season in the 'killing' department. I wrenched the Reaper in every direction as I struggled to cling to his back.

He heaved himself forward, almost throwing me clean off. I clutched his neck as tightly as I could, doing everything possible to prevent the man from centering his aim at Val. Desperate, I unlocked my grip, only to dig my fingers into his face. I could feel his skin ripping off as it collected underneath my acrylic nails. The scratches stretched from his cheeks up to his eyebrows, cutting into the Reaper's eyelids. The man hurled his weight forward, and without my grip on him, I was thrown off his back. The Reaper blinked furiously, trying to see as his eyes teared with blood. Now lying in front of him, I leveled my foot into his groin, and he dropped instantly to his knees. I jammed the butt of his gun into his nose for good measure.

"Is it wrong that I'm totally turned on right now?"

I looked over my shoulder, finding Blaine ogling me with that devil-may-care grin. Of all things, I laughed, feeling an adrenaline rush that left my entire body buzzing. And it only heightened as more men approached. Two Reapers grabbed a hold of me as another advanced with a syringe. Blaine's takedown moves definitely came in handy, letting me throw the first to the ground before I nailed the other in the sternum. When the third tried to strike me with the needle, Blaine's own instincts seemed to take over, because my body acted on its own accord. I grabbed his arm, twisting it at just the right angle that I heard a sickening pop as I ripped his shoulder out of its socket. My hand chopped the Reaper in the neck and he hit the dirt instantly. Reynolds's other men weren't fairing much better. One of them made a grab at Carly and immediately incurred Val's wrath as he sent the Reaper toppling off the overlook into the ravine below.

That luck seemed to run out though as twenty-plus men raced down the hillside towards us.

"Get Carly back to the car!" Blaine ordered his brother.

"What about you?"

"I've got an idea."

Val and Car raced off the path, disappearing into the brush.

"You don't actually have a plan, do you?" I panted, following after Blaine as we darted down the other way, off the trail.

"Apart from getting their attention away from my brother and your friend? Not really, no."

The confession should have been disconcerting, but the adrenaline seemed to drown out any rational fear the harder we pushed ourselves. Our shoes kept sinking into the muck as we battled our way through the wetlands. In spite of the inhospitable trails, Oakland Leap happened to be quite the welcomed sight the moment we fell out of the brush and onto a paved trail. Rakkin River, which divided the park, rested below as we raced over the wooden bridge.

The scenery was stunning, but not overly helpful. Despite the wintry months, a lot of the trees still had leaves, given that the park was mostly made up of evergreens and pines. It was next to impossible to see anything on the other side of the river. To make matters worse, the sky was now painted in amaranth amid the overcast as the light of day sank behind the treetops. If Reynolds's men had machine pistols, it stood to reason that they'd probably have night vision as well, leaving us at a distinct disadvantage.

"Over there!" a voice called out.

Quickening footsteps trampled across the floorboards as several Reapers raced over the bridge after us. I yanked Blaine to our left once we reached the other side of the river. The trail winded about the waterfront, and we didn't dare steal a look behind us as we ran without objective. My feet pounded into the earth so hard it made my feet burn. Something rumbled up ahead, accompanied by a loud horn. A truck! Through the masses of evergreens obstructing our view, the vague outline of a bridge—a *real* bridge—rested ahead. It was only about a quarter mile away, and with our speed, we reached it in under a minute. Although, the road wasn't even with the path, forcing us to slog up the narrow, uneven steps of concrete that led up to the bridge.

Something rang out behind us, and Blaine turned around, only to throw me to the ground as gunfire hammered into the guardrails. Either they were ignoring Mr. Reynolds's orders, or they safely assumed we were harder to kill than initially credited for, because Reapers were shooting at us from below like we were bull's-eyes at a firing range. To our horror, there wasn't any traffic heading towards us in either direction, until...

Two SUVs came barreling down the road, screeching to a halt not twenty feet from us. Reynolds, along with five other Reapers exited the vehicles.

"Surrender now, or my men will put silver into every

last one of your limbs," the Alpha declared.

The roar of straight pipes sounded behind us, bringing this holdup to an abrupt end. We all knew they couldn't risk being seen by pedestrians. Blaine grabbed me, readying to yank me behind him, but I threw him back.

"Kat, don't—"

The energy inside me soared to its crescendo as my fists balled up at my sides. Every last weapon was wrenched to the ground.

"Stop!" Blaine ordered behind me. I didn't need to turn to know he wasn't talking to me anymore. The guttural crackling of the motorcycle came down the stretch, slowing to a halt right beside us, just as the Mage had commanded.

Reynolds stepped forward, and my Omen rune burned brighter as he fetched out a hunting knife from his back pocket. His gaze wasn't fixed on me. It was on the Mage behind me. So much for rules... My curled hands only tightened, and a chorus of gasps and curses followed as the gravel on the roadside suddenly levitated, along with the rocks off the riverbank.

Nathan froze, seeing my arms shaking from the surge of power as I raised them up. His fingers settled on the hilt of the blade, but I didn't give him the chance to throw it. The second he brought up his arm, I slammed my hands together in front of me. Every last stone hurled at the SUVs. The men barely had time to drop to the pavement as glass shattered and the paint was stripped off the vehicles. Debris slashed through the tires, and with a wave of my hands, the Reaper's guns disappeared into the water below. I focused my energy at the discarded knife by Reynolds's head as he cowered on the pavement, but nothing happened. The runes on my arm petered out, and my legs suddenly felt shaky beneath me.

"Sorry, but we need to borrow your bike," Blaine declared. "Get off."

I turned to see the biker beside us do as he was told, and the Prince swung his leg over, gesturing me aboard.

"You didn't see this," Blaine whispered to the man.

"See what?" the biker muttered numbly.

"Exactly."

I got on behind Blaine, wrapping my arms around him. My thighs tightened around his as the motorcycle lurched before we tore off down the road.

Echo

The cool breeze batted my face as I slumped against the warmth of Blaine's body, feeling the muscles work in his stomach with every turn and bend in the road. Fatigue worked its way over my eyes, and the lethargy threatened to pull me under. A hand settled over mine, squeezing my fingers ever so slightly.

"Don't fall asleep on me, love," Blaine's voice ordered to my thoughts.

I forced my eyes back open, but couldn't seem to concentrate on any of the scenery until we rumbled our way up to the familiar gates.

"No, everything's fine," he said, turning off the engine. I hadn't even realized Blaine was talking on the phone. "Yeah, I'll call you a little later. Okay... Bye."

I tried to get off the bike and wound up stumbling to the ground.

Blaine caught me before I face-planted into the asphalt. "Hey."

He held my arms, steadying me in his hold. Before I could lift my gaze to him, his lips met mine. I wanted to pull away, but it felt so good. Warmth spread into my limbs, and the relief was immediate. It was like a shot of epinephrine, jolting me awake instantly.

Blaine pulled away, taking the sensation with him. "Feel better?"

I staggered back a step. Not out of exhaustion, but pure confusion. "What the hell was that?"

"I transferred some of my energy to you." Before I could respond, he simply turned and trotted up to the front porch like it was nothing, disappearing inside the darkened foyer of Haven Crest Manor.

Trying to get my head straight, I followed after him, noting that my legs were no longer weak. He'd offered more than just 'some' of his energy.

"Close the door," Blaine ordered, seeing me lingering in the entryway.

I did as he commanded, putting the lock into place as he disappeared down the corridor. Blaine returned a moment later with a bottle of Johnnie Walker in hand. He shrugged off his jacket and haphazardly tossed it at the chair in the corner before unbuttoning his shirt.

I could only imagine I looked like a deer caught in headlights as I openly gawked at the sight. "Uh...what are you doing?"

"Taking my clothes off."

"I can see that. *Why?*"

"Well, in my experience, I find it makes things simpler when they're not in the way."

"Excuse me?" My eyes practically bulged out of my

head, watching him unscrew the bottle of whisky and take more than a healthy swig.

Who the hell did this guy think he was?

Sure, he saved my ass back there, but that didn't mean I was obligated to give him sex in return! And by his continual alcohol intake, it wasn't exactly flattering that he apparently needed to be drunk off his ass to be with me.

Blaine merely cocked a brow. "Can you come over here? I can't do this by myself."

"What?"

"Well, I mean, I *can*," he shrugged, "but it'd be a hell of a lot better if you helped."

"You can't be serious." I whirled around, ready to storm upstairs.

"What? You afraid of a little blood?"

"Am I...what?" I turned back around and outright gasped as Blaine shrugged off his unbuttoned shirt. "Oh my God!"

Blood stained the length of the outside of his chest, coming from the inflamed circular hole in his shoulder.

"You were *shot*?"

"Yeeeeeah." His featured twisted further in confusion, and I knew immediately when it had happened. He'd thrown me to the pavement on the bridge just as they started shooting at us. "What did you think I was talking about?"

"Uh...nothing."

Understanding must have settled in, because he smirked. "Give me a hand, please."

"Aren't you just going to self-heal?"

"It's not that easy. The bullet didn't exit, which means—"

"The wound will heal around it if you don't get it out."

I cursed under my breath.

"The damn thing hurts like a Mother as it is. I don't want it stuck in there." Blaine dragged out a large camping sack from the floor of the coat closet and began rummaging inside it. "We have to be quick about this."

He pulled out a nylon rollout bag armed with various knives and headed into the bathroom, taking a seat on the ledge of the counter. Blaine grimaced, dousing the wound with whisky, before he plucked out a long, thin blade from his cutlery collection.

I hesitantly stepped into the doorway, but immediately recoiled as he held out the handle of the knife to me.

"Ready?"

"What? No!"

He groaned. "You said you'd help."

"No, I didn't!" I clarified. "And you said 'help.' This isn't helping; this is waaaay beyond that."

"Well, the bullet's stuck in my right shoulder, and it's impinging it. I can't raise my hand up high enough, which is a problem since it's my dominant side. I'd rather not do this with my weaker hand."

Bile threatened to rise in my throat as I looked between the blade and the wound. I nearly threw up in Bio once when we had to dissect a squid.

"Then don't think of me as a squid," he gnashed, clearly able to hear my thoughts. "And I certainly don't want you dissecting me either. I just want the bullet out. And it doesn't have to be pretty."

I wanted to help, but I didn't think me retching would be helping him any.

"You ever play Operation as a kid?"

"Yeah."

"Well, think of it just like that. But instead of a heavy-set naked guy with a red light bulb nose, it'll be a devilishly handsome scoundrel with a six-pack."

I glared at him.

"I'll strip all the way down, too, if that'll help."

"It won't," I gritted.

"Please. If I don't get it out now, I'm gonna have to stab myself open later after I've healed. I'm already in agony, and I really don't want to go through this all over again. I trust you." He peered at me with pleading eyes, and I wanted to kick myself for what I was about to say.

That 'trusting' sentiment quickly dissolved as his teeth grinded into the towel Blaine had lodged into his mouth to muffle his screams. It'd been ten minutes, and I still couldn't recover the bullet.

He finally yanked the cloth from his mouth with a laborious gasp as I pushed the knife deeper into the wound. "You're a bloody butcher!"

"Well, I'm sorry, but it's not like I'm digging around in here for fun," I snapped, still trying my best to hold down the contents of my stomach.

He gave a pitiful groan. "I'd take Leatherface over you right about now."

"Hey, if you want me to take a chainsaw to you, just say the word. I'd be more than happy to at this point."

"You don't see it at all?"

"No, and it's getting harder for me to move around in there."

"Shit. The wound's closing up." Blaine slumped sideways against the wall, the empty whisky bottle dangling from his fingertips. The new position gave me a clear view of his back in the mirror, and I groaned at the sight. "Do I even want to know?"

"I think I found your bullet..."

He cocked his head up at me, following my line of vision behind him. "You've gotta be kidding me."

One look in the mirror, and the circular bump protruding under the skin on his upper back was unmistakable.

I wasn't sure if his accelerated healing pushed the bullet all the way through to the other side or if perhaps I had during my excavation, but I nevertheless apologized.

Blaine wasted no time dousing the back of his shoulder before snatching up a larger knife. In one swift motion, he pressed the blade to his skin and completely swiped away the portion covering the bullet head. Blood immediately gushed from the wound, and I raced toward the toilet, ready to gag.

"You okay to do this?" he called out.

To hurl? Yes.

I tried composing myself again as I resurfaced to the counter. "What do you need me to do?"

"Pull the bullet out."

"How?"

"Just use the knives like chopsticks. Get a hold of the bullet on each side and pry it out as far as you can. Then just dig it out with your fingers."

Yeah, that was all. No biggie...

He turned around in front of the counter so that he was faced away from me, and I shuddered at all the blood trickling down his back. Uselessly trying to clean up the mess with masses of tissues, I finally found the bullet beneath all the profuse carnage. To my surprise and utter relief, the bullet eased right out that I didn't even need to use my fingers...thank God. The bullet clanged onto the floor, and I had to use hand towels to help soak up the blood pooling down his back. Between the bullet wound and the carved up flesh, I had to fetch more.

"Who's Danika?" I asked upon returning.

Blaine grimaced as I pressed the fresh towel to his back. "It's complicated."

"I'm sure I can keep up."

He didn't say anything at first, keeping his gaze fixed on the floor.

"Was she Val's girlfriend, or something?"

"Or something." Blaine gave a grievous sigh, resigning himself to the situation. "Dani was his fiancée and high school sweetheart."

"And Mr. Reynolds...he killed her?"

"Evidently."

"But Val said he never had a mate—"

"She wasn't his mate, but he loved her. And she was a human."

"Then why would Nathan kill her?"

"Reapers see themselves as a necessary evil. They do whatever they have to in order to stay five steps ahead of Hell. But you have to ask yourself, if you forfeit your own humanity in order to combat them, are you really any better than those you're fighting against?"

I could tell it was a question he'd ask himself more than once, seeing the muscles work in his jaw. And the knot in my stomach only grew.

"A couple years back," he said, taking another brief pause, "some Reapers found out my brother was the next Crown Prince. They ambushed him at his house, not realizing he wasn't alone. Dani had already been waiting for him inside for when he got off work. By all accounts, everybody assumed she didn't know what he was, because she appeared to be human. But when she tried to intervene, the Reapers there discovered she was allergic to the silver they were using on Val to take him away."

"So she *wasn't* human?"

"She was. What most Reapers don't know is that human women develop our demonic weaknesses when they're pregnant with our children."

I dropped the bloodied rags in my hands.

"She'd just found out the week prior, but they didn't believe her. From a Reaper's standpoint, the best case scenario was that she was demonic *and* lying about the pregnancy. Or the worse case: she was still something demonic and carrying the child of a Dark Prince. Either way, she was a threat." Sadness flickered in those pale eyes. "I wasn't lying when I said Dark Mages could turn off their emotions. Val managed to escape, but he was too late to save Danika. After that, he couldn't cope with it— any of it. He did the only thing he could think of. Now, he prides himself on being a high-functioning sociopath. The only feeling he claims to experience is the thrill that comes from hurting others, and that's his only real motivation, to tear down the people who hurt him, no matter the cost."

"That's not true. I mean, he definitely enjoys tormenting other people, but he wouldn't have reacted like that when he saw Reynolds if he didn't *truly* care."

"Just don't tell that to Val. He doesn't like being accused of having sentiment."

"He does realize that if he *didn't* care, it wouldn't bother him if we suggested it, right?"

Blaine laughed quietly. "What can I say? My brother's a stubborn son of a bitch."

"I think that's a familial trait."

His eyes lifted, finding mine in the mirror.

"You have a nasty habit of taking bullets for me," I clarified, pressing another fresh towel to his back. "Thank you, for both times. But I am curious, why didn't you just use that invisible shield you created when Donovan tried shooting you?"

"That was kind of a freak accident. I'd only ever made it that one time. And with you, I guess I panicked. I wasn't about to risk your life trying to make the shield again, so I did the only thing I could think of."

"The blood's beginning to clot." I grabbed the bandages Blaine had handy in his first-aid kit. Though, I really wouldn't call it that. It was more of a miniature hospital, chalk full of gauze, shears, scalpels (which probably would've been more useful in recovering the bullet), along with antiseptic wipes, pads, and even a suture kit. Thankfully, I wouldn't have to sew, seeing as how the wound was already healing. Given the amount of energy we'd both used, I suspected it was going to take him a little longer than usual.

"Given any thought on what you're going to say to Blackburn?"

"As far as…?"

"You don't find it the least bit odd that his father, an *angel*, just so happens to be involved with the very people who want you dead?"

"No, I don't," I said flatly, shooting him a dark look. "And I'm not doubting each and every last one of the points you brought up in the limousine ride either, because I'm a gullible idiot."

My anger flared as I pressed a fresh bandage to Blaine's back, and he cringed. My runes still hummed lowly, but they thankfully didn't have enough power to do any serious damage. It still probably hurt like hell though, making me grimace.

"Sorry," I lamented, taking better care this time as I secured the bandage down with tape. "I just want this to be over, you know; I want to go back to being normal."

"No, you don't."

My TLC suddenly came in short supply as I slapped the last of the adhesive tape around the wound. *"Excuse me?"*

"I'm not saying you don't *think* you want that, but deep down, you really don't." There was no hint of amusement in his voice. He firmly believed that.

I threw the discarded wrappers into the garbage and prepared to storm out of the bathroom when Blaine's hand caught my wrist, hauling me back to him.

"Don't," I warned.

"I heard you, in the darkness..."

All the rage inside me vanished, replaced by panic.

"...When Reynolds's men took you." His fingers were suddenly tracing the base of my back, and I shuddered at the goose bumps left in their wake, feeling the enthralling sensation cascade all the way up to my neck. "You couldn't hear me, but I could still hear you, ever so faintly. You called to me, pleaded with me to find you."

Tears pricked behind my eyes at the very mention, at the reminder of how utterly pathetic I had been against Nathan's men. I had never felt so weak, so *helpless* in my entire life.

Both his hands tightened on me. "You are not weak," he whispered. "Don't ever believe that. Everything you need is already inside you, Kat. You just need to stop fighting it. Allow the energy to become a part of you."

I couldn't even open my mouth to speak, struggling to hold back the tears threatening to spill out over my lashes.

I can't.

"All you've asked for—all you've *begged* for—these past two months is to be normal again, and you got your wish that night. No power, no discernible hint of our bond. But it didn't give you freedom." His breath stirred my hair as he drew me closer. "All you wanted in those moments was to have it back."

I couldn't move. Couldn't breathe.

Because he was right.

"As much as you claim to hate the darkness in you, you secretly revel in it." The inexpressible warmth in his voice was like sinking into a hot bath. It eased into my bones, my muscles, offering me the sweetest relief. "I felt that primal thrill rise inside you when you sensed I was coming. That darkness you hate, the thrum of it coursing through your veins, it's not evil. It's an extension of you. And you felt that tonight. The moment you stop resisting your true nature, it'll stop lashing out against you to break free. Let it become a part of you."

"And what will I become?"

"What you were always meant to be: a fighter."

29
MERCY

I 'm sorry, you want to do what now?" Dr. Madsen didn't seem overly keen on my proposed plan, but it wasn't like we had much of a choice.

"The Sagax agreed to meet up with us, but since she's technically angelic, she isn't allowed to be seen by any humans. And she refused to meet us anywhere outside, because she doesn't feel it's secure," I said, having to speak louder over the static interfering with the phone call. "And there's no way in hell anyone is going to want to invite her inside their house. Can you think of somewhere we could go?"

"*I still don't understand why you would wish to summon her. Taking up company with creatures like the Sagax isn't something to trifle with —*"

"It's complicated." I looked to Blaine who merely

nodded. "I just want to know if there's anything I should be aware of before I talk with her. Is there, like, some kind of protocol?"

"For every question you ask, she's allowed to ask you one in return, and you have to answer it…" A heavy sigh. *"I don't like this, Kat."*

"I know, but I need answers."

"Well, you're not meeting her alone. How about you invite the Sagax to the University? The dorms just closed for Winter Break, so nobody will be at the library. You can come meet me at the study room where we convened last time."

"You mean when you pointed a gun at me?" I jabbed, half-laughing at the flabbergasted expression Blaine shot in my direction.

"You are joking?" he mouthed.

I shook my head.

"How's seven o'clock sound?" asked Madsen.

"We'll be there."

Blaine slowed down to a stop on the side street next to the college, pulling out a pair of binoculars from his bag in the backseat. Holding them up and adjusting them accordingly, he shook his head. "I don't like this."

"What's wrong?"

"The security cameras aren't on."

"So? Everybody's gone. The security staff probably shut them down. Or maybe Madsen did. Maybe the Sagax can't risk being caught on tape." I hit the redial on my phone, only to meet the same voice messages. No one was picking up. Not Reese, not Madsen, not Val, not Mark or Carly.

He cut the engine to the Cutlass and placed a spare key

in my hand. I turned it over, realizing it was for the car. "If something happens in there, promise me you will run. Promise me you won't stop, for *anything*. If things go sideways, you leave, with or without me. Understand?"

"Blaine—"

"Do you understand?"

"...Yes."

"Okay."

We climbed out and locked the doors behind us, slinking through the shadows until reaching the side of the building. Blaine peered around the bend, motioning me forward. It was like *The Town That Dreaded Sundown*. There wasn't a single car on the street or in the nearby lot, and not a single soul could be seen down the long stretches of sidewalks. We snuck up to the front entrance and tried each of the doors. Thankfully, the left one pulled open. Neither of our Omen runes was glowing, but that didn't stop Blaine from taking some precautionary measures. He shut the door behind us and fastened the lock on top.

"Stay behind me," he whispered, heading into the foyer.

Our eyes shifted across the entire place, still not seeing another soul in sight. I pointed to the map on the wall, indicating where the library was stationed. He nodded. We darted into the closest corridor, creeping alongside the wall as we moved further along. Without the sunlight gleaming in from the windows, the dimly lit halls cast shadows across half of the space. The cold breathed its ways through the glass, and the icy winds batted into the panes, causing the windows to creak. I couldn't discern a single thing from the darkness outside, leaving me with the aching suspicion that someone could be watching us.

We navigated our way through the maze of corridors,

eventually reaching the dining hall. Blaine held up his hand, signaling me to stay put. He headed out into the commons with knives gripped in both hands. A *thump!* echoed from an adjoining hall, sounding like a heavy door closing.

"Go," mouthed Blaine, shooting his glance up the nearest staircase.

I scampered across the room and darted up as he followed behind me. He shoved me against the wall as footsteps reached the commons from the ground floor. We peeked around the bend to see a young husky guy sporting a university sweatshirt saunter through the dining hall with a gym bag slung over his shoulder. Blaine turned the corner to meet me and rested his back against the wall as well, letting out a much needed sigh. He didn't waste another second after that. Hustling through the next three corridors, we finally reached the library.

Towering oak bookshelves greeted us as Blaine pried open one of the dual ornate bronzed doors, the hinges squeaking shrilly across the vast open space. The library was sparsely lit, the cathedral vaulted ceilings not even visible overhead in the darkness as we headed in deeper. I looked behind me, seeing the entrance shrinking in the distance. With each step, the harder the pang in my gut hit me. Nothing felt right, and Blaine sensed it all too well. Still, our Omen runes weren't igniting.

"About time."

I shrieked, whirling around to my right. Mark and Carly were seated at the set tables just off to the side of the private study room. Blaine's shoulders finally slackened, spotting his brother pacing in the specified doorway.

"Cutting it close, eh?" Val gestured to the askew face of a large antique clock at the end of a bookcase in the distance. It was only a couple minutes to seven. "The doctor with you?"

"Madsen?" I shook my head. "He isn't here?"

"No, and we're gonna have to close up shop," said Reese, emerging from the study room. "The Sagax won't show if Mark and Carly can see inside."

The pair was sitting far enough away that it shouldn't have been a problem, but we pulled the shades to be safe.

"Give a holler if you hear anything, okay?" said Val.

Mark gave a thumbs-up while Carly just rolled her eyes, feigning annoyance. Her heel was tapping nervously against the carpet, a sign that she was still far too rattled from earlier.

Reese's cell sounded off a moment later, officially declaring it to be seven o'clock. With no sign of Madsen, we had to draw the door closed.

"Hey, Princess." Those boyish dimples lit up Reese's face the moment he came to me, and the sight, the nickname, all of it—it felt like a sucker punch to the gut. Thankfully, the dimples disappeared as he scowled, spotting who was behind me. Then his gaze fell to my clothes, to the blood still tarnishing me. I hadn't even realized it was all over the bottom of my shirt. "Jesus, Kat! What happened? Are you hurt?"

Reese raced around the table, and panic replaced his glare as he grabbed me, looking for any sign of an injury. When he couldn't find anything, his hands cupped my face, and I couldn't fight the tears as I pulled away from him.

"Kat? What's wrong?"

"You guys having any problems with your phones?" Val asked.

"Yeah, my calls keep dropping out, and hers won't even go through," said Blaine. "We'd been trying to get a hold you, but you weren't answering."

"Mind telling us why we're here?"

Neither of us had any intention of answering, but it didn't matter. Black mist filled the corner of the room, and an all-too creepy figure emerged from the billowing cloud. The pale woman had opted to abandon her previously pallid dress for a black gown as inky as her bone straight hair. The Sagax was only a couple inches taller than me and definitively thinner, yet her unnatural presence even spooked the likes of Val as instinct sent both him and Reese recoiling at the sight of her.

"A truth for a truth, my darling." Her pale green eyes immediately locked on me, and she strode forward. The Sagax's attention however cut to the young man standing beside me. "You brought your mate, I see."

She took her time examining Blaine, and he angled himself in such a way that he placed himself between the Sagax and me, clearly not trusting the individual who stood before us. The woman smiled, or at least appeared to. Her pale lips merely stretched, baring a glimpse of startling white teeth.

Val grimaced, trying to mask his repulsion. "If looks could kill," he mouthed.

"Why have you summoned me, royal girl?" the Sagax cooed. She took one look at me, and immediately spotted me stealing a glance over towards Reese. "Ah-ha, you wish to know the truth regarding your beloved."

Reese stiffened. "Wait, *what*?"

"How long have you known?" My mind replayed every

moment we'd shared, and I had to bite back a sob. "How long have you known about me? About what I am?"

Reese shook his head, confused, and Blaine cut him off before he even had a chance to speak, handing over his cell. "I'd choose my words very carefully if I were you."

Reese looked at the screen, and any hope I had vanished as he paled. It wasn't shock, or surprise, or even confusion on his face as he looked at the image of his father. It was guilt.

I staggered back, feeling something deep within me snap.

He knew.

"So what then? Did your father order you to spy on me?" Reese tried to step closer, but I shoved him back. "Is that why you suddenly wanted to be around me? Was all of this just some sick game for you?"

"What? No!" He was shaking his head again. "It wasn't like that."

"Then tell me what it's like, Reese!"

"Kat…" His gaze kept drifting around the room, at the audience all gawping at us. "Can we talk about this, alone? *Please.*"

"No, I want the truth, now."

"It's not that simple—"

"Did you know who I was when we first met?"

"What? No."

"When did you find out?"

Reese looked over at the woman, and she simply gestured towards me. He had to answer. "Right…right after I left the theater." He had told me later that demons attacked him, and it didn't take a bond for him to know where my thoughts had gone. "I didn't lie about what happened. It's just… I was ambushed. I wasn't strong enough at the time to defend myself against an entire pack of demons. They were about to haul me away when my old man showed up. He ran out on my mom a week after I was born, so it was the first time I'd ever seen him that I could remember."

"What did he tell you about Kat?" Blaine demanded.

"He said I needed to stay away from her." Reese swallowed hard. "He claimed that she already knew what she was, and that all she would be was trouble. Demons were planning on using her for something, and the ones who had showed up outside the theater were there for her, to keep an eye out on her. He wouldn't tell me what they wanted with Kat, but he said that if I interfered, they'd come after me...after my mom. It was why he abandoned us all those years ago."

"What do you mean?"

"Right after I was born, an old friend of my father's tipped him off. There was a bounty on his head for something that he had meddled in, and if the people who were after him learned about my mom and me, they'd use us against him. So he did the only thing he could. He ran, to protect us."

"But I didn't know what I was!" I cried.

"And I only figured that out after you were killed in the accident." Reese's glare cut to Blaine. "Or should I say 'car crash,' seeing how it wasn't very accidental?"

"Don't push it," the Dark Mage warned. Bitterness poured off him, engulfing my senses as Blaine tried to wrangle in his own anger.

I shook my head, demanding myself to refocus. "Did you give me up to Reynolds? Or was that your father?"

Reese froze, and that guilt immediately vanished, replaced by utter indignation. "You honestly think I would do that to you?" I didn't amend my accusation, only further inciting his ire. "No, I didn't tell anybody *anything* about you. Ever. Not my old man, and certainly not that piece of shit."

"I don't believe him," Blaine growled.

I couldn't ignore that Reese's nickname for me happened to be exactly what I was about to become, I didn't know how Reynolds's men tracked me down, and I now knew that his father was somehow involved with the very people who wanted me dead. But against all better judgment...I did. I still believed him.

I looked to the Sagax, and she nodded. Relief and guilt simultaneously crashed into me. Reese was telling the truth.

The woman strolled over to him, seeming to appreciate his face. "You do look an awful lot like your father." Her hand brushed his own for an instant, but it was enough to startle him. "Oh, how history repeats itself. Though I do believe it will end quite differently."

He recoiled from her, defensive. "What is that supposed to mean?"

"You Uriel men certainly seem to have a penchant for the women of the Ravyn bloodline. Unlike her mother however," the Sagax gestured to me, "*she* reciprocates your affection. Something Katalin never granted your father. You may be hurt by your beloved's misgiving, child, but do not doubt her love. For what she has endured, it would be foolish of her to not be guarded. She cares just as much for you as you do her."

Reese returned my gaze, and although his hurt was still evident, understanding filled those amber eyes.

The Sagax's head tilted as her gaze drifted back to Blaine. "I cannot, however, say the same about you, Prince.

I saw many things in your mate's heart last time I touched her. Not only do you scare her, but she truly hates you."

Unable to swallow the lump in my throat, I inadvertently pulled my eyes from Reese to look at him.

That icy gaze was already locked on mine. Only, Blaine smirked. "Can't say I'm surprised."

The raven-haired woman clicked her tongue, and immediately, Blaine grimaced, looking like someone had just smacked him upside the head. The expression only worsened as he squeezed his eyes shut. What started as mild annoyance suddenly twisted into physical pain as Blaine's hands gripped the sides of his head. He bit back a scream, sinking to the floor. I wanted to make a move for him, but the Sagax's merciless gaze left me glued in place as she observed Blaine's agony in utter indifference.

"Lie."

It was only then that I realized what she really was. The Sagax didn't force you to speak the truth. She punished you for being dishonest.

"Why would that surprise you?" she asked flatly, peering down at the Prince.

Blaine didn't answer. I wasn't sure it was because he was afraid to, or if maybe the pain was so unbearable that he *couldn't*. By the veins bulging in his face and down the length of his neck as he panted, I suspected the latter.

The Sagax knelt down, stroking a finger beneath his chin. Blaine's entire body locked up with what I could only assume to be the same glacial sensation I'd experienced from her touch. He gasped, obviously wanting to pull away, but his body betrayed him, keeping him rooted to the spot. The Sagax's eyes rolled back into her head until only the whites showed. She sighed, her pale green irises returning mere seconds later. Blaine wheezed as he doubled over, trying to regain his bearings the moment she released him from her hold.

The Sagax studied him with the most peculiar expression, or at least as much as her limited features would allow. "She doesn't know, does she?"

When Blaine finally lifted his head, blood seeped from his nose. *What the hell had she done to him?*

"No," he spat.

"Why not?"

The Dark Prince's shoulders shook with quiet rage, but he didn't dare cross her again. "It wouldn't change anything."

The Sagax seemed to consider this.

But I wasn't having any of it. "What are you talking about?" I demanded.

She looked to Blaine, as if waiting for his consent. He only glared at her as he rose up from the floor. When it was made clear she would get no such thing, the Sagax continued, speaking on another subject I had no interest in hearing. I needed answers, and I would be getting them, even if I had to beat it out of someone.

Refusing to look at me, Blaine whirled around, heading right for the door. He shoved his weight into it, only to find it wouldn't open, despite the locks not being in place. Blaine shot the woman a murderous glare, and she apparently relented, because he shoved it open a second later, disappearing into the library.

Reese and Val called out after me, but I was already out the door, in hot pursuit.

"Blaine!" I was forced to run just to keep up with his long strides as he charged towards the exit. "What was that back there?"

He didn't so much as slow down, plowing right

through the doors into the hallway.

"Blaine! *Will you stop?*" I finally managed to reach him, snatching hold of his arm. Energy burned beneath his skin, and I realized I was touching his runes. Instantly, everything went black.

"Kat? You okay?" Blaine's voice echoed in my mind.

The darkness invading my vision slowly faded away, leaving me to observe the massive bonfire burning in the distance. Loud music blasted through the air, the heavy bass vibrating the ground beneath my feet. I whirled around, seeing all my old classmates.

"Whoa," he chuckled.

I spotted Blaine amongst the many partygoers, just as he caught...*me*.

Not ten feet away stood a seemingly drunk version of myself, now safely secured in Blaine's arms. My breath caught as I stumbled back.

The bonfire.

This was the night I died.

I'd gone inside Blaine's mind.

"You know, I've been hoping you'd show me some interest for awhile now, but I never imagined you'd *literally* throw yourself at me," he laughed uneasily, trying to steady me in his hold.

God, I couldn't even stand upright. What had he really done to me? Drugged me? Used magic of some kind?

"Kat?" The Prince deserved a freaking Oscar, because he appeared genuinely concerned as he brushed the hair away from my face. "How much have you had to drink?"

Vanessa and Carly howled something at the two of us,

but my attention redirected to Blaine's eyes. I followed his gaze, spotting Daniel who was leaning contentedly against a concessions table. Carly's ex cast him a shit-eating grin, tapping the watch on his wrist.

Blaine's spine immediately stiffened. "Hey, how about I take you home?" he whispered to me, reaffirming his hold around my body. "You don't look so hot."

Why was I seeing this?

I followed after Blaine as he directed the drunken version of me across the field to his car. Just as he helped me into the Mustang and fastened my seat belt, I heard it. Loud and clear.

"Kat!" It was a male voice. Unmistakable.

Reese.

I spun around. Blackburn's rust bucket pick-up truck stood out like a sore thumb amid the mass of luxury cars parked around the tree line of the open field. Reese leapt out from behind the wheel, the engine still running, and started pushing his way through the hoards of tipsy classmates.

Blaine closed the passenger door, his eyes frantically darting between Blackburn and Daniel. He looked...horrified. The Dark Mage hastened around the car to the driver's side as Reese barked out, "Ryder!"

But Reese wasn't fast enough. The Mustang roared as the car turned over, kicking up grass and dirt in its wake as it revved and drove off across the field.

"KAT!" Reese bellowed, clawing his hands through his hair. He doubled over, out of breath, watching in dread as Blaine's car disappeared after turning onto the nearby road. "Shit."

He knew what was about to happen. He'd seen the omen when I ran into him back at the gas station. He had tried to warn me, but I just thought he was crazy…

In an instant, the scenery vanished, replaced by the eerie quiet of some remote rural back road. The only light came from the crescent slice of moon resting overhead.

"You got the paperwork ready?" remarked a cool voice. Its owner tossed the remains of a lit cigarette to the ground, grinding it out beneath his boot heel as he pressed the phone back to his ear.

Val.

"And does it say specifically that it was 'decapitation'? That's very important." He appeared to like the answer on the other end of the call, because he grinned. "We need an ambulance and some squad cars. What's your E.T.A.?" The smirk turned baleful. "Terrific."

Tucking the phone back into his jacket, the black-clad Mage strode out into the street, affirming his place in the middle of the right lane just as a roaring engine hummed in the distance. The all too familiar Mustang raced around the deep bend, barreling right at the man. Tires squealed as the car suddenly wrenched sideways, narrowly dodging Val as it went into a tailspin. In an instant, the vehicle plowed into the boulder just off the road. The devastating impact sent debris hailing out all around me, and I shrieked as a jagged piece of metal went sailing right through my phantom figure.

Val whistled what sounded like "Don't Worry, Be Happy" as he casually sauntered down the road towards the wreckage. He plucked out his cell again as he peered into the passenger window…at my broken, bloodied body. Of all things, the Dark Mage snapped a picture. Of me, and then one of Blaine.

The pictures I'd been receiving weeks after the accident…

I couldn't breathe.

Val strolled around to the driver's side, finding the flashlight function on his phone to be useless. He plucked out an actual flashlight and sighed as it better illuminated the inside of the crushed interior. The Dark Mage unsheathed the massive blade holstered around his waist, studying Blaine's beaten body.

Using the butt of the sword, the ruffian smashed the window, letting out a hearty laugh. "'The thief comes only to steal and kill and destroy.'"

Val reached inside and unlatched the lock, prying the crumpled door open. Blaine barely managed to cough as his brother pried his limp body from out of the driver's seat. Val scowled, dropping him onto the pavement thoughtlessly as he noted the blood now staining the cuffs of his jacket.

"Come on, Prince Charming," he scoffed, giving Blaine a light smack on the cheek.

Blaine's eyelids fluttered as a small Sowilo healing rune glowed on the outside of his forearm. I had the same one, obviously, but had never ignited it before. He coughed again, this time with a little more relief.

"That's more like it." Val straightened up, wiping the blood from his hand. "Don't want to leave your mate waiting now, do we?"

Realization seemed to dawn on him, because Blaine's eyes flew open with a start. He painfully angled his head in horror over to the opened driver's door of the car. At me still inside. "Kat…"

"No."
"No."
"No."

He kept muttering the word as he tried scrambling up from the pavement. Resistance sent him back into the ground though, and he let out a stifled yelp. Considering the amount of blood soaking his entire body, it was safe to assume he had more than just a few broken ribs. His whole face was even masked in red. The pain didn't keep him down for long. Using the door for leverage, he managed to lift himself enough to stagger upright. The Mage gnashed his teeth the instant he stood. Limping on only one foot, he hobbled around the backend of the car towards the passenger side.

"Not so fast." His brother pressed his boot into Blaine's left ankle. It was already bowed at a grotesquely unnatural angle, and the pressure only snapped it further, sending the young man crumpling back to the ground in blinding pain. Val just shook his head with a bemused chuckle. "That's why I told you to turn it off. So long as you still have your emotions, pain will continue to be your greatest weakness."

"Why?" Blaine seethed. His entire body shuddered from unadulterated agony, but his eyes were bright and alert, ablaze with a murderous rage.

"Why?" Val mocked.

"I told you I was going to take care of it. You didn't need to hurt her!"

"Is that right?" His brother only smiled, kneeling down in front of him. He fetched out a small vial from his jacket pocket and dangled it in his face. "No worries. I already did 'it' for you. "

Blaine lunged forward, forcing Val to grind his foot

harder into his brother's twisted ankle until the boy aguishly fell back against the bumper of the ruined car. *"What did you do to her?"*

Val shrugged, admiring the tiny vial still in his hand. "Just got your buddy, Daniel, to line the rim of her soda can with my special formula. A few more minutes, and she would've been as dead as a doornail, regardless."

"Then why do *this*?" Blaine sneered, gritting his teeth as he gestured at the wreckage.

"To teach you a lesson." He rolled his eyes, exasperated. "Be grateful, brother. At least *you* get the luxury of bringing her back." Despite the cruel mask he was donning, the restraint in Val's voice was all too obvious. "You're not ruining this for us, not out of petty sentiment."

"I did everything you said. I told you I'd handle it!"

"Then, pray tell, where were you speeding off to?" Val's gaze shifted over the backend of the car, down the vacant stretch of road. "You obviously knew there was something wrong with her. And this place is crawling with private roads and scenic views. You could've taken her to any one of them and just waited for her to die so you could work your magic. Yet, here you are, having gone out of your way to head to...where else?"

I took a closer look down the winding path to the quadrangle road sign in question. It was blue with a large white H printed in the middle of it. Beneath, it read, *"5 Miles."*

The hospital.

Blaine had been trying to take me to the hospital.

Like a kick from a mule, my body rocketed backward and I stumbled away from Blaine as my vision snapped back into place. I couldn't fight the tears. My entire body was shaking with an emotion I would never have a name for. And his eyes... His eyes were so wide and petrified that it only shattered what little there was left of my sanity.

"You killed me!" I had screamed at him, time and time again. *"You* killed *me!"*

His answer every time: *"I brought you back."*

I'd always assumed he meant that he resurrected me after he *purposely* crashed his car. But the figure in the road... I'd seen it that night.

"No." I just kept shaking my head, stumbling back, back, back. I tried to speak, tried to find the words I needed to express the chaos in my mind, but all I found was a handful of spare letters. "Why?"

Why didn't you say anything? Why didn't you tell me?

Why?

Why?

Why?

I wasn't sure if Blaine could hear those thoughts, but I suspected as much, seeing a faint tremble ravage his body. My chest tightened all the more. Someone so seemingly resilient was standing before me, visibly gutted and vulnerable.

I finally managed to take a step forward, but he immediately cowered back.

"Don't," he whispered.

"You tried to help me."

He scoffed, redirecting his eyes to the floor. "A lot of good it did."

"It...it wasn't your fault."

He matched every step I took toward him, refusing to let me come closer. His back finally met with the wall, only inciting his chest to rise and fall faster.

"It wasn't your fault."

"Stop."

"You brought me back."

"Please, *stop*," he pleaded, his voice so weak the words were barely audible. Blaine flinched, as if my very touch singed him, feeling my fingers cup his jaw. I angled his face to meet mine, and he forced his eyes shut.

"Look at me." *Please*. He heard the word spoken only to his mind, and all attempts at control vanished. I'd never done that before. I'd never felt my thoughts travel through that bond. But I'd felt it this time. His eyes snapped open. "Why didn't you tell me?"

"What difference would it make? It was still my fault. You'd still hate me..." He tried pulling away, but I secured my hold on him.

"I don't. I *can't*." I didn't fight back the tears pouring from my eyes. "You scare me—*terrify* me even—because I don't know who you are. You're the caring stranger I met at a party, and the man I thought I killed, and the crazed lunatic who's as damned as he seems, and the boy who's so beautifully broken... I *am* scared of you, but I can't hate you."

Blaine stopped breathing.

Why did you put a hex on me?

He laughed the strange sort of laugh that wasn't a laugh at all. "I didn't."

My hands slipped from his face. "...What?"

"I never put *anything* on you."

"But your mark..."

382

"I never put anything on you."

What did that mean? Who put it there? Did Raelynd? How?

His finger ran over the bottom of my lip, tracing the curve of my mouth. "Tu es meus verum coniunx."

He said that to me once before, the night of my Great Rite. What did it mean—

His hands dropped to my jaw, angling my face up to meet his as he repeated the words against my lips. He kept saying my name, and his every touch was the cure to an ache I didn't even realize I had. "I never meant to hurt you."

I was suddenly sobbing, remembering the last time he had tried to tell me, when I had lashed out at him, when I had told him that no one could ever love him, that *no one* could ever care about him.

Thank You For the Venom

The low grunt sent ice prickling up my spine as I pulled away, watching Blaine's jaw tighten. We didn't need to look down to know what runes had ignited.

"Go back inside," he ordered. "Lock the door."

I turned, and immediately regretted it. The being standing at the end of the hall appeared human in the dim lights, but as it emerged from the shadows, its full features proved it to be far more formidable. The creature didn't appear to be much taller than Blaine, but its naked body was built of muscle upon muscle upon muscle. Every vein in its body bulged out, the color a sickly black over its hardened gray skin. The beast roared, stressing our eardrums as the tyrannosaurus howl bounced off the high ceilings of the corridor.

If its body didn't do you in, its mouth certainly would. What was with these creatures' aversion to clothes and penchant for serrated bites? The beast had what happened to be a human-esque nose, but its jaw jutted out into a sharp point like a reptilian snout, revealing an equally ferocious set of teeth, so massive that they rivaled a raptor's. It even had an elongated tongue that wove around its notched bite, as if preparing to clean for its next meal.

The beast didn't have claws, for those same serrated teeth made up the jagged ends of its fingers. They even protruded out from the muscles in the center of its chest. With the simplest flex, the teeth atop them shifted, stretching out like a Venus flytrap, ready to clamp its carnivorous snare shut the moment the beast's arms locked you in. And same as the previous creature Blaine and I encountered, it wasn't affected by the wave of magic the Dark Prince threw at it.

"Go!" Blaine demanded, but I didn't move. Not when I saw an exact replica of the monster on the other end of the hall over Blaine's shoulder. Each wielded a large tool of some sort in their hands, and as the flat metal end illuminated in the dim light, I could see that it was some kind of medieval sledgehammer. He wouldn't have been able to take on both of these things alone.

And Blaine knew it. He shoved me over to the library doors and yanked me inside. To my relief, he followed after me, throwing the locks into place. The ornate bronzed doors prove to fend off the assault as the metallic material pounded and thudded from the opposing side as Blaine and I raced down the main aisle back to the study area. The remains of the Sagax's smoke dissipated upon our arrival. Seriously? Was this woman really that useless when it came to confrontation?

Val appeared to share in the sentiment, because he suddenly cursed. "Gee, thanks a pant-load, lady."

Before either of us could give the command to leave, Val and Reese immediately met us at the door.

"Don't bother. We already know," growled Blaine's brother. "She just said as much before pulling her whole Keyser Söze vanishing act. How bad is it out there?"

The crash of metal exploded across the towering ceilings as the doors finally gave in, no doubt. "I don't feel like staying around long enough to find out," said Blaine, yanking me backward.

Val grabbed Carly as Reese barked at Mark to run the moment we reached the reading center at the end of the study hall. We all raced down the main aisle to the other end of the library, hitting identical bronze doors. Blaine threw all his weight into it, and it proved useless. The damn things wouldn't give.

"Watch out!" I yanked him sideways as a sledgehammer suddenly swung right at him from behind. The mallet drove past us and pounded into the column beside the frame of the doorway. The annihilating impact sent bits of stone raining down on us as Blaine and I fell to the floor.

Quickly recovering to our feet, we looked up to see the other half of the Gruesome Twosome charging right for us from the other end of the library. A scream lodged in my throat as Blaine pounced up in front of the closest creature. The beast heaved its arms to the side, preparing to drag the hammer right into him. Blaine lunged rearward, his back hitting the library doors.

The club drove precisely into his position, but Blaine managed to sweep out of the way with not a second to spare. The bronze doors thundered as the hammer obliterated a hole right where the locks had just been. Blaine swooped into action, grabbing the handle of the sledgehammer. The creature and he fought for its possession as the beast tried to pull him in. Val hauled Carly away from the assault and dove right into the other creature's path as it, too, tried to make a play for us. He wasn't as lucky as his brother. The beast barely managed to haul him up against its chest, allowing its secondary set of teeth to snap shut. The serrated chompers clamped down on Val's right arm, pinning his blade to his side.

The Mage cast the creature his darkest smile, not the least bit affected as the ferocious bite drew blood from his bicep. "You really shouldn't have done that."

Seeing where his knife was positioned, I grimaced. Bad way to go.

Sure enough, Val pressed the blade against the beast's exposed genitals, and with the flick of his wrist, he sliced the entire package clean off. The creature bucked and roared, snapping its jaw at anything and nothing as it crumpled down onto the floor in a blithering heap of cries and moans and pooling black blood. Blaine nailed the other creature in its jaw, snapping its head up before it could take a bite out of him. He'd lost his blades in the midst of the scuffle, and I immediately snatched out my own, leaping on the creature's back as it prepared to pull Blaine in for a second time.

Before the beast could haul him to its chest, I jabbed Reese's pocketknife into the creature's brainstem, just as Blaine had demonstrated with the creature in the mall parking lot. The beast lurched backward, hurling its weight into the end of the book aisle. With me still clinging to its back, the wind was ripped clean out of me from the

VICTORIA EVERS

crushing impact. When I didn't let go, it threw itself forward, and repeated the maneuver. Only this time, I did let go. I barely managed to snake myself out of the way just as it rammed itself again into the end of the bookshelf. Without my body providing the necessary space, the creature had inadvertently thrust the handle of my blade only deeper into its brainstem. As soon as we heard the sickening *squish*, the beast collapsed onto the floor, not five feet from its creepy companion.

"What the hell were those things?" bellowed Carly, shaking like a leaf as she cowered into the corner.

I'd forgotten. This had been her first encounter with such a thing. Sure, Hellhounds were terrifying, but they still just looked like black wolves on a massive scale. *These* beasts were the things from your darkest nightmares.

"Lich," said Val, using the fabric of his pants to wipe the blood from his knife. "They're hired trackers, meaning whoever hired them shouldn't be far behind."

Blaine tossed his weight into the doors again, and with the lock busted, they flew open. The six of us hurried our way through the labyrinth of hallways. Unfortunately, in our desperation to escape, we seemed to have lost track of where we were. It wasn't very hard, seeing as how every hallway in the second floor was identical to the one we just came from. Eventually coming across an unfamiliar stairway, we decided that getting to the ground floor was the best objective.

Blaine suddenly cussed, looking out through the second story window. "We've got a problem."

"*What?*" Amid the suffocating darkness outside, I couldn't distinguish much of anything.

But then a shadow zipped across the lawn. Then another. And another.

"We've got company," the Prince growled. "And lots of it."

The only way to reach the other wings of the school was from the main hall, forcing us to retrace our way back to the front entrance. I started to race across the foyer when Blaine suddenly pinned his arm against my chest, forcing me to a stop. I looked over at him, seeing his gaze fixed upward. My eyes drifted from the dark pool staining the lobby floor up to Blaine's line of vision. Everyone else followed in suit. Carly threw a hand over her mouth to catch her scream as Reese and Mark cursed.

No, no, no, no!

Blood trailed off the ends of Madsen's fingertips as he lay strung upside down from the rafters, his face frozen in a state of primitive horror from the gaping wound sliced in the middle of his chest.

All our gazes fell to the fallen bulletin sign for Madsen's seminar. The word *"Traitor,"* was painted in crimson red smears across his picture.

"As the good ol' Bible says, 'Show no mercy to wicked traitors.'"

The six of us whirled around to face the unwelcomed lilted voice, finding no one in any of the adjoining hallways. A soft, birdlike whistle followed, pulling our attention back up to the lower half of the rafters.

"Same goes for you, boyo," the stranger added, gesturing to Reese. He swept the cap off his head, swinging off the beam beneath him. The Irishman landed as gracefully as a cat onto his feet, despite the fifteen foot drop. His pinstriped vest and matching shirt were pressed with such deep wrinkles that it looked like he'd just woken up from a two-day bender and hadn't bothered to change his clothes.

Normally, it would have been next to impossible trying to determine if he was a Mage or not. Unruly dark hair framed the Irishman's forehead and cheekbones, the only parts of his body I could see that weren't covered in tattoos. With his sleeves rolled up, the pale blue lights emitting from his left forearm highlighted the remaining ink on his skin. Strange tendrils snaked up his neck, their intricate designs crawling up over his jaw and chin. The one side of his neck had a seared handprint of black and red with the warps in the palm made to look like the outline of a ghoulish face screaming. And the other side…a snake wrapped around two crossed blades, consuming fire. My drawing.

Getting Away With Murder

"I t's one thing to fight alongside *them* when you are one," the Irishman continued, pointing the tip of a twelve-inch Bowie knife towards Blaine and me. "But to betray your own heavenly duties to save them... Now, that's just sacrilege. Like father, like son—no doubt." The stranger gave a wicked grin as he surveyed Reese. "Oh, I'm gonna have fun with you."

Blaine let out a low laugh. "I wouldn't threaten him in front of the lady," he said, nodding to me. "Things won't end well for you. Trust me."

"I don't make threats, Prince. I make promises."

The world thundered behind us. I looked at the base of the dual front doors, seeing shadows lurching from underneath the doorframe. Our little get-together was about to become an all-out event.

"Let's see whatcha got." The Irishman beckoned us on, aching for a faceoff. Blaine was only too happy to oblige. The two threw fists, even with ten feet still separating them. Magic crashed against magic, making the air ripple as runes lit up the entire lobby. I knew Blaine still hadn't regained his fullest strength, but this Mage had to be pretty skilled nevertheless to parry his attacks. The distance closed, until flesh finally met with flesh and dagger met with dagger.

None of us could intervene, finding a new batch of opponents filing in the south hall. All bared black ink covering their eyes as they charged inside. Carly and Mark braced themselves for combat, but even with weapons at the ready, every last demon rushed past them as if they were invisible. Their sights were set on me, and I found myself taking on two, three, four demons at a time. I couldn't stab them, too afraid to hurt the people whose bodies the demons were possessing, but as effective as my roundhouse kicks were, I couldn't fight them off like this. There were too many.

Val was ripping as many of them off me as he could, but as more demons poured into the room, it was clear we had been overrun.

White light flashed to my left, and I whirled, seeing the Irishman throw a fistful of what looked like red powder into Blaine's eyes. The Dark Mage staggered back, trying to wipe the content from his vision, but he wasn't fast enough. The jolt to my chest was immediate as another blinding white light exploded. Blaine's body flew across the foyer, hitting the marble floor with a crack. Red filled my vision, seeing the Irishman wink at me. My fangs had come out, and they'd locked their sights on their intended target. Raising my hands, the entire room rattled. I threw my closed fists down, watching the chandelier looming overhead tear off its hook. The Irishman leapt forward, rolling himself into a somersault to narrowly avoid the broken remains of the metallic fixture shatter around him as it crashed into the floor.

My fingers flexed out, and everyone standing, including my friends, was all thrown off their feet. They'd only caught the blast wave of my magic, dazing them for a brief moment. My aim had been centered on the Irishman, and it was a direct hit. He slammed into the floor with an equally painful blow as the one he'd delivered to Blaine, but he merely choked out a laugh as he pulled himself up. The bastard was egging me on, taunting me into a one-on-one.

And he'd get it.

But not yet.

More demons flanked me, and I promptly addressed the attack. One of them slashed a knife at me, forcing me to meet their proposal. I used Reese's pocketknife to counter it, and even managed to sweep the weapons to the side, leaving my opponent exposed. The demon dropped the blade in hand and I grabbed his remaining arm, disarming any further movement. I quickly yanked him to me and drove my fingers into his jugular notch, watching him crumpled to his knees with a sickening wheeze.

The victory was short-lived.

A heavy fist pounded into the back of my head, and the world dimmed for a woozy moment. Just as I regained my bearings, I stood upright. A polite *tap-tap* hit my right shoulder, and I turned, catching a glimpse of wild green eyes before the Irishman blew a mass of red powder into my face. I'd expected it to have the same effect as silver or holy water, making my skin sizzle. The dust burned my eyes as I tried to blink through the tears, and it irritated my throat as I choked on the thick air, but the powder didn't seem to affect me beyond that.

Clearly having found enough amusement with me, he vanished back into the throng of bodies. Still wrestling with two demons, Reese was suddenly thrown back by the collar of his coat as the Irishman hauled him toward the front desk. He didn't miss a beat. As soon as the Irishman loosened his grip on him, Reese nailed an uppercut to his jaw. The stranger's head snapped back, but he refused to let go of him, reinforcing his hold on the Light Mage. A pulse of energy slammed into Reese's chest, and he staggered back, only to have the Irishman force him into a chokehold.

I couldn't see what the bastard had pulled from his pocket, and I wasn't about to find out as the Irishman brought his closed fist up to Reese's face. Blaine seemed to notice the same thing, kicking his knife across the floor to me. I snatched it up, and without a moment to lose, I let instinct take over. With a snap of the wrist, the blade didn't even spin as it sailed through the air. It cut through ten feet of opened space before slicing into flesh. The Irishman had been fast enough to avoid the direct blow to the head, but the blade still hacked into his cheek.

He pressed the back of his clenched fist into the grisly gash, and his slow smile only further stretched the cut. "I like a girl with some fight in her," he snickered, tightening his hold on Reese until the boy choked.

"Then you're gonna love me." The air rang with a metallic reverberation as Carly grabbed the silver-plated vase from the reception desk and slammed it into the back of his skull.

The Irishman didn't even have enough time to turn around to face her as she nailed it into the side of his head. The second blow delivered the knockout hit as we watched him slump to the floor, down for the count.

The atmosphere seemed to shift in the room, because the demons suddenly didn't appear too keen on simply ignoring the vase-wielding blonde. It became an all-out assault, on *everyone*, as the remaining demons began lashing out at both Carly and Mark.

"Everybody, get down!" Reese hollered, finally managing to catch his breath. The space around him burned bright blue as half his runes roared to life. Mark ripped away the wiry-haired man trying to claw at me and yanked me down as the five of us dropped to the floor. The air resounded with a low rumble before the blast came. Everybody left standing was catapulted across the room, half of them crashing into the far wall.

I tipped my head back against the cool marble floor and finally sighed as the space around us went silent. Any relief I had vanished the moment I looked up at Reese. He swayed to the side, barely managing to catch himself on the edge of the reception desk as his legs buckled out. I shot to my feet and raced to his side, feeling the clamminess of his skin as his hand touched mine.

He had used too much energy.

"Look at me," I demanded, watching his eyes sink shut. *Why, why, why would he do that?* He knew it would be too much.

It wasn't until everyone was left in unconscious heaps on the floor that the scope of the situation sank in. There had to be close to eighty people lying all around us. Eighty people, against six. If Reese hadn't done what he did, we wouldn't have been walking out of here.

But as he lurched forward in a pathetic attempt to prove he was steady on his feet, it was evident he wouldn't be doing much walking, regardless. Reese muttered that he was fine, but I couldn't help recall Blaine saying the same thing before he nearly died.

The fastened doors at the front entrance pounded, bowing in under the pressing weight from the outside. And more footsteps echoed from the east wing corridor.

"Where are you guys parked?" I asked the guys.

"West Entrance, off the main drag," Val and Mark both confirmed.

"Take Reese, and get out of here. Call Raelynd."

Val was shaking his head, but Blaine nodded. "We'll lead them away."

"Are you crazy—"

"They're only after Blaine and me," I barked. "The Cutlass is right off the side street here. We'll be fine. Get Carly and the guys out of here, now!"

Val looked between us, knowing damn well we wouldn't relent. "Well, shit…" He took hold of Reese and nodded, letting Mark help distribute the Light Mage's weight as they turned and hurried down the hall with Carly in tow.

Blaine canvassed the foyer, calculating the odds. "This was a bad idea, wasn't it?"

"Terrible, actually."

"You know a better way out of here?"

"The closest exit still takes us too far from the car," I said, pointing down to a nearby corridor.

"I don't think we have another choice." Blaine snatched a hold of my hand and directed me to the hall to our left, but we both crashed to a halt as figures suddenly emerged from down the corridor.

We spun back around, only to see a sea of people flood into the entrance hall from the main doors as they burst open. Not to either of our surprise, every last one of them had black orbs for eyes.

Blaine rattled the knob to the door beside us, but it wouldn't give. "Stand back!"

Before I could move, he drove me away from it. His vision tunneled as he threw his hands out. The entire door blasted right off its hinges, falling in broken bits inside the top of a lecture hall. Blaine cursed though, gripping his arm as the lights atop it sputtered. He shook it off, taking my hand again and propelling me down the rows of seats. He charged over to the elevated windowsill off to the side, and prepared to blast the glass out of the pane, only to find the energy crackle uselessly at his fingertips. I pushed him aside and took out the window with my own runes. It worked, but I buckled over as the power thrashed inside me. The energy was still alive beneath my skin, only it felt like a teeming dam with nothing but a tiny spout to evacuate the building pressure.

That red powder!

Whatever the Irishman had thrown at both of us was blocking our energy. We still had use of it, but it was mere scraps compared to what we should have had.

Blaine hoisted me up to the window and thrust me right out of it. I flew out headfirst and barely managed to tuck under before falling into the snow covered grass on the other side. My body crashed down hard, the wind escaping my lungs as I hit the ground on my back. Blaine's boots squeaked as he ran up the wall. His hands and arms came into sight, and he grunted as he struggled to pull himself through. A roar of footsteps clamored behind me, and he only just managed to snake his body through the casement before a pair of hands grappled at the windowsill from inside.

Blaine stealthily recovered to his feet, and we sprinted across the campus lawn. A sharp whistle shrilled behind us, and that seemed to be a signal to the others. More people came darting out from the front of the building, catching sight of us as we raced toward the side street where the Cutlass was parked. My legs frantically carried me forward, and I almost lost my footing on the small hill leading to the road.

Unable to stop myself in time, I hammered into the passenger side as Blaine slid over the hood of the car to get to the driver's door. Since there weren't electronic locks on the vehicle, he had to unlock it manually. Blaine pried the door open and hit the button to let me inside. I practically fell into the seat, wrenching the door behind me just as a sea of riotous people rushed at the vehicle. Armed with crowbars and other unsavory tools, they came with their arms raised, prepared to take out the windows.

Blaine punched the keys into the ignition. The tires squealed furiously across the dampened pavement before gaining traction. The Cutlass lurched forward, and we tore off but not before someone managed to take a swing at the backseat window behind me as the man ran alongside the car. Blaine jerked the wheel and the Cutlass's backend swerved, bumping right into the guy. The force knocked him to the side, and the man stumbled off back down the hillside. It took us a few minutes before Blaine confirmed that we were in the clear. We hadn't been followed.

The others hadn't been so lucky. Val called not a moment later, barely audible over the mass of static interfering with the call. They'd made it, but not without catching a few stragglers along the way. Since the demons weren't interested in Mark and Carly, they had taken off in McDowell's Camaro while Val led the rest of the trailing demons away with Reese in the Mercedes. But they'd made it out.

Blaine rambled on about our next plan of action, but the words were lost on me. Dark masses of trees flew by the passenger window as we rocketed down the forested stretches of streets. The scenery blurred as tears began clouding my vision.

"Kat?" Blaine gave me a soft shake. It was only then that I realized he had asked me something.

"He's dead." Of all the thousand of thoughts racing through my mind, that was the only one I could verbalize. Madsen was dead, and it was all my fault. He'd only ever tried to help me, and they had killed him for it. Every muscle in my chest contracted, stealing my breath as I began sobbing.

"Mystic Harbor - 10 miles."
The road sign came into view, and the very site seemed to fuel something in Blaine, because his foot slammed down harder on the accelerator. We were only fifteen minutes from the manor. Fifteen minutes to safety. The sound of the Cutlass's roaring engine drowned out the world around us, making the low drone humming behind us nearly undetectable until it was right on top of us. Blaine and I both looked at one another, seeing our Omen runes simultaneously ignite.

The whirr grew louder, and just as Blaine and I turned around, blinding headlights shone in through the rearview window. The vehicle revved, and it came so close, I could see the two men sitting in the front seat of the large black pickup. The truck jolted forward, ramming into the back bumper of the Cutlass.

"Shit!" Blaine tried regaining traction, but a patch of

black ice sent the whole backend of the car into a tailspin.

The drift sent me slamming into the passenger door, and Blaine's immediate rotation of the wheel tossed me back again. The car fell into a fishtail and Blaine managed to recover, pushing the car as hard as she could go once we straightened out. We seemed to be gaining ground on the truck, until the vehicle floored it. In mere seconds, the truck barreled down on us, slamming once again into the backend of the car.

"Oh, Sitri!" wailed a snide voice. "Come out to play!"

The truck swerved over into the oncoming lane and sped up until it was right beside us. The two men in the truck barked and howled, their eyes visibly black as we raced beneath the streetlights overhead.

"Hey, Princessssss!" The man sitting in the passenger seat pointed to me. "Time to face the music, missy!"

The driver jerked the wheel, and the mass of the truck pummeled into the side of the Cutlass. Blaine pumped the brakes in an attempt to slow down, but between the impact and the fact that we began hydroplaning, he couldn't keep control of the car.

The truck plowed into us again, and the nose to the Cutlass dipped down into the ditch. Blaine barely managed to recover, but it only incited more catcalls.

"Not so fast there, Speed Racer!" The truck repeated the maneuver, smashing into us once more. Harder.

The car wrenched off the shoulder again, the front end drifting to the right. In an instant, the front of the car nose-dived into the ditch. The trunk of a tree was suddenly illuminated by the headlights before the car crashed right into it. With the Cutlass's speed and the fact that the back end was in the midst of a spin out, the momentum wrenched the car to the side. The world spun viciously as the Cutlass jackknifed, flipping over.

Again.

And again.

And again, before plummeting into the ditch.

My vision slowly came into focus as the nauseating smell of burning rubber filled the car. An excruciating pain seared all the way through my ribcage, and the veins in my head throbbed as vertigo set in.

"Blaine…"

A dampness streaked across my forehead, but the liquid was running up to my hairline. That's when I noticed it. I looked up to see the ends of my blonde locks dangling above me. I was suspended upside down. Lights flashed through the passenger side window, and I could see the inverted view of the road. The truck was just down the stretch.

"Blaine…"

Every little movement I made awakened another pain in my body as I tried to unlatch my seatbelt.

"Blaine!" I looked over at him, seeing blood dripping all over his face. He lay motionless with his arms limply hanging down. Another pair of headlights roared into view, stopping alongside the truck. I tried rolling down the window, but the crank broke off in my hand. I called out for help, pounding my fists into the glass.

A few brawny figures stepped into view from the other vehicle, and laughter resonated in the air as everybody strolled down the road toward the flipped car.

Shit.

They weren't here to help…at least not me.

One of the men sauntered over to us, twirling a crowbar about in his hands as he practically skipped along.

"Blaine!" I reached over and started shaking his frame, begging him to wake up.

He didn't.

I continued fiddling with the busted seatbelt, but it wouldn't give. I grabbed the holster around my ankle, only to find it empty. Where was my pocketknife? Frantically looking around the car, I saw the silver glinting on the roof a few feet from me. As hard as I tried, my fingers couldn't grab it. The knife was out of reach.

"Awww, look what we have here." The man with the crowbar laughed, bending over and peering in through the passenger window as he approached. "She's a pretty little thing, isn't she? Sure we can't have some fun with her first?"

The whole gang chuckled.

"Sorry, boys, but the bitch is damaged goods," remarked another man. "It is a shame though, isn't it?"

"Indeed." The man with the crowbar grinned and winked at me. "Best cover your eyes, sweetheart. Wouldn't want anything to happen to that face now."

He drew the lever up and I shrank away, frantically trying one last time to free myself from my seatbelt. It wouldn't give. The glass exploded into the vehicle from the crowbar's impact, splaying over me before falling down to the roof of the car. He dropped the tool and reached inside to grab me, only to get a face full of claw marks as I scratched and tore furiously at his eyes.

"Feisty, I see." He pulled out a switchblade, and the knife sprang free with a push of a button. "I like that."

I instinctively froze as he drew the blade over to me. It grazed down my torso before digging underneath the seatbelt harness strapped around my waist. With a flick of his wrist, the blade snapped the material apart, and I crashed down onto the roof. He grabbed hold of me, but not before I snatched up my own pocketknife.

As he heaved me out of the car and into the drainage ditch, I jabbed my blade into his arm. The guy immediately let go of me and screamed, prying the knife out of his bicep.

"You like that?" I sneered, driving my heel right into his kneecap. He dropped to the ground and I clawed my way up the other side of the drainage ditch to the woodlands, but someone grabbed a hold of my legs.

I face planted as the brute yanked me down, and I was heaved up the hill back to the road.

"Somebody sedate her already," grunted the guy holding me. He dragged me over to the pavement and hurtled me onto the asphalt as another member of the crew immediately plunged a needle into my neck before I could fight back.

I tried to peel myself up from the street, but my knees buckled and my vision swayed. A heaviness drew over my limbs, and I struggled to keep my eyes open. My body caved into the drug almost immediately, dropping to the ground in seconds. All I could see were the headlights reflecting off the dampened road as all the men headed down into the ditch to the Cutlass.

"He's not dead, is he?" asked one of them as the car creaked.

"Nah," confirmed another. "At least, not yet."

Muffled laughs droned in my ears as everything went black.

Knocking On Heaven's Door

My head banged into the fiberglass floor of the van as I jolted awake. The massive bumps in the road sent me flying, only making it more difficult to sit up as it aggravated the pains already raking throughout my body. But the sight of Blaine lying beside me gave me the motivation I needed. I shot upright, whispering his name as I shook his unconscious frame.

There was no one else in the back of the van with us, and the divider resting between the cab and the cargo space was shut. The only light we had came from the two small windows built into the back doors of the vehicle. I shook my arm, trying to get my runes to ignite, but they only let out a gentle hum. That powder was still blocking the energy from releasing. I continued to rattle Blaine, and to my everlasting relief, his eyes groggily opened.

"Hey." I brushed the hair from his blood spattered face,

seeing two gashes ripped across his cheekbone and forehead.

He looked around the van confusedly. "Where are we?"

"What'd you last remember?"

"Being on the road, and…" His eyes widened at the recollection. Blaine gritted his teeth as he wearily pulled himself up off the floor. Straining to hold his hands outward, he tunneled his focus toward the back doors, ready to obliterate them away. The van jostled, and Blaine barely caught himself against the wall as the vehicle took a sharp turn. His eyes fluttered dazedly, and before he could catch himself, his legs buckled beneath him.

"Blaine?" I knelt down beside him, seeing panic settle into his features.

"Something's wrong…" He lifted his rope-bound hands up to his aching shoulder, and his jaw slackened. He felt along the top of the joint. "My runes aren't even igniting."

"What? *Why?*"

He leaned over, exposing his battered shoulder. There was something metallic jammed into the muscle beside his neck. It looked like a twisted iron rod, but the smoke seared from the wound. "It's suppressing my energy."

Even in the limited light, I could see how insipid his skin had become. And he was ice cold. "We have to get that thing out of you." Struggling to prop him upright, I tried to grapple my hands around the small, warped piece of silver. I bit back my cries, feeling my palms searing at the simplest touch. It only worsened as my grip tightened, but I didn't care. "At the count of three. Ready?"

Blaine nodded.

On my mark, I pried the device up as hard as I could.

His guttural yelp was nothing short of feral as he tried so desperately not to scream. "Stop…Stop."

I let go, and he crashed back against the side of the van.

"It's not coming out," he gritted.

Blaine was right. I had given it everything I had, and the silver didn't budge.

"What do we do?" Just as I spoke, the two of us got tossed about the cargo space like a couple of rag dolls as the van slammed to a halt.

"Hey, where's the road?" called out a voice from the cab.

"This is as far as it goes," replied another voice in the distance. "You gotta walk down the path if you want to get to the field."

My pounding heart stopped.

Field?

I could hear the front doors open, and the weight of the van lifted as I suspected the men up front climbed out.

Blaine's frozen fingers wrapped around my wrist. "Run."

"What?" I turned to see his exhausted eyes boring into mine.

"The first chance you get, you run."

"Blaine, don't talk like that—"

He let out a pitiful laugh. "Look at me, Kat. I'm not going anywhere."

"But—"

"You still have a chance. I'm gonna try to cause a distraction. The moment you find an opening, you run."

"If you die, *I* die. Remember?"

"Not necessarily." Before I could question him, he grabbed hold of my arms and drew me right up in front of him. His lips met mine, the touch so heartbreakingly gentle. *"Vos autem semper quod digna id."*

"What?"

"You will always be worth it." He murmured the words against my mouth, taking one final look at me, to study my face, to appreciate the shape of my eyes, to marvel at every shade in them, before he kissed me. Not like before. It was desperate and urgently strong, making my inside go flush as the phenomenon left me lightheaded and wanting more.

And I recognized the sensation immediately. Energy. *His* energy. He'd just transferred the rest of it to me... "Blaine," I gasped. "What are you doing?"

The slightest smile tugged at his lips. "We all have to go at some point, right?" His left hand reached up to the shrapnel lodged in his shoulder. He poised his ring finger over it, and swiped it across the jagged edge until it drew blood.

I grimaced, feeling my own hand burn. The mating bond... Where it had been a solid band of intricately woven tendrils around my ring finger, a thin, naked patch of skin appeared, running down the length of the rune exactly where he had cut his own. Slowly, the black ink turned a metallic gray. It...It was severed.

"So long as they kill me before it has time to heal, you'll be okay." Those beautiful eyes glinted in the blaze of flashlights as the back doors yanked open.

I choked on a cry. "Blaine..."

"I'm sorry." He sprang up from the floor, hurtling himself out into the sea of men awaiting us outside.

The first guy he reached tried taking him down, but Blaine slammed his elbow right up into the man's face. As another guy grabbed Blaine from behind, he used his weight and kicked up. His riding boots jammed directly into someone else's jaw. An all-out brawl of fists and feet and thrashing overwhelmed the spectacle. Everyone else moved in on the prince, attempting to secure him.

Blaine got lost in the pack, but as all eyes focused on him, he bellowed, "Go!"

The closest Reaper to me snatched a hold of my jacket as I leapt from the van, but I threw my arms back and let the fabric slip right off me as I darted past him.

"Grab her!" demanded one of the men as I sped off into the forest sprawling out in front of me.

I blindly thrashed my way through the tangled mess of bare tree branches clawing at me as I raced through the wooded abyss. The only source of light came from the sliver of the moonlight resting overhead, and it barely illuminated the outlines of the trees in front of me.

Multiple voices called out behind me as a gun blast detonated. Splinters of bark blasted beside my face as I sprinted past a tree.

"Don't kill her!" barked one of the men.

My fingers burned with a familiar surge and I whirled around, ready to relinquish the energy. The air rippled as a wallop resounded from my mere palms turned outward. The men were instantly knocked back by the rush, and I didn't waste a second as I whirled around to continue running.

"That is a wonderful trick," laughed the man who suddenly appeared ahead of me. "But do ya' really think it's fair? Perhaps we should level the playing field."

I crashed to a halt, raising my hands at the Irishman. His cheek still brandished the knick I'd given him, and he hadn't bothered cleaning the blood from his face, only adding to his unruly demeanor.

The Irishman clicked his tongue. "Oh, that's not very nice."

Another blast erupted from my palms. He swiftly

ducked the attempted strike, taking coverage behind a tree as it absorbed the impact.

"Not too shabby." He sauntered back out into the open again and batted his raised hand to the side. As if my body was suspended by marionette strings, I was suddenly flung sideways, catapulting through the air until I slammed into the trunk of another tree. I crashed back down to the earth, feeling all the oxygen escape my lungs.

"Only problem, lass," remarked the Irishman, "I'm better." He skipped over to my beaten frame, kneeling down beside me. A low laugh followed as he rolled me over onto my stomach. "Forgive the informality, but there's somewhere ya' need to be, and we can't spare the time in you dawdling." The Irishman gripped the neck of my shirt and began dragging me through the woodlands as if I weighed nothing more than a backpack.

I tried bringing my hands up again, but the energy was gone. All my attention was focused on just trying to regain my breath. Every time I inhaled, it felt like someone was stabbing me with dozens of daggers all down my back and chest.

"Don't die on me yet," he laughed, taking notice to my condition.

Chanting echoed from afar, and the sounds grew louder the further he dragged me. My feet helplessly kicked at the foliage beneath me as I struggled to wrestle out of the Irishman's hold. Vibrations at last coursed up my arm, but the relief was short-lived. The ground beneath me changed to ambient lit grass, and every last ounce of my magic went still. Cloaked figures soon came into view as the Mage dropped me. I looked up, seeing I was now ensnared in the middle of a circle made up of people. Reynolds's coven. The embers from all the torches surrounding us crackled as everyone fell silent upon command.

Foliage crunched beneath footsteps as someone drew nearer. "Good work."

The voice was cold, hard, clipped. Unfamiliar.

Fingers clutched me by the neck, and I was pried up to my knees. "What a ride, this one. Quite fetching," the Irishman crooned.

A pitiful wheeze escaped me as I dragged my gaze up at the spectator as they approached, my heart clenching at the sight of the long leather duster.

Death.

I could see the hilt of the Sanctus blade peeking out over his shoulder, secured inside the scabbard strapped to his back. That's why my runes had died out.

I wasn't sure what I'd been expecting, but as he drew the deep-set hood back from his face, I shrank away. The Irishman snickered, his fingers digging deeper into my neck to the point that I nearly cried out at the applied pressure.

The Angel of Death.

Samael.

My father.

His square jaw was cut at hard angles, accessorized by his five o'clock shadow and goatee. Being as how he made up half my DNA, I'd expected him to share at least some familial features, but with his bronzed skin and charcoaled hair, I couldn't say I did.

Leather-sheathed fingers extended to my chin, cupping beneath my jaw as to hold my bobbing head upright as he knelt before me. Those jade green eyes scrutinized every detail of my face. "You look just like your mother." He let out a long, dissatisfied exhale, releasing his hold on me. "Pity."

"May I do the honors, slitting her throat?" the Irishman tittered giddily behind me.

"I'm afraid the Prince will be the only one paying with his life, at least for tonight," my father growled.

"What are you talking about? We need to spill her blood."

"No, we only require one sacrifice to rebuild the ward. And unfortunately, she's the only thing that could draw her mother out of hiding. I still need her alive. The blade will sever the bond, so Katrina won't die with that cretin over there."

"What are you going to do with her in the meantime?"

"She'll be spending her foreseeable future in the crypts," said Samael. It wasn't even indifference in his voice. That was pure hatred.

"The crypts, ay?" Gratification laced the Irishman's words as he leaned into me. "It appears you and I are about to get *very* well acquainted."

Several of the cloaked figures around me stepped forward and took a hold of me. Still struggling to catch my breath, I batted weakly at them, but it didn't do me any good. They bound my wrists so tight that the ropes cut off the blood circulation to my hands.

"I thought you were supposed to be all holier-than-thou," I spat. "Since when do you work with demons and Mages?"

"The first matter is simply a means to an end. The second..." He surveyed the Irishman. "A Light Mage *can* still be corrupted by the darkness, but I've found ways to prevent that probability."

"By hiring the craziest one you could find?" I scoffed. "Well done, *Dad*."

His lips peeled back into a sneer at the mention, but my

attention was ripped away from my father as coffee-hued hair and Victorian clothing landed in a heap to my left, just outside the circle. Blood marred the side of his head. I shot up in blind panic, only for the Irishman's hold on me to tighten, yanking me back into place.

Reese.

"We found him with Sitri's bastard brother. Ended up in quite the wreck," one of the men laughed. "We tried to grab the other one, but he got away. Nearly took off Jenkins's head in the process."

Samael turned and faced the boy, bemusement riddling his features. "That's not the one we need. Where is the Prince?"

Groans immediately howled in the distance, and no sooner did Blaine emerge from the woods with three other men flanking him. His cheek was still marred from the accident, accompanied by a collection of fresh bruises. My heart splintered with every step he took, his feet dragging along as he buckled over. They'd beaten him. Not just with the blows they'd exchanged while fighting him. They had thoroughly battered him, to the brink of death. And he seemed so resigned to it, all too willing to accept his fate.

Until his eyes met mine.

His boots dug into the ground as dread twisted his features.

"No."

"No."

"No."

That single word kept echoing through my mind. The voice; it was his.

"Speak of the devil, and he shall appear." Mr. Reynolds entered my field of vision and approached my father as the other men fought against the Prince's newfound vigor.

Someone slammed the butt of their gun into the back of Blaine's head, and he at last crumpled to the ground as they threw him down into the edge of the circle not ten feet in front of me.

To my everlasting horror, my father unsheathed his blade...and handed it to Reynolds. There was not a single ounce of remorse as the Reaper turned and faced Blaine, the Sanctus blade in his grasp. "Time to pay the piper, my boy."

"No!" The mere effort of my desperate, pleading scream had my lungs ripping apart as my broken ribs scraped against the organs.

"Sorry, lass, but he has a debt to pay," the Irishman cackled behind me.

"Nathan, please!" I bawled. "Stop this. I'll do anything you want!"

"It is because of this pathetic creature that any of this remains possible," Reynolds spat, yanking Blaine's head back by his hair. "The barrier will be destroyed because of the perversion your unholy kind brings to this earth." He pinned the blade against my mate's throat.

"Stop!"

"It's too late."

"Nathan, please, don't!" The men holding me fastened their grips around my arms as I sprang up from the ground. "You don't need to kill him to reverse the cast."

"It requires a sacrifice," my father snarled.

Blaine's nostrils flared as the blade pressed into his skin teasingly.

"Then kill *me*."

"No!" Blaine barked. "Stay out of this, Kat!"

I wouldn't.

I wouldn't let someone else die to protect me. "I'll give

you your sacrifice," I said. "Just promise me you'll let him go."

Mr. Reynolds's gaze snapped up to meet mine, feeling the Prince go still in his hold. "You would do that?" That wasn't surprise in his voice. It was absolute disgust.

Unmoved by my plea, my father held up his hand. "Proceed."

"Nathan, don't!" I shuttled up from the grass again, only to be slammed back down. "I beg of you! Please!"

"*I'm sorry*," Blaine's voice whispered, only to me, brushing a warm caress through my mind one last time. I barely heard the words over my own screaming as Nathan brought the blade to the side of Blaine's throat.

There was nothing merciful about it. He pressed the edge of it in until a small trail of blood trickled down his neck. The Reaper wouldn't be swift about it. It wouldn't be a clean death. He deliberately dragged the sword across the entirety of his neckline as slowly as he could, letting the blade's cruel power sear the skin apart with its unholy fire. A painful gurgle erupted from Blaine's mouth as the blade at last fell away, exposing the gaping wound.

My cries howled into my plea as I desperately thrashed, and bucked, and kicked, trying to break free from my captor, as if I could actually do something to help him. I was immediately slammed to the ground the moment I tried to rise, knocking the wind right out of me.

Mr. Reynolds released his hold on Blaine, throwing him down at his feet as others cheered. And all I could do was helplessly watch as Blaine's hands grappled at his neck in vain. Red slowly painted his neck, his chest, his torso. I cried out again, tears clouding my vision as Blaine continued choking and gasping for air that wouldn't ever come.

That everlasting warmth that promised me he was near…it leeched from my chest. The life drained so quickly from his eyes as he crumpled over into the ground, and I sobbed. My whole body convulsed as I buried my face, gnashing out an inconsolable scream that broke through the pain tearing into my lungs.

I was dying.

Not my body.

But my soul. It was being ripped in half.

The Wars To Come

The trees clattered all around us as harsh December winds came barreling down over the field. Debris and dead foliage blew across the ground by us, but the atmosphere within the circle of cloaked men remained unaffected by the blustery airstreams.

But the ground rumbled beneath us.

Pale blue lights set the forestlands on fire as a blast wave suddenly hurled out across the field. All the Reapers standing outside the circle were knocked off their feet, their weapons sent flying into the brush. In seconds, dozens of men stormed the field, half of their arms lit with primed runes.

"Your magic won't do you any good!" the Irishman cackled. Sure enough, with every passing step, the Dark Mages' runes petered out more and more. With the Sanctus blade here, their runes were useless.

"That's why it pays to have a Plan B." Val emerged from the group, taking center stage, with a rifle in hand. He staggered with each step, his face a painful collection of bruises and swelling. "Don't bring magic to a gunfight."

My father cursed under his breath as Reynolds rushed to his side. He tried to make a move towards me, but bullets whizzed through the air, cutting him off. Samael glowered down at Reese. "Tell your father next time you see him that we still have a score to settle."

"Do it!" Nathan ordered, looking behind me. Samael grabbed hold of him, and in a split second, they both vanished in a mist of black smoke.

The Irishman threw up some kind of invisible shield around the remaining members of his crew, stopping the bullets in midflight. The air rippled. "Well, fuck me."

His wall wouldn't hold. He barked at the others to go before he grabbed me. "Have fun with Lover Boy," he purred. Before I could process the remark, he pounced on Reese, yanking him off the ground. An odd flat stone rested in his palm, and he pressed it to Reese's neck. Despite his grogginess, Reese screamed as the rock turned bright orange, searing his skin like a hot poker. The Irishman gave him a parting wink before darting off into the shadows of the woods behind us.

With no one holding me back, I clawed my way up to my feet, falling down beside Blaine the moment I reached him. My wrists were still bound, making it nearly impossible to turn him over onto his back. Seeing the quiver still running through his body, my runes flared to life, connecting with every cell in my body, becoming one with *me*. I snapped the ropes right off my wrists and heaved him over.

Blood.

There was blood everywhere. All over my hands, all over my clothes.

My vision.

I screamed for his brother, watching Blaine's eyes flutter as his body convulsed. I held him in my arms, trying to prop his neck up enough to help slow the bleeding. "You're going to be okay... You're going to be okay..." No, no, no, no. There was too much blood...

"VAL!"

The gunfire had ceased, but magic tore through the field, taking hold of every last Reaper and witch who hadn't yet managed to flee. All the cloaked figures, both men and women, dropped their extinguished candles and crumpled over as they grabbed their heads. They pleaded for mercy, but Val turned his knuckled fists, and an aching snap resonated as each of the witch's necks wrenched to an unnatural angle.

The coven lifelessly collapsed to the ground.

"VAL!"

The Mage finally heard me over the commotion, whirling around to find his brother cradled in my arms. He tried hurrying to my side, but his leg was crooked at such a grotesque angle. It didn't matter if he couldn't feel pain. The limb refused to cooperate as he dragged himself over to me.

I needed to transfer my energy to Blaine, but how? The only thing I read about it was in that journal, and it didn't give the necessary incantation. "What is the phrase?" I screamed.

"'Dare enim vos anima mea.'" Val reached me a moment later, and actually staggered back at the sight of his brother. "Kat, don't—"

But I did. I pressed my lips to Blaine's, replaying the

words over and over in my head. His shaking began to subside, but his heartbeat only slowed. He was slipping away. I finally pried my mouth away, choking on the blood that he'd coughed up. "It's not working!"

"Kat, I'm sorry. It's too late—"

Mate.

He was my mate.

"When the Crown Prince of Lust chooses a mate, his Mark is the source of their bond." That's what Reese had said.

But which mark? The mating bond? The tattoo on my ring finger was still severed.

The training room. I could feel his energy when I touched his runes. His Mark. The Mark of Sitri.

I gripped his arm. Where the energy had once been magnetic now rested a weak hum, but it was still there. Everything around me suddenly felt so far away as instinct seized control of my body. Val muttered something, but I didn't hear it. Still gripping Blaine's arm, I turned him over.

He wasn't breathing.

He'd gone wholly still.

No, no, no, no, no. Stay with me.

I yanked the fabric away from his neck, finding the scarred marks I'd given him. Without hesitation or assistance, my fangs jutted free, slamming down into his flesh.

'Dare enim vos anima mea.'

'Dare enim vos anima mea.'

I wasn't going to allow him to suffer in Purgatory. Not for me. Not after everything he had done.

I give my soul unto you.

The world around me fell away, dimming until all I could see was black.

"Kat!" Someone was shaking me. "Stop! You're going to kill yourself!"

I didn't dare move, even as the voices dulled to hollow whispers in my ears. I didn't dare stop, even as I felt my pounding heart slow, felt myself slipping free from my body...until I was yanked back.

My fangs. They'd been pried out of Blaine's neck. I could faintly hear someone scream, not sure if it was me as hands ripped me away from him. Fighting my way through the darkness, I tried to find him again, but I couldn't feel anything. Not his body, not the hands on me, not the frozen grass beneath my fingers. I could feel nothing.

34
Rise Up

The pain was the first thing to register, even before I managed to open my eyes. Every inch of me felt like I'd been hit by a car. My muscles ached without movement as I remained lying down, and my head only throbbed harder as bright lights poured into my eyes. I pressed them shut again just as fingers combed through my hair, cleaning the stray strands from my face.

Despite the pain of enduring the brightness, I forced my eyes back open, finding a gentle amber gaze staring back at me.

"Hey, Princess."

The walls were starch white, along with the sheets and furniture. Everything was so suspiciously sterile. I tried lifting my hand to his, but something spiny shifted in my arm, making me wince. I looked down, seeing a needle shoved into my vein. Blinking through the grogginess, reality seeped back in as I took in my sights more clearly. There were monitors and machines all around me. I was in a hospital room.

"What..." My throat was raw, making me cough on my dry vocal chords. "What-what happened?"

A head of blonde hair appeared on my other side, and I nearly gave myself whiplash as I turned to face them.

Wrong.

It was all wrong.

It was the wrong shade.

Carly brushed her butterscotch bangs out of her eyes. "How are you feeling?"

NO.

Tears whelmed up inside me as my chest caved in. Reese sat beside me, but I still didn't feel that warmth. I didn't feel his warmth. I didn't feel *him*. I felt empty.

"Where is he?"

The two just glanced at one another, uneasy.

"Where is he?" No one answered, and I suddenly ripped the IV from my arm.

"Sweetie..." Carly tried coaxing me back down, but I slapped her hands away, wrestling out of the hospital bed.

I fell over the guardrails, attempting to land on my feet, but I was too weak. My knees buckled, and I collapsed onto the linoleum floor. Reese and Carly immediately came to my sides, but all I could do was scream at them to get away from me as I coiled into myself and wept. Hands took hold of my shoulders, and I batted at them, only to be pried off the floor and swept into someone's arms.

Worn black and white leather pressed against my cheek. With the inhale of cigarette smoke and cologne, I didn't need to look up to know who it was.

Val.

He was carrying me, back to bed I was sure. I just clung to him, and he only held me closer. It wasn't until I looked over his shoulder that I realized he'd carried me someplace else entirely. He turned the corner of the hall, where we passed a large sign that read *Critical Care Unit.*

Someone said something to him about visiting hours, but they didn't push further as he whispered something back.

And it hit me.

It was barely detectable, that flicker of warmth in my chest, but it was there. Val turned, letting me face a large sliding glass door. It was closed, but the curtains inside weren't drawn.

A warm kiss pressed to my temple. "He'll pull through," Val murmured.

There were wires and tubes and so many machines. His throat was wrapped in layers and layers of gauze and bandages, but he was alive. Blaine was alive.

"Though, he'll have one hell of a scar," his brother added. Indeed he would, considering it had been the same blade that had marred them both before. "It might do him some good. Blaine was a little too pretty before."

Amid my tears, I laughed. Actually laughed.

It took me two whole minutes to discover my bed had been implemented by the Spanish Inquisition. That much I knew for sure. The damn thing was one of those stupid "smart beds" that adjusted itself every time you shifted, and it only got harder and harder, pressing up into all the wrong spots. I never had back pain before, but after an hour of laying in it, I was only in more agony. Plus, when Val returned me to my room, the nurse wasn't particularly pleased to see that I'd taken out my IV. And after what I did, giving up nearly all my energy, I apparently didn't have enough to help me heal any faster. With the bruises staining my arm, it felt like someone jammed a pencil into my veins instead of a needle when the nurse reinserted the IV.

Thankfully, the hospital outside of the ICU didn't have set visiting hours, so Carly and Reese stayed by my bedside while Val continued to make his rounds, leaving every half hour to check on Blaine. He assured me since angels were forbidden from being seen by humans, my father wouldn't be able to even enter the hospital. And no one was stupid enough to think they'd be able to waltz into a heavily watched care unit and kill a patient without being caught, including a Reaper or even a crazy Irishman. But it didn't hurt to keep an eye out.

"I'll be back in two shakes of a lamb's tail, Doll Face," affirmed Val at the top of the hour. "Any requests from the vending machines?"

"Anything with caffeine," said Carly.

"Anything edible," I added.

Reese just shook his head.

The Dark Mage bowed, giving me a wink upon departure. I wanted to plead with him to stay, if only just to save me from the awkwardness that always ensued when he left. Carly and Reese would just sit there, attempting to make small talk, but it was painfully obvious. They were trying to say anything else except the one thing they really wanted to. *Why had I done it?*

Apparently, I'd been unconscious for over five hours

before I woke up in the hospital. And during that time, Blaine's own recovery was rather touch-and-go. Because of this, Val continued slicing the rune on my ring finger so that I wasn't bound to the mating bond, just in case things with his brother took a turn for the worst. And this was something he'd made a point of explaining to Reese and Carly.

Which begged the big question: If I knew my life wasn't tethered with his, why didn't I let Blaine die? Or better yet, why would I risk my own life in a pathetic attempt to save his? If he was gone, half my problems would have disappeared in an instant. My hex would be null and void, Raelynd would have no further use of me if I didn't have a mate, and I would no longer be the next Princess of Hell.

How could I explain that Blaine wasn't as awful as everyone thought, or that he hadn't intentionally killed me? How could I explain that I saw a part of myself in him? He didn't have a choice in what he had become, same as me, and we'd both been abandoned and brutalized by the people who claimed to love us. How could I explain everything without sounding incredibly naïve or brainwashed?

I couldn't.

So I didn't.

I just lay there in the unbearable bed, pretending not to notice the uncomfortable glances and awkward pauses in conversation as everyone tried to find something else to talk about.

Reese rubbed an aggravated hand against the dressing bandaged on the side of his neck.

"It still hurts?" I asked.

He nodded. "The damn thing won't stop burning."

"I thought you guys were supposed to heal, like,

superfast," said Carly.

That very fact had been clearly bothering him since I'd awoken. All his other injuries had already healed hours ago, almost immediately after he regained his lost energy. He started peeling off the tape that secured the dressing and headed into the bathroom.

"Should you be doing that?" Carly asked. "I mean, it was pretty nasty when you came here; looked like someone literally set your skin on fire. It probably just needs a little more time."

"What the hell...?"

Carly and I both stole worried glances at one another, and she immediately helped me out of bed as we hurried to the bathroom. Reese had pulled the entire bandage off, and not a millimeter of his skin was still scorched. But that wasn't what any of us were focusing on. In place of the once burned flesh rested a perfectly polished tattoo...of a snake wrapped around two crossed swords, appearing to consume a flame.

"Dare I ask why you're all in here?" drawled Val, appearing in the bathroom doorway. One look at Reese's neck, and his eyes went as wide as our own. *"Holy shit. What the hell happened to you?"*

Reese's hand fell away from the mark as he staggered back from the mirror. "I've been hexed."

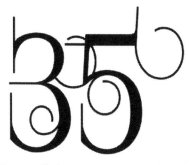

Night Of the Hunter

It didn't make any sense. The sigil branded on Reese was used for summoning and wielding power, and it was always used on surfaces like floors and grass, so it could generate portals. What the hell would it do when imprinted onto a person's flesh?

By morning, Blaine still hadn't woken up. Without Doctor Madsen, and the fact that Val had never heard of anything like this before, I only had one other person to turn to. If my calculations were correct, I still had a few questions saved in my piggy bank, and it was time to cash in on them.

I couldn't remember the Sagax's number, and if I spent another minute trapped in that hospital bed, I was going to Hulk out, runes or not. With Val's assistance, I 'persuaded' my doctors to release me and had him drop me off at the manor so I could retrieve the business card Nick had given me.

Since I'd lost my jacket after having to abandon it outside the van last night, Val had been kind enough to let me commandeer his, something he apparently had *never* done before. The leather racing jacket obviously held a lot of sentimental value, another sign that he hadn't completely shut off his humanity. As we headed into the foyer, I thanked him and returned the trusty jacket before making my way upstairs. It had started snowing outside, so I could only pray that Reese had grabbed another one of my warmer jackets from my aunt's house as I perused the suitcases he'd packed for me.

The first two bags were a bust, so I moved on to the third, unzipping the main compartment. I peeled open the cover, finding a black and white apparel box sitting on top, its red silk bow flattened from the compression of the other luggage. Blaine's gift. The one I'd never opened. I hadn't told Reese about it, because I'd sworn to myself that I wouldn't entertain Blaine's head games by seeing what was inside.

A corner of the envelope tucked beneath the ribbon poked out, and I at last surrendered to my curiosity. I expected to find the same letter inside, which had simply said, *'Bygones?'*

Instead, I found a piece of stationery written in inked calligraphy.

"Benjamin Franklin once said to never ruin an apology with an excuse. For the moment, I cannot give you reasons for my actions, and I know what I have done cannot be forgiven. But if you let me, I would like to return what is yours, even if I can only do so in the smallest way…"

I unfastened the bow and slid the ribbons off the box. Being as how I'd thrown it out the window and into the side of Blaine's house, the crinkled corners of the box put up a little bit of a fight as I struggled to pull up the lid.

I laughed.

Inside rested my beloved leather jacket that Daniel had taken off me when I was unconscious the night of my Great Rite. I'd thought I'd lost it for good, but its vintage studded shoulders and familiar smell greeted me as I pulled it out of the box. I gasped, spotting the white fabric underneath. I'd spent hours trying to find the shirt online, but no retailer had it. Only the little vintage shop I found in New York had ever carried it, and they were long out of stock. Even if it was a little battered, I would have kept the one I already had, but considering the holes and the cuts and the amount of blood I'd accumulated, it was fit for nothing but the trash. Yet, a strikingly identical off-the-shoulder Sex Pistols tee sat inside the box, and it just so happened to be in my size.

Wanting to save the coveted shirt for a special occasion, I nestled it safely back into the box, but still opted to sport the jacket. The lush lining immediately secured my body heat inside the fabric, warming me instantly.

"What's the holdup, Doll Face?" Val called out from the foyer.

I grabbed the business card from the bedside and hurried back downstairs.

Once again using the burner phone Reese had given me, I dialed the number. I expected to hear the Sagax's usual greeting when instead she said, "Corner of Nickels and Colonial," before hanging back up.

Sure enough, when we convened with Reese at the intersection of Nickels Street and Colonial Boulevard in the rather shady area of Mystic Harbor's West End, we found a foreclosure property with the front door already open. I took Reese's hand as we headed inside, with Val bringing up the rear.

Surveying the vacant space, I stepped into the living room, only to shriek and dart back into the foyer, hiding behind Reese as if to use him as a human shield.

"Scared of Morticia Addams, are we?" the Dark Mage chuckled.

"No!" I shot him a dirty look, pointing to the entrance of the room just as a rodent scampered out of it and raced past our feet. In fact, calling it a mere rodent didn't do it justice. The rat was actually the size of a small cat!

"There are far worse things in this world to fear, my darling." The cooing voice sent us all whirling around to the staircase, watching the Sagax descend the steps with such fluid grace amid the long, flowing skirts of her dress. While it seemed the rest of us couldn't avoid making a racket, I truly suspected the woman in question just floated above the ground, because not a single floorboard of this dilapidated house creaked beneath her as she headed into the living room.

Without any furniture, the three of us just stood awkwardly in the entranceway as the Sagax strolled about, seeming to admire the cracks in the wall and the water stains on the ceiling.

"Oooookay," Val mouthed, clearly finding the woman to be a few fries short of a Happy Meal.

I finally cleared my throat, hoping to regain her

attention. The sooner we got out of this dump, the better. "We wanted to ask you—"

"What is the mark on your beloved's neck?" she mused, her gaze fixated on the fireplace mantel as she dragged a finger across its dust-covered surface. "It has been around for millennia, though I haven't seen it used in quite some time. Its purpose is to summon power to a Mage, or to wield control over one." The Sagax finally turned to face us, her attention fixed on Reese. "When branded on one's skin, it transcends being a mere spell."

Reese already knew that much. "A hex."

"Indeed. Its effect may not be immediate, but the power inside you will eventually begin to bend to your Master's desires."

"What does that mean?" I blurted, instantly wanting to kick myself for using up a question like that. I needed to be specific. And I needed self-control. But I couldn't help it. The panic surging in me was making my arm burn as my Distress rune hummed wildly. Yet, its power remained at my fingertips, waiting patiently to be used, if need be.

"Allow the energy to become a part of you."

At last, I understood what Blaine meant. For the first time, I wasn't afraid of my magic. I wasn't fighting it, and in turn, it wasn't fighting back.

"When summoned," the Sagax cooed, "your beloved will not have power over his actions. Whether he wants to or not, he will have to do as his Master wishes of him. And when the hex takes over completely, his mind will be lost as well."

Reese's hand went limp in my hold. All the blood drained from his face. He was shaking his head. "No…"

Now I knew how he felt, when he learned of my hex. Hopeless, useless, desperate. I couldn't do anything, or even say anything to help him. I just squeezed his hand tighter.

The Sagax looked down at my other hand, at the clenched fist as the pale blue light poured out of my left sleeve. Her eyes traveled back up to meet mine. Of all things, she looked surprised. "You have already seen this."

Reese snapped out of the daze he had fallen in, his head snapping in my direction. *"What?"*

I shook my head, but the Sagax extended a hand out, her long, slender finger gesturing to his neck.

"Touch it, and see for yourself."

Reese staggered back, trying to pull himself free from my grip.

"For God's sake." Frustrated, Val grabbed my other hand and yanked it over to Reese's neck, clamping it down on the sigil.

Exhausted.

I was...exhausted, and the bitter cold burned my lungs more and more with every inhale. I blindly hastened through the thicket, desperately yanking at the fabric of my skirt as it continued getting caught on the clawing branches all around me. I could feel the skin on my arms breaking the further I batted my way through, but at last, a gold glow appeared in the distance. I repeatedly stumbled and fell as my feet snagged on tethers of tree roots and foliage.

Finally, I burst out into the open, gasping in horror at the grisly sight. The torches lining the forest were the only source of light in the dead of night, but the shadows couldn't conceal the carnage. Countless bodies lay contorted across the distance of the battlefield, the earth soaked in pools of blood. Lifting the hem of my skirt, I frantically hustled out into the gory meadow, cautiously maneuvering my feet between the corpses sprawled out all around.

A faint figure stood crouched down in the distance, their back faced towards me. Warm brown hair eventually became visible as I came closer.

"Reese!" I cried out, racing to him with no other objective but to throw myself into his arms.

The thought fleeted though the moment I arrived not ten feet from him. He was knelt down in front of a particular body, and I could barely make out the plastered black locks splayed across the corpse's forehead.

"No." The word barely escaped my lips as my knees buckled under me. I forced myself up and hysterically raced over to the two, falling down right beside Reese to confirm my worse fear. "No, no, no, no!"

I frantically combed the raven black hair from the obscured face, only to be met with striking, blood-spattered cheekbones and frozen blue eyes staring blankly into the void of the night sky.

Blaine!

My chest dragged on each agonizing breath as a downpour of tears expelled from my own eyes. I continued to coddle his face in my trembling hands, pleading desperately for him to come back to me. A fading warmth still lingered on his skin, and it only made the anguish hit harder.

I couldn't get to him in time.

I crumpled over, burying my face into the crook of his neck as inconsolable cries stole my breath. My hand trailed down from his shoulder, and I sat paralyzed in place as it fell into a grimy cavity on the left side of his chest. I barely managed the strength to pull myself up as I looked down at my blood-soaked hand, my gaze fretfully then following down to the massive hollowed crater in Blaine's ribcage.

His heart.

It was gone.

Ripped clean out of him.

"Reese," I muttered. "What...what happened to him?"

Of all things, the boy beside me let out a raw chuckle.

"Babe?" I turned to him, seeing blood dripping from his fingertips as he mused contentedly at Blaine's body. "Reese?"

He lifted his left hand, watching the blood trickle down from his nails to the cufflinks of his jacket. He laughed openly again, this time baring a bloodstained set of teeth. Crimson liquid trailed down the corners of his lips as he placed two fingers into his mouth, releasing a gratifying moan at the taste of the blood.

"R-Ree-Reese..."

He rose to his feet, and I stumbled sideways.

"Reese, w-what've you done?" I whimpered, suddenly noticing the massive filigree blade sheathed on his right side as he turned to face me.

"Call it...just desserts," he crooned, removing the sword from the scabbard.

"Reese—"

"Your precious 'mate' got what was coming to him, something you're about to learn for yourself all too well." His grotesque grin didn't subside as he strode toward me with the blade gripped securely in his grasp.

"Reese, what are you doing?" I cried.

He rolled his shoulders in preparation, the high collar of his jacket sliding down his neck just enough to reveal the pale light seeping from the horrid rune marring his skin. "Settling the score, *Princess*."

Backpedaling hopelessly on the ground, I finally managed to climb to my feet as he patiently ambled closer. Mania drove my body, forcing each foot in front of the other.

Leaping frantically between the corpses of slain men, I started to gain some distance between Reese and me. A blast abruptly detonated, and a searing pain suddenly ripped through the back of my shoulder to the front of my chest, whirling me around as my body crashed to the ground. Desperately attempting to climb up again, I was only sent back down into the soil as all the muscles on the left side of my chest felt like they were being ripped apart.

"You didn't honestly think I'd make it that easy for you to scamper off, did you?" Reese laughed as he placed what I now saw was a pistol back into his jacket. He picked up the Sanctus blade from the ground, admiring the blood already staining it. "It's finally your turn."

I couldn't help but cry from the excruciating pains tearing through my shoulder, but I couldn't yield to it. Tossing my weight over, I lay on my stomach and began crawling across the grass with only one functional arm to help pull me along.

"'And I will strike down upon thee with great vengeance and furious anger, those who attempt to poison and destroy my brothers,'" annunciated Reese, his footsteps reaching closer and closer. I screamed as the heel to Reese's boot suddenly dug into the gunshot wound on my back, pinning me face-first into the ground. "'And you will know I am the Lord when I lay my vengeance upon you.'"

He booted me over so hard, the impact knocked the

wind right out of me as a rib cracked.

"Reese," I gasped, "please...don't—"

"Oh." He knelt down over me, brushing the mess of hair out of my eyes. "It's only fair, *love*. You broke my heart; now I take yours." Reese lifted up the blade, taunting me as he traced the tip of it above the organ in question.

I turned my face away, seeing Blaine's lifeless body lying in the distance. My stomach lurched, and my fist closed around a small rock I filched from the ground beside me. Rocketing as much momentum as I could muster, I heaved my arm up, slamming the stone right into Reese's temple. He crumpled over with a howl, and I barely managed to scuttle out from under him.

"Bitch!" He snapped up to his feet and rushed right at me.

The earth swayed woozily as I frantically tried to outrun him, but an arm hooked around my waist and I was hurled down into the dirt with another brutal impact. Reese lunged on top of me, his fingers clenching around my throat. I tried batting my good arm at him, clawing my nails into his face. He let go of my neck and ripped my hand away, leaving me completely pinned under his weight. No matter how hard I wrestled and kicked, I couldn't get his weight up. And with that sword so close, my runes wouldn't work.

"Poetic, isn't it? The bastard and the bitch die together, yet again," Reese sneered. The Sanctus blade appeared in his right hand. "Sanguis quia sanguis."

"I love you! Please, Reese, don't do this!"

"Awww, I love you, too," he crooned, casting me another fiendish, bloody grin. He slowly drove the steel down, savoring the moment as he merrily watched the blade plunge into my chest. "I just happen to hate you a whole lot more."

"Kat?"

I screamed, my entire body heaving in hysterics as I ripped my fingers away. Amber eyes glittered in front of me the moment my vision refocused, and I cried out again at the sight, flailing out from Reese's hold as his hands tried steadying me.

"Have fun with Lover Boy," the Irishman had laughed.

Another set of hands caught me just as I fell back. "Kat? What happened?" asked Val. "What did you see?"

The fear radiating from Reese's eyes brought me to tears as his hand clasped over the marking on his neck. I looked back to the Sagax.

She merely tilted her head. "I told you, child, to protect your heart."

My...heart. Not in the emotional sense, but... "It wasn't my dad."

"What are you talking about, Doll Face?" Val further insisted. "What happened?"

"My vision. It wasn't warning me about my father," I muttered, slowly peeling my eyes back to the beautiful boy in front of me.

It was *him*.

ABOUT THE AUTHOR

VICTORIA EVERS is a paranormal fiction writer who feels really awkward referring to herself in the third person.... When she's not vacationing in Narnia, you'll probably find her reading, watching horror movies, spending time with her AMAZING family, or daydreaming about the newest story in her head.

Stalk Me Online At:

Twitter:
https://twitter.com/victoria_evers

Facebook:
https://www.facebook.com/AuthorVictoriaEvers/

My Blog:
http://victoriaevers.blogspot.com/

Goodreads:
https://www.goodreads.com/author/show/16046914.Victoria_Evers

Made in the USA
Middletown, DE
30 January 2020